A NICE CUP OF TEA

ALSO BY CELIA IMRIE

The Happy Hoofer
Not Quite Nice
Nice Work (If You Can Get It)
Sail Away

A NICE CUP
OF TEA

CELIA IMRIE

BLOOMSBURY PUBLISHING
LONDON · OXFORD · NEW YORK · NEW DELHI · SYDNEY

BLOOMSBURY PUBLISHING
Bloomsbury Publishing Plc
50 Bedford Square, London, WC1B 3DP, UK

BLOOMSBURY, BLOOMSBURY PUBLISHING and the Diana logo are
trademarks of Bloomsbury Publishing Plc

First published in Great Britain 2019

Copyright © Celia Imrie, 2019

A catalogue record for this book is available from the British Library

ISBN: HB: 978-1-4088-8326-6; TPB: 978-1-4088-8327-3; EBOOK: 978-1-4088-8325-9

2 4 6 8 10 9 7 5 3 1

Typeset by Integra Software Services Pvt. Ltd.
Printed and bound in Great Britain by CPI Group (UK) Ltd, Croydon CR0 4YY

To find out more about our authors and books, visit www.bloomsbury.com and sign
up for our newsletters

To all my brave friends in Nice

PART ONE

PAIN PERDUE

Literally, Lost Bread – in the UK known as French Toast.
Serves 8.

3 eggs
200ml milk
1 teaspoon orange-flower water
20g golden caster sugar
ground nutmeg, to taste
80g unsalted butter
8 slices bread or brioche
icing sugar, sieved

In a large bowl or a concave plate, beat the eggs, then
add the milk, orange-flower water, sugar and nutmeg.
Mix well.

Melt the butter in a frying pan, taking care not to let it
burn. Dip the slices of bread into the mixture until they
are well covered, then drop them into the melted butter.
Fry until golden, turning at least once.

Serve after sprinkling with sieved icing sugar. Add fruit,
lemon juice or jam to suit your taste.

ONE

B ELLEVUE-SUR-MER. The name translates as 'beautiful view on sea'. Looking out from Bellevue-sur-Mer certainly gave a beautiful view *of* the sea, along with the hazy headlands of the Côte d'Azur. The beautiful coast and its sheltered harbour had made Bellevue. At first, just a few fishermen's cottages were built on the shore; then, during the nineteenth century, Bellevue grew into a small village with its own shops and church. Slowly the village spread out from the waterfront and up the hill until it became the town it was today.

Tucked neatly into a corner of a horseshoe-shaped cove, the old harbour was now a busy *port de plaisance*, a public marina, crammed with rows of brightly painted fishing boats, which bobbed in rhythm on the turquoise waters alongside the great white motor yachts of the rich. Luckily – or perhaps not – for the town, the waters were not deep enough for cruise ships, or the boats of the mega-rich which used a town a few miles along the coast. But for the medium-rich, the retirees and the businessmen out to impress, Bellevue-sur-Mer marina was a popular port of call, where they could moor their boats, restock and recharge their electricity while taking lunch.

If you were lucky enough to own one of those floating gin palaces, you might sail out into the bay and, once you hit the horizon, turn and glance inland. It was worth doing, for, from out at sea, the sight of Bellevue was as pretty as a picture-postcard village, with its pastel-painted cottages rising sharply up the hillside, the twisting lanes and roads zigzagging up to the brow of the green hill, behind which loomed the grey craggy foothills of the Alpes-Maritimes. If you visited during the winter months, from December to May, you might see the snowy caps of the ski-stations, a few miles inland.

Along the shoreline of the town there were cafés and little shops selling the usual tourist tat – everything from tea towels and lavender bags to calendars and tin trays. There was even a casino.

Near the Gare Maritime stood a small house, divided into two apartments – the kind of building which in England would be called a maisonette.

In the lower apartment lived Theresa Simmonds.

When the bottom fell out of her life, Theresa had left her home in London and moved here permanently. She had been coming up to the age of sixty when she lost her job; she had no pension yet and was left with no income and nothing to do. So, on a whim, she had sold up and moved to Bellevue-sur-Mer.

For the last three years Theresa had been part of a tightly knit gang of expats, who had been running La Mosaïque, a small restaurant on the seafront, a few doors down from her flat.

Theresa cooked. Her friends William, Benjamin and Carol managed the front of house, taking the positions of welcome desk and bookings, maître d', hostess, sommelier and waiting tables between them. They also did the lion's share of the boring stuff: checking that their licences and insurance were up to date and filling in the annual tax returns. Ex-actress Sally Connor, formerly Doyle, helped out all round, in particular doing the publicity and driving the van to pick up supplies, like the daily fresh fish from a stall on the shore in nearby Cagnes-sur-Mer. Zoe, very much older than the others (though, if you had been rude enough to ask her, she would deny it), had invested her money in the restaurant, and between trips to spas in Switzerland, from whence she returned home with puffed lips and a dubiously smooth forehead, she brought many of her well-heeled friends to La Mosaïque to eat and spend, spend, spend.

Theresa, at a mere three years' residency, was the newcomer among the gang. And, as her French was still not good enough, she was unable therefore to do anything demanding public-relations skills, unless it was in English. But, anyway, she was happiest behind the scenes in the kitchen.

The purchase of the restaurant had come with the unexpected benefit of a unique mosaic medallion which had been cemented into the pretty floor by the previous owner. The mosaic turned out to be a self-contained, signed work by Pablo Picasso.

Today was an exciting day for Theresa and all the other owners of La Mosaïque, for the mosaic medallion, valued by experts for at least one million euros, was about to go under the hammer at Sotheby's in Paris.

The gang had had to wait a long time for this. The artwork was taken to the French capital, where it was checked out and researched. After several months it was proved to be a genuine creation of the famed master of twentieth-century art.

Once estimates and reserves, along with very costly insurance and storage costs, had been put on the medallion, it was photographed and advertised all over the world, and, after what felt like a very long time indeed to the owners of La Mosaïque, it was finally put into the annual Sale of Important Modern Art.

Today was the day when all would be decided and they would know how rich they had become.

Theresa was totally on edge. William and Benjamin had pulled the straws to be the two who went up to Paris to attend the sale, while the others sat round the table in Theresa's apartment, waiting for the phone to ring with news. When the draw happened Theresa felt relieved to be staying at home, but now that the sale was imminent she wished she was in the saleroom as the anticipation was starting to make her feel queasy.

She had made sandwiches and tea, but felt unable even to look at them. Carol and Zoe hunched over the table. The phone sat in the centre, pride of place, like a Sunday roast.

Sally was with Theresa, wiping down the tops and packing the dishwasher, fussing around her while she laid a tray with plates, cups and cutlery.

'I just need to keep busy,' Sally said as she sprayed a whiff of surface cleaner over the fridge door and dabbed at an imaginary smear.

'It's like waiting for a prison verdict,' said Zoe.

'I'd prefer to think it's more like knowing whether or not we have the X-factor,' drawled Carol, a beautiful American from Muncie, Indiana, who had in fact, before undergoing surgery to become herself, been christened and brought up as Mark. 'Even if we get the lowest estimate, I feel I have to say that. Only half a million? Gee, I'd be happy as a clam being forced to share that half a million between the six of us. But if we hit the bingo, and we bag several millions each, well ...'

'Dream on, dear,' Zoe interrupted Carol's reverie. 'If we get the lower estimate, you'll only be sharing what remains of the half million after you've paid *me* back, paid off all our creditors and got La Mosaïque back on its feet.

And as the debts are mounting daily, frankly, dear, what remains to be shared from five hundred grand would be mere pin money.'

'If there's anything left at all,' added Sally, puffing the spray at a nearby light-switch and polishing it. 'We have to strike it big or we are doomed.'

The problem was that, for the last three years, the owners of La Mosaïque had steered their way through extremely rough waters. And their difficulties had not been brought on by their own lack of industry or imagination. Twice, since the joyous opening, the restaurant had come really close to bankruptcy.

It was only a few months after they opened that the result of the Brexit vote had shaken them all, leaving them worried that, depending on how the whole catastrophe was managed, they might be left high and dry, unable to continue working or even living here in France. The worst scenario that they could imagine had them all being forced to give up everything they had worked so hard for here, and obliged to return to a country which, for the majority of them, had not been home for a very long time. Theresa felt she had only just upped sticks to settle here, and the thought of doing it all in reverse was too horrible, particularly as she would then consider it all to have been a failure. It would certainly look that way, she knew, to her not-so-close friends in London. Not only did the referendum result leave the gang of six owners of La Mosaïque in limbo, but it impacted the profits of the business too. The other local expats, who made up a fair percentage of their regular clientele, started pulling in their horns, preparing for the worst. It was obvious why they did this. The first thing that people who feared for their future cut back on was inevitably the unnecessary expense of dining out. Tourism from Great Britain also diminished during this time.

They were quite unprepared for the second enormous blow – a tragedy which occurred only three weeks after the Brexit vote.

The nearby city of Nice was hit by a devastating terrorist attack.

On 14th July 2016, right after the annual firework display, held to celebrate the Fête Nationale, a machine-gun-wielding terrorist had ploughed through the crowd in a heavy lorry, killing eighty-six people and hospitalising almost five hundred more.

That night the restaurant had been closed for the holiday.

Theresa and Sally had gone into Nice together to have some fun. When the lorry struck they were caught up in that terrified crowd. As they ran for their lives, Theresa injured herself trying to leap over a set of overturned bins in a side street. She was left for six months with a bad limp, and had been unable to stand for long periods, which made cooking difficult.

Although Sally stood in, she herself was in no state to work, and as a result the restaurant had no choice but to take on a temporary chef.

Though not physically injured, Sally was badly shaken. For two months she was unable to drive, as whenever a lorry came towards her she went into the shakes and had to pull in to get herself back together again.

Carol took on her duties as van driver.

Even now, almost three years later, whenever either Theresa or Sally heard a police or ambulance siren, they still broke into a sweat and their hearts battered in their chests. Post-traumatic shock took some getting over.

Carol and William were particularly assiduous in their care of Sally and Theresa, but no one quite foresaw the next direct result of the dreadful attack.

Many foreign tourists, mainly the English and the Americans, cancelled their holidays on the Côte d'Azur, while local people simply stopped going out after dark. Even during the day the streets were markedly quieter. For the first week the city was eerily silent and still, and for months afterwards it was a ghost of its former self.

As if the attack itself were not bad enough, the city of Nice and all its satellite towns and villages suffered an enormous financial downturn. By the end of the year 30 per cent of bars and restaurants in the area had closed, including establishments which had been successful and well known for decades. Some of the busiest streets, like the famed Marché aux Fleurs in Nice, were suddenly lined with boarded-up buildings which, before the attack, hosted thriving brasseries, cafés, burger bars and restaurants.

It was a miracle that, principally thanks to Zoe's continued financial support, La Mosaïque had survived at all.

But for the owners of the restaurant, their joint faith in the future had been secured by the knowledge that they owned this Picasso mosaic, and that it was proceeding through the stages towards a sale at the auction house. Hopefully the mosaic would achieve a great price, with which they would pay off their debts and then divide the profit.

'We're lucky,' said Zoe. 'The economic downturn means that more and more people are turning to tangible things like Bitcoin and art.'

'But I thought Bitcoin was only virtual,' replied Sally.

'Who cares?' Zoe knocked back her cup of tea as though it was a shot of eau de vie. 'Truthfully I'd think we're likely to reach about six mill.'

'A mill each,' crooned Carol, munching on a langue de chat.

'La la la la la!' Theresa put her fingers in her ears. 'Please, Zoe, let's not tempt fate.'

'Theresa's right,' said Sally, moving over with the second tray, and taking a seat round the table. 'It's not as though this will be pin money for us. After the events of the last couple of years, well … If we don't get good money, we're all done for.'

Theresa laid the platter of sandwiches next to the teapot. She still couldn't face eating, she felt so tense. 'Not totally done for, Sally; we're still scratching along. It's not over … yet.'

'For one awful moment,' Zoe put her hand to her wrinkled chest, 'I thought you were going to say, "It's not over till the fat lady sings," and then … God forbid, you were going to sing to us.'

Theresa did not like the implication that Zoe thought she was fat, even though, as she smoothed her hands down her sides, she could feel definite rolls of flab around her waist. She preferred to think of herself as slightly embonpoint.

'I still don't understand what we're doing huddled around this phone?' asked Carol. 'Wouldn't it be easier to link up on the net? Then we could see it live and not be dependent on those two keeping us informed.'

'No unofficial filming allowed.' Sally grabbed a tomato sandwich and took a bite. 'I imagine no one wants to have their buying splurges recorded and put on Facebook for their husbands or wives to see.' She took a second bite just as, with a loud shrill tone, the phone rang.

Everyone leaned away from the table.

'Well, go on.' Zoe jerked forward. 'Somebody answer it.'

Theresa put down the teapot and picked up. 'Hello?'

All four faces strained to listen to the voice in the phone applied to Theresa's ear.

'*Oui, Cyril. Évidemment.*'

Everyone slouched back to their original positions.

'*Actuellement, il reste le même que d'habitude. Oui. Je t'aime. À demain.*' She put the phone down. 'That was Cyril. About the meat delivery. Did we like the new sausage? Do we want to increase it up to the old level yet.'

All four women let out a sigh and reached out for the sandwiches.

'"*Je l'aime*", Theresa.' Sally corrected her French. '"*Aimez-vous la nouvelle saucisse?*" Correct response – "*Oui, je l'aime.*" Not "*Oui, je t'aime.*" Unless you want Cyril to think you love him.'

'*Je l'aime,*' repeated Theresa. 'I always get that one wrong. *Je l'aime.*'

'*Moi non plus,*' added Zoe, making a reference to the 1960s racy song '*Je t'aime … mois non plus*'. 'But to be fair, I do adore his sausage.' Zoe laughed alone at her own joke.

'How can Cyril be so stupid? He knows why we're cutting back – like everyone else around here.' Sally swallowed the last of her sandwich. 'And, anyway, he could have asked me yesterday. I was chatting to him at the market. He was asking whether we'd all move away from Bellevue-sur-Mer once we were rich! Marcel seemed very worried by the idea.'

'Why would Marcel care?' asked Zoe. 'He owns the brasserie next door. I'd think he'd be whooping it up at the idea of us all buggering off. His business would double without us.'

'This is nerve-racking.' Theresa fiddled with the teapot. 'Why don't they just get on with it?'

'Perhaps lots 1 to 254 are taking longer than expected,' said Carol. 'The timings they give are mere approximations, you know.'

'Like the estimates they give us on the works of art, you mean?' said Sally, reaching for a second sandwich.

Carol held up her large hands. 'I don't know why we're all being like this. After all, whatever we get is a win. No?'

'If we get the lower estimate, it's only a mini-win,' said Sally.

'Stop moaning. It would still get us out of hot water.'

The phone rang again. This time Theresa didn't wait, and snatched the receiver. '*Allô?* ... William! Any news?'

'Put it on speakerphone,' said Zoe. 'Let us all hear.'

Sally fiddled with the phone base and eventually got the speakerphone turned on.

'There's an internet bid of two million,' said William. 'They're *starting* at two million.'

Carol crossed herself and rolled her eyes up to look at the ceiling.

They all leaned in towards the phone, straining to hear the auctioneer as he called out the bids.

'Two million five hundred thousand ... Two million eight ...'

'Can you hear all right?' William said.

'If you'd shut up we might,' snapped Zoe.

Sally hushed her.

'Three million ... Do I hear three and a half? Madam? The gentleman in the green tweed suit?'

'I hope he isn't accidentally bidding while he's waving his phone about,' said Zoe. 'A green tweed suit sounds quite William's style.'

'Four million ...'

'Alleluia!' Carol made jazz hands.

'I need a stiff drink,' said Theresa.

'Four million five ... Yes, sir. Five million ... Six million ...'

'Six million and rising!' hissed Sally, closing her eyes. 'There is a God.'

'Seven million ...'

'With seven million we won't need to run a restaurant,' said Sally. 'We can just live the life of Riley.'

'Who is this Riley?' asked Zoe. 'I've often wondered.'

'Shut up, Zoe!' Theresa was still leaning over the phone.

'Spoilsport.' Zoe scoffed. 'I think we can all sigh an enormous sigh of relief now. Can't we?'

'Wait a minute ...' William said.

'Is there a bottle of champagne in the house?' yelled Carol.

'What?' It was William, whispering hoarsely into the phone. 'WHAT?'

'WHAT?' replied everyone, excitedly pressing in around the table. 'WHAT???'

'I don't believe it,' said William. 'I don't believe it.'

'Someone's jumped up to ten million. Haven't they?'

William's breathing echoed loudly down the line.

'William?' said Theresa, trying to sound level. 'What's going on?'

'Tell us!' echoed the others.

'Just a minute, Theresa.' William had cupped his hand over the receiver. They could hear the muffled sounds of him talking in French with someone in the auction room.

'Perhaps they leaped up to twelve!' shouted Zoe in the direction of the phone on the table. This received no more than further muffled sounds from William.

Then he said abruptly, 'I'll call you back,' and hung up.

As Theresa put the receiver back into the base, a strange silence fell on the group. All smiling, but biting their lips with anticipation.

'Perhaps someone fainted?' suggested Sally.

'Probably Benjamin, thinking about all those drugs he could buy.'

'Shut up, Zoe.' Sally slammed her cup down on the saucer. 'You know he's stopped all that stuff.'

Carol grabbed the receiver.

'What are you doing?' asked Sally. 'He said he'd phone us back.'

'I can't wait. I'm phoning him.'

Theresa wrestled the receiver from her hands. 'Carol. Sally's right. Something has clearly happened. Someone's been taken ill or whatever ... I'm sure William, of all people, will phone us back the moment he gets a chance.'

Carol rose from her seat and strode round the room like a prisoner trapped in a cage. She threw her arms up and cried to the ceiling: 'I just can't stand the waiting.'

'Shall I make some more tea?' suggested Theresa, also rising from the table.

'No,' everyone called in unison.

'But a stiff gin wouldn't be out of the question,' added Zoe.

Theresa went to the kitchen cupboard and pulled out a bottle of Bombay Sapphire and plonked it down in the centre of the table beside the phone, then went back for glasses, bottles of tonic and a lemon.

At this moment the phone rang again.

Zoe was first to grab the receiver. 'William, dear boy, how rich are we?'

The others were silenced.

Sally reached forward once more, trying to activate the speakerphone button.

'What do you mean? ... But they can't do that. You're not serious? So now what? The bastards. I understand. I'll tell them. Yes.'

Zoe put the phone down. She sat well back in her chair and whispered, 'Sod it!'

The others gathered like vultures around a dead cow. 'Well?'

'We're bolloxed.' Zoe grabbed the gin bottle, poured some into her teacup and knocked it back in one. 'Zero,' she said. 'Nil, nought, nothing, bugger all. The bastards!'

'But ...' As she sank into her chair, Theresa felt oddly calm. 'How can that be?'

'The sale was stopped and the mosaic was withdrawn.'

'By William?' Sally slammed her fists on the table, rattling the gin bottle. 'Has the man gone mad?'

'You won't believe this.' Zoe sighed and poured another measure into her teacup. 'Lawyers arrived ...'

'Lawyers?'

'From the Picasso Estate. They got there just at the crucial moment and halted the sale.'

'Halted the sale?' echoed Sally.

'But they can't?'

'They did.' Zoe took another swig from her teacup. 'They say that the work was illicitly taken by Old Mother Hubbard, or whatever her stupid name was, and *never* did belong to her. They say that she was never Picasso's mistress – she was his cleaner. And, while cleaning, she had stolen it. And if the mosaic did not ever belong to her, equally it does not belong to us.'

'So who does it belong to?' Theresa took a deep breath.

'According to those lawyers, it belongs to the descendants of Picasso.' Zoe shrugged and started to shout. 'As though *they* needed the money, the little, spoilt, grasping, tight-arsed, nappy-wearing, ugly little sods.'

'So there's no sale?' Carol put her face in her hands. 'Oh Gaaadddd.'

'Do we get some kind of compensation?' asked Sally. 'We must get something?'

'Nothing.' Zoe shook her head. 'As I said: zip, zilch, sod all.' She quaffed some more gin. 'Actually I'm wrong. We not only get sod all, we will be given the present of a massive bill from the auction house for administrative costs, photographs, insurance, storage, advertising … and the rest.'

Theresa felt as though she was about to fall through the floor. Suddenly everything was blurred. She feared she would pass out. She stretched forward for the gin.

'Now what?' she said, gripping the blue glass bottle to steady herself. 'That is the question.'

'Well, I suppose the first thing …' Zoe looked at her watch ' … would be for you lot to go to La Mosaïque and open up. You've got one booking for tonight. Table for one. Me.'

'Oh, thank you, thank you, thank you, Zoe,' said Sally. 'Thank you for still having faith in us.'

'Who's talking about faith? I'm quite aware that you won't be able to pay me back the money you owe me in pounds, shillings and pence, or even in euros for that matter, so instead you can pay me in kind. Starting tonight.'

———

Whey-faced, William and Benjamin had arrived in La Mosaïque at the end of the night's service, having flown down from Paris immediately after finishing the dire business concerning the mosaic.

The group stayed in the dining room of the restaurant and talked until late into the night about the consequences and choices of the day's debacle.

They could choose to engage lawyers to fight the claim, but having no evidence of the sex life of the late Widow Magenta, the previous owner, or of her relationship with Pablo Picasso, they knew that, by hiring anyone to defend them, they would probably only be throwing good money after bad. After all, the Picasso Estate was obviously not short of a bob or two, and would have enough dosh to buy the best legal team in the world to fight their case.

'Tomorrow the restaurant is shut, as usual, and I propose we use our day off to get the accounts straight. I will do this myself, with your help, Theresa, if I may.'

Theresa paced about the room. 'Well, I don't know much about money, but I did used to work for a solicitor, so I vaguely know my way around the law, albeit the law of Great Britain.'

The way things were going she feared she would be back working in a London solicitor's office all too soon.

'Once we know exactly where we stand financially, then we can choose whether to sell up or struggle on.'

'When will we get your verdict, William?' asked Carol. 'In here, tomorrow evening?'

Sally piped up. 'No. That's too sad. Let's meet at mine. For once I'll cook. I'm no Theresa, but it'll be like the old days.'

Everyone agreed that that would be a good idea. Sally would prepare the main dish, Carol would bring starter and dessert and Benjamin would get the wine.

'Honestly, William, what are our chances of survival?' asked Theresa, her stomach filled with the dull ache of fear. 'Now that we won't be getting this money which we'd all been depending on.' Her head was so full of the grim thought of being forced to sell up and move back to dreary old Highgate that she barely listened to his reply.

William shrugged. 'Let's say we're going to have to be very creative. I suspect our best chance of staying out of jail is by selling up our interest in the restaurant and going our own different ways. And if necessary taking the first steps towards declaring insolvency.'

Theresa slumped into the nearest chair.

TWO

IN THE COLD MORNING LIGHT, Theresa wrapped her turquoise mac tight and resolved, even though it was drizzling, to walk along the shore before going up to William's house to start the accounting.

This mac would always remind her of her first days here in Bellevue-sur-Mer, meeting Carol and the others, the beginning of what she realised had been the happiest years of her life.

She did not want it all to stop now. She would hate to find herself aimless, penniless and forced to return to London, where she knew she wouldn't have a chance of surviving, either mentally or financially.

If La Mosaïque were to fail, and close down, which certainly seemed the most likely way forward, she would have to find another means of getting by. And by getting by Theresa realised it wasn't simply a financial concern. She wanted to have a decent reason to get up each morning. She needed something to look forward to, something to love.

She stepped carefully down the stone ramp to the small pebbly shore. With a loud cry a seagull swooped and dived into the water, chasing a fish.

Theresa picked up a smooth, flat stone and, like a child, skimmed it across the dark blue surface of the water.

It was important, she realised, to try and keep positive. Once you let yourself slide down that black hole of depression, who knew where you might end up? She had to stay positive. And here, in this lovely little town, there was plenty to keep positive about. Around three hundred days of the year without rain. No freezing-cold winters. A beautiful turquoise sea to gaze at, calming and enlivening at the same time. A gang of really great friends. And last, but certainly not least, wonderful food. Theresa understood how important that was to her. Certainly, here on the Côte d'Azur, even the cafés and market stalls served wonderful things – from *socca* and *panisse* to pissaladière and pizza; hand-held snacks, but all quite delicious.

She flopped down on to a rock and sat staring out at the sea. She had about ten minutes before she'd have to trudge up the hill and start the hellish day of accounting. At the bottom of her heart, even though she couldn't extinguish a flicker of hope, she knew that in all likelihood the day's work would end with one decision: La Mosaïque was finished; La Mosaïque had to go.

With a piercing cry the seagull was suddenly back, circling round a stretch of water which appeared to have a slightly different surface from the surrounding sea. The bird dived again and this time came up with a fish in its beak. Within minutes, as though from nowhere, scores of seagulls appeared, all circling and diving into the same patch of water, which obviously contained a shoal of fish.

Everything needed to eat. Not only everything but everyone. La Mosaïque and her dreams of being part of a restaurant might go up in smoke, but there had to be other ways she could use cooking to continue her life here.

She reached into her bag and pulled out a notebook and pencil. And as she jotted down the first few ideas, the sun came out and shone so strongly she needed to take off her mac.

Sally drove the van along the coast road to Cagnes-sur-Mer. She was visiting a little fish stall from which she frequently bought red mullet and sea bream for the restaurant. She hoped to buy something good – a treat which she could cook up for everyone at tonight's dinner of fate.

As she climbed out of the driver's seat, the sun emerged from behind a black cloud.

It felt so lovely, especially after the dismal weather this morning, that she couldn't resist running out on to the beach and darting about, abandoned, springing up like Isadora, dipping in and out of the water, even though she was wearing shoes.

When she had exhausted herself with her little display, she flung herself down on the sand and closed her eyes.

That was exhilarating!

She felt like one of those blonde-haired girls who used to twirl around in misty 1970s adverts for Polaroid or Nimble and other long-forgotten products. As Sally recalled, those girls usually seemed to steal an apple somewhere along the line, and so pretty were they that nobody ever arrested them for theft.

What a turn-up! Only this time yesterday she had thought that today she would be rich. This morning it was all change. Her dreams of round-the-world cruises and new wardrobes of lovely clothes right out of the window. Not only that but she was much worse off than she had been a few years back before plunging much of her savings into La Mosaïque.

She closed her eyes, basking in the warm March sunshine, and felt guilty because, despite everything, she still felt happy.

It was inexplicable. Immediately after the bad news came, she felt terrible. But once she was out of Theresa's flat and walking up the lane to her house a kind of thrilling pall fell upon her. She wondered whether this wasn't a leftover from her years in the acting business. That sense of not-knowing what will come next, the wide dark hole which opens up as every job ends, understanding that you might never work again, but, at the same time, now you were again available to all offers and it was possible that your next job might take you to Hollywood, riches and world fame. Sally realised that, like most actors, she was addicted to those adrenalin surges, and living a life which was like walking a tightrope. She could never have been happy sitting around, smug, behind a desk, with a pension lined up, guaranteed promotions in the pipeline and safe, reliable security all round.

She bit her lip and winced.

It was a pity that the others felt so very bad about the end of La Mosaïque.

Of course it would be a struggle for them all. She felt slightly foolish for having put quite so much of her spare cash into the place, but, until yesterday, nothing about that seemed to be risky. In fact, the whole project seemed to be just like a game they were all playing while waiting for the spoils.

Her feelings towards La Mosaïque reminded her of moments when she was a child, running a post office with one of those paper kits your grandparents invariably gave you every Christmas. Little pink, yellow and blue envelopes; stamps with teddy bears and bunny rabbits on them; a rubber stamp and a red ink-pad …

Now she and her friends were running a toy restaurant, only this time the food was real and customers were spending real money, not plastic tokens. But Sally and her friends carried none of the actual pressing anxiety that all the other local establishments must have been feeling over the last three years.

For, at the back of the minds of the owners of La Mosaïque, whatever came to pass there was always that safety net lurking: the cosy, warm security of the Picasso.

She opened her eyes.

Damn! Damn! Damn! Damn!

She laughed aloud, even though she was lying alone on the beach. She peered along the way to see if anyone had heard her.

It reminded her of when she played Eliza Doolittle in *My Fair Lady* for one of the better northern repertory companies. Hadn't Higgins said that when she slammed the door on him?

She looked around to make sure no one was staring. But the other people there all seemed too preoccupied with digging out their sunglasses and blowing up beach balls to care about anyone else.

Now that La Mosaïque would soon meet the dust Sally also realised that she was going to have a lot more time to herself, which might be fun.

She could get back to classes at the Sea School. See if she could get that Yachtmaster Certificate. Or perhaps she could try something else. A course in wine or perfume. There was so much opportunity if you went out to find it.

A shadow fell across her face.

At first she presumed it was someone passing by, looking for somewhere to set down their blanket for the afternoon. But the shadow remained.

Sally felt quite irritated that these people were blocking her sun. She wished they would just settle and get out of her ray of sunshine.

She kept her eyes determinedly shut.

'Oh, yes! It is.'

'I don't believe it.'

They spoke English, too. How awful! She prayed it was not fans who remembered her from years back when she was well known on English TV.

'Sal? Is that you?'

Sally opened her eyes. She could barely see who was looking down, but could tell it was two people, a man and a woman.

'I don't believe it. Sally Doyle! Salzy, old darling! How faberoo *de vous voir.*'

Sally shielded her eyes but could still not make out the identity of the man and woman who loomed over her.

'It's Eggy, darling! Eggy and Phoo.'

Sally sat upright, rather quickly.

Edgar Markham and his wife Phoebe Taylor were the most famous married couple of English showbiz, known to the tabloid press as 'The Magical Markhams'. Edgar – 'Eggy' – was renowned for playing classical roles on stage and diplomats and barristers on film, while his wife had been the queen of TV sitcom, in particular the immensely popular long-running TV series, *Paddy and Pat*. Taking the role of Pat, Phoebe, known in the business as Phoo, officially became a 'National Treasure'.

'Oh God! Eggy! Phoo! What on earth are you doing here?'

'*En vacance*, darling; like you, I suppose.'

'No, no.' Sally scrambled to her feet. 'No. I live here. Well, not here, exactly, but just along the coast.'

'And you come to this beach to run around like a woman possessed!' Phoo laughed. 'Eggy and I almost expected you to leap on to a broomstick and fly away.'

Sally took the implications of this remark with a pinch of salt.

'How lovely to see you both. Are you staying here in Cagnes-sur-Mer?'

'No, no, darling. We're in a very chi-chi establishment in St-Tropez. But as we have the car we thought we'd take a spin along the coast to see the rather less salubrious areas.'

Sally winced. How could anyone even think of this lovely little town as anything less than gorgeous? 'Will you be here long?'

'Only a few days left of our fortnight, *malheureusement*. I'm loving it, of course, cos I've a cosmopolitan soul. But Eggy's missing his home comforts, aren't you, darling?'

Eggy pulled a hound-dog face. 'Haven't had a decent cup of tea since we arrived. And no toast for breakfast for ten whole days. Never seen the point of those crescent things. Bacon, eggs, toast, marmalade and a nice cup of builder's for me. I'm finding the froggy food insufferable. Yearning to go home and get a proper meal.'

'Oh, Eggy darling, you are so silly. You know you're enjoying Odile's food well enough. You practically lick the plate clean. Or are you just hypnotised by her 48 double D?' Phoo laughed and elbowed Sally in the ribs. 'Odile is our landlady. Well, she's an old friend really, I suppose.' She giggled like a schoolgirl, something strange to see in a woman who must be in her mid-seventies. 'Men are so transparent, aren't they? I've often said that Eggy's a bit of a twitcher. He's always transfixed the moment he sees a pair of great tits looming.'

'A mature man's hobby.'

'Second childhood, more like.'

'You're right, of course, Phoo. Nanny did have a pair of big balloons.'

The three had strolled away from the sands and were now sauntering aimlessly along the seafront.

'But enough of all us, Salzy.' Phoo turned and stood facing her, hands on hips. 'You're being as evasive as ever you ever were. Come along, woman, tell all. You're living over here – is there a handsome rich chap on the scene? Do you still tread the boards? Or are you wildly, independently rich? Five kids? Run an orphanage? What gives?'

Sally was desperate to save face in front of these two, who, early on in her career, had intimidated her so cruelly. She was not going to tell *them* that her restaurant was on the skids. So she told them about La Mosaïque, as it had been in its glorious heyday. How the Hollywood actress Marina Martel had attended the opening night and even offered her a part in her film, but she had been too busy then to accept. How her son Tom ran a very successful art gallery in Vieux Nice and how her daughter was big in finance, working in London – the City – happily betting with other people's money.

'And you *own* this restaurant?'

'I have partners. Theresa Simmonds ...'

Eggy, not listening or waiting for a reply, raised his hand, pointed it forward, and a distant car bleeped and flashed in response. Sally noticed that it was a very expensive-looking classic BMW convertible.

'I suppose we can't give you a lift anywhere?' he asked.

'No, Eggy. Thanks for offering but I'm here in the van.'

'Oh, you do deliveries too, do you?' said Phoo. 'Like Pizza Hut.'

'No, actually,' replied Sally. 'I'm picking up supplies.'

'Ever the busy little worker bee,' said Phoo. 'Do you remember when you were an ASM on that tour we did? Can you recall, Eggy? She was always so earnest while setting the props table. Oh, you did make us laugh.'

'Lovely to see you again, anyhow, Salz,' said Eggy. 'Chin up, old girl! Enjoy the rest of your holiday.'

As Sally watched them walk away she felt a rush of relief. She ran back to the van and turned on the engine. She pulled out into the moving stream of traffic, wondering why it was you always bumped into the people you really did not want to see, while those you had lost touch with and missed never came your way.

Her mind went back over the three times she had worked with the Markhams – that early stage-manager job where they mocked her incessantly for taking her duties too seriously, but the one night when she placed the letter in the wrong corner of the table, they reported her to the company manager and almost got her sacked; then the TV job where she played their dimwit maid, and off camera they treated her as though she really was their dimwit maid; and, finally, the show where she was queen, *Sssaturday Sssslamerama!*, in which (as she did to everyone who came on the show, be they rock stars, movie stars or royalty), she glooped them. Everyone had to answer questions about themselves, and if they went wrong or hesitated, a bucketful of brightly coloured gloop landed on their head. But the Markhams did not take their glooping with the grace displayed by everyone else. They all knew beforehand that glooping was an inevitable part of the show. But not the Markhams. Oh, no. After the live transmission they behaved as though she had glooped them spitefully, just to mock them and have her revenge on them for reporting her when she was ASM. But they surely knew that being mocked was the entire point of the programme, so if they hadn't wanted to be glooped/mocked, why had they agreed to come on the show at all? She knew why, of course. They had a tour to promote, and *Sssaturday Sssslamerama!* was top of the ratings, so at that moment they needed her more than she needed them.

But they couldn't possibly admit that.

And then, stupidly, still intimidated, at the after-show drinks, out of mere habit, Sally had felt obliged to apologise over and over.

As she sped along the autoroute she could feel her face getting hot with fury and embarrassment. Why on earth should things which happened so long ago still cause her to feel so low?

Anyway, so what? She'd bumped into them today, and now, with any luck, that sharp dose of the Markhams was over and done with, forever.

Sally was almost home before she realised she had not actually bought any fish and now had nothing to contribute to tonight's dinner.

She hastily turned back towards Nice and drove to the large hypermarket to buy some fish there.

After getting the fish, she wandered up to the back of the vast shop and put two luscious-looking gateaux into her shopping basket. Eggy might go for English stuff, but for Sally nothing bettered French patisserie for comfort food. Quite unnecessary, really, but a huge chocolate cake was just what she needed as an antidote to her chance meeting with the monstrous Markhams.

THREE

EVEN TO THERESA, who was used to lawyers' meetings, the evening's discussion felt as though it went on for ever. As they discussed all the possibilities left to the owning partners with regard to La Mosaïque, she found herself engaged one moment and the next gazing out of the window at the sea: deep blue, sparkling and tempting. She felt utterly trapped.

She and William had sat in her flat and thrashed everything out all day, with paper, pencils and a calculator. Even as they ate their sandwich lunch, they were noting down figures and drawing up columns of numbers. All day they had dealt only in facts – bank balances, debts, income, tax, licences, gross expenses, net profits.

It was a horrible day. And once all the team were gathered at Sally's home, suddenly mathematical reality went up in smoke and emotions took over, for Theresa as much as for the others. Carol and Benjamin were still dreaming of a revival, full of hope and future success. Zoe nodded off, then woke up and demanded answers to questions which they had dealt with in minute detail while she was asleep; while Sally seemed to be mentally absent. Theresa had simply hoped that someone might have been able to come up with a magic answer. But that was folly. And this was reality.

So far, the ideas presented had all been idealistic, pie in the sky, mostly depending on a great imagined upsurge of custom, despite the fact that it was already early March, the height of the slow season, with the post-Christmas tightening of the belts in the run-up to Easter.

For what felt like the twentieth time, William laid out the options: 'One: we sell up the premises and the business as one and move on. Two: we struggle on, hoping for a reprieve. Three: we cut our costs, dramatically. We work without pay and employ no covers until we are out of the red. Four: we reduce the quality and style of our menu, replacing top-end products with cheap and quick convenience food.'

Carol let out another heartfelt sigh. 'I just want it to be like it was before ...'

William groaned and lowered his face into his hands, while Theresa had to stop herself throwing up her arms and yelling at Carol to shut up.

'Sally? What are your opinions?' William leaned his elbows on the table and scrutinised her face.

Sally sat to attention. 'Um. Well, er ... I ...'

'Are we boring you?' William pursed his lips. He was in for the kill. 'For the last hour you've been in another world.'

Sally apologised. In truth her head was back on the beach at Cagnes-sur-Mer and those preposterous Markhams.

'We've been going around and around in circles for hours now.' Theresa stood up, her chair scraping on the parquet floor with a high squeak. 'For God's sake, let's eat. And, Benjamin, open a bottle of something alcoholic.'

'There must be a way we can get more people in to La Mosaïque.' Carol beamed, as though she had had divine inspiration. 'Couldn't I walk around with a sandwich board, handing out leaflets?'

'No.' William banged his forehead on the table. 'No, Carol. You cannot. This isn't Coney Island. Yes, we need more customers. And, yes, we also need more time. But our debtors are pressing and, to be frank, since the dreadful events of the summer before last, we have all been living in cloud-cuckoo-land. That bloody stupid work of art gave us false hope, and an imprudent sense of security. If it hadn't been for that bloody medallion, we'd have called it a day long ago.'

'How about if we—'

'Nooooo!' shouted William. 'Don't you see, Carol. It's all over.'

Theresa moved to the window and looked out, wishing she was anywhere but in this room. The birds were gathering over the dark sea, as the evening drew in. She watched them swooping and whirling up again from the teal-blue waters. 'Everybody has to eat,' she murmured.

'Including us,' said Sally, clearing the papers and pens from the table and bustling towards the kitchen. 'Carol, lay out that salad and bread, while I get the fish going.'

In silence they prepared the food and laid the table. Benjamin handed everyone a glass of rosé, and flopped into an armchair.

'Perhaps we should all run away to sea,' he said. 'And Sally can drive us.'

'On what?' said Zoe, already topping up her glass. 'The raft of the *Medusa*?'

'At least none of them had to pay meat suppliers,' replied Benjamin.

'No.' Theresa downed her glass of wine and slumped down at the table. 'They ate one another.'

By ten o'clock they were all well fed and rather tipsy. Sally put on the latest album by French superstar Calogero, and they sprawled out on the sofas while the music played.

They had unanimously raised their hands to approve the vote that, from now on, they would work twice as hard, adding extramural activities, like home deliveries, to their restaurant schedule. That way they hoped to keep the place afloat. The aim was to make the restaurant seem as attractive as possible to potential buyers. Then, as soon as the time was ripe, and the websites were full of recommendations, they would sell up and go their separate ways.

It was disappointing but at least there was a tiny glimmer of hope. Theresa put her faith in this new optimism.

Meanwhile they tried to think of ways to enhance the restaurant's profile, and at the same time to make more money through it. Priority number one was to get more five-star reviews on the FaveEats website. They already had many, but, obviously, the more the merrier. By branching out into out-of-house catering, they hoped to fill the financial gap which had been caused by the drop in tourism.

As people fired more ideas into the air, Benjamin uncorked another bottle.

Even William was now laughing at the wild suggestions proffered by Carol.

'Seriously, though,' she grabbed one of the petits fours and ate it with flair. 'Even when we offload the property, we must be able to find a way to make a living out of something related to hospitality. We have the equipment and the expertise.'

'Equipment?'

'Pots and pans. Spoons. You know what I mean.'

'And what expertise do you have, exactly, Carol?'

Carol ignored William's remark and took another sip of wine.

'You could always go on the game, Carol,' quipped Benjamin.

'You, too, for that matter, sweetie,' she replied with a tart smile.

'Poke and Rogers,' said Theresa, attempting to lighten the atmosphere. 'You've certainly got the right names for it.'

'I'll buy fifty per cent of the shares in that one,' said Zoe, trying to grin through her latest application of Botox. 'I'm in!' She pulled out her chequebook. 'Seriously. I am in. When does the brothel open?'

'Rogers and Poke sounds better,' said Theresa, earnestly repeating the name to herself. 'Rogers and Poke.'

'We could do sailors.' Sally sank down on to a leather pouf, her back banging against the wall. 'Sailors Are Us.'

'I'm astonished at you, Sally,' said William. 'I thought that you, of all people, would take this matter more seriously.'

'Shouldn't it be Sailors Are We?' asked Zoe.

'I am taking it sherioushly,' Sally slurred and blinked her eyes a few times. 'As sherioushly as anything. What I meant was – we could make packed lunches, cater for dinner parties, picnics, all that jazz, for all those vishiting those horrible big gin palaces. I doubt they want to cook themselves. So it would be a sort of meals on wheels … only without the wheels.'

'Mulls on hulls?' said Zoe. 'Mails under sails?'

'But, look, I've got the little boat. You lot can cook and pack and I'll ship it out to them, direct to their boats.'

'Shore to ship, rather than ship to shore.' Theresa grabbed a chocolate and popped it in her mouth, savouring every morsel of flavour. 'That's a good idea. It could work.'

'While we're at it we could all dress up as French maids,' said Benjamin. 'They'd love that.'

Theresa snatched the pad which lay in the centre of the table and added 'Shore-to-Ship Catering' to the list.

'Obviously we'll have to put in extra man-hours in the mornings – I imagine people going out on boats for day trips will need the provisions delivered early. And we'll have to take someone out of the dining room to pack up the home deliveries during the evening service.'

Benjamin, Carol and Sally raised their hands.

'A little too keen to wiggle out of dealing with the public, I think.' William's face was as pinched as his tone.

'On the whole, William, as you well know, the public are pure hell.' Benjamin raised a challenging eyebrow.

'The customer is always right.'

'The customer is usually wrong, and not only that but ignorant and rude.'

'I always drive the van. So I can drive the van and the boat to do the deliveries.' Sally could see that this was quite a clever way of edging out of the actual restaurant while still being part of the team and doing her bit.

William gazed at her for a few seconds, then agreed that that was a good plan.

Theresa felt rather pleased that she would be in the kitchen, doing what she always did, even though she would be having to provide twice or three times as much.

She was keen to get on, to move things along.

Yawning, she glanced at her watch. 'Almost the witching hour. Come along, folks. We've got to be up early tomorrow to get all these plans started, so I, for one, am heading home to bed. See you early in La Mosaïque.'

T HE MORE SALLY KNEW she had to get up, the more she wanted to remain snuggled up in bed, watching the clouds as they cast navy-blue shadows on the turquoise sea.

The whole atmosphere of doom had got Sally thinking. She thought about her dead mother, and how much she missed her. She thought how lucky she was to be alive after the atrocities of the terror attack of 14th July. She added up her years and realised that if she was lucky she'd have at most fifteen good years ahead. She recalled the past and felt disheartened by how much time she had wasted over trivia: the years spent pining after her no-good husband, wishing she'd kept her career going after she married, wondering why she hadn't held on to her self-respect when her husband's infidelities ground her down, regretting the hours she'd spent worrying over her kids.

Sally turned over and pulled up the covers.

It was all too depressing.

Then the phone rang.

She answered it.

'Hmmmmm?'

'Hangover?' It was William. 'No excuses. We have our first Shore-to-Ship order.'

'How come? We only came up with the idea last night?'

'No idea. Perhaps it was the advert Carol craftily managed to drop when she phoned in to the English-speaking radio station this morning, pretending to answer some quiz question.'

'Oh.' Sally wasn't sure why she felt so disappointed that things were already so quickly on the move.

'Chop-chop! You'd better get that brigantine of yours bobbing along on the bubbling briny asap. Theresa is already in the kitchen, and Carol is tying everything up in pink ribbons. All we need is Able Seaman Sally to climb out of her pit and get behind the steering wheel of that boat of yours.'

He put the phone down.

Sally wondered whether, last night when she was drunk, William had installed CCTV. How otherwise could he know she was still in bed?

She groaned and slumped through to the bathroom. She looked a sight. She pulled on some clothes, quickly brushed her teeth and washed her face, then went down to get the boat key and her safety kit.

The streets were busy this morning. Most of the people shoving up the hill, which she was trying to get down, were definitely Brits. Salmon-pink faces, wobbly arms, midriffs bulging out of their embarrassing T-shirts, bearing utterly unfunny slogans like 'I'm With Stupid ☞' and 'Keep Calm Woman and Pour the Tea'.

Sally growled to herself as she pushed through the thrusting, chattering throng. She knew when crowds were this thick it meant that a cruise ship had come in along the coast. Hopefully some of them would take lunch at La Mosaïque.

At the bottom of the hill she found the quay also bustling with slow-moving tourists.

Tugging the collar of her waterproof jacket up, she scuttled along at the water's edge. The last thing she needed now was one of them recognising her, and telling her how much older she looked than when she was on telly twenty years ago.

She shoved through the doors of La Mosaïque to find Carol, holding out a large cardboard box and tapping her watch. 'The ship's name is on the box. Presumably you know how to find an address which is just "somewhere out here on the water"?'

'No more details?'

'It's a 52-footer,' Carol read from her notes. 'Which probably means more to you than me.'

Sally grabbed the box and peered at Carol's felt-tip-marker writing. '"*The Bitch Got The House*"?'

'Apparently that's the name of their yacht.'

'What kind of a name is that?'

Carol shrugged. 'Ours not to question why ...'

'And they didn't tell you anything other than the boat was on the water?'

Carol proffered Sally her notebook.

Laying down her safety kit, Sally flicked through the scrawled pages.

'It's a Sunseeker, 52 foot?' Sally rolled her eyes. 'Well, that narrows it down a bit. Did they even say they were off Bellevue-sur-Mer? They're not at Villefranche, Èze or Cap-Ferrat, perhaps? The Côte d'Azur is a huge stretch of water.'

'Stop fussing, woman.' Carol thrust the box at Sally. 'I'll get hold of them again and then phone you with the details.'

Sally stood, waiting.

'No, Sally. I mean you go, now. I will phone you with further info.'

Sally did not like the way Carol was talking at her as though she was simple.

'Come on, Sally. Vamoose! We want to start this business with a good reputation.'

Suppressing her desire to reply, Sally turned on her heels and went out again into the open. She nimbly steered the picnic box through the pressing crowds, then took the steps down to the quay where her little fishing boat was moored.

This Shore to Ship was such a stupid idea she regretted being the twit who'd thought it up. She also realised that she was going to have to look slippy, because, if it didn't work, she would be the one to take all the blame.

Jumping aboard her boat, Sally stowed the box in the wheelhouse where there would be no spray. It was only then that she realised she had not picked up the safety kit.

Ah well. She'd never ever needed it before. Fingers crossed that she wouldn't need it this time.

———

To Theresa, getting in an hour earlier and making up a box of picnic fayre had not been too much of a strain.

She was now busily peeling potatoes, while singing along to the radio.

They had a pretty full house for lunch, which was probably due to the cruise ship which had moored just up the coast for the day. On the other hand, tonight's dinner bookings amounted to one table for three.

She hoped that the adverts going in the local papers and on the radio stations would bring in a few home deliveries.

Potatoes finished, she cleared away the peelings and went to the store cupboard for flour.

Theresa loved pottering around in this kitchen. But pottering, of course, was not the ideal state to be in. If she were racing about, wiping sweat from her brow, it would be preferable because then they would be earning money rather than propping up the place while it descended into ruin.

Opening the fridge, she took out a slab of butter, and laid it on the stainless-steel top, to soften up. She realised she should have done this before the potatoes, but frankly, since the disappointment of the auction, she had not been thinking efficiently.

She moved across to the vegetable racks and pulled out a handful of carrots and placed them in the sink. She knew she'd also want red peppers later, so she went to the salad rack. Lying across the lettuces was a red rose. How lovely! Someone had sent her a pretty flower to cheer her day. She filled a jug of water and put the rose in. Unfortunately the neck was too wide so it kept flopping out.

What a gorgeous little token to brighten a dull day. As she set to work on the carrots, she wondered who might have left it. She wondered whether it was the actual vegetable-delivery guy, or perhaps the driver. How romantic! Maybe it was one of the team at La Mosaïque.

No doubt whoever had left her the sweet gift would own up later on and it would be a terrible disappointment. She sighed and glanced up at the wall clock. Half eleven! She was well behind.

Snatching the rose from the jug, Theresa dropped it into a glass of water. Tonight she'd take it home, put it in a slim tall vase and leave it on her windowsill.

Then she turned up the radio, picked a good sharp knife and started chopping.

Sally navigated through rather choppy waters, squinting at all the motor yachts anchored in the bay. She hadn't realised how many had clever-clever long names. She had thought that the particular name she was headed for would be easy to spot due to its length, but not when you had others called *Three Sheets to the Wind*, *Stocks and Blondes* and *Eat, Drink and Remarry*. She sensed a fair amount of bitterness in boat naming.

Sally was also amazed at the number of British ensigns dangling from the stern staffs. Many of these boats seemed to be registered in every conceivable tax haven, from Jersey, Guernsey and Bermuda to the Cayman Islands.

So many loaded people.

And if the Picasso had sold as intended, she might have been one of them. Sally gathered control of herself. Even if the mosaic had made what she considered to be mega-bucks, she still wouldn't have arrived at anywhere near the level of wealth of these people. And presumably they had something more up their sleeves than just striking it lucky. If they had worked for their money, there must be some feeling of fulfilment, something which in her own mind she lacked.

As she left the waters of Bellevue-sur-Mer and pulled out into the open sea, she turned the wheel of the helm and pushed the throttle forward.

Where was this ruddy boat?

Her phone rang.

Carol.

'You were right. They're not at Bellevue-sur-Mer. They're actually at the end of the Rade at Villefranche.'

Sally sighed.

Carol continued: 'To be fair, they admitted to me that they didn't actually know where they were but described their surroundings, saying it was a big bay, with hills either side and that they could see "a kind of polygon-shaped white lighthouse" nearby at the end of the land …'

'Cap-Ferrat,' snapped Sally. 'I'm on my way.'

'Good.' Carol hung up.

Sally slipped her phone back into her pocket. Carol didn't need to be quite so brusque. Sally felt utterly disgruntled.

Why had she got involved in the stupid restaurant in the first place? It really wasn't her thing at all. She must have been having a mental fit that day. Her friendships with the others had been so much easier before. Now practically everything made her feel guilty.

Sally steered the boat towards the lighthouse, all the while thinking of the fuel she was getting through. This Shore-to-Ship idea was going to cost them so much more in gas than they could ever make in profit from a few sandwiches. She couldn't see how they could make it work if she had to race miles and miles around the Med …

As the boat hurtled through a wave, spray drenched the windscreen. Sally laughed. Really, she was relieved to be out at sea in the boat rather than hovering around the restaurant surrounded by all that disappointment, tension and fear.

Perhaps, for the moment, she wouldn't say anything.

She could see a yacht ahead.

Bare, white, oiled bodies sprawling on the foredeck. They must be mad. The sun might be shining, but it wasn't *that* hot.

Sally threw the fenders over the side, pulled in towards the stern of *The Bitch Got The House* and gave a shout.

'Hi there! La Mosaïque! Your luncheon order.'

A plump dark-haired man in nothing but a pair of white shorts leaned over the side. Sally noticed his greying temples. 'I'll send the boy down.' Even if he hadn't spoken

Sally knew as soon as she set eyes on him that he must be English. No one else would dress like that at the end of March. It was sunny but cold.

A teenaged boy slouched down the steps and took the box from Sally. She went back into the wheelhouse, ready to move off. But the dark-haired man called down: 'Before you go I'll have to check it. I know all about you fly-by-night outfits.'

Sally gritted her teeth.

She was really not in the mood for this.

With no sense of haste, the man lay back down on his lounger and waited till the boy arrived at his side with her box. Sally could hear female giggles; presumably the girlfriends she'd seen earlier on the deck, now out of her sightline.

Slowly the man untied the pink ribbon.

Sally could hear the females whispering to him.

'Apparently this is not what my, er, pretty friends ordered.' The man stood, hands on hips.

Sally took the receipt from her pocket and read it aloud.

'Two portions of hake, green beans, peas and, um, toast.'

'I'm sorry?' said the man, gripping the starboard guard-rail and leaning down. 'No. No. This will not do.'

One of the women appeared behind him – a young blonde with unnaturally large lips and breasts, wearing a bikini so skimpy it was barely more than two pieces of string. Sally could see goose-pimples rising on the flesh of her arms. How mad to wear swimwear, simply because the sun was out and they were on a yacht! Hadn't they noticed that on every passing yacht the crew were fully clothed?

'Tell her, Snooky.'

'It's OK. I have this under control. Don't worry your pretty little head about it.'

The girl took a step forward, looking down at Sally in every possible way. Another surgically enhanced girl moved into the picture. They both snuggled up to 'Snooky'. Sally barely managed to disguise her revulsion as they started stroking 'Snooky's' impenetrably dark, hairy chest.

'I'm just the delivery service.' She couldn't help thinking that the man's chest looked like a dirty doormat. 'I have brought you what you ordered.'

'Now look here, you old bint. You people might want to work up all this healthy-eating malarkey, but when a customer orders baked beans, toast and chips, that's what the customer wants, and it is your bloody duty to provide it. Not this pretentious rubbish. We don't want it. I want my money back.'

He tipped the box upside down, emptying the contents into the water. A large hunk of lightly grilled white fish and a single haricot landed on Sally's windscreen.

'Come on. Cough up.' 'Snooky' thrust out his hand. 'I'll send the boy down for the cash.'

The teenager slouched on to the bathing platform. At least he was more suitably dressed, in a T-shirt and jeans. He bent down and whispered to Sally. 'Wish I'd never agreed to come on this ship. He's a pig.' He held out his hand. 'And those girls are more my age than his. Except they're so boring.'

Sally had no cash on her other than the contents of her purse, a few coins and a five-euro note, and she wasn't giving that up to Snooky.

She mimed putting money into the boy's palm and muttered, 'Tell him it will be credited back to the card he used.'

The boy leaned forward and said conspiratorially, 'Thanks, Theresa.'

45

'Sally,' said Sally, dashing back into the wheelhouse. 'You must have spoken to Theresa earlier.'

She started up the engine.

How odd of the boy to think that the same person who must have taken the call also made the delivery.

As she pulled away she glanced back at the gin palace. The boy gave her a furtive wave. The little boat swerved, and she could hear the two girls screaming abuse after her. But she pushed the throttle and manoeuvred the boat past the rocky shore, whizzing around the headland and away.

PART TWO

TARTE TROPÉZIENNE

St-Tropez Tart, a Provençal classic, is sold in all patisseries in France. It was created in 1955 and named by Brigitte Bardot to celebrate her home town. Serves 8.

For the cream
500ml semi-skimmed milk
1 vanilla pod, split in two
3 eggs
100g icing sugar
50g plain flour
200ml double cream, whipped
4 drops orange-blossom oil
2 pinches salt

For the brioche
5g dried yeast paste
50ml water
250g plain flour
salt, to taste
30g icing sugar
3 eggs
125g unsalted butter, cut into small pieces and at room
   temperature
zest of 1 lemon
15g sugar crystals
50g unsalted butter, cubed

Decoration
50g icing sugar, sieved

First make the cream filling. Boil the milk with the vanilla pod, then vigorously whip the eggs with the icing sugar until it resembles a thick cream. Fold in the flour. Pour in the boiling milk and mix well. Put it back on the heat for about 3 minutes, or until thickened. Once the cream mixture is cooked, pour it into a bowl, cover with cling film and leave to cool (as quickly as possible). When cool, whip using an electric mixer. Add a third of the double cream to the mixing bowl, still beating vigorously. Then gently stir in the remaining cream, orange-blossom oil and salt.

Next make the brioche. Dilute the yeast in lukewarm water. Mix the flour, salt and sugar in a food processor. Add the eggs and the diluted yeast to the mixture and blend using a dough hook until slightly sticky. After 8 to 10 minutes' low-speed kneading, the dough should be smooth and elastic. Then add 125g of butter and continue to knead gently until it is completely incorporated. Stir the lemon zest into the dough, then cover with a cloth and leave at room temperature to rise for approximately 1 hour (or until it has doubled in volume). Preheat the oven to 200°C. When risen, knead the dough by hand until it returns to its original size. Leave it to rest in the refrigerator for a minimum of 15 minutes. Spread the brioche mix into a 20cm-diameter greased cake tin. Leave to rise until once more doubled in size. Sprinkle the top with the sugar crystals and butter cubes. Bake in the oven for 20 minutes. Take it out and let it cool, then cut into two through the centre to make a sandwich.

To assemble the tart, use an icing bag to squeeze the cream over the lower part of the brioche. The filling should be at least as thick as each of the two slices of brioche. Put the upper part of the brioche on top of the cream. Sprinkle with icing sugar before serving.

FIVE

THERESA FOUND LUNCH SERVICE utterly depressing. Cruise days were always terrible. The customers were so used to the fine dining on board that all they wanted onshore was fry-ups.

Three tables had sent their *panisse* chips back, mistaking them for simple potato chips, rather than the delicious *Niçoise* speciality made from chickpeas.

How to start explaining?

It had certainly not been their plan to run a greasy spoon. And even if they did change the menu to cater for these people, where would that leave them on ordinary days when there was no huge white whale of a ship in the nearby harbour?

The locals wanted good food, well prepared.

She thought of Marcel, who ran the brasserie next door. After the service was over this afternoon, she would go there for a glass of wine and have a chat with him. He must have similar problems. It would be interesting to hear how he dealt with it.

Theresa found herself trying to compose a reply to another table which had just sent four tartes tatin back, wondering why their apple pie had arrived served upside down, when Sally burst into the kitchen through the back door.

'I hate being insulted by people. Did you not listen to the order?'

'I'm sorry, Sally,' Theresa put the ice cream back into the freezer and dropped the scoop into the hot-water jug, 'but I haven't a clue what you're talking about.'

'The Ship-to-Shore or whatever it's called.'

'Hake, beans, toast and peas?'

'Exactly. Or as they would have had it: baked beans on toast and toasted cheese.'

'What?'

'Exactly.'

'If they wanted that why did they phone us?'

'You tell me. You spoke to them.'

'No, I didn't. Carol took the call. As usual. I don't do the phone.'

'Whatever!' Sally turned on her heels and slammed through into the restaurant.

The next half hour continued in similar vein. Theresa was very happy when the last order was called. She wiped down the tops and left through the restaurant. Carol and Benjamin were laying up for dinner, and William was at the desk totting up. No sign of Sally.

'Shore to Ship not such a success, apparently,' said William. 'But she's out now in the van, doing a home delivery to a local couple, so that should be all right. Carol clearly didn't understand their Essex accents.'

Theresa didn't want to get involved in another dispute, so she passed quickly out into the open air.

The afternoon sun was dazzling. Not bad for March. She took a deep breath and felt again the sudden delight at the beauty of the bay with its sparkling turquoise water.

As she strolled along the water's edge, Marcel from the brasserie gave her a wave. Theresa had always thought him a rather good-looking man. Typical *Niçois* – lean, small twinkly eyes, swarthy complexion, with a head of dark curls, sprinkled with grey.

That determined her.

She crossed the road and took a seat on his terrace.

'*Un verre de Côtes de Provence, s'il vous plaît, Marcel,*' she said. '*Un grand!*'

'That bad?' he asked.

She nodded and sighed. They spoke in French. Theresa's was faltering, but at least it was getting better all the time. She seemed to be able to understand much better than she could speak. And she knew her accent was pretty terrible.

'Thank God for you, Marcel. How are things going here?' she asked.

'The usual,' Marcel shrugged. 'Some days busy but, like today, with idiots; other days very quiet with no one here but our regulars.'

'Are you cutting back on the suppliers?' she asked. 'We're not sure where to turn. Your advice would be very valuable to me. You've always been very generous with us, Marcel.'

'It's different for us, with a brasserie.' Marcel sat down at her table. 'We make a great deal of money on people who come here to sit and read a paper with a coffee or a glass of wine. If we had to rely only on our food, I think we'd also be in pretty bad trouble.'

'We're trying to consolidate,' said Theresa. 'And then sell up. *Voilà!*'

'*Désolé.*' As Marcel said this – so sorry – he really did look desolate.

'Ah well, that's life.' Theresa smiled. 'It was fun while it lasted. And when it's all over I will be free to do as I please with my time, which is not such a bad thing.'

She couldn't help but notice a slight twinkle appear in Marcel's eye. His enterprise might be a bar-brasserie, but perhaps, when there was no competing restaurant along the way, his mealtime covers would increase.

'You were very brave to open when you did. The timing was bad luck,' he said. 'Who could know ...' He left the subject dangling. No one liked to talk about what had happened in Nice a few years back. 'What will you do next? You're not leaving Bellevue-sur-Mer?'

'How could I leave you?' Theresa pointed to the surroundings – the sea, the town, the sky. 'I was thinking about maybe setting up in a small van and doing stalls at festivals and marketplaces.'

Marcel pulled a typically Gallic face which indicated lack of faith in the idea.

Theresa knew that he was right. There was no point in doing anything when you were only doing it as a stop-gap. Unless you were full of enthusiasm for a project, how could you expect it to succeed?

'Well, Theresa, I wish you all the luck in the world.' Marcel started to move away to deal with a customer in the corner.

'You're adorable to give me your time.' She raised her glass to him as he went. 'Thank you, Marcel.'

After the drink Theresa went home. She sat for half an hour staring out of the window, watching the sea, feeling depressed and rather scared. She was still four years away from getting her pension. Now that La Mosaïque was so deeply in debt, even once they sold up she would be no better off. She was going to have to find some way of stay-ing afloat and supporting herself.

She got up to turn on the kettle.

She could hear people moving about in the flat above her. It used to be quiet most of the year, but she realised that the owners, who lived in Paris except during holi-day times were letting it out as an Airbnb, whenever they weren't here themselves.

She sighed.

Life was changing in so many ways.

Maybe she really would have to give up her dream of living here and go back to live in London.

But now she wouldn't have a hope of buying anywhere, and where would she get money to pay rent? Would she end up loading shelves at B&Q, along with the other silver stackers? All told, it would be cheaper and easier to stay here and beg in the streets.

She called and left a message at the old solicitor's office in Hampstead, where she was once secretary, just to see if there was any work going. No doubt she would hear nothing. She'd been laid off. Why would they want her back now that she was even older?

As Theresa poured her tea, she decided to phone home. Perhaps talking to her daughter would help.

Imogen picked up.

'Hello?' She sounded stressed. Instantly Theresa realised it was not great timing. With the hour difference, Imogen would have only just got home from work.

'Hi, darling. Just phoning to say hello.'

'Oh, Mum. Hi.' Theresa picked up her lack of interest. 'Look ... I'm a bit pressed at the moment. Only just walked through the door. Here. Speak to Chloe.'

Chloe was Theresa's eldest grandchild.

'Hi, Gran. How's sunny France?'

Theresa waffled on for a while. She could hardly ask a fifteen-year-old for career and life-choice advice!

'Gran, I was wondering ... ?' Chloe left the phrase dangling.

'Yes?'

'Is Bellevue-sur-Mer near the French Riviera?'

'Bellevue-sur-Mer *is* the French Riviera.' Theresa laughed. 'The Riviera is just an English phrase which means the coast of south-eastern France, the whole coast along here, around Bellevue-sur-Mer.'

'So you live in the French Riviera?'

'Well, yes. But over here it's called the Côte d'Azur – the blue coast. Is this for a geography class or something?'

'Something like that. Here's Lola. Talk some sense into her.'

Theresa was amused that Chloe was picking up her mother's way of talking.

Lola wanted Theresa to look out and send her a copy of the photo she had taken of her and her two sisters by the wall plaque of Catherine Ségurane, the sixteenth-century *Niçoise* heroine who had saved the city by baring her backside to the fleeing hordes. 'I'm writing a project about women soldiers,' she said. 'And I'm going to say that she won the war by showing the enemy her bottom.'

Theresa looked across the room at the bookshelf. She could see the orange spine of her photo album at the end of the row of art books. She promised she would do it right away, laughing at how fixated children always were with bottoms.

Theresa spoke briefly to her third and youngest grand-daughter Cressida then ended the call.

Almost instantly the phone rang again. She picked it up, hoping it would be Imogen to continue where Cressida had left off. But there was just a silence. She must have done that thing where you put the phone down too violently and it rings the bell.

She laid the receiver carefully back and looked out across the road at the sea.

The gloom was still upon her. The physical gloom outside, as the sun set, did not help.

It was almost time to go back to work. Time to face the sombre music. Time to prepare the dinner service.

After Sally had driven back and forth all afternoon doing the usual restaurant shopping, picking up ingredients from Theresa's list at the huge cash and carry, she had barely a few minutes before she was on the road again, this time making the evening home deliveries.

This afternoon had been problematic. What with the stupid shenanigans of Shore to Ship she had lost the vital morning time when the markets were open. Instead she had to rush about sourcing fresh things from more dubious outlets.

Luckily most of the dinner home deliveries so far this evening were in Bellevue-sur-Mer; only one was outside the town, a few miles along the coast in Nice itself.

She motored along in the dark, the passenger seat and footwell loaded with the boxes of dinner all tied with a pink ribbon within their insulated bags. The van laboured up the hill. It was badly in need of a service. She wondered how long this situation could last, with everyone working all hours, just to try to scrimp a bigger profit and earn some good reviews on the online sites.

She was dog-tired. Or was she simply depressed?

The traffic signal turned green and the van lurched forward, on the descent into Nice – the yellow horseshoe of street lamps lining the curve of the bay, the distant multicoloured twinkling lights of the airport.

The atmosphere in the restaurant itself was so horrible that she was glad she was out on the road doing deliveries.

If this was how it felt after a day, what would they be like in a week, a month?

She pulled up at another traffic light, and watched the flashing sign for a fast-food joint near the port. She knew that businesses around here had had a triple whammy as they had also been disturbed by work on the new tramway. Once the tram was running, business here should not only pick up, but multiply.

Back in Bellevue-sur-Mer they had no such hope.

Damn that Picasso!

If they hadn't had that expectation of an unearned fortune, they might have thought more clearly, and thrown in the towel while there was still a chance of making good for themselves.

Now the weight of everyone's disappointment was too heavy to bear.

Sally prayed that they would find a buyer for La Mosaïque soon, offload the premises, dissolve the partnership and save their friendships. The strain was already showing. Theresa had been short with her, and she with Theresa. William was even more bossy than usual, if that was possible. Benjamin was as likely as she was to go off the rails, and as for Carol …

Their friendships had been so strong before this restaurant fiasco.

Though, to be honest, after La Mosaïque was gone, she had no idea what she would do with her days.

If she could even get back her investment, or even the better part of it, she should be OK. But she realised she had got so used to being busy that an everlasting spread of long days of nothing to do held no great fascination for her, especially now that she was living with these thoughts of being old and, inevitably, death.

The phone rang. Carol again. While Sally was delivering in Nice could she please pick up some things for the restaurant.

'Like what?'

'More takeaway tin trays, and large cans of tomatoes?'

Sally glanced at the clock. Somewhere in the city there should still be a supermarket open this late.

Carol said she'd send the complete list by text.

Once Sally had delivered the last dinner, she promised to go to the big hypermarket near the Riquier station.

The clients this evening, unlike those in this morning's fiasco, seemed genuinely delighted with their food boxes. Life was looking up.

The supermarket was insanely bright. The lighting had that neon white which made everyone look utterly washed out.

She was exhausted and dreaded to think what she must look like.

Taking out her phone, Sally scrolled through the list while she fumbled about in her pockets for a coin to release a trolley.

Nothing.

She stood for some time in a queue at customer services and was eventually provided with a plastic token.

This shop sold everything from potato crisps and wine to top-end televisions, bicycles and garden trellis.

As Carol had not written the shopping list in any particular order, this meant Sally had to traverse the same departments over and over. She was too tired now to think clearly and was in no mood to walk a marathon in the shopping aisles. She leaned on the trolley and suppressed a yawn. Her *petit pause* was interrupted by a siren, warning all shoppers that the shop would soon be closing and that as soon as possible they should make their way to a checkout.

Sally bent over and went through the contents of the trolley, checking everything off against the text, then she joined what looked like the shortest queue, only to discover it was restricted to customers with a specialist loyalty card which she did not possess.

She spun the trolley round and shoved it along, diving towards the next shortish line before more people arrived.

'*Attention!*' called a woman with a high-pitched, affected French accent.

Scraping her hair out of her eyes, Sally turned to apologise, only to find herself face to face with Phoo Taylor-Markham.

'Salzy! Of course it had to be you crashing into me. You were never the greatest driver.'

Phoo held out her shopping basket. 'I suppose I couldn't squeeze in front? I've only a few paltry items.'

Reluctantly Sally agreed, knowing that now she would have to spend a few minutes in polite conversation.

'Eggy and I were laughing this morning, remembering how clumsy you always were. And all those problems with biscuits! Don't you remember? Trying to charge us for all those expensive biscuits? And it was so clear to us that you were a secret biscuit binger. In those days you were rather large, weren't you? Well done, by the way, getting all that flab off. You're not nearly so fat these days. Must be the famed Mediterranean diet that everyone's always going on about.'

Sally tried to find the conversation amusing, but found it difficult to crack a smile. Why did Phoo have to remind her of her nervous start in the business? Why bring any of it up now, so many years later? Sally thanked her stars that the merry theatrical couple were only here on a two-week holiday.

'Making the most of your last few days?' she asked.

'Sorry?' Phoo looked puzzled. 'I don't understand you.'

'Didn't you say you were going back to London at the weekend?'

'Oh lord, no. Well, yes. We were *meant* to be going back on Saturday. But it's all change now, I'm afraid. We're staying on because Eggy and I ...'

'Phoebe!'

Phoo was interrupted by the shrill call of a heavily tanned woman, with hair dyed so blonde it was almost white. The woman was skimpily dressed for the season, but Eggy who marched doggedly at her side was bearing a huge fur coat which no doubt belonged to the blonde.

'Let the peasants form the long lines. I 'ave the special card for the short queue. Come with me, Phoebe.' The blonde clicked her pearly-pink taloned fingers in the air; a collection of bracelets on her bronzed arm jingled. 'You are now shopping with Odile de la Warr!'

Odile dragged Phoo away to the special priority queue.

'Oh, ye gods! Sal, old girl!' exclaimed Eggy. 'What on earth are you doing here?'

'Shopping?' she suggested. 'Rather like you.'

There was a pause.

'I presume the fur coat is not your own?'

'It might suit me rather well,' Eggy pulled a face, 'if I was playing a character in *Game of Thrones* – I should be so lucky ... But no. It's Odile's. I am her mere slave boy.'

'I hear you're staying on for a while. That'll be nice for you.'

Eggy seemed to ignore her remark.

'Odile's quite splendid, don't you think?' He cast his eyes back in her direction. 'My idea of the perfect ultimate Frenchwoman.'

Sally squinted along the rows at the loud woman with her mahogany skin, scraped-back hair and surgically enhanced breasts and lips. In her own opinion she thought a perfect idea of a Frenchwoman would be something more along the lines of Simone Signoret or Jeanne Moreau.

She remained silent.

'Would you like to join us for a drink, Salz, old girl, once we've put the shopping in the Beamer?' Eggy looked around. 'God knows where the exit is to this place, but there must be something resembling a bar nearby. After all, this is France.'

'I don't think I can manage tonight, Eggy. I have to get all this back to the restaurant.'

'Which restaurant? We could all go there, perhaps, for supper?'

Sally started to panic now. She looked at her watch. Ten p.m. She was relieved to see that it was the deadline for last orders.

'I'm so sorry, Eggy. It's miles away. We'll be too late, tonight. Maybe another day.' She took a few steps forward and was now nearly at the till. 'How long will you be here?'

'In this shop?'

'No. I mean when do you go back to England?'

Eggy gave an enormous sigh. 'That, my dear Sally, is in the lap of the gods. Things have popped up and we are both going to be around for quite a bit longer.'

'Any particular reason?' Sally didn't really care, but could see that Eggy was leaning out to be asked.

He gave her a coy smile. 'Can't say, I'm afraid, Salzy.' He looked around then knocked his own head. 'Superstitious, you know. Touch wood.'

Sally had now reached the cashier. She started unloading the contents of her trolley on to the conveyor belt.

Moving away, Eggy made a mime of a telephone with his fingers.

'We'll meet up soon. When I have a better idea of what's what. Ta-ta, old girl.' He turned away and twisted back. 'Did Phoo tell you how we were all laughing with Odile the other day talking about how hopeless you were as an assistant stage manager? Oh, how we howled. I bet you're glad to be out of all that showbiz stuff, Salzy, and being over here, on easy street.'

Sally gave a wan smile and nodded. 'Sure.'

While she was paying, Eggy was summoned by a cry from Odile, who needed her coat. He obediently trotted away, leaving Sally to stack the paid-for items neatly back in the trolley. Then, grinding her teeth in fury and dismay, she shunted it down the ramp to the car park.

She wasn't a useless actress. She had had quite a success, in her day. But when she thought of the reality of the present, with the restaurant and all its problems, that didn't polish up so brilliantly.

Eggy was right. She was a failure.

She felt desolate and dreaded the promised call where she would have to put up with more humiliation.

It was only when she was in the lower car park, steering the trolley towards the van, that she realised with enormous delight that Eggy didn't actually have her phone number.

SIX

THERESA HAD WOKEN LATER than she planned and it was only when she was closing the front door that she remembered she had promised to send Lola the photo of herself with her sisters, posing next to Catherine Ségurane's wall plaque in Nice.

She quickly unlocked, snatched the orange photo album from the shelf and flipped though, looking for the photo. After a few minutes she gave up, shoved the book into a string shopping bag and left for work.

The kitchen was in chaos. Sally had dropped off all the stuff on the shopping list last night, but no one had put it away, then the vegetable man had stacked boxes of fruit and veg on top of the supermarket bags. This meant that when Cyril arrived with the meat delivery, there was simply nowhere for him to rest his box.

Carol and William arrived in time to help move things about.

Cyril grumpily shoved past them, and tried to get the fridge door open using his elbow. Plump and rosy-cheeked, Cyril had blond hair, which was thinning out, leaving a balding circle. Theresa noted that it was getting worse by the week.

'Just stop, Cyril!' Theresa shouted. She could see that his efforts were annoying everyone else. 'Don't be so stupid. Wait by the door and I will tell you when to come in.'

In a sulk now, Cyril gave a shrug and walked to the back door, where he stood, barely disguising his irritation.

Carol stacked boxes to one side while William traipsed up and down the stairs to the cellar with the dry goods and tins.

Then, amid this confusion, Marcel wandered in through the back door, pushing past Cyril, saying that he needed to speak to them all.

'Oh, please, Marcel,' cried Theresa. 'One minute. It's like Piccadilly Circus in here. Just go through, darling.' Marcel clambered through the mess of boxes, bags and packaging strewn on the kitchen floor and sat down in the dining room.

Theresa then called Cyril inside.

'Thank you so much, my dear Cyril.' She took his box and dismissed him quickly. 'As you can see, today, I'm afraid, I have no time to chat.'

She kissed him on both cheeks, in the usual French manner, and waved him goodbye.

Tying her apron on, Theresa shoved the photo album under her arm and came through to the dining room. The others were gathered round the tables, waiting to hear what Marcel had to say.

Sally lingered near the front door with Benjamin.

Theresa could see that they all looked very tired. Although it was morning, she herself was exhausted.

What would they all look like if it went on for months?

'My friends,' Marcel addressed them in French. 'I know you are all suffering. I am aware, thanks to Theresa, of the status of events, all out of our control, which have come to pass. I too have had my own problems. And I am here to suggest a solution, which I hope will suit us all. I realise you will need time to digest my offer, but I make it in good faith.'

Theresa could see that Marcel had caught William's and Carol's attention, even if Sally and Benjamin were still huddled together giggling about something else.

'I wish to buy you. Everything. La Mosaïque, the premises, the equipment, the goodwill.'

Theresa gasped. 'You don't mean it?'

Marcel's surprise suggestion even made Benjamin and Sally sit up.

'First, I will need to see the accounts, discuss them with my accountant, and if you agree in principle then we will discuss the price.'

He stood, smiling encouragingly. He placed his chair carefully into the table, taking care not to scrape along the mosaic.

'Can you bring round the paperwork, William, and leave it with me. Give me forty-eight hours to go through everything and we can meet in here same time the day after tomorrow. Yes?'

Everyone echoed his yes.

It was Theresa who reminded them that, before deciding on anything, they were obliged to let Zoe take part in the vote, and that Zoe was off in Switzerland on one of her 'mini-breaks', which they all knew were a few days under the knife or being injected with sheep's placentas, under the guidance of some famed surgeon who promised her eternal youth.

But Marcel must remember that any decision on behalf of La Mosaïque had to be unanimous, and that a majority would be against the terms of their original contract.

He said he understood and moved towards the front door.

Theresa put out a hand to touch him as he passed. 'Thank you, dear Marcel.'

When he had gone, the buzz in the room was palpable.

'It will save us so much misery,' said William. 'And he's right. It would be in all our best interests. After all, we're all planning to stay on in Bellevue-sur-Mer, so we might as well be on friendly terms with the local eatery!'

Aware that she needed to catch the last post, Theresa busily flipped through the orange album, skipping past old photos of her wedding and those of Imogen as a teenager, and extracted the picture of the famous wall in Vieille Ville, Nice, in which she and her granddaughters posed in front of the bas-relief of Catherine Ségurane. She took an envelope from the welcome desk, addressed it to Lola and inserted a brief note, before sealing it. Explaining to the others that she would be back in a matter of minutes, she ran out to the postbox.

As she trotted past the brasserie, she could see Marcel inside talking earnestly with a small group of people.

She had just popped the envelope into the box when the postwoman's van drew up. Theresa felt happy that the photo was on its way home.

The grandkids had once been a bit of a problem for her, but the magic of this town had changed all that. They had come over here, and learned that she was not the enemy.

She was now so fond of them, and clearly they of her.

As she passed the brasserie for the second time, Theresa gave Marcel a wave and he winked and mimed a kiss in her direction. She blew him a kiss in return, using both hands.

Cyril's van pulled away.

In the dining room of La Mosaïque, William was on the phone to Zoe. Even from as far as the kitchen door-way, she could hear Zoe's excited 'yes'.

Theresa had barely settled in the kitchen when her mobile phone rang. She glanced down to see that it was Imogen on the line.

She knew she shouldn't when she was already running late, but she decided to take the call. Squeezing the phone between her neck and cheek, she started to scrub some new potatoes.

'Hello, darling. How lovely to hear from—'

But Imogen immediately cut her off.

'She's gone. I don't know what to do. I can't stay away from work. But someone has to be here in case she comes home.'

'I'm sorry, darling, I don't know what you're talking about.'

'Chloe. Chloe has gone missing.'

A chill ran though Theresa.

'Since when?'

'We don't know. She wasn't here this morning when I went to get them all up.'

'Did the others see anything?'

'No. They last saw her when they all went to bed. So she could have gone at any time between nine last night and now.'

Theresa looked at the wall clock. Eleven-thirty.

'She's not at school?'

'No.'

'Have you called the police?'

'Of course I have, Mother. I'm not a fool.'

'Might she be with friends?'

'No.' Imogen let out a sob. 'I've phoned all her friends. They're all at school.'

'Her father?'

'Don't be ridiculous. He's off travelling somewhere with that bloody au pair of his.'

In the ensuing silence, Theresa's mind raced through possibilities.

Imogen sobbed again and said, 'I'm at my wits' end.'

'What do you want me to do?'

'I know it's hard for you …' Imogen's voice was feeble with crying. 'But could you come home, Mum? Please?'

Theresa panicked. She knew she should be doing something, but what?

'I'm at work now – at school,' continued Imogen. 'But really I should be at home. Or in both places at once, but I can't.'

Theresa knew she must go back to London.

But how could she break it to the others at La Mosaïque? How could she leave them all now, when everything here was at such a crisis point?

But for Theresa there was no choice.

While preparing the lunch, she made a quick check on flights to London. There was one with an available seat, which flew out of Nice in three hours. With security, and check-in, that meant she would have to leave here within the hour.

She ordered a cab to come to the restaurant in forty minutes and take her straight to the airport.

Throwing herself round the kitchen, slamming dishes into the oven, preparing rows of desserts and putting them into the fridge, Theresa tried to think of ways she could prime the others before her departure. She would try to do as much as she could now, working on the basis of the covers for an average lunch service.

Carol ran in with an order for a strange little man in the corner who had changed his mind, and now wanted a different main dish. Theresa realised she should have tried to tell Carol, then and there, that she was leaving. But instead, she presented the new dish, saying nothing.

She knew Carol would want her to stay and also knew that she could brook no argument, or waste time while the others tried to persuade her.

So Theresa made up her mind that she would break it to the others only as she walked out of the door, for then it would be too late, and she didn't want to deal with their sympathy and suggestions.

She was certain they could manage without her. (And although actually she doubted the truth of that, she tried to suppress all her qualms on this subject.)

Because Theresa knew that she really had no choice.

She had to go to her family.

SEVEN

W HEN SALLY HAD PRESENTED the fuel bill for the boat's trip to Villefranche and back, Carol had seen her point. This meant that, unless a massive order came in for a ship moored nearby, the Shore-to-Ship project was effectively shelved. If anyone phoned with a small order, Carol would simply tell them that they had just missed the boat, literally.

But Sally was still on for picking up and making deliveries in the van.

As she unfastened her seat belt, back from a mid-morning early-lunch delivery, she watched the paltry gang of diners shuffling into La Mosaïque and taking their seats. They had the air of holidaymakers, French ones today, perhaps from Paris or the north.

Following them inside, she fiddled with her phone, all the while thinking about her bizarre meetings with Eggy and Phoo. She couldn't believe that people held on to those petty grievances for so long. But then she too was still nurturing the pain from the intimidation they had inflicted, and still was, deep inside, rather frightened of them, as though she was a mere child and they were serious adults. Those two chance encounters had left her feeling pretty nervous about driving the van around. She certainly did not want to bump into them a third time.

Just as the first orders started being served, Theresa arrived in the dining room and made her startling announcement, telling the whole group that she was leaving, with immediate effect, and that she did not know when she would return. Despite her initial shock on Theresa's behalf, Sally felt sure that the fourteen-year-old she had met last year would be off somewhere having a laugh with her friends, not imagining how this might scare her family. While Theresa was away, Sally would be secretly pleased to take her place, thereby retiring from the world of deliveries to hide in the kitchen. This would enable her to remain out of sight while still making her contribution to the team.

Thus, with no qualms, she volunteered. Carol, she suggested, could take on the deliveries, if and when they came, and in the meantime, at this low level of custom, the dining room and welcome desk could be easily served by William and Benjamin.

Having seen Theresa into the waiting cab, Sally rushed through into the kitchen, threw on an apron and set to work. Theresa had done most of the tricky business. All that was left to Sally was to put things into and take them out of the oven. She also had to whip up the odd thing on the stove-top. But Sally loved cooking, so all was well.

A large orange book, a photo album, was taking up most of the counter to one side of the sink, so Sally stowed it next to the delivery and order folders, and some small trays which stood vertically in a side cubbyhole under the counter, near the back door.

She swirled pureed beetroot on to warm empty plates, ready for the pies, heating up in the oven and almost ready.

As she found her way around Theresa's kitchen, Sally felt as though she was prying into someone else's world.

Poor Theresa. She hoped all would work out well, and the little girl would turn up soon. Children could be such a worry, especially if they were secretive or stubborn. Sally had had some close moments with her own two. But hopefully Chloe would be found soon; with any luck before Theresa even landed at Heathrow.

Sally pulled the tray of pies from the oven and swept it round, but her cloth caught the edge of a small glass, spilling slightly foetid water all over the countertop. The glass swirled round, then rolled across the counter and down on to the terracotta floor, where it smashed into pieces.

Flicking the broken glass out of the way, Sally briskly plated up the pies. It was more important that they should be served piping hot than cleaning up the mess on the floor. After William arrived and whisked them through to the dining room, Sally got out the dustpan and brush and knelt to sweep up the glass fragments.

'I hope I'm not disturbing you ...'

Sally jumped with surprise.

She turned to face Marcel who had sneaked in through the back.

'I'm just returning the account books. I'll come again during the break. Theresa not here?'

Benjamin was at the dining-room door calling for three cheese platters.

'No. She's not.' Sally wiped her forehead with the back of her hand. 'One minute, Benjamin.'

'Sorry! Sorry!' Marcel threw up his hands. 'I'll see you later.'

For heaven's sake! The man worked in the restaurant trade. What was he thinking about, coming here at the height of the lunch service?

Sally wondered if it wasn't to get a glimpse of how things were going in the kitchen before he made his offer. She smiled. Of course in most restaurants the 'height of service' would be rather more than eight covers – which was all she was coping with. But, still, for Sally, taking over from Theresa like this, unprepared, even catering for a few tables was something of a baptism by fire.

Sally washed her hands and got back to work, cutting tranches of cheese, snipping small branchlets from a bunch of grapes and arranging them on plates.

She hoped that she would find tonight easier. Once she felt she was in control of her own kitchen, and her own work, rather than finishing off someone else's, and feeling uncomfortable in their space, it had to be easier.

Didn't it?

As Sally moved across the kitchen to return the cheeses to the appropriate shelf, her foot went sliding and she found herself hurtling towards the door, then the floor. Without thinking, she grabbed on to the hot cooker-top to steady herself. She landed on the tiles on all fours, one hand burnt.

'Damnation.' She looked down to find that the cause of the slip was the remnants of a red rose which had fallen with the glass. Where had that been hiding? She threw the wretched thing into the bin, and held her palm under the cold tap for a few moments to ameliorate the pain.

The timer pinged, alerting her to another batch of pies due to come out of the oven. She pulled an oven glove over her sore hand and grasped the hot baking tray, only to find once more that, due to the awaiting cheese plates and the restaurant's books, which Marcel had thought-lessly laid on the other counter, there was nowhere to put it down. Balancing the tray on the edge of the sink, with her other hand Sally chucked the books down into the cubbyhole under the counter.

All would be well. She *would* master this kitchen.

This afternoon was a one-off.

It had to be.

Theresa spent hours going through security. Luckily she had her passport, which she tended to keep in her handbag in case she ever fancied going across to Italy, as nowadays there were random checks on the trains. Plus, of course, if you ever wanted to enter the casino at Monte Carlo, it was necessary to take a passport.

As her little win there had been the final deciding factor on her move to Bellevue-sur-Mer, the Garnier Casino had become rather a totem in her life.

But as she had not planned on leaving the country this morning, she only had her handbag with her, which should have made things easier. It did not. For naturally it was full of things which are forbidden in carry-on luggage.

As the security official dumped Theresa's bottle of very expensive perfume into the bin, he gave her a bright smile. Her favourite penknife, a pair of nail scissors and a box of matches, which she always kept with her in case the cooker burners failed to ignite, followed the perfume. She was then taken aside and interrogated for some time regarding why she would be travelling today without anything but a handbag, especially as she had no return flight booked. What was she running from?

She was eventually let through and on to the flight, where her thoughts were concentrated on the trouble which waited ahead in London.

She ran through many ideas of how to continue the search for Chloe. It seemed clear to her, from what she knew of both Imogen and Chloe herself, that the most likely scenario was a secret boyfriend.

Despite the loud and constant chatter of a couple seated beside her, Theresa's thoughts managed to remain fairly focused. She inadvertently learned an awful lot about them. They lived in a chi-chi village outside Stoke-on-Trent. They disagreed violently about whether red or rosé wine was superior, and spent much of the two-hour flight squabbling about that and other trivia.

Theresa realised that she had no clues about where Chloe might have gone because she always thought of her as a child rather than a person. She knew about all those things which were associated with childhood: the exams Chloe had passed and was due to sit, her grades, her hobbies and how she had excelled in the annual school play. But she knew nothing of Chloe's real desires or those inner flames which every human kept burning, leading them hopefully towards some kind of better tomorrow. She recalled her own childhood, and realised that she could still remember yearnings she had had when she was only six. So, as Chloe was fifteen, Theresa knew that the best clue to finding her would be to search out these private desires.

'I suppose you're going to tell me next that you prefer Beaujolais to Rioja,' said the male from the trendy village outside Stoke-on-Trent.

'Absolutely. In my opinion Rioja tastes just like saddle soap.'

'You spent a lot of your youth licking saddles, did you, dear?'

'When I had ponies, I loved my life. They were my happiest years,' said the woman from the village near Stoke-on-Trent. 'I should never have married a man who's never even been to a gymkhana.'

'I regularly have a bet on the horses. That's as far as I am prepared to go. But, no, dear, I cannot see the delight of a weekend's hacking.'

Theresa ran her mind back over the time Chloe had spent in Nice. That was when she had known her best. To

Theresa, Chloe had always appeared to be the rip of the family. A bit of a tomboy. The leader of the pack.

But as children moved into the teenage years, Theresa realised that even a few months could make a massive difference in behaviour. When those hormones kicked in, everything turned on its head.

'If you feel that way, perhaps you would have done better to marry a horse.'

'I married the nearest thing,' replied the wife. 'I married an ass.'

Theresa was very happy to get off the plane.

She took the Tube into town and went straight down to her daughter's house in Wimbledon.

A policewoman was with Imogen, who was now visibly distraught, quite unlike the stern head teacher Theresa knew.

As Theresa sat down Imogen sprang across the room and started putting on her coat.

'You can find out anything else you need to know from my mother,' she said, opening the front door.

The policewoman jumped up. 'Mrs Firbank, I strongly advise you to stay here. Leave this to us.'

But the door slammed and Imogen was gone.

'I realise that it feels useless staying put, Mrs, er ...'

'Simmonds,' replied Theresa.

'But it really is the best thing.' Tapping her pencil on her notepad, the policewoman shook her head. 'People always want to take action. But, for one thing, your daughter is in no fit state to drive.'

'She's not drunk?'

'No,' replied the policewoman. 'But she is extremely agitated.'

'Of course she is. Who wouldn't be?' Theresa decided to take control of the situation. She had seen enough TV shows to know what she should do. 'But my daughter is a very methodical person. She is probably going to visit all of Chloe's haunts. Meanwhile we shouldn't waste any time. Shall we look around her bedroom?'

'I think that would be very useful, Mrs Simmonds.' The policewoman laid down her pad and put her hat back on. She followed Theresa up the stairs.

While rifling through her granddaughter's things, Theresa felt guilty, but knew it had to be done.

'Does the child have a mobile phone?' the policewoman asked.

'Everyone has been ringing her.' Theresa moved towards the chest of drawers. 'But it appears she has turned it off.'

She pulled open a drawer.

'And here we have the solution.' A pink mobile phone was lying there, nestled between Chloe's T-shirts and underwear. 'It is most unusual for a young girl to leave without her phone, wouldn't you say, officer?'

The policewoman looked grim. 'Unless she was abducted in the night, which seems highly unlikely without some evidence of a break-in, I would suspect that this means she has a second phone. Perhaps a pay-as-you-go. But I'm afraid that it does make things look rather more serious.'

Theresa sat on the bed. She knew what the officer was about to say.

'Men who groom children frequently buy them these phones so that they can have more control over them. It would also indicate that some planning went into her disappearance.' The policewoman bit her underlip. 'Do you know if she has a passport?'

'Yes. I live in France. I remember suggesting it, just in case they ever needed to come over to visit me without their mother. I have seen her passport.'

'Then we must find out whether she took it with her,' replied the policewoman. 'Do you know where the household passports might be kept?'

Theresa shook her head. 'I don't live here, I'm afraid. When my daughter gets back ...'

Theresa illuminated Chloe's phone. She hoped there might be something of a clue left on it. She scrolled through a long list of missed calls, all from her mother and sisters. The recent texts were only about homework and other school-related activities.

The policewoman held out her hand. 'If you don't mind, I'll take that. It's more than likely that the child—'

'Chloe.'

'That Chloe would have deleted anything she felt scared her mother might see. Frequently, if a departure from the parental home is planned, the child can be very wary about leaving any clues. Luckily the police have ways of retrieving old and deleted files.'

Theresa handed over the phone.

The policewoman took it, made her excuses and left.

Left alone with time to think, Theresa felt rather giddy. It was all so dreadful. On top of the turmoil she realised she had eaten nothing since breakfast. It was now around 7.45 p.m. French time, 6.45 here. She went to the kitchen and fumbled around trying to find something which would instantly appease her rumbling stomach.

As she was spreading a slice of toast with butter, the front door opened and Lola and Cressida were ushered in by a self-styled bohemian type with flowing black hair.

'Hello. I'm Frances, the girls' drama teacher.' Frances thrust forward a hand with multiple cheap rings and bangles. 'Imogen asked me to bring them home as soon as my rehearsal session was over this evening. She said you'd be here.' She lowered her voice. 'Dreadful business.'

Theresa excused herself. 'Pardon me for eating, but I've had nothing since breakfast.'

Frances clapped her hands and the two girls stood to attention. 'I presume you have homework?'

The girls nodded.

'Then would you kindly take yourselves to your rooms and start on it, while I talk to your grandmother.'

Theresa was amazed to see their immediate obedient reaction to her command.

Frances lowered her voice. 'We have all been taken by surprise over this. Of all the children in the school, I would never have expected Chloe to do something like this. She's always been the reliable girl.'

Frances leaned against the countertop, took an electronic cigarette from her pocket and put it to her lips. 'You don't mind, do you? My nerves are shattered.'

'Did Chloe have a close friend who might know anything?'

Frances took a long drag and puffed out a cloud of strawberry-scented vapour.

'Alice. Poor child has been given the third degree by all and sundry throughout the day. Watching her, I fear that she is devastated by the whole business, but mainly by the fact that she really didn't guess anything, and that Chloe, her supposed best friend, held it back from her.'

Theresa's hopes deflated a little further.

'And there are no boyfriends lurking?'

Frances chewed on the stem of the vape.

'No. Last autumn when she played Juliet in the school play, I did wonder about the boy who played Romeo. She was quite intense in her reading of the role, and—'

'And the boy, Romeo … What has he to say?'

'I rather think that he was more interested in Mercutio and Tybalt than poor Chloe.' Frances laughed. 'But she was certainly gone on him.'

'Is he still at school?'

'Yes. And, like Alice, has been grilled all day long. He's barely spent any time with her this term.' Frances emitted another sickly-sweet puff of vapour. 'We haven't sat idly on our hands, you know.'

'No one else from school has gone missing?'

'Absolutely not. Look, I'm glad to share information with you, but please don't imagine we have left any stone unturned. I think Imogen needed you here because of the other two kids. Poor things.' She took another puff of her vape. The scent niggled Theresa with some long-forgotten memory, and suddenly she remembered what it was. A childhood 'treat'. On Sunday mornings, her mother had opened a can of strawberries and laid a few on top of her bowl of cornflakes. Her recollection had them as something like limp, red, sticky surgical swabs. The drama teacher looked at her watch. 'Oh God. Look at the time. Must rush. We're rehearsing *Treasure Island* tonight. All that ship business and X marks the spot. It's all go.'

When Frances had gone Theresa made her way upstairs to speak to Lola and Cressida. But she feared she would get no further than the teachers had done.

———

Once lunch was over, Sally gave herself an hour to refresh herself and then returned to the kitchen and started getting everything ready for the evening service. She did not want to be caught out. She spent the early afternoon becoming familiar with the kitchen and the arrangement of the store-cupboards so that the dinner would go extremely smoothly.

In the light of both Zoe's and Theresa's absences, Marcel had postponed his meeting with them to discuss his offer for the restaurant. He knew that their decision had to be unanimous and, without the presence of two pivotal partners, he didn't want to waste his time. Sally thought there might be an ulterior motive lurking there too. He probably wanted to pounce in the style of agents selling timeshares. He would arrive, make an offer and give them only hours to accept or it would be withdrawn. That kind of thing. And for that ploy to work everyone with a vote had to be present.

Sally placed the last of the glass bowls of mandarin fool into the fridge, ready to be served. The potatoes were parboiled, ready to mash. And she had already chopped the little fat discs of *panisse* into the same shape as chips, ready to fry.

Through the dining-room door she could hear Benjamin squabbling with William. It was a comforting sound. There was a brief silence then somebody turned on the restaurant's music, which was about as far from lift musak as you could get. Most of the songs were French, and had a soft, lilting, relaxing feel, a bit like the music which was played in an upmarket hotel bar. Some Stéphane Grappelli, Le Hot Club de Paris, Charles Trenet, and even some modern songs by the likes of Emmanuel Moire and Julien Doré. Music was the signal that the doors would soon open to the public.

Sally swayed to the gentle rhythm as she started work on the breadcrumbs for tonight's fish dish, a pan-fried *merlu* – or hake. She glanced at the clock: 6.50. Ten whole minutes till the restaurant opened, and the handful of customers booked this afternoon dribbled in.

She felt rather smug.

She was on top of this.

84

Theresa sensed that Lola and Cressida were unsettled in more than one way by Chloe's disappearance.

Cressida sat forlorn on her bed, hugging her teddy bear and sobbing dramatically. Theresa wasn't sure whether the tears were for missing Chloe or for herself.

Lola was more insouciant. It was obvious to Theresa that she had information which she was holding back.

'You didn't see her packing a case then?' Theresa asked.

Lola shrugged and shook her head.

'Do you know what she took with her?'

'How should I know?' Lola started picking at the duvet cover with paint-stained fingers. 'She left while we were asleep.'

'When did you last see her?'

'Last night.'

Theresa glanced at Lola's multicoloured fingers. 'You were doing art this afternoon?'

'It's always art today.' Lola let out a huge sigh which implied that Theresa was a fool. 'Tomorrow afternoon it's games.'

'And you like games?'

'No, I do not,' Lola growled. 'It's cold and horrible, your legs go blue and you get covered in mud.'

'I suppose the boys like games, though?'

Lola hunched her shoulders. 'They like football.'

Theresa lobbed in a trick question: 'Did Chloe's boy-friend like football?'

Lola laughed and said 'No' in that querulous tone which implied that Theresa had made a ridiculous suggestion.

'You don't like her boyfriend?'

But Lola suddenly wised up to Theresa's wiles and looked directly into her eyes to reply. 'I don't know any-thing about him,' she said, defiant.

Theresa clapped her hands and rose from the end of the bed where she was perched. 'Bath-time!'

'It's too early for a bath.'

'Not when I'm in charge, Lola.'

Theresa went into the bathroom, turned on the radio and ran a bath, then marched Lola in. 'I want you clean as a new pin. Fingernails included. After that I will cook you both a very lovely supper.'

'Can we have chocolate tiffin?'

'We'll see.'

Once Lola was established in the bath, Theresa went back into the bedroom to quiz Cressida without the watchful and determined eye of her elder sister.

'I bet you miss Chloe, don't you?' she asked, watching Cressida as she pulled out her pyjamas and laid them on the bed.

'I want chocolate tiffin too,' the youngest grandchild replied.

'Of course. It's important to share.' Theresa picked up a book from Lola's backpack and pretended to be interested in it. Idly turning the pages, focusing on them rather than her grandchild.

'And do *you* like Chloe's boyfriend?'

Cressida bit her lower lip and said nothing.

'Does she meet him at school, or after school?'

'Don't be silly,' replied Cressida. 'He's gone abroad.'

'Abroad? Like me,' said Theresa calmly, though her heart had started to thump. She recalled Chloe's remark on the phone, asking about the South of France. 'French Riviera,' she said.

'How do you know that?' said Cressida. 'No one is allowed to know.'

'Chloe told me on the phone yesterday.' Theresa dangled the bait. 'He must be handsome, this young boy.'

Cressida looked at her warily. 'You're making a joke, aren't you, Grandma?'

'Of course. He's not that handsome, is he?'

'Of course not. He's fat, and bald.' Cressida pulled a face and added an afterthought. 'And he's not a young man. Actually he's very old.'

———

Sally was in the middle of her worst nightmare. Or at least she wished it was only a nightmare, rather than real life.

Just when things were going swingingly in the kitchen, a huge gang of British tourists arrived demanding 'nosh'. They were on a cruise, but, due to some technical disaster, the ship's coach couldn't come to pick them up for two more hours, so they had all decided to use the time here to take supper.

The main problem with this was that they wanted serving with snacks, and they wanted serving now.

William had politely explained that this was in fact not a café, but a restaurant, and that they could not just sit here for two hours sipping a coffee or a glass of wine. However, if they chose to remain, he would be delighted to serve them dinner.

They all stayed put.

A man in a shell suit stood up and shouted above the sound of the chatter that William should turn the music off; or better, replace it with some decent English music, like Rihanna. Everyone at his table cheered.

Drained of all colour, William snapped the music off, while Benjamin rolled his eyes and headed for the relative quiet of the kitchen.

'Prepare yourself, Sally. Tonight is going to be hell,' he warned her. 'I suppose you don't have any Valium, do you? I think it won't be long before William is going to lose it.'

'Why would you think that I have Valium?'

'Because you're an actress.'

Sally threw the spatula down on the countertop.

'What a ruddy assumption! Don't you actually think that if I had Valium I wouldn't have already taken five this evening?'

'You look as though you have. You seem so much calmer in here than you did after that incident with the man on the boat.'

William arrived and stood behind Benjamin's shoulder.

'They all want the fish and chips *Niçoise*. That's twenty. Twenty fish and chips *Niçoise*. I tell you, Sally, it's like a horror story out there. I don't think that in all the years I've lived here I have seen so many ugly outfits in one room.' He pulled both hands back through his sleeked hair, then slammed his palms down on to the serving surface with a deep sigh. 'I need a Valium.'

'Told you!' Benjamin gave a little pout.

The sound of the bell, indicating new arrivals, summoned William back to the dining room.

Sally and Benjamin gave him just enough time to get out of earshot before bursting into laughter.

'Where's Carol?' asked Sally, wiping a tear away.

'Delivering to one of our regulars who's down with *la grippe* or *les hémorroïdes* or something equally unsavoury.'

They both grabbed the countertop and rocked with silent hysteria.

'Oh lord, it's like being at school or something. Why are we laughing?'

Benjamin shrugged. 'Better than wringing our hands and sobbing, I suppose.' He sniffed and turned away.

'Benjamin! Where do you think you're going?'

'Back into the restaurant from hell.'

'No, no. I need you in here.' Sally picked up a large, sharp knife.

Benjamin held up his hands in supplication. 'Be gentle with me!'

'Well, then, darling, roll up your sleeves and start slicing the *panisse*, while I get on with breading the fish.'

William appeared again, looking even more tightly wound up than the last time.

'That was Daniel and Constance. They took one look at the room, said they'd had enough and have decided tonight to go home to eat.'

'But they're regulars ...'

'I do know that, Benjamin. But they didn't like the ambience, and I don't blame them. They thought they were coming in for a romantic *diner à deux*; instead they've got a bun fight.'

'Oh God! We don't want to start losing customers; now, of all times.'

'Fine.' William took off his velvet jacket and handed it to Benjamin. 'If you think you could have handled it better, get out there. It's Armageddon.' He looked around. 'Where's Carol?'

'Delivering to one of our regulars who's down with *les hémorroïdes*,' said Sally and Benjamin in unison. Then they both collapsed again with laughter.

'Did you even take note of the order?' William asked tartly. 'Twenty – oh, eighteen – fish and chips *Niçoise*.'

Snatching his jacket back from Benjamin, he turned on his heel and returned to the fray.

———

Theresa sat waiting in the living room for her daughter to return. She had rung Imogen and asked her to come home at once. Theresa knew that the information she had got from Cressida had to be discussed face to face, rather than on the end of a phone.

She was nodding off on the sofa, exhausted by the emotional day, when the key clicked in the lock.

She rose and straightened her clothing. It was strange how she behaved with her own daughter as though she was being hauled before the headmistress.

Imogen put her head round the door. She looked unlike she ever had before: hair awry, make-up smudged, vaguely shell-shocked. 'What is it?' she asked, moving swiftly into the living room.

Theresa told her exactly what Cressida had said.

'Did she have a name for this bald old pervert?' Imogen's hand hovered over her mouth; Theresa could see that it was shaking. 'I have a direct-line number for the police. We have to give them his identity right away.'

Her words faded out and she staggered, tilting backwards and landing on the sofa.

Once sitting, she started to wail.

Theresa sat beside her and softly put her arm about her daughter's shoulder.

'Cressida wasn't making much sense. She was on the verge of sleep. I think they've had a pretty weird day too.'

'Name?' snapped Imogen. 'Just give me the bloody name.'

Theresa took a deep breath. 'She didn't *exactly* give a name. But she said his name was "Fire".'

'"Fire"? What kind of a name is that?'

Theresa shrugged. 'Perhaps it's an avatar. It seemed to me to be the kind of name you'd get on a computer game or internet chatroom.'

'You do a lot of gaming, do you, Mum?' Imogen shook off Theresa's arm and stood up. 'I'm going to wake Cressida and force it out of her.'

Theresa followed. 'I don't think that's a good idea, Imogen. The child is exhausted.'

Imogen ran up the stairs, with Theresa in pursuit. She swung round the newel post and went straight into the girls' room. She sat on Lola's bed.

'But it was Cressida—'

'Yes. Yes,' snapped Imogen. 'But I know these two. Cressida only parrots what Lola tells her. If Cressida told you that much, Lola knows so much more.'

Imogen shook Lola.

The child's forehead was damp with the sweat of sleep. Lola blinked a few times and looked at her mother.

'What's wrong, Mummy? Is it a fire drill?'

'Lola. I need you to tell me everything you know about the man Chloe has gone off with.'

Lola bit her lip. Theresa could see that she was struggling with divided loyalty.

'I don't know anything,' she said. But her voice wavered.

'I'm sure Chloe told you not to say anything to your mother,' said Theresa, low but firm. 'But it really is very important. Chloe might be in danger. Please, Lola.'

Lola looked up at Theresa. A flash of fear lit her eyes. She licked her lips a few times, like a kitten at the vet's. Then she spoke, in a voice a little above a whisper. 'He's old and fat,' she said. 'He's bald, and he wears a dress.'

'A dress?' Imogen covered her face with her hands. 'Stop it, Lola. Tell me what you know. Don't make things up.'

Lola shrank back under the covers and whimpered, 'Chloe said he was a lovely kisser.'

As Imogen sobbed, Theresa took a small step forward.

'Did he promise to take her to the French Riviera?'

Lola shook her head. 'She was upset because he had gone there without her. But he was in Spain too. And Italy too, somewhere with a fishy name. Like Sardineland.'

'Sardinia,' muttered Imogen. 'The bloody man's every-where.'

'Does he really wear a dress, Lola, or are you making that up?'

'No. He does wear a dress. Brown with knots on.'

Theresa shot a look at Imogen. She stooped and whispered into her ear. 'Perhaps we should give that information to the police now.'

Imogen appeared not to hear her and she bent low over Lola's cowering face.

'Did you see him yourself, Lola? Or is this something Chloe told you?'

'I saw him, once. But that was a long time ago.'

Imogen shook Lola's shoulders.

'How long? Where did you see him?'

'It was before Christmas. Last term. At school. But I don't remember anything. I didn't know Chloe even liked him till yesterday.'

'Do you have a name for this man?'

'I think he used to be called Laurence, but he changed his name after Christmas and Chloe didn't tell me what it is now. But he's gone away before with lots of young girls with no clothes on, even though it's cold. He told her.'

Imogen's jaw was shaking.

Theresa was frightened for her.

She reached out and gently touched her daughter's back, whispering: 'We should go downstairs now, Imogen, and make that call.'

───────

William stood in the kitchen, his face the same shade of purple as his velvet jacket.

'I can't take it any more.' He flung up his arms. 'I just can't.'

Sally was rather relieved to find that William too was feeling distraught. The last two hours had been up there among the worst times in her life. Even the first performance of *A Long Day's Journey into Night* at St Andrew's Rep had come nothing near it, though that had been like a five-hour nightmare, rather than tonight's two.

'Don't look at me!' Sally watched William's meltdown turn into a simmering volcano of rage. 'Or, for that matter, at Benjamin. We've been working our arses off in here.'

William stamped his foot, and simultaneously threw a menu up to the ceiling. 'But everybody hates everything. They've sent it all back and now they're refusing to pay.'

'It's all been prepared exactly the same as normal. Red mullet in batter, with *panisse* chips.' Sally took a step forward, challenging. 'And don't think it's been fun sending out perfectly good dishes only to get them back three minutes later.'

'They think *panisse* is French for potato, so they're all grimacing and saying that the chips are "slimy".'

'Let's face it, people like that don't want anything we serve here,' added Benjamin. 'They want ketchup and vinegar, hamburgers and mushy peas.'

'He's right …' Sally backed Benjamin up. 'It states quite clearly on the menu …'

William silenced her by shouting, 'I know what it says on the bloody menu. I wrote the bloody thing. But it's in frigging French and they only speak bloody English. They think they're on a sodding day trip to the end of the bollocking pier at Blackpool not to a classy little chic restaurant in Bellevue-sur-Mer.'

'It's too late now to save the situation—' Sally started, but William cut her off again.

'I'm on the verge of a nervous breakdown, Sally. Really. If someone doesn't restrain me, I'm going back in there with a carving knife to finish them all off.'

Benjamin put out a hand, resting it on William's arm, but he shook it off, saying, 'Tomorrow, Sally, you can wait-ress. You have social skills, garnered from all your years "treading the boards". I'm just a crusty, old ex-English teacher who loathes and despises these low-lifes.'

'But can you cook, William?' Sally ventured.

'Of course I can't,' he squealed. 'But with this lot, who needs to actually be able to bloody cook?'

Sally realised how upset William must be. Normally such a fastidious speaker, he had just split two infinitives.

Benjamin removed his apron and crept towards the dining room.

'I'll try to salvage what I can,' he said quietly. 'William's too upset.'

'Didn't they see the word *Niçoise* after fish and chips?'

'You don't honestly think that means anything to them, do you? One of them thought it was pronounced "knick-ers". "I'll have the fish and chips knickers." She actually said that to me!'

William collapsed on to the bentwood chair in the corner and started fanning himself with the menu.

'Truly, Sally, why don't we just throw in the towel and sell up as it is now? Leave the place dark, as they'd say in your *métier*.'

'You know why, William. We need to sell it as a thriving business. With decent accounts and recommendations.' Her voice faded out as she realised that tonight was demonstrating the exact opposite. 'But our locals like us, the regulars. Perhaps we could ask them to go online and—'

'Sally, don't be ridiculous. You don't honestly think that people who live round here have got the time to fiddle about on phones giving stars and writing reviews of their favourite restaurants? They're French! They simply come out to dine, expect it to be wonderful, and then go home replete and happy. And quite right too. Only an imbecile writes reviews of a meal without being paid for it. Once upon a time that's how it was here, every night at La Mosaïque.' William hung his head.

Sally couldn't be sure, but she thought he might actually be crying.

'The cruise ship will be gone tomorrow, thank God,' Sally suggested quietly.

'Perhaps. But who's to say another one won't arrive?' Suddenly he looked up, his face earnest and suspicious. 'And another, and another. And we'll have a constant stream of people who mistake our gastronomic restaurant for a greasy spoon. Give me a moment. I'm just popping out.'

He strode past Sally and out. A few minutes later he was back.

'That bloody Marcel. His terraces are certainly *not* full. Nor are the tables inside. He just dumped that lot on us, knowing what would happen.' William rolled up his sleeves, and made again for the back door. But Sally grabbed hold of him, just in time.

'Please don't do it. Just know that we're on to him. Remember that, at this moment, Marcel is our best hope of a buyer. And naturally he wants to drive down the price. In his position, wouldn't we? Seriously, William ...'

William was about to respond when Benjamin arrived back in the kitchen. He was sobbing.

'That does it,' he wailed. 'One of them just vomited all over my new trousers.'

Once the two policewomen arrived to take down this new information, one in uniform, cap in hand, the other in plain clothes, Theresa sat in the corner of the living room and let Imogen do all the talking.

'We've put out an alert at the airports,' said the detective sergeant. 'And so far no one with Chloe's name has gone through on any airline. I gather Chloe has her own passport. I need you to check that it's here. If it's not here, I'm sure you appreciate, that changes everything.'

Imogen rushed through to her office. Theresa could hear her pulling open drawer after drawer.

To fill the awkward pause, Theresa introduced herself as Chloe's grandmother.

Imogen returned with three passports in her hand. She flung them down on to the coffee table.

'Mine, Lola's and Cressida's.' Her face was pale as she added quietly, 'Chloe's is gone.'

The uniformed policewoman rose and started to speak brusquely into a wireless handset fixed to her shoulder.

'Now, Mrs Firbank,' said the detective sergeant, 'we need to know why exactly your children have their own passports? Was it to visit anyone in particular?'

Imogen shot Theresa a look. 'It was *her* idea. For some ridiculous reason she now lives in France, when she could have lived around the corner here in London. Then she had the bright idea that, if the children ever needed to travel over to see her, it would be easier if they had their own travel documents.'

Theresa winced from the unfairness of the attack. She recalled that once, when she had suggested moving to live round the corner, Imogen had made a cruel remark: 'Better to keep a bit of distance. After all, we don't want you spying on us.' It had been the tipping point in her decision to move to France.

When Theresa looked up she saw that the detective sergeant was silently surveying her.

'Clearly you are not in France, Mrs Simmonds. Therefore, I presume your grandchild isn't currently paying you a visit.'

Theresa didn't know how to respond. 'I left as soon as I heard what had happened. Today. Early afternoon.'

'Do you live alone in France?'

'Yes. I have a small flat on the Côte d'Azur.'

'In Southern France, I believe? A few miles from Nice, is that right?'

'Yes.'

'Does Chloe have a key to the flat?'

'No. She did ask me on the phone the other day whether Bellevue-sur-Mere was in the Riviera. At the time it didn't seem to mean anything, but maybe it did ...'

'No one else lives with you?'

'Not with me. It's the lower part of a maisonette. There are people in the flat above mine. But it has a separate front door. It's an occasional short-holiday let. But my flat is currently empty.'

The detective nodded and returned to her notes.

'Mrs Firbank, do you have any connections with these other places your daughter referred to: Spain, Sardinia?'

Imogen sighed and said no.

'Returning to the subject of this man, Laurence. Your other daughter told you he was seen before Christmas at the school which they attend, and of which you are headmistress?'

'That's right,' said Imogen. 'I presume she meant in the playground rather than the school building. But I cannot think that a strange man, lurking in a school playground wearing a brown dress, would not have been reported to me by one of the supervising staff.'

'And do you have any idea how they met?'

Theresa decided to put forward her theory. 'Cressida told me his name was Fire. I'm wondering if that isn't one of those internet names from a gaming site?'

'Interesting.' The detective scribbled again in her note-book and said, 'I realise that it's very late now to wake the other children but I'm sure you realise that time is of the essence ...'

Theresa watched the uniformed officer return to the room. She stooped to whisper in the detective's ear.

It was not going to be good news.

The detective nodded, turned to Imogen and said in a sombre tone: 'We have a report that this morning your daughter boarded a ship sailing from Dover to Calais. She is now somewhere on the European mainland.'

Theresa started wishing that she had stayed in Bellevue-sur-Mer. Perhaps Chloe was heading down there. She suggested the idea to the detective who pursed her lips and replied that mentioning the Riviera hardly narrowed it down. The South of France was a big place, and Chloe could be heading anywhere. Her sisters had already mentioned three separate countries she had spoken of in connection with this man, and there was no guarantee there weren't more: Germany, Sweden, Greece. It was easy enough to get anywhere, even without taking a plane. 'You must concentrate your efforts on discovering the identity of this "Laurence",' she added. 'Could he be travelling with her?'

The policewoman said that her colleagues were in talks with the ferry company, who were at this moment inspecting their CCTV.

Theresa vaguely remembered a case a few years ago, when grainy photographs of a child on a ferry had been shown on the news. The girl had run off with her teacher.

'The trouble is,' the detective continued, 'the man might possibly have a car. Or, they might be going onward by train; that train could be heading for an airport, in Paris for instance, from whence they could fly to Alabama or Bangkok. The options are incalculable.' The detective stood up. 'Now, I think the best thing for you two is to get some sleep and leave this bit to us. Believe me, Mrs Firbank, we will do everything we can.'

When they had gone, Theresa made her daughter a hot whisky toddy and told her to try and rest.

In her own bed Theresa tossed and turned. Why yesterday afternoon had Chloe asked her about the French Riviera? Surely that must indicate that she had some interest in going there. Maybe her 'friend' was heading there with her. And if they were to visit the South of France, surely Chloe would steer him to Bellevue-sur-Mer, which she knew? If they had left for Calais this morning, and changed trains at Paris, they'd be pulling into Nice near midnight.

What if they needed somewhere to stay?

Theresa knew she had to contact someone to keep a lookout at her flat.

NINE

SALLY WOKE WITH A START. The phone was ring-ing. She squinted at her bedside clock: 03.17. Who on earth could be calling her at this hour? Dreading it would be bad news, she stretched out to pick up.

'Hello?'

Silence.

'Hello?'

She cursed and replaced the receiver. Someone had clearly misdialled.

She turned over and tried to get back to sleep.

A few minutes later the phone rang again.

She could hear fragments of speech, interspersed with crackling and sonic noises that sounded as though they were coming through a tunnel.

Again a click of a phone going down.

She thought she heard the word 'shit'.

She sat up and waited. No doubt there would be another attempt.

Almost immediately the phone rang. She snatched the receiver.

'Hello?'

'So sorry, Sally, it's Theresa. I know it's an unholy hour but there is a possibility that my granddaughter is heading towards Bellevue, with some weird, fat, old, bald bloke. I just need to know if you might keep an eye on the front door of the flat. Just in case … You know.'

'Why couldn't this wait for a normal time? I know it's terrible and everything but for heaven's sake, Theresa, I'm hardly likely to see him in the middle of the night.'

'Sorry, Sally. I should have texted or something. I wasn't thinking.'

Sally hung up and snuggled down into bed.

Once more the phone rang.

Sally considered ignoring it, then thought again.

'What?'

'Sally? I realised I hadn't asked how it's going down at La Mosaïque?'

'Don't even ask. It's been a catastrophe. We need you back soon. Today William is cooking.'

'But he—'

'I know. He doesn't cook. But he's refusing to do front of house and, frankly, in these circumstances, I am sick of being in the kitchen too … Look, Theresa, I know you've got more important things on your plate but when you get back, don't worry, I'll give you a blow-by-blow account.'

'Another thing is that I left my photo album in the kitchen. Could you put it through my door, or safely downstairs in the cellar or something. Some of those photos are really precious to me and the grease …'

'Sure, sure.'

'Sorry again, Sally.'

'Me too, Theresa. You get some sleep. I hope you get some better news soon.'

Though Sally tried to drop off again she could not. She lay gazing out of the window at the dark sea, with tiny red, white and green lights of moored yachts bobbing their bright reflections on to the ink black.

Sally next got to thinking of Theresa's granddaughter. How horrible if she had really run off with some old bald man. She couldn't just do nothing. If that had been Marianne at fifteen, she would have been terrified. She decided to text Carol who would be out in the van tomorrow morning. She sat up and tapped out a text asking her to keep an eye on Theresa's flat whenever she parked up on the quay and to keep her eye out both for Chloe and some old bald man.

Although Sally felt worried about Theresa's missing grandchild, she felt a touch of bitterness too. Her own children had not been the settling-down kind. Marianne was now commuting between London, New York and Zurich on her incomprehensible financial adventures. Sally's daughter was far too self-preoccupied to think of giving her grandchildren, while her son Tom, though living in nearby Nice, where he ran a small art gallery, was the flipside of the Marianne coin – too much the hippy. He showed no signs of wanting to marry or finding a nice woman to give her a grandchild.

Sally felt sorry for herself, that was true. What had she achieved? Years ago she had been *someone*, a respected theatre actress; then a TV star with a high profile. But she gave it all up in order to marry a two-timing liar. Or rather she married the liar and he was jealous of her life so persuaded her to surrender it so that she could live his kind of life. But then ... Oh, it was such a waste of time going back and wishing you'd done things differently.

She'd been happy enough since moving out here to Bellevue-sur-Mer. But, until the restaurant, she'd just been bobbing along, doing nothing really – living from day to day. And now, thanks to circumstances entirely out of her hands, the restaurant was on the floor, and any savings she had had gone down the drain with it.

She turned over once more. She felt restless and miserable. She wanted to run away, take the Trans-Siberian express, spend a year in India, jump on a liner to America, see the world.

But to do things like that you needed money, and Sally had none.

———

Theresa slept fitfully. At 6 a.m. she decided there was no point staying in bed, so went down to the kitchen. Imogen was sitting at the table, fully dressed. She looked up and gave Theresa a wan smile.

'What can we do, Mum? I simply can't sit around doing nothing. It's not my way.'

Theresa understood exactly what Imogen meant but wondered what on earth they *could* do.

Her phone buzzed in her dressing-gown pocket. She glanced down. An unknown number with a French prefix. It could be her.

Theresa answered.

'Hello?'

Silence.

'Hello?'

A click. The call ended.

'What was that?' Imogen was alert.

'Don't know. Wrong number, I think.'

Theresa hastily returned the call. The ringtone was definitely somewhere abroad. But no one picked up. She wondered if it was perhaps Chloe trying to contact her, but didn't want to suggest that to Imogen.

Theresa's mind flooded with images of Chloe having regrets and trying to dial her for help, of the bald old man snatching the phone out of the child's hand and throwing it away.

But then the call could have been from anyone in France calling her on restaurant business, perhaps simply phoning her from a car or a train and going through a tunnel.

'We could go into school, maybe,' Theresa suggested. 'Ask whether anyone saw him hanging around the playgrounds or at the school gates.'

'Do you think I haven't already sent emails to all my staff asking them exactly that?'

In silence Theresa prepared herself a cup of tea, and sat down at the table to drink it.

'I can't see why I didn't see it coming,' said Imogen.

'Children can be very secretive. It's sometimes hard to read them. And when they are determined, well ...'

Imogen scraped her chair back. 'Oh God, I hate these chairs. They're always wobbling.' She stood up and strode through into the living room, where she flung herself down on to the sofa, feet up, and stared out into the darkness of the street.

Cradling her cup of tea, Theresa followed, sitting on an armchair near the coffee table.

In her pocket, her phone vibrated, then rang.

She answered.

It was Cyril, about today's meat order.

'Sorry, Cyril, you'll have to speak to Sally or William. I'm terribly busy.'

'I wonder, Theresa, if today you might like some fresh—'

'I'm sorry but my granddaughter has gone missing. I'm in England. I really don't care about the meat. You'll need to speak to someone who's actually in the kitchen.'

'I'm very sorry to be disturbing. *Pardon.*' Cyril hung up.

Theresa watched Imogen and realised that there was little she could do but be here for her.

Her phone rang again.

Imogen spun round and said furiously, 'Don't mind me, Mum, I'm only out of my mind with worry. Carry on, please, with your business calls.'

Chastised, Theresa rose and answered the phone while climbing up the stairs.

It was Carol.

'Darling. Now I'm just sitting in the van in the parking opposite your flat, so I thought I'd better keep you up to date.'

Theresa had no idea what she was talking about.

'Really, Carol, I've no time for La Mosaïque at the moment … But I—'

'Sally told me you wanted me to keep an eye out on your place.'

'It really doesn't matter …'

'All right. But for your information there is, at this very moment, a balding man peering through your front window. He's literally got his face crushed up to the glass.'

Theresa was pulled up short. She turned and sat on the top step.

'Sorry, Carol, tell me that again.'

'A man with a bald head – not entirely bald, you know, not Captain Picard, more of a tall Winston Churchill – is looking through your front window in a rather earnest fashion.'

Theresa was now furious not to be there in person. From here what could she do?

'Is he fat?'

'I can only see his back.'

'Can you go and question him?'

'And ask him what?'

'I don't know. He may be the man who's run off with my granddaughter. You remember her? Chloe? She's gone off with some old bald man.'

'I'm on it.' Carol cut off.

Theresa remained immobile at the top of the stairs. She knew it would be unwise to say anything to Imogen until she heard again from Carol.

She got up and made her way to her bedroom. As she reached the door, Cressida came out of her own bedroom, rubbing her eyes.

'Oh, it's you, Grandma. I thought Chloe was home.'

Theresa gave Cressida a squeeze.

'The man – you know, Chloe's friend. Was he in the playground or at the gates, or where?'

Cressida gave a shrug as though Theresa was stupid, and said in that swooping tone, 'Noooo! He was in the assembly hall. But he was a long way away. I didn't really see him. I was bored.'

Theresa's fingers gripped Cressida's shoulder.

She was getting somewhere.

But at that moment the phone in her pocket buzzed again.

'Hi, Theresa. I ran across the road but once I'd locked the van he'd vanished. I can't imagine how he disappeared so quickly. Really. I can have only averted my eyes for fifteen seconds and whoosh – gone!'

'Did you look up the hill?'

'Of course. I looked in every direction. I'm beginning to wonder if he wasn't a hallucination.'

Lola, already dressed in her school uniform, came out of the bedroom and dragged Cressida back inside.

'Oh, and by the way, you'd better get back here pretty damn quick, or La Mosaïque is going to fold in days. Three days ago we might have been in the ketchup, but now we're positively swimming in it.'

From downstairs, Imogen let out an anguished cry.

'I have to go, Carol. Speak soon.'

Theresa ran down the stairs as fast as she could.

Imogen was standing in the kitchen, holding her hand under the cold tap. 'Burned myself. Stupid.'

'Shall I ... ?'

'Just leave me alone.'

Theresa crept back up the stairs and quickly dressed. When she came back down Cressida and Lola were tucking into breakfast.

'I've decided to go into school today,' said Imogen. 'With the girls. So please could you stay here, just in case. Hold the fort.'

Theresa said yes. What else could she do? But she wondered why on earth she was here.

After they had gone, the house descended into an eerie silence, with only the ticking of the kitchen clock to break the monotony. Theresa wandered around for a while. She sat on Chloe's bed and pulled out the drawers hoping something would prove to be a clue to her whereabouts. But it was only the usual things you'd find in a teenage schoolgirl's room: socks, T-shirts, pants and weekend clothes.

Theresa went downstairs, made herself a coffee and flopped down on to the sofa. She tried to put herself into Chloe's mind. But the impossible thing was to imagine her mind under the influence of some bald old man. She felt sure now that Cressida was fantasising or confused about his wearing a brown dress. Unless perhaps this Laurence was a transsexual teacher ...

On the shelf beneath the coffee table there was a pile of magazines and the orange spine of a photo album, exactly like her own, which she had been so worried about during the night.

She wondered if she hadn't gone mad and inadvertently thrown the photo album into her bag and brought it with her and not left it on the counter back in the kitchen of La Mosaïque. As she reached forward and pulled it out, she vaguely recalled a Christmas when she'd absent-mindedly bought two for the price of one albums, gave one to her daughter and in the end kept the other for herself.

Theresa flicked idly through the pages of fading photos of christenings and children's parties. Chloe in a fancy-dress costume, dressed as a witch. A goose-pimpled Lola, blue with cold, standing by the school pool, holding up a swimming medal. Cressida, shy and knock-kneed, in a huge school hat. Probably her first day, thought Theresa. Some pictures of a pantomime. It was hard to see through the make-up and work out whether any of her grandchildren were involved. She presumed they must be. Why else were the photos in here? She felt happy that Imogen kept up this book. After all, in these days of camera phones, very few people kept hard copies of photographs.

Theresa turned the page to a lovely full-length photo of Chloe in her costume as Juliet. She wished she could have seen the production. Chloe looked perfect in the part. So eager and innocent. Her hair down, flowing over the shoulders of a beautiful ivory and gold gown.

On the next page was another gorgeous photo – Romeo stooping over Juliet, who lay on top of the tomb. A hand-some lad, in a maroon doublet and hose. This was followed by a photo of Chloe, this time in a line-up with some of the boys in the play. It had obviously been taken in the dressing room. Reflections showed other people who were not in costume looking on, laughing. Another with Chloe resting her head on the shoulder of Friar Laurence while two costumed boys, Romeo and probably Mercutio, gazed into one another's eyes. Underneath was a handwritten label: 'Love give me strength!'

Theresa smiled and closed the book.

How funny.

She went back into the kitchen and popped another pod into the coffee machine.

She pressed the button and the machine made its usual roaring noise. As she strolled back to the sofa, Theresa warmed her hands around the cup of extra-strong coffee.

Juliet in love with Friar Laurence! That would be a turn-up for Shakespeare's plot!

She gripped the cup and slammed it down on to the tabletop so hard that it cracked.

She pulled out the photo album again and flicked urgently through to the back.

Fire! Laurence! A bald, old, fat man in a dress, who Cressida had barely noticed in the assembly hall, because she was too bored.

That was it!

She crammed the photo album into her tote bag, ran out on to the street and hailed a cab.

PART THREE

TÊTE DE MOINE ET SES LÉGUMES

Serves 8.

head of broccoli
4 carrots
4 courgettes
2 fennel bulbs
1 shallot, finely chopped
150g butter
1 cup white wine
salt and pepper
prepared chestnuts, to taste
200ml maple syrup
lemon juice, freshly squeezed
fresh parsley, chopped
Tête de Moine cheese, with its curler

Chop the vegetables and cook them in boiling water, making sure to put them in in order of hardness so that they all reach the same consistency (carrots first, courgettes last). When still al dente, drain and put aside.

Meanwhile gently cook the shallot in 50g butter, in a large frying pan, until transparent. Spoon in the white wine and increase the heat until the liquid reduces. Add a pinch of salt, a grind of pepper and the rest of the butter.

In a small frying pan, drop the chestnuts into a knob of melted butter and fry, then pour on the maple syrup, keeping the heat up until the liquid reduces.

On a gentle heat, put the drained vegetables, and chestnuts, into the wine sauce. Toss well and sprinkle with the lemon juice, salt and parsley. Decorate with frilled 'flowers' of Tête de Moine.

TEN

SALLY QUITE ENJOYED the lunch service, which luckily consisted of many locals coming for the wonderful *prix-fixe* menu.

Cyril, the butcher, was there, sitting in a corner with his wife, a busty, smiling woman with an earthy laugh, who seemed very concerned on Theresa's behalf. Cyril kept asking frequently if Sally knew when Theresa would return. Sally wondered whether it was because he was genuinely concerned about Theresa's missing grand-daughter or maybe that he preferred her cooking.

Towards the end of service her own friend Jean-Philippe came in and, as everyone else was already on desserts by then, it was easy to hang around his table and chat with him. He had bought a new boat. A 35-foot sports motor yacht. He wanted her to come out on it whenever she had a day off. She had to explain that until things here in the restaurant were a bit more stable she'd have no time, but after that – try and stop her!

Before signing off for the afternoon Sally went into the kitchen to check on William and Benjamin who seemed very calm and merry as they tidied up after the lunch service.

Sally walked out into the street and sat on a post on the quayside.

The sea was a deeper blue than usual today, and glassy-still. The sun was very warm. Her coat was de trop, so she shook it off and threw her face back to bathe in the sunbeams.

'Darling!' Carol's voice was a positive croon. 'Well, have I got news for you.'

'You haven't found Chloe?'

'No, darling. I've been propositioned.'

Sally opened her eyes and stared at Carol.

'By whom?'

'By a charming Englishman, with the most dreamy voice I think I have ever heard. Well, since the death of Richard Burton, anyhow.'

'I thought you were off men?'

'I'm only off lying, cheating criminals and husbands who've slyly slipped their wedding ring into the inside pocket of their vest.'

'Vests don't have pockets. Do they?'

'Lost in translation, darling. Remember, I'm from Muncie, Indiana.'

'Where did this pick-up happen? Not at the cash and carry?'

Carol gave one of her deep-throated laughs. 'No, silly. Here. Right here in this very street.' She pointed to the hill. 'Or, rather, that one. Remember you told me to watch out for any activity at Theresa's apartment? Well, I was watching early this morning, and I saw the backside of some bald man peering in through the front window. I gave chase but he vanished. A little later, when I came back to bring in the fish, I saw him again marching up the hill. So I challenged him. He told me I had a sexy voice and wondered if I might be around over the next few days to join him for an aperitif. So, anyhoo, upshot is I'm on for drinks with him in Nice. He wants me to show him around the Vieille Ville – as they say!'

'And the *vieille dame*, while he's at it?'

'Hey! You! Enough of the old.'

'He's not a local then?'

'Oh no, he's staying around here for a few weeks. He was very "So British", as they say over here.'

'But what was he doing gazing through Theresa's window? Did he say?'

'Something about his work with sound reverberations. Acoustics or something. I don't know. I wasn't really listening. He must be at the Astra. They usually are. I didn't have a clue what he was on about, actually. I was just transfixed by the seductive tone of his mellifluous vocals. So I told him the owner of the flat was away; meanwhile he could make as much noise as he wanted, and when she got back then if he wanted to continue, he could explain everything to her. That seemed to please him.'

'And you're sure he's nothing to do with Chloe?'

'It seems not.'

Sally glanced at Theresa's place, up to the small square windows of the flat above and beyond to the looming shadow of the Hotel Astra.

'You don't think he's up there? What if he has her locked up?'

'I'd say he seemed not the type to be interested in children. After all, he invited me out on a date!' Carol laughed her deep, warm chuckle.

Sally was still worried. The man might fancy Carol, who due to her past life had a certain handsome allure, but that did not rule out his having other interests of a sexual nature. She looked up once more. 'Wonder what he's getting up to up there that he doesn't want Theresa to hear?'

'Chopping up the bodies, perhaps!'

Although Carol had only said what Sally herself was thinking, she said, 'Carol, you're beyond beyond.'

'I am what I am!' Carol swept off in the direction of the restaurant van. 'Anyhoo, honey, don't worry. When we're out on our date I'll probe him.'

Sally laughed. 'I bet you will.'

When she arrived at the school, Theresa was shown straight up to Imogen's office. She opened the photo album and displayed the photo of Chloe with the boy playing Friar Laurence.

'Fire! Laurence!' she said. 'Bald, fat, old … and he wears a brown dress – with knots on. It's him.' She stabbed her finger down on the photo. 'Another boy from this school. Over to you, Imogen.'

'Oh, that's something of a relief.'

'It's a huge relief, darling. It's not a real old, fat, bald man who lured Chloe away. At least it's someone of her own age. So where is he?'

'I don't remember who that was.' Imogen peered at the photo, then pulled open a drawer in the filing cabinet at her side. 'Behind all the make-up. *Romeo and Juliet* was the school play, last November.' She took out a file marked 'Drama', and flipped through to the printed programme. 'I just leave all that theatrical stuff to Frances. And the boy is so well padded-out and bewigged I've no idea who it was.'

'Don't you have a boy who's missing from school too?'

'Friar Laurence …' Imogen ran her finger down the cast list. 'Oh, no. I don't believe it. Neil Muffett. Not Neil.' She slid the *Romeo and Juliet* programme over to Theresa and flung herself back in her swivel chair.

Theresa was worried by Imogen's reaction to the discovery of the boy's name. 'He's a troublemaker? A bully?'

'Not exactly.'

'But is he absent from school?'

'Worse than that. He *left* the school at the end of last term.' Imogen rose and moved over to another set of filing cabinets. 'I doubt I have anything much of use on him in here now.'

She stooped over the desk and pressed the button on the intercom. 'Nadia, please could you find out the address and phone number of a boy who left the school last Christmas. Neil Muffett ... That's right. Neil.'

Imogen took her finger off the intercom and leaned forward to speak to Theresa.

'Neil was a strange boy. Always gazing out of the window. Full of daydreams.'

'Was he expelled? Is that what you're trying to say?' Theresa could imagine Chloe finding the lure of a daydreaming 'bad 'un' rather irresistible.

'No. Neil was not expelled. Absolutely not. He was more of a sloth than a wild boy. He thought he could just sail through his education without putting in one iota of effort. He truly believed he'd get by simply on his ravishing smile. He left, I seem to recall, because his parents moved away from the area. There was a huge divorce. Mega-bucks involved.'

The intercom buzzed and the voice of Nadia said that she had the address of the boy's mother. A house in Streatham.

'Come on, Mum.' Imogen picked up her bag and coat and strode through to Nadia's office to collect a written copy. 'Let's go.'

Twenty minutes later Theresa and Imogen pulled up outside a house with a large driveway and a garage. It had obviously once been rather grand, but now seemed slightly dilapidated. The borders of the driveway were overgrown with weeds, the paintwork round the windows was peeling, the glass dusty and uncleaned in months.

'Can this be right?' Imogen peered forward, then pointed at the address card. 'I always thought they were frightfully well-off.'

Theresa double-checked the card.

'Yes. This is it. It does look like a very big house. Perhaps it's better inside.'

'Come on.' Imogen got out of the car. 'Now we're looking for Cynthia Muffett.'

Theresa wondered whether anyone lived here at all. It looked as though the owners had been away for a long time.

Imogen stepped up to the front door, rang the bell, then wiped the tip of her finger with a tissue.

They waited, but there was no sign of life inside.

Theresa stooped and looked through the letterbox. She was thinking there would be a mound of mail lying there, but no. Then something caught her eye. The slightest movement at the end of the hall. A skirt disappearing round the architrave of a door.

'I saw someone,' she whispered. 'There's a woman inside. She's hiding behind a doorway.'

Imogen pushed Theresa away and shouted through the letterbox. 'We know you're inside, Mrs Muffett. You'd better answer or we're going to call the police.' She stood up and pressed her finger on the bell. She left it there. It was a shrill bell.

To help, Theresa rattled the letterbox.

Eventually feet shuffled along the hall. Then the door, on a chain, opened a crack. Two eyes, make-up smeared, peered through the gap.

'Yes?'

Only one word, but enough for Theresa to smell alcohol fumes on the woman's breath.

'Mrs Muffett?'

'Who are you?'

'It's Imogen Firbank, Mrs Muffett. I was Neil's headmistress.'

The fingers of one hand curled around the edge of the door. 'What's he done now?'

'We just need to come in and talk. Neil isn't in trouble. But, if we don't have a word privately with you first and try to sort things out, he could be in very bad trouble.'

The woman slid the chain off and tentatively opened up.

'Who's she?' She pointed at Theresa.

'I'm the child's grandmother.'

'Which child?'

'Chloe Firbank, the underaged girl Neil has run away with.' Imogen stepped into the hall.

'Aren't you Mrs Firbank?'

'Yes,' said Imogen. 'I am Chloe's mother.'

'So he's run off with a young girl.' Mrs Muffett, still in dressing gown and slippers, her hair unkempt, shrugged. 'Like father like son.'

Leaving a trail of Martini fumes in her wake, Cynthia Muffett slopped down the hall to a large, open kitchen which looked out on to an impressive garden. Theresa and Imogen followed.

'Where does your son go to school nowadays, Mrs Muffett?'

'What do you mean?'

'I mean what school does he attend? He's fifteen years old, Mrs Muffett. By law he has to be at school.'

'Drink?' Mrs Muffett sat on a high stool and topped up her glass from the bottle.

Theresa and Imogen declined.

'How would I know? His father won custody. His father wins everything.' Mrs Muffett gulped back the Martini in one. 'I suppose Neil's at a school near to where his father lives.'

'And his father lives where exactly?'

'I don't know. Everywhere. Nowhere. Last seen in Ibiza. Or was it Tenerife? I can never tell the difference between those common places.'

'Do you perhaps have a phone number for your husband? Or an email address? Some way of contacting him? It is crucial that we find your son, who it appears has eloped with my daughter. I should point out that they are both underaged.'

'I used to have Roger's number.' Mrs Muffett poured herself another drink. 'But he changed it because I would phone to talk to Neil.'

'And Neil? Doesn't he have a phone? Do you have a number for him?'

'He sometimes contacts me on one of those app things.' Mrs Muffett suddenly put her face in her hands and started sobbing. 'Once upon a time I had everything. And Neil was such a sweet boy. And Roger is such a pig. But boys will be boys. Roger kept saying that. Boys will be boys. And when Neil and adolescence collided, the little boy got it into his head that he wanted to be like his father, the big boy ... and ... When Roger left me ...'

Mrs Muffett dissolved into a mess of tears.

Theresa moved in softly.

'I know what that's like, Mrs Muffett ... when a marriage breaks up. I'm sure your son is still the sweet boy you love. Children go through many changes while they search for an identity of their own, but you must understand that we need to talk to him, urgently. If only to make sure that my granddaughter is safe.'

'There!' Mrs Muffett pulled her phone out of her dressing-gown pocket and dropped it on the countertop. 'If there's anything on there you can find. He usually uses the one with the pink 8 sign.'

Imogen opened the app and fiddled with the phone while Theresa kept Mrs Muffett talking.

'Did Neil have any ambitions at all?'

'He wanted to be Jack Sparrow.'

'No desire to be in any job? Footballer? Actor? Banker?'

'No. He used to help me out at the brasserie sometimes, for pocket money. But then his father swanned off with that young girl and he changed—'

'Brasserie?'

'Nothing great. La Cour. It was just down the road. I loved running it. But the swine even took that joy away. He got it in the settlement, and sold it. So now I not only have no family, but no work.' She gave a stifled sob. 'It was meant to be called La Coeur – French for "The Heart" – but the idiot signwriter missed out the "e". Good thing really because I would have had to change the name to La Coeur Brisée. "The Broken Heart". As it is, I had to live with smug French-speakers constantly pointing out that it should be *Le* Cour. Bloody stupid signwriter.'

'And when did your husband go away?'

'The divorce became final over the summer. And Roger was gone by Christmas, taking Neil with him. He took my brasserie and my son. The only two things I ever cared about. The bastard. And I adored him.'

Mrs Muffett put her head down on the countertop and sobbed uncontrollably. 'And I thought he adored me.'

Theresa could see that Imogen was still busy scribbling down notes from the phone.

'Didn't your husband realise that it was illegal to take Neil out of school, Mrs Muffett?'

'Cynthia. I hate Mrs Muffett. After all, I'm not really Mrs Muffett, am I?'

'Neil – not in school … ?'

'Roger always believed that he was above the law.' Cynthia shrugged. 'He didn't give a toss about "interfering officialdom", as he called it. And, as he constantly pointed out, he managed to become a successful businessman without one examination to his name, not even a swimming certificate.' She raised her head, her mascara now smeared down her cheeks. 'I've got six GCSEs, three A levels and a BA.' She sobbed and looked imploringly at Theresa. '*And* I've got a gold medal for swimming!'

Theresa had no idea what to reply, except a feeble 'I'm so sorry.'

'Neil's more like me than Roger. Or he was when he lived here.'

'He's a good swimmer, then, Neil?' asked Theresa.

'No. A hopeless swimmer. But Roger sang his siren song, dangling all those presents and promises. He won't be arrested, will he?'

Theresa was lost to know to which male of the Muffett family Cynthia was referring, so said nothing.

But Imogen spoke, brusquely. 'As Neil is also under-age, if he has touched my daughter he will probably be cautioned. But if your ex-husband is implicated in the kidnapping, it is quite possible that the police will charge him with all sorts of things.' She put her note-book back into her handbag. 'Thank you, Mrs Muffett. I wonder if you could give me your password for that networking site. You understand that it's for your bene-fit as well as our own – I have to find Neil before the police do.'

Cynthia Muffett looked at Imogen. Theresa could see the slow dawning of understanding cross her face. She reached for her handbag and, fumbling inside, pulled out a scrap of paper on which was written '160905Neil!'

While Imogen scribbled the password down, Theresa worked out that the numbers must be the boy's birthday.

'If I find Neil, I will let you know right away, Mrs Muffett. I promise.' Imogen signalled to Theresa to follow her out. 'Meanwhile I suggest that you put that bottle away and start cleaning up. Paint the windows and clear the front entrance. Neil won't want to come home to this. Pull yourself together.'

As Theresa left with Imogen through the front door, they heard the noise of a glass breaking. It sounded as though Mrs Muffett had sent it flying in their direction.

———

Sally bumped into Marcel coming out of the little boulangerie up the hill.

'Thanks for last night,' she said without a smile.

'Why do you not look pleased?' Marcel seemed puzzled. 'I thought it would help you. All those extra covers.'

'All those rude people who wanted only junk food, you mean?'

All innocence, Marcel replied, 'But as they were English, I thought you would know better how to handle them.'

Sally realised that this subject was trickier than she was prepared for. She scrutinised his face. Either Marcel was a first-class liar, or he really did think that those people would be happy eating the type of food they served in La Mosaïque.

'They were time-wasters, Marcel. They really just wanted somewhere to sit while they waited for their boat to take them away. I believe the cruise-ship's tender had broken down. If I'd known what they'd be like, I'd have rowed them out there myself, one by one.'

Marcel laughed.

'I'm sorry, Sally.'

'The result is that tonight William is in the kitchen.'

Marcel pulled a shocked face so extreme that he looked almost like a clown.

'Ooh lor lor! And when will Theresa return?'

Sally shrugged a 'don't know'.

'I see.'

'But for the future, Marcel, when you are recommending us to your cast-offs, I should tell you that we're looking a little more in the area of the *BCBG* clientele. Those last night were, let's see, I don't think we have a phrase in French for it. In England we'd say ...' And Sally reverted to English to say: '"End of the pier". Which, Marcel, literally translates as: *Fin de la jetée.*'

'So that you could throw them off!' replied Marcel, leaving Sally realising that some things really did have no translation.

Once loaded with baguettes she staggered down the hill to the restaurant and dropped them by the kitchen door. William and Benjamin were standing silently at separate counters, chopping and peeling.

It appeared that serenity ruled.

Rather than disturb the peace, Sally turned and swiftly moved through into the dining room. She spent the next hour putting on the tablecloths and laying up. She glanced quickly in the bookings ledger and saw that there were two tables reserved for dinner tonight. Both with French surnames.

As she put the ledger back under the counter, she remembered that Theresa wanted her to post her photo album through the front door.

She went through into the kitchen.

Benjamin turned and smiled serenely. As she passed him, William also looked up from the blender and grinned. This was spooky. It felt like something out of *The Stepford Wives*. She sidled past them and stooped to find the photo album. She pulled out the menu book. Then the order book. After that the accounts book. She scraped her hand to the back of the shelf. Nothing else there.

'Boys?' she asked. 'Did either of you see a large orange folder? It was Theresa's photo album. Only it's not here.'

Benjamin and William shook their heads.

'Right. OK. I'll just have a quick root about down in the cellar.'

But down in the cellar there was nothing. Someone had left a rose – a pink one this time – laid on a piece of paper inscribed with a large pink heart on the desk. As William and Benjamin were acting so strangely, she presumed it must be something to do with them.

Thinking of Theresa again, Sally realised that she should update her on the mystery of the bald man looking through the window. She went upstairs and out through the back door, moving along the narrow alleyway till it turned on to the open seafront.

To make the call she sat in her usual place, perched on the sea wall, looking out to the bay.

Theresa's phone went straight to voicemail, so Sally left a message telling her that the bald man was just an English tourist snooping about who, as far as they could see, had nothing to do with Chloe, especially as he had just asked Carol out on a date.

She hung up and looked at her watch. It had been a conscious decision not to mention the photo album, which Sally felt sure must have got mislaid during the chaos last night, and would certainly turn up when they were looking for something else.

She had a good hour before she needed to be inside the restaurant. So she phoned her son Tom.

That was a mistake.

Tom told her in too much detail about some woman he'd been going out with, who had since dumped him. She was French and local. He loved her, especially as she was a conceptual artist and used her own body and its secretions and excretions as works of art. Feeling quite sick, Sally ended the call, claiming she needed to go to work. It sounded to her as though Tom had had something of a lucky break. She didn't like to imagine what form those artworks took, but at least now Sally would be spared having to attend an embarrassing private view where she would have to scrape together enough compliments to satisfy the wretched girl. Adieu, and *merci*!

The sun went down and suddenly Sally was freezing cold. She saw the restaurant van pulling into the parking space, and watched Carol get out. Sally admired the way Carol always looked so well groomed, and loved how she shook her hair into place whenever she got out of a vehicle.

Sally followed her into the restaurant. As they turned on the lights, and started work, placing candles on each of the tables, Sally whispered how oddly tranquil both William and Benjamin seemed in the kitchen.

'That's just as well, dearie,' Carol replied. 'I was dreading the day I'd be called to cooking service. I can't even boil an egg.'

The phone rang.

An order for a delivery at 8 p.m.

'Ding-dong!' said Carol. 'Let's hope there are many more of those tonight, as I've become quite partial to doing the rounds.'

'Tomorrow is D-Day,' said Sally.

'D for what? Disaster?'

'I hope not. No. Marcel is going to name his price.'

'I thought he was waiting for everyone to come back?'

'No. He's telling us the price but we don't have to reply until we've made a unanimous decision.'

'Fine!' Carol crossed herself. 'It's enough to turn one to religion. Oh to be free!'

She looked around the dining room. 'Though, candidly, once this is all gone and we've all got our money back, I'm not really sure what I'll do with my time.'

'To tell the truth,' replied Sally, 'me neither. But we can't carry on like *this*, can we?'

'No, not like this.' Carol walked from table to table, doling out side plates from a large pile. 'But I'm going to find a way to lead us back to glory days ... Jeez, we've got to. I'll never be able to keep up my paradise pad without regular spondulix. You know, hon, Nice *is* starting to pick up.' Nudging Sally, Carol winked. 'The Italians are back and I—'

The phone interrupted her. Another home-delivery order. This one for just after eight.

'So, Carol, at the busiest time, you'll be off on the road. Leaving me to it.'

'Oh, you'll be fine, darl. Yesterday was a freak day. Get in, gal – it'll be gorgeous tonight. You mark my words.'

ELEVEN

Theresa sat in Imogen's office while Mervin, the technology teacher, fiddled about with the smartphone.

'The trouble with these programs,' said Mervin, pulling on his shaggy beard while shaking his head, 'is that to communicate you can ask a person to be your friend, but before you can converse they do need to accept. And why is he going to accept you, Mrs Firbank, when you are his ex-head teacher?'

Imogen let out an exasperated sigh.

'I have an idea that lying, perhaps pretending that you're one of the kids in his old class, would make it quicker getting through to the lad.' Mervin sat pushing the ends of his beard up towards his lips with nail-bitten fingers. 'This social-networking stuff is more their domain, after all.'

'I wonder what I pay you for,' snapped Imogen. 'You're meant to know more than your pupils, not go to them for assistance.'

Theresa felt the need to save poor Mervin from Imogen's misguided wrath. 'Perhaps Neil had a friend in his class who might *already* be in touch with him.' Her suggestion obviously made an impression, for Imogen pressed the intercom button and barked to Nadia to bring Frances to her office immediately.

'Can't you just locate phones these days?' asked Imogen. 'I saw a programme once which—'

'That only works if you previously set up a program to find it before you lose it. Neil might well be able to find his own phone,' Mervin pulled the beard from side to side, 'or the police could quite likely locate it, but not a mere tech teacher like myself.'

Within a few minutes Frances put her head round the door. 'Can I help, Imogen?'

'Did Neil Muffett have any particular friends?'

'Mmmmm ... Not that I recall.' Frances screwed up her face into a thinking mode. 'He was a bit of a loner, actually. Sat on his own in the corner writing poetry. He was excellent as Friar Laurence in—'

'Yes, yes, Frances, we know all about that. I just need to find someone who might have been in contact with him since he left this establishment.'

Frances's face brightened. 'Oh, but I'm in touch with him. I needed to communicate about rehearsal times, and notes on the show. And since he left I've kept in touch.'

'You what?' Imogen got up from her desk, thrusting out her hand. 'Give me your phone.'

Frances took a step back. 'But, I—'

'I need your phone, Frances. Neil Muffett has run off with my daughter Chloe.'

'That's highly unlikely, Imogen.' Frances rooted about in her handbag for her phone. 'You see, at the moment, Neil is in the South of France.'

'Whereabouts in the South of France?' Theresa rose from her seat. 'Which part?'

'The Riviera, of course.'

'Saying "the Riviera" is exactly the same as saying "the South of France". Can't you be more specific?'

Frances opened her phone and swiped her fingers across the screen, opening a messaging program. She peered down and read: 'The last stop he told me was somewhere called Roquebrune-Cap-Martin. Reading between the lines, I believe Neil was feeling unhappy with his father. And also feeling rather lonely and sorry for himself.'

'Cap-Martin! That's just along the coast from me,' said Theresa. 'When was Neil there?'

'Um … yesterday,' said Frances.

'Why do you say "the last stop"?' asked Imogen.

'He's touring with his father. As far as I can see they seem to be staying in a new place every day. Three weeks ago they were in Olbia.'

'Sardinia,' whispered Imogen.

'Where was he last?' Theresa wondered which direction they were taking. 'Day before yesterday, before Cap-Martin? Which town?'

'Somewhere called Cagnes-sur-Mer. And before that, Antibes, Cannes and Saint-Raphael.'

Theresa realised that they must be heading towards Italy. 'So perhaps next stop Ventimiglia or Bordighera?'

'I'm not sure about that,' said Frances. 'Their path does seem rather random. They were in Italy only last week. In San Remo for lunch on market day.'

Despite the variations towards the east and west, Theresa could see a pattern emerging. When she thought about it, most towns Frances had named were within a few hours' driving distance from Nice.

'If she has indeed run away to join this boy Neil in the South of France, I should get back there right away.' Theresa stood and turned to Imogen. 'I'll leave now. Please come out and join me, Imogen, whenever you like, but meanwhile keep me up to speed with any developments.'

As Theresa reached the door Mervin suddenly shouted, 'I have a ping back!'

'What are you talking about now?' Imogen loomed over him.

'He's acknowledged me. Only it wasn't me, "Mervin", you see. I chose a female name. I called myself "Theresa" after you.'

'So what happens next?' asked Imogen. 'Can we speak to Neil directly?'

'As Theresa, yes. And when you say "speak", you realise we actually don't physically use our voices, just our thumbs.'

'Anything you like, Mervin.' Imogen looked up at Theresa. 'Can you continue this? I'm not sure if you have the technical know-how, Mum.'

'But why me?' Theresa didn't like the thought of being the only person responsible for communicating with Neil. 'Won't he immediately assume that I am in touch with Imogen and therefore am the enemy?'

'I am hardly the enemy.' Imogen glared at her mother.

'He knows you live in the South of France, Theresa,' said Mervin, trying to alleviate the tension. 'And therefore you are a potential refuge there.'

Imogen sighed. 'So, Mum, are you up to it?'

'I know how to text, Imogen.' Theresa wondered why her daughter imagined she was so out of touch. She turned to Mervin. 'Is it Messenger or—'

'No,' said Mervin, without looking up from the tiny screen. 'If you hand me your phone, I'll install the app and sign you in as Theresa, then once you arrive in France you can take over.'

Theresa fumbled about in her bag for her phone.

'To keep continuity I'd suggest that for the rest of the day I will pretend to be you, Mrs Simmonds. And we can communicate; then when you want to take over ...'

Theresa looked to Imogen, who nodded agreement.

'What's the plan, Imogen? What should Mervin say to Neil?'

'Once they're chatting, Mervin – as Theresa – will invite Neil over to see you in Bellevue-sur-Mer. To your restaurant or something. With or without the father.'

'I'll keep my eye on the app,' said Mervin. 'Then if Neil is responding and you don't appear to be on the ball, I'll pick it up, OK?'

Theresa wondered why this bearded man would expect her to not be on the ball.

After a brief demo with Mervin, Theresa stowed her phone away, kissed her daughter goodbye, left the school and headed for the Tube. While the trains were still running in the open and she still had a decent signal, she bought her ticket to Nice airport. She was booked on a flight at half past eight. She'd touch down just before midnight.

———

After Sally had given the first table their menus, she went into the kitchen to check on Carol, who was packing up the thermal boxes with the first batch of the evening's deliveries.

'Frankly, Sally,' Carol drawled, 'once we relinquish this place we should set up a full-time home-delivery service. This restaurant may be on its last legs. But the delivery joint is jumping. We could easily do it from home.'

Over at the range, Benjamin threw some *panisse* into the fat fryer which emitted a loud hiss.

Carol zipped up the last bag, and strode out through the back door.

William and Benjamin turned to Sally and smiled beatifically.

She was starting to wonder if they weren't both on drugs. She'd never seen them so merry, quiet and content. Normally, wherever they were, they could be heard squabbling and sniping at one another. Maybe it was the simple act of cooking which had calmed them. Kitchen life obviously had a tranquillising effect for some people.

Sally pushed back into the dining room to take first orders.

Another table had arrived and seated themselves.

Strange, she had not heard the bell. But maybe it had pinged when Carol was talking. Her voice was sometimes loud enough to drown out a thunderclap.

A woman was standing, glaring, near the desk. She spoke in French: 'As no one was here to welcome us, I sat my guests at the corner table.'

Sally felt as though she had seen this woman before somewhere but couldn't exactly place her. She was a typical Côte d'Azur beach-woman – flashily dressed, tanned, blonde, her stretched forehead shiny from Botox, her pale-pink glistening lips bursting with filler.

Sally moved to the desk to mark off the table on the plan.

'Madame de la Warr?' she asked.

'*Exacte!*' spat the woman. 'Odile de la Warr.'

Again, the name sounded familiar to Sally.

Bearing three menus, she walked Madame de la Warr to her table, where, rather rudely in Sally's opinion, the other two had already seated themselves.

As Sally pulled out a chair her eyes caught those of one of the diners at Madame de la Warr's table.

'Salzy, darling! Bet you didn't think you'd see us again so soon, did you, poppet?' It was Eggy Markham.

'Erm no, I suppose I ... What are you doing here?'

'Well, what with one thing and another, we've decided to stay a little longer and we thought we'd surprise you!'

'One had no idea you were the *waitress* here, darling,' said Phoo, putting on her spectacles as she picked up the menu. 'The way you spoke to us about the place, we imagined you owned it or something.'

Sally's spit dried up.

Through her shock she managed to stammer out: 'How did you find me?'

'Name on the van you were driving, old gal. "La Mosaïque" writ large. Quaint foreign spelling and all that. Then when we saw the place in the flesh, as it were, while passing through the village, we decided we must pay you a visit toot sweet.'

Sally wondered how anyone would 'pass through' Bellevue-sur-Mer. It was away from the main road, and you could only really get down as far as La Mosaïque if you were coming expressly to the bay and in fact to La Mosaïque itself. The only thing beyond it was the *port de plaisance*. The Markhams must have come here deliberately searching her out.

'Well, then? Are you going to stand there gaping like a fish?' pressed Odile. 'Might you take our orders before we die of famine?'

Sally caught a brief exchange between the two women: Odile rolling her eyes, and Phoo pursing her lips in reply.

'Of course.' She poised her stylus over the order pad. 'What can I get you?'

Having taken the orders, Sally returned to the kitchen. She didn't think she would be able to put up with a whole night of this.

'I need to swap places with somebody. One of you will have to take the service. I can't do it.'

'So *now* you see what we had to deal with last night.'

'No, William, this is quite different. These are people I know from way back. They didn't like me then, and they don't like me now. And while we're at it I have to confess that I don't like them either. It's personal.'

'You're an actress, aren't you, Sally?' William gave her a cold glance. 'So act. There is little difference, surely, serving at table or performing on stage.'

Sally thought she would like to brain William with the order pad.

'Really? Sally?' Benjamin took a step back and gave her a wry look. 'You're old friends with Odile de la Warr?'

'Not her. No. I never saw her before in my life. Well, that's not exactly true. I met her once in a supermarket queue. How do you know her?'

Both William and Benjamin threw back their heads and made goggle eyes.

'She's famous, dear. Fay-mous. *Très célèbre!* She's always posing in those glossy mags, in backless dresses or see-through blouses, standing next to French pop singers and models at parties. "Glamorous Odile and friend" kind of thing. When we knew that she was coming here we were both rather excited.'

'Odile de la Warr, Sally, is the Queen of St-Tropez,' added Benjamin, exasperated. 'Or should I say the original Tarte Tropézienne.' He laughed loudly at his own joke.

'Chop-chop, Sally. What are they eating? Madame de la Warr is an extremely demanding creature. And she has a big mouth.'

'Well, perhaps she shouldn't have injected her lips with so much filler—'

'I mean, Sally dear, that Odile's opinion really counts.'

Sally took a deep breath. 'Thanks, Benjamin. Thank you, indeed. That's all I need.' She reeled off the orders; then, as she returned to the dining room, said under her breath, 'The sooner this place is sold, the better.'

Both William and Benjamin laughed aloud.

But Sally knew that the entire evening service was going to be hell.

The other tables slowly filled up with passing trade. Carol did not come back from her delivery round. Sally really could have done with some help. She tried to get through to Carol a few times, but the phone went straight to answer. She presumed today's deliveries must be in distant valleys or people who lived in tunnels or something. She left a message begging Carol to return soon.

Odile de la Warr sent three dishes back: one too cold, one too salty, one because she had changed her mind about what she fancied.

To make matters worse, Sally kept dropping things, and once even tripped over someone's handbag, which was lying on the floor by their seat, and upturned a whole trayful of desserts, which had to be remade.

Towards the end of service a family of six, all dressed in matching shell suits, arrived at the door.

The man of the family spoke in English and made no attempt to try even a *'Bonsoir'* in French. His opening gambit was: 'We need a drink of water.'

'Not in here, I'm afraid,' said Sally, as quietly as possible. 'This is a restaurant. If you want a drink, you could try the bar-brasserie next door.'

'Did I say a drink?' The man pushed forward. 'I said we want a drink of water.' He said the word 'water' in a loud and aggressive way. 'My family is thirsty.'

'I've already told you, monsieur,' said Sally calmly. 'This is a restaurant.'

'So you won't give us a glass of water?'

'If you have a meal, of course we serve water. But this is not a bar. We don't serve drinks alone.'

'All right. Have it your way.' The man took another step forward, scanning the dining room. 'Do you have a table for six?'

'You're lucky, monsieur. It's the last one.' Sally escorted them to the only remaining table, which was right next to the Markhams. She handed out six menus.

'Do you have a toilet?' asked the woman, who Sally presumed was the man's wife.

Sally pointed towards the corner and the sign reading *'Toilettes'*.

The four teenaged children trooped off in the direction of the facilities.

'I know you,' said the wife, staring at Phoo Markham, sitting at the adjacent table. 'You're on the telly, aren't you? Isn't she, Danny? She's famous. She's on the telly.'

'How lovely to be recognised so far away from home.' Phoo gave a sickly-sweet smile of acknowledgement. 'And might I say, what a charming family you have, my dear.'

Sally watched while the woman continued to simper and coo over Phoo, then turned on her heels and disappeared into the kitchen to take a few deep breaths.

'What are you doing in here?'

'Taking a mini-break. What does it look like?'

'Fine. So you won't mind if I go in and introduce myself to La Belle Tropézienne.' Benjamin took off his apron and waltzed past Sally, heading into the dining room.

After a moment or two gathering herself, Sally moved after him.

By the time Sally reappeared, the shell-suit family were all seated back in place, holding up menus which hid their faces.

Another group of six stood waiting at the door, near the desk.

The man held up six fingers.

'I'm so sorry,' said Sally. 'But tonight, as you see, we're full.'

The group grimaced a look of disappointed resignation and left.

Wishing that the latter party of six had arrived a few minutes earlier, Sally took the order pad and walked across to the English family.

'A few more minutes.' Danny lowered his menu. 'We're still deciding. You know kids. Could we have that jug of water, please. Just tap will do. Adam's Ale. None of that fancy stuff you charge a fortune for.'

As Sally turned, Phoo threw her a look of sympathetic pity and stage-whispered, 'Poor Salz! What a busy night.' She grabbed Sally's hand. 'We've been laughing with your friend Benjamin about how funny you were in those dark, distant days when you thought you wanted a career in acting.'

Phoo gave a throaty laugh.

As Sally walked away, she noticed that Benjamin was now grovelling on one knee before Eggy and Odile as though they were the King and Queen of Fairyland on the verge of granting him three wishes.

In the kitchen once more, as she stood at the sink, filling the jug, Sally let out a growl, which caused William to fall into a fit of giggles.

Sally then smoothed down her apron, and returned to the shell-suit table where she poured out six glasses of water.

'Two more minutes, please,' said Danny. 'Such a lot of choice!'

Another table hailed Sally over to the far side of the room for their bill. Simultaneously Odile jangled her bracelets and demanded three coffees, *express*. She suggested that they should come with petits fours.

Before Sally could reply Benjamin told her that they did. 'Believe me, Odile,' he gave her a winsome smile which Sally imagined he had practised at the mirror, believing it to be cute – personally such sycophancy made her want to vomit, 'Sally will bring you a plate of petits fours to die for.' Beaming from ear to ear, he then swanned off back to the kitchen.

Sally managed not to say out loud, 'And with any luck they will choke you.' She hastily placed the bill on the nearby table and retired once again to the kitchen to fetch the coffees ... and the petits fours.

'What's bitten you tonight?' asked Benjamin. 'Everyone is so famous and glamorous. And you actually *know* two of them! If I had famous friends I'd be over the moon.'

As she poured the coffees Sally gritted her teeth. Benjamin was right. She did seem to be in a foul mood all the time these days. She wondered what was wrong with her. She felt stupid and hurt. It was how she remembered feeling in the school playground. But how could she have let two people from her past get to her like this? She was happy with her life out here. Wasn't she? She'd escaped from an unhappy marriage and divorce and regained her independence here in Bellevue-sur-Mer. And yet, in just a few days, her whole outlook had changed so violently. She had been perfectly content until that stupid mosaic medallion failed to bring in the promised fortune. How shallow had she become? And these two shadows from her past were probably the only people in the business who had made her feel so small. No other job cast a shadow. But it was all so long ago. She was no longer a lowly assistant stage manager. They couldn't report her to the company manager and get her sacked. If they wanted to carry on living in the past, that was fine. But she was the person with a lovely house here and a life full of sunshine and great friends. She must pull herself together and make the most of everything she had now, rather than suffering for a world of long ago.

When she got back to the dining room, she was just in time to catch the shell-suited family of six trooping out into the street, sated after their free and gratis water and lavatory break. 'We don't like any of this stuff you serve here,' Danny's wife called over her shoulder. 'We really wanted a kebab, not this foreign muck.'

It took every ounce of self-control Sally possessed not to crash the tray of coffee down on to the mosaic floor and stand there screaming till she passed out.

As she approached the Markhams, Sally caught Phoo and Odile giggling into their hands.

Calm! Calm!

But it was impossible.

She plonked the coffees down.

'No need to take it out on us, old girl,' said Eggy. 'A simple glance at that lot, you could tell that this place was not for them. They were hardly sophisticated. You should have told them where to go before you let them sit down.'

'You were caught, love,' interjected Phoo.

'*Candid Camera* and all that.' Eggy mimed taking a picture. 'Gotcha!'

'Taken in by some very common people. Taken in, my love, hook, line and stinker.' Phoo laughed as she slurped her coffee. 'But, poor old Salzy. As I recall, you always were a teeny bit slow on the uptake.' She turned to Odile and cooed intimately, 'Sally used to be our stage manager, Odile ... but she never quite got the hang of it.' She turned back to Sally. 'And in those days Sally was rather pudgy. Weren't you, darling? You've done ever so well, you know. All this rushing around, serving at tables, has taken off pounds.'

'We'll have *la addition* now, please, old girl,' said Eggy, brushing the crumbs down his bulging shirt front. '*Tempus fugit* and all that. And we have an early start tomorrow.'

'Sparrow's fart,' added Phoo. 'Plus, I have a few frightfully important phone calls to make. *Entre nous*, I'm angling after a very juicy film role. And I'm pretty confident that I'll be a shoo-in.'

Sally trudged back to the desk to print out their bill. She hoped that, once they'd paid, the Markhams and friend would quietly disappear never to be seen again.

But it was a good half hour before they left the restaurant. Odile queried every item on the bill, before finally agreeing to pay two-thirds of the actual cost.

'So, I hear through the grapevine that this restaurant's up for sale,' she laughed. 'And no wonder!'

Take-off was delayed 'due to staff shortages', meaning that Theresa's plane didn't touch the runway at Nice Côte d'Azur airport till a few minutes before 1 a.m. Despite sitting squashed between a boy who spent the whole journey crunching his way through jumbo packs of crisps, and a woman listening to a beeping kind of electro-pop music through leaky headphones, for most of the flight Theresa managed to get some sleep, slightly relieved by the knowledge that it was not some fat, bald old paedophile who had lured Chloe away, just a boy at her school. But teenagers were unpredictable and the situation was far from over.

Bleary-eyed, she shuffled through customs, and went out on to the forecourt where she climbed into a cab to take her home to Bellevue-sur-Mer. She knew that a taxi ride of that distance would cost around 100 euros, but at this time of night what other way did she have to get home?

Chloe's disappearance was turning out to be not only a disturbing but an expensive business, to be sure.

The ride home was much too fast and swervy for Theresa's liking. But, when the driver eventually skidded to a stop outside her front door, she found she didn't have the right money in small notes. The driver claimed not to have the right change, leaving Theresa no option but to overtip him wildly.

She watched the tail lights of the taxi disappear up the hill as she let herself into the dark flat.

It was strange. Even before she stepped inside she thought that the place felt different.

Above all, there was a lingering smell of aftershave.

She flicked on the lights.

As she shoved the door open, a pile of rose petals spread themselves across the Welcome mat.

How had they got there? Had someone been in here while she was away? Who had keys?

Only Sally, and she wasn't the rose-petal-delivery type.

Or had they just been emptied through the letterbox?

Nervously Theresa moved further into the flat. 'Hello?'

Tiptoeing around, slamming open the wardrobe doors, she checked every cranny to make sure she was alone.

She inspected the small back yard, too, even though the only ways anyone could get into it were by coming through her flat as she had done, or by jumping from a window in the Hotel Astra or the upstairs flat.

She peered up into the darkness. Most of the windows which looked out on the courtyard were small – probably lavatory windows, except in the hotel; but you'd really have to be very fit to make that jump and land one piece. And then, how would you get up there again?

As Theresa moved back inside, still looking up behind her towards the yard, she heard a great thump coming from somewhere near the front door.

She froze.

What was that?

Breathing heavily, she took a few tentative steps into the living room.

Another thump.

Then a blood-curdling scream.

She dashed through the living room and stood beside the front door, ready to open up and run for it.

She could hear footsteps above her. She glanced at her watch. Almost 2 a.m.

Perhaps it was a tourist, renting the flat, packing for an early flight. They would have to leave soon if they were booked on the first flights out of Nice at 5 a.m.

A diabolic laugh from above.

What was going on?

She could hear a woman's voice now, pleading. She sounded terrified.

The man laughed again and once more a loud thump.

Silence.

Barely daring to breathe, Theresa opened the latch on her front door and went out into the street to take a look up at the windows of the flat above.

The curtains were drawn, but a sliver of light spilled through the gap.

Theresa looked around her.

No one was in the street, and the lights in every building except the flat above her own were extinguished.

The only sound was the gentle wash of waves rattling the pontoon.

Should she go and knock at her upstairs neighbours' door?

Where would that place her? What if he was in the middle of killing a woman? Would a murderer let her go so that she could run to the police?

On the other hand, what if it was a couple involved in some sex game? Everyone had read that *Fifty Shades* book. And Theresa had read that, since it first came out, sales of velvet handcuffs and whips had gone stratospheric …

The lights upstairs went off. Silence reigned. Whatever they had been up to, they were now clearly settling down for the night.

Theresa moved discreetly back into her own apartment.

Once safely inside, she went straight through to the bedroom and flopped down on the bed.

Her phone beeped.

She sat up and pulled it out of her handbag. It was a text from Imogen: 'Have you arrived yet?'

———

Sally had tossed and turned for hours, blushing with horror at how small she felt whenever the Markhams mocked her. It was just like being back at school, being picked on by the playground bullies. But she had to get back the old rhino-hide. Just because these two treated her like a walking joke who'd been completely useless at the job, that wasn't to say she hadn't been a good actress. She had had nominations, won awards and been showered with wonderful reviews from national newspapers to prove it. So why did it matter so much?

Sally realised that it was because it affected her life now, her life here in Bellevue-sur-Mer. It was as though the Markhams had arrived here, moved among her friends and constructed a totally new past for her. And now her current friends looked at her differently.

She was disappointed in Benjamin.

He had not helped her situation by being quite so obsequious with them.

Sally turned over and curled up into a ball. She hadn't felt so low since those grim days which followed her husband dying in his secretary's bed.

If she hadn't felt such emptiness, she would have cried herself to sleep. Instead she lay awake until she drifted off into a nightmare in which Odile de la Warr, wearing a black witch costume and armed with a pair of flashing silver Japanese kitchen knives, was chasing her through a dark, moonless forest.

The phone rang.

Sally opened her eyes, thankful to have escaped from the dream.

'*Allô?*'

'It's William.'

Sally flopped back into the pillows, dreading what he had to say that was so important.

'Well, dear, you made a right cock-up of tonight. Benjamin and I have been discussing it for the last hour, and we both feel assured that a good mention by Odile de la Warr in one of those local magazines would have got the whole project rolling again. Instead we get another anonymous one-star diatribe. Odile obviously hated the whole experience and, thanks to you, the night was a disaster ... And now we're a laughing stock. And, yes, Sally, before you jump in to make excuses for yourself, I do lay it all at your clumsy feet.'

Sally tried to get a word in, but William was on a roll.

'And as for those two theatrical types with her ... Handled properly they might have given us a bit of prestige too. Not to mention the faux pas of the night ... What were you thinking letting those awful chavs in, and losing us a whole table for the last service? This is not working out, Sally. You've bolloxed up the Shore-to-Ship deliveries, you couldn't hack it for your one night in the kitchen, and now you've proved you cannot manage the heat of working front of house. So tell me: what can you do?'

'I don't know why every disaster turns out to be my fault.' Sally felt seriously aggrieved and wished they could be shot of the restaurant tonight and never have to set eyes upon it again. 'I was too pressed. Where was Carol? That's what I'd like to know. It was too much to manage on my own.'

'Poor Carol is still stuck up in La Turbie.'

'What on earth is she doing up there?'

'That's another thing which counts against you. You've broken the delivery van, putting an end to one of the most lucrative parts of our failing enterprise.'

'What are you talking about now?'

'The van broke down up in La Turbie. According to the man who came to fix it, "*somebody*" forgot to put in any oil.'

'I did put in oil. Last week.' Sally sat upright again. Why was Carol trying to frame her? She thought they were friends.

'Well, there was none in the engine tonight, and as a result the gearbox or the bearings or the big end or something has gone to hell. My brain clouds over when anyone talks about technical things to do with cars. But I understand money and the repair bill comes to nine hundred euros plus tax.'

Sally gasped.

'Exactly. That's yet more dosh draining out of La Mosaïque's dwindling coffers. Or should I say empty coffers. The only thing we appear to be accumulating at the moment is debt and bad will. And now the choice is a new van, or hiring one for the foreseeable future. Oh, and paying Carol's hotel bill for tonight. She's stuck. The last bus left La Turbie at six p.m. and there's no other way home but taxi, which would cost double the price of the B&B.'

'I don't know what to say, William. I'm sorry. Really.' Sally sighed. What else could she do? Tonight she hated everything and everyone, including herself. 'If I had any money I'd resign my share right now and pay for my escape.'

'Dream on, love. The only income you have is us. And until that van repair is paid off, your pay is docked. Face it, Sally. You are a flop. Anyway – see you tomorrow, if you can be arsed to get off your backside and come in to work.'

Sally put down the phone, laid her head back on the pillow and cursed the world.

Her phone rang again.

She picked up.

'Just bugger off and leave me alone to get some sleep now, all right?'

'Sally? It's Theresa.'

'Oh, sorry.' For the moment Theresa's predicament had entirely gone out of Sally's head. 'Any news of Chloe?'

'No. But I'm back home. Down the road.'

Sally froze. She hoped this was not really bad news.

'Chloe is somewhere here, in France. And we think she's in this area. It turns out it was some schoolboy she's run away with, not a bald fat man, after all. I know it doesn't make it that much better, but at least it's not some mad old paedophile.'

Sally wondered why Theresa was phoning at two in the morning to tell her this.

'I just wondered, Sally.' Theresa lowered her voice. 'While I was away have you let anyone into my flat?'

'No.'

'You didn't give my keys to anyone?'

'No. They're hanging up in the cupboard in the restaurant cellar. I saw them there tonight. Someone had left me a pink rose and a heart.'

'That's strange,' said Theresa. 'That's why I thought someone had been in my flat. There are pink rose petals by my door.'

'Carol did see some man hovering around outside yesterday,' said Sally. 'He was worried about the acoustics or something.'

'That might explain the noises, maybe. But not the rose petals.'

'You don't have a secret admirer?'

'Not unless he's keeping it a secret from me. Or has a key. You're sure you haven't lost mine, have you?'

'I told you, they're in the cellar cupboard. Could someone have posted the petals through the letterbox?'

'That's what I think.' On the other end of the line, Theresa paused – presumably to look. 'Yes. That must be it. But who?'

'A secret admirer. So what are the noises?'

'All quiet now. But half an hour ago, some couple was making a hell of a racket. It sounded as though they were killing one another.'

'I gather they're tourists,' said Sally. 'Maybe they're on honeymoon, or a dirty weekend. Carol met the bloke, and he was warbling on about acoustics. Obviously worried that you'd be able to overhear their romantic dalliance.'

'Oh yes. Once they get out of England people do go rather sex-mad, don't they? Kinky stuff, I expect. Anyhow, it's good to catch up, though I'm not sure if I'll see you tomorrow or not. Until we find Chloe, I'm going to be rather distracted ...'

'It's all right, Theresa. I understand.'

'How's it going your end?'

Sally knew that she couldn't burden Theresa with her woes, so she replied, 'Oh, I'm fine. But if you're worried about the flat, Theresa, I'd put the chain on.'

'Don't worry, Sally. It's already on. And I've got chairs balanced up against both doors. And tomorrow I'm getting the locks changed.'

After hanging up, Sally turned out the light and lay in the dark. Once more there were too many thoughts flitting through her mind to be able to settle down to sleep. She gazed out at the black horizon. A shaft of moonlight drew a neat, white, sparkling strip down the centre. In the distance she could see a brightly illuminated cruise ship sailing silently into port.

She hoped Chloe was safe. She remembered the worries her own two kids had put her through and dreaded that all starting again with a new generation.

With a groan, she faced the wall.

She had been such good friends with William and the others. But the vagaries of fortune at La Mosaïque had put paid to all that goodwill.

Sally wished again that she had never got involved in this stupid restaurant business. Thanks to it, she was sinking further and further into debt, both financially and socially.

Bloody William.

She wished he'd get off his high horse. True, she had not handled the last service very well, but surely everyone was entitled to an off-day? True, the restaurant was failing, but it wasn't all her fault. Why blame everything on her? After all, William himself was no angel.

In fact now she wished that she had reminded him of his own failed night as a waiter.

Next time he started accusing her she was determined to fight back.

The phone rang again.

Sally turned over and grabbed the receiver.

'NOW WHAT!' Silence. 'Hello? Hello?'

All she needed – a wrong number.

'Hello?'

No doubt someone wanting a taxi to Monaco or some equally annoying misdial.

'Hello?' said Sally. 'Sorry! Wrong number.'

She slammed the phone down. It rang again immediately.

'It's fucking three o'clock in the morning, you bastard.'

'Sorry about that, Sally. These time zones always get me fuddled.' A woman with an American accent.

'Who is this?' Sally was truly in the dark.

'Is that Sally Doyle?'

'Who wants to know?' asked Sally.

'It's Marina Martel. I'm phoning from my offices in West Hollywood.'

Sally leaped out of bed and stood to attention.

This was Marina Martel, the Oscar-winning American movie star, on the other end of the line.

'Now, Sally,' Marina continued. 'Here's the thing ... I'm sorry if it's the middle of the night with you, but I have a little emergency, and you might be able to assist.'

Sally's mind raced.

Why on earth should Marina Martel be needing her help?

'I realise that last time things didn't work out for you, because you'd just bought that lovely restaurant with the dazzling floor, but I'm sure that, over the last couple of years, things have settled down a little.'

Sally knew she couldn't bore Marina Martel with the details of why that last phrase was so very wrong, so instead she simply said yes.

In fact 'yes' seemed to be the only word she had felt able to pronounce since she knew who was calling.

'So, now, Sally.'

'Yes.'

'You remember me telling you how, when I was a kid stationed with my dad in the UK, how much I admired your work as an actress. How I caught up with all your stage work and got the videos of those classic plays you did before *Ssssaturday Sssslamerama!*'

'Yes.'

Sally could not imagine where this conversation was leading.

'Well, the thing is, I have a little project going on over in your area,' Marina Martel continued. 'You're not far from Monte Carlo, right?'

Sally once more let out a feeble yes.

'You see, we've been rather badly let down.'

'Right.' Sally felt triumphant that she had managed to find a new response.

'And, Sally, I would like you to take part in the filming, which starts tomorrow.'

Sally had images of herself doing the catering, serving in a commissariat or from the chuck wagon.

'It's only small, but it's actually a wonderful part. And I want you to play it.'

Sally was dumbstruck.

'She's a nagging wife. Very funny role. And she always gets the last laugh. The husband's a real twit. In fact they're both a pair of bumblers. But they come out on top.'

'But, Marina, I ... I haven't acted for years ...'

'Don't be silly, Sally. As well you know, acting is just like riding a bike.'

'But I can't ride a bike.'

Marina guffawed down the line.

'There you go! That *is* the character. I realise you'll probably want to think about it, honey, but we're very pressed and I really do need your answer in the next half hour. And, also, Sally, do you have email?'

Sally reeled it off. She didn't think she could take up this job offer, but at least she could write her refusal to Marina Martel in an email reply. That would be much easier.

But Marina was still talking. 'Of course I know you must realise that someone dropped out at the last minute. Stupid woman took herself off skiing at the weekend and is now laid up in some French hospital with two broken legs, a broken nose and a black eye, meaning she can't walk, and even if we tried some trickery – shooting her in a wheel-chair – her face looks as though she's been in a prize fight. And certainly won't settle before we finish the shoot. Oh, and by the way, it's only a week's shoot. All along the French and Italian Riviera. You'll to have to reshoot the shots she's already done, which will set us back a bit. Obviously it's too late to get someone out there from Stateside without losing another couple of days, and so, as you're right there, I immediately thought of you. If you say yes, you start shoot-ing tomorrow morning. We'll put you up in a lovely hotel, of course, but if you prefer to stay at home, naturally we'll provide a car and per diems in lieu. It's full Equity, but the fee's not great. I don't know if you have an agent ...'

Sally's mind now sped through all her old contacts in the business, wondering if any of them might negotiate this contract for her. She was shocked to realise that by now all of her old agents would probably have retired or maybe have died.

'But it's all pretty straightforward SAG rules and so on, Sally, a standard contract ...'

Sally was once more thinking it would not be right for her to walk out on the others at La Mosaïque just so that she could follow her own dream.

After all, she had William breathing down her neck.

But then again, would another chance like this *ever* come up in her lifetime? She was almost sixty-five, for heaven's sake. Time was running out.

But when things were going so badly, to let the others down ...

'I'm afraid the fee isn't much to write home about, Sally. We'd pay you in euros or pounds, or whatever you like, but I'm afraid I could only offer you twenty-five thousand dollars.'

Theresa woke to a bleep from her phone. She grabbed it and peered at the tiny screen. It was exactly 6 a.m.

The message was only some totally irrelevant suggestion sent by one of the apps recommending 'attractive' hotels in the vicinity. She saw the screen long enough to notice that the Hotel Astra had a score of 3.1 out of 5, which was three points higher than Theresa would have rated it.

Awake now, albeit reluctantly, she opened the socialising app which Mervin had installed yesterday, wondering whether now would be the time to try to contact Neil. She then remembered that teenage boys were famous for not getting out of bed till noon, so she laid the phone down on her bedside table and turned to face the window.

She looked up at the back windows of the hotel and wondered how many of the people sleeping there last night had been recommended to book a room by their very annoying phones.

She vaguely recalled a bit earlier hearing noises coming from the upstairs flat, followed about half an hour ago by the sound of someone clomping down the stairs, followed by the slamming of car doors. Maybe whoever it was had been heading into Nice for an early flight.

Theresa tried to nap but kept being haunted by thoughts of Chloe. Where would she have slept? Last night it was cold. She prayed that the child had found somewhere decent and warm to lay her head.

If she came by train, might Neil have been waiting for her at the station? Would she have had enough cash on her to take a cab to wherever she went? Chloe couldn't possibly realise that Nice cabs were three times the price of those in London. What if the driver had suspected she couldn't pay and dumped her out somewhere along the way?

Could she be walking distance from where Theresa lay, or might she be miles along the coast, at Menton or Toulon?

Theresa wondered whether she should do that thing which people did when they lost a cat – get a photograph reproduced and put it up all over the place – but simultaneously she knew that that would be a horrible thing to do, and that if either Neil or Chloe saw something like that it would be the finish.

Having a photo of Chloe always in her pocket, though, wouldn't be a bad idea. First things first. Theresa had to find a recent photo of Chloe, then at least she could go around local cafés and hotels asking if anyone had seen her.

Theresa wished she had brought that photo of her with Neil taken after the play. Though, in full Friar Laurence gear, complete with bald wig, Neil would be unrecognisable. She might as well tout around a photo of Friar Tuck, thought Theresa. All you could see was the fatness, the baldness and the brown dress. If only she had asked Neil's mother for a photo. But on second thoughts, perhaps not.

So first things first. She would get up, go to the restaurant and find a photo of Chloe in the photo album.

Then what?

Take it to the police?

She thought Imogen would not like that. One thing she did know was that she must run everything past Imogen first and not go jumping into things on a whim.

She decided to phone her daughter to discuss tactics. Then she remembered that England was an hour behind, so there it was only 5 a.m. Even during an emergency that was much too early to call, especially as she had no news to impart.

The letterbox rattled. The postwoman delivering something. Theresa climbed out of bed and went through to the living room.

Something lay on the mat. Probably only news of a sale at the local supermarket. She stooped to pick it up.

It was a photograph of herself, all made up and wearing posh clothes. She flipped the photo over but there was nothing written on the reverse. It was obviously a picture of her which had been taken ages ago, perhaps at one of the children's christenings. She recalled that it had been in the photo album.

Still in her nightie, Theresa opened the front door and peered into the street to see if the person who had posted it was still there. But there was nothing moving outside except a street-cleaning machine operated by a council workman, which was a hundred metres away, noisily sucking at the gutters and spraying the pavements.

She went back inside and sat at her glass table, staring at the photo. Perhaps it had fallen out of the photo album when she was walking over to La Mosaïque, and some kind person, recognising her from the picture, had posted it back through her door. But that was a few days ago now, and, if she had dropped it in the road, the street cleaners would have swept it off early one morning, along with the discarded sweet wrappers and cigarette ends.

After a quick shower, Theresa dressed and walked along to the restaurant. She let herself in through the back door.

It was just after seven.

No one was inside.

She would have expected someone to have been in by now. The van was not parked outside, so maybe whoever was picking up the fish this morning was already on their way to bring in the daily fresh goods.

She spent some time searching the kitchen for the album. Everything had been moved around since she'd not been here. Obviously other cooks had their own methods, which was fair enough, but she had to go through every cupboard and drawer before being certain that the photo album was not here, near to where she had left it when she departed for London.

She went down to the cellar.

Pieces of paperwork littered the table: bills, receipts and invoices. She sat at the desk and started going through the filing cabinets, searching each folder, just in case it had been hurriedly put inside to get it out of the way.

Almost an hour later she gave up the search.

Sally had not returned the photo album. Theresa wondered if she might have taken it up to her house for safekeeping.

As Theresa came up the stairs to the kitchen, the back door opened.

'What a shock!' Bearing a large box, Cyril stood at the door. Theresa could see that he had visibly paled. 'I thought you were at London.'

'Yes,' explained Theresa. 'And now I am back.'

'You gave me fright!' Cyril put the box on the counter and asked Theresa to sign for its receipt. 'It's lovely that you are back. Your granddaughter is returned?'

'We're not sure where she is yet.'

Loud chattering echoing in the tiny lane outside fore-told the arrival of Benjamin and William.

On the sight of Theresa they stood stock-still for some seconds.

'What are you doing here?'

Sensing tension, Cyril buried his head in his order book checking his deliveries against the dockets.

Suddenly he let out an exasperated sigh and banged the heel of his palm on his forehead.

'*Merde*, I've forgotten the pork. I'll be back later.' Cyril excused himself and hastily left.

'We were about to put up the "Due to unforeseeable circumstances we are closed" sign.'

Theresa could see a nasty glint in William's eye. He was spoiling for a fight.

'As we seem to be the only two people left working in this enterprise, we thought we might as well just shut up shop and be done with it.'

'I'm sorry, William, you're going to have to explain.'

'Oh, don't worry. We will,' snapped Benjamin. 'First, *you* waltz off without so much as a by-your-leave. Next thing Carol gets stuck up in La Turbie, along with the van, and now Sally has buggered off as well. By text message, if you please! The rats have deserted the sinking ship, leaving Muggins and Friend.'

'Excuse me, Theresa!' William shoved past her, heading for the dining room and the front door of the restaurant. 'There are things to do here. Like watching a ship with no lifeboats smash into an iceberg.'

'Thank God, you're back.' Benjamin lowered his voice to talk to Theresa. 'It's been a hellish couple of days. You cannot imagine. And he's gone right off the rails.'

'Sorry, Benjamin, but I'm not exactly back—'

'You have to be back, Theresa. You are physically stand-ing in front of me.'

'But I was—'

'Please do the lunch today. Please!' He threw himself to his knees. Theresa was worried for his designer trousers. The floor looked none too clean.

'There's nothing here for me to cook,' she said. 'Do get up, Benjamin.'

'There's meat.' Benjamin rose and indicated the box on the countertop. 'And we have potatoes, rice, pasta ...'

'You do realise that my granddaughter is still missing? And anyway, what's wrong with Sally?'

'This is all we know.' Benjamin held up his mobile phone and read: '"Something has come up – sorry! Cannot be in to work for the next week or so. Sally. I will buy myself out."

'You understand, Theresa,' he said, while she glanced at the text to see whether it might have another meaning. 'Sally is in a sulk because of the hideous goings-on in here last night. That's all this is.'

'Good riddance.' William was back, and in for the kill. 'She's a sanctimonious drama queen and I, for one, have had enough of her.'

Five minutes later, Theresa had her apron on, and was preparing today's special – cottage pie – while Benjamin and William got the dining room ready.

She reasoned that, until some contact was made with either Chloe or Neil, there really wasn't much she could physically do to aid the search. She had made numerous attempts to get through to Neil via Mervin's app. He had not replied.

About five minutes before the house was due to open to the public, with a bright 'Coooeee', Zoe popped her head round the back door.

'Only me!'

It was lucky that Theresa knew Zoe's voice, as, after undergoing the new Swiss treatment, her face was unrecognisable: a glossy forehead, something about her eyes which gave her an oriental appearance, and lips so full they looked as though she might have bought them in a joke shop. 'Just wanted to hear any news. All running smoothly since I went away, I hope.'

William and Benjamin arrived abruptly in the kitchen, waving their mobile phones.

'Has anyone seen this?' cried Benjamin. 'It'll be that bloody Marcel and his cronies.'

'A whole batch of one-star reviews on *FaveEats!*' William leaned against the countertop. 'I never read these stupid internet things, but look! Even the burger bar in the garage up on the autoroute now has a higher rating than us.'

'According to this other foodie site,' Benjamin swallowed hard before continuing, 'we are the lowest-rated eating establishment in Bellevue-sur-Mer.'

Zoe grabbed the phone from Benjamin's hand, and peered down at the screen. 'Can't see a thing.' She looked up and blinked her false eyelashes, not realising that one of them had unhinged itself and fallen across her right eye. 'It's gone awfully dark in here. I don't know how you work in these conditions. Anyone got a magnifying glass?'

'Does anyone seriously read those star-review things before choosing where to eat?' Theresa would never consider the opinions of total strangers.

'Only everyone in the world,' snapped Benjamin. 'Nowadays there's no strolling around looking in at places you fancy. People are like sheep. They rush to the suggestions at the top of the list, and steer well clear of the ones at the bottom. It's a self-perpetuating load of rubbish.'

'Couldn't we get someone to march around the streets with a sandwich board telling them to ignore what's on the app?' Zoe looked up. The stray false eyelash finally lost its grip and fluttered to the floor. 'Hello? Did somebody turn the lights on?'

The restaurant front door slammed and Carol stepped into the kitchen. 'That doggone van. I love her but ...' Carol's face was streaked with oil and her hands were black. 'I persuaded the garage to do a patch job, just to get me home,' she announced. 'But the darned old girl broke down trying to climb up the hill to get on to the main road. I've spent the last three hours jacking her up, lying on my back underneath her, giving her the once-over, and finally she's on the road again.'

'As the bishop said to the actress,' added Zoe.

'I didn't think that Mech. Eng. would have been quite your scene,' said Benjamin, curling his lip at the sight of Carol's soiled clothes.

'What do you mean, darling? I've always adored engines. I'm fascinated with everything mechanical.'

'But did you manage to collect the fish and veg?' William stepped forward, his mind forever practical.

'I'm not Louis Hamilton.' Carol threw down the keys. 'I thought you'd be pleased with me for getting the van back in one piece. Did they find the girl?'

'What girl?' asked Zoe.

'My grandchild. No.' Theresa moved towards the oven to turn it on, getting ready to start baking some potatoes. 'But I volunteered to do lunch. This afternoon I have to devote my time to finding Chloe.'

'I thought we were here to offload this restaurant ... sorry, I mean this money-disposal unit ... to the irritating twit next door?' Zoe boomed.

A sharp rap on the back door, and Marcel walked in.

'I may be French,' he said, 'but I realise that a "twit" is not necessarily a good thing.' He glanced at the tray of individual pies on the counter. 'I see you are back, Theresa.'

Theresa forced a smile.

Marcel did not return the gesture. '*Restaurant sans terrace, trente couverts,*' he said. 'For a swift sale I will offer you two hundred thousand euros. Final offer.' He turned towards the door. 'You have till this time tomorrow; after that the offer is withdrawn.'

'That's less than we paid for it.' Zoe attempted a look of horror, causing her remaining eyelash to tumble down and land on her cheek.

'It's an insult!' screeched Benjamin.

'If your reviews are anything to go by, overpriced.'

Zoe wiped a finger over her cheek and the eyelash slid down on to her décolletage. 'Agh! A spider!' She jumped back. 'Or is it a cockroach?'

Marcel left.

———

Sally sat in the make-up chair, going through her lines. She had four scenes to shoot today, and, according to the sides she had been given when she arrived on set this morning at six-thirty, it was only in the last scene that she actually spoke. The other scenes involved: 1. walking out of a front door, 2. going into a boulangerie and coming out with a baguette and 3. coming into a public toilet, where she put on a wig and coat, and going out again. All without a word spoken, which was great.

Last night – or, rather, earlier this morning – after she had hung up the call from Los Angeles, Sally had wanted to sleep, but was too excited, so that when the car drew up outside her front door at 5 a.m., she was already waiting, fully dressed, having barely slept at all.

The make-up wagon was parked up, jammed among all the other movie vehicles in an open car park on the outskirts of Monaco.

Judy, the make-up girl, was charming, and immediately arranged with the Third Assistant to get a cup of tea and some pastries brought in for Sally.

While Judy applied Sally's make-up base, Sally asked her a bit about the film. The current fashion was always to keep actors in the dark – only give them the pages they were featured in – so it was difficult to get a sense of the whole story.

'Wish I could help,' said Judy. 'I only started today too, I'm afraid, Sally, and everyone else is off with the main unit, which is doing some car stuff up on a high road where Princess Grace Kelly shot some movie with Cary Grant and later died in a crash. Frankly I'm glad to be down here. IMO sounds like an unlucky place to shoot.'

'You don't have a cast list on you, do you, Judy?'

'Sorry, Sally. Please could you stop talking for a moment. I need to concentrate on your lips.'

As Judy applied the lip brush, Sally mentally went over her lines again for the scene this afternoon. It was an exchange with a man named Gilbert, a scene which ended in a snog. Lord. She had forgotten this unpleasant side of showbiz. A roomful of people staring at you from every possible angle while some total stranger had his tongue down your throat. The glamorous life!

The caravan bounced a few times as someone came up the steps.

'Sally Doyle!' A tall man in a sheepskin-collared leather jacket held out his hand. 'Daniel Sullivan. I'm the director of this little caper. *So* pleased you're joining us. Marina is producing from LA, the London casting director's gone into premature labour, and, well, you don't want to hear about our problems. But the upshot is, at the eleventh hour, in total desperation, we've got you here with us, and ... *hoorah*.'

Sally wasn't sure whether the young man was aware how rude he had been, but she smiled as best she could manage without moving her lips for Judy.

'So, anyway ...' He glanced down at a clipboard in his right hand. 'We're off to a flying start with a few scenes from towards the end of the movie, on the day of the heist.'

'It's a heist movie?'

'What other kind of movie gets shot in Monte Carlo?'

The Red Shoes? thought Sally. *Grand Prix*?

'So far we've had terribly bad luck. Bloke originally playing Gilbert, your husband, caught mumps and had to pull out a week after we started rolling. Who gets mumps in this day and age? We'd already shot some of his scenes, but on the last day he looked less like a suave Englishman and more like a pantomime Mr Toad, so ...' Daniel kicked his foot out. 'Order of the boot for him. New fellow has some relationship with the pregnant casting director, and managed to squeeze himself into the role as replacement. Then Lia, the silly cow, whose plum part of Louise you've managed to snitch, decides, contrary to clearly stipulated contractual rules against such Eddie the Eagle recreations, that she's a downhill racer and—'

'Will I get a full script at all, Daniel? Only I'm a bit in the dark about the story.'

'I'll get all your sides printed out and delivered to your hotel room ...'

'I'm actually coming in each morning from my home in Bellevue-sur-Mer.'

'*Ooooh la la!*' Daniel said. 'A proper little *vedette*! We're all staying at a frightfully posh place here in Monte Carlo.

The Grand Hotel Astor. All mod cons, gym, 24-hour room service, ravishing views of the Med, swimming pool, bar, four-star restaurant. But I suppose your own place must beat that.'

Sally hated the way everyone assumed that if you lived down here you owned a moated palace. But she had more pressing worries than correcting his presumption. 'And the story?'

'Blah-blah-blah, really. All you need to know is that you are playing one of a cameo couple of amateur burglars, who accidentally ruin things for the main characters who are pros at the burglary business. They of course are being played by Marina Martel and Steve Baxter, *real* stars, who arrive over here in a few days, by which time hopefully you'll be gone and out of our hair ...'

Judy coughed, and threw a glance at Daniel.

'So, anyway, I'll leave you in the capable hands of Janey, here ...'

'Judy.'

'Judy! Yes, that's right. Sorry about that.' He banged his forehead. 'Judy! Judy! Judy! Isn't that a quote in some ancient, long-forgotten film? Anyway, as you gather, we're picking up all the scenes we'd already shot with the queen of off-piste slalom, and we've a hell of a lot to cram into the scant hours of daylight, *aujourd'hui*, so "one-take wonders" are the order of the day, lady.' Daniel raised his eyebrows. 'I've gathered you're an old pro at the game, so I'm sure you'll be fine. I usually find veteran actresses very efficient.' He ran his fingers through his hair and held a pose for a moment. Sally wondered if he was about to vogue down the steps. But instead he inspected his clipboard. 'See you down on set, erm, Sally. We have a rather fancy bakery for you to enter, but I can't attest to the public conveniences, and as for the door ... Well, as Shakespeare once said: a door is a door is a door.'

If Marina Martel had chosen this man as director, Sally presumed that he had to be good at his job, even if his social skills had certainly not been nurtured in the Barbara Cartland charm school.

Daniel's phone rang. He pulled it out of his pocket and answered.

'Who?'

As the voice at the other end spoke, Daniel rolled his eyes in the direction of Judy and Sally and continued: 'Not that old bag *again*. Doesn't she understand English? The role is cast, cast, cast, and, no, I do not want to see either her CV or a show reel ... Yes, I'm sure she knows quite a few important people in the business ... No, no, no. Tell her under no circumstances should she fly out to the set to meet me.' Resuming the conversation at the top of his voice, Daniel turned on his heels.

'Now, Sally,' said Judy as Daniel bounced away down the stairs, rocking the make-up wagon so that Sally's seat felt as though it was on a trampoline, 'before I start on the hair, I'm just going to try out a few wigs for scene 102.'

Sally sat back. She mustn't let her nervousness get in the way of this opportunity. Nor must she become obsessed with the idea that she was totally out of touch with the business, just because she had been living in France for so long. She might not be so young any more, and could even qualify as a 'veteran' performer, as Daniel had so keenly reminded her, but Sally felt she was still *au courant*.

Judy advanced with an auburn fringed wig with flick-ups. She hovered behind Sally, then pressed the wig down on her head.

'Oh. I say!' Looking at herself in the mirror Sally laughed. 'Very Mary Tyler Moore.'

'Who?' said Judy.

FOURTEEN

THERESA STARTED TO TAKE her apron off. What if Chloe had been ringing on her home telephone? She had an urgent desire to be in two places at once. To keep her promise to her friends and her business but also to be available should Chloe make contact. She knew she had to sneak out and check.

Benjamin entered the kitchen. 'Where are you going?'

'I've prepared the lunch service, Benjamin, but I really do need a breather now.'

'But we're supposed to be having a meeting about the insulting offer from Marcel. We need you to take part in the discussion.'

'Frankly what is there to discuss? We just say no and tell him to come back with a sane and genuine price. Why should we gift him the building along with all our hard work? We had a good reputation.'

'*Had* being the relevant word …'

'I've told you my opinion.' Theresa pulled her phone out of her handbag and walked past Benjamin and out through the dining room.

She was very relieved to be in the open air. The sun was shining, but this afternoon the royal-blue sea was topped with white horses. A fierce wind blew in, whipping up Theresa's hair and catching her scarf. As the long strip of cashmere flew off along the quay, Theresa ran after it, stamping like a Spanish dancer every time it came near to touching down on the pavement.

Once she had snatched it and wound it back around her neck, this time with a solid knot, she had passed the moored multicoloured rowing boats and little white fishers, bobbing on the swaying sea.

As she put her key into the front door, she felt the phone buzz. She glanced down at the screen.

One missed call. When had that come in?

An unknown number, but it looked like an English mobile phone.

Hoping it might be Neil, while walking into the flat, she immediately redialled the number.

'Hello?' A female voice. 'Is that you, Grandma?'

'Chloe?'

'Yes.'

'Oh, God. Are you safe?' Still wearing her coat, Theresa flopped down on to her armchair, cradling the phone close to her ear. 'Please tell me you are all right.'

'Yes.' Chloe spoke very softly. 'I'm fine and I'm happy.'

'Is this your new phone number?' Theresa intended to store it immediately the call was over, so that, when necessary, she could phone her back.

'No. Neil lent me his phone. I knew people would be worried by now. But this call is to let you know that everything's all right and not to bother looking for me.'

Theresa stopped herself from replying. She was quite aware that, whatever Chloe thought, the situation was not 'all right'. Far from it. A fifteen-year-old girl should be in school, not gallivanting around the Côte d'Azur with a fellow truant. She was committing a criminal offence, for heaven's sake.

'Neil wants to know if you're the strange woman called Theresa who keeps buzzing him on Instatalk, and writing in a creepy way that sounds like some weirdo pretending to be young?'

'I'm so sorry, Chloe. That was someone from your school trying to find you.'

'Please don't tell me it's Mum?'

'No. A teacher going by the name Mervin.'

'Oh, that freak.' Chloe laughed. 'He's a real perv, Grandma. And he smells.'

'To be truthful, Chloe, I didn't get close enough. But he was doing his best to help us.'

'You were in London?'

'Yes. But I'm back home now in Bellevue-sur-Mer.'

Theresa was not sure how to get the best out of this call. The most important thing was not to make a thing of it and scare Chloe away. She had to be sure that Chloe kept in contact. She didn't want to spell out the panic which had taken up the best part of her last forty-eight hours.

'I was wondering where you were, darling. Someone said that they thought you were in the South of France, somewhere near me.'

There was a silence. Chloe did not take the bait.

Theresa pressed on. 'And, if you are, why don't I treat both Neil and you to lunch?'

'Is this a trap?'

'No, darling. Of course, it isn't. But, as you know, I love cooking. And it would be good to see you. And I can advise you about some interesting local places to visit.'

'I'm not on holiday, Grandma.' Chloe sounded determined. 'This is my new life. Being with Neil.'

Theresa had to grab the conversation back from this dangerous topic, grab it back to the merely casual.

'You could come to the restaurant, or to some neutral space, a café or somewhere, or perhaps to my flat, whichever you like. Are you in Nice?'

'No,' Chloe replied.

'Somewhere nearby, though?'

'I'm not really sure where we are, to be honest. Nor is Neil. But it's very windy here. I can barely stand up.'

As Theresa had walked here, she had almost been blown over by the wind. She wondered how far these weather conditions might stretch. Could it be that the two kids were only a few miles up the road, or were they well along the coast in San Remo or Saint-Raphael?

'You're warm and have somewhere to sleep and eat, I hope?'

'Really, Grandma, stop worrying. Neil's dad is a very generous person and I've got a lovely bedroom, so it's all fine. I think he's one of the nicest men I've ever met. He's such fun.'

'Is that Neil or his dad?'

'Oh, I meant his dad. But Neil is even better.'

So, she had got some information out of the child. Now to press on.

'Well, if you have a little think, conflab with Neil, then name the day and pop over to Bellevue-sur-Mer and I'll cook you some of your favourite things.'

'Can we have tiffin, Grandma? I've told Neil about it.'

Theresa heard a low voice in the background. Could this be Neil or was it the father?

'I have to go now, Grandma. Love you!'

And she was gone.

Theresa thought about redialling but decided against it. She put the phone back into her pocket.

The dilemma now was how much to tell Imogen? If she didn't tell her daughter that Chloe had phoned and then Imogen found out, all hell would break loose. But Theresa did feel that she had Chloe tentatively hooked. They were joined each end of a thread, even if that thread was made of the most fragile silk. One false move and Chloe could truly disappear. But if she kept hold she might be able to reel her in.

Theresa moved through to the kitchen, to check the answering machine, as that is what she had come to do.

Almost immediately the landline phone rang. It was going to be William summoning her back to the restaurant.

'Hello?'

Silence.

'Hello?'

She could hear someone breathing, but nothing more.

'Anyone there? No? All right then. Goodbye.'

She replaced the receiver and looked at the handset screen for the call log.

Number Withheld.

As she scrolled back she noticed that over the last few days there had been quite a few Number Withheld calls.

No doubt it was some awful marketing robot. She poured a quick glass of water and knocked it back. She needed to get to the restaurant to complete lunch, but still felt so divided by the feeling she should be doing something more active to find Chloe.

'I've got a lovely bedroom, so it's all fine,' Chloe had said. So did that mean that Neil's father had a property out here on the Côte d'Azur? Chloe's sentence didn't sound as though they were staying in multiple hotels as Theresa had been imagining. When people stayed in hotels they rarely called them bedrooms – just rooms.

Perhaps Roger Muffett had bought some chateau in the country, or a large city flat, and they drove out each day for lunch in various places.

Though, to be serious, that didn't sound right, either.

It might be that Mr Muffett was house-hunting. That would certainly explain them bobbing around from town to town. Maybe he had rented a place to stay, probably in or near Nice, then they ranged out every day to various towns and villages along the coast on his property search.

She moved towards the front door but the landline phone rang once more.

Theresa answered but this time said nothing.

After a moment or so's silence at the other end, a female voice said, 'Mum? Are you there?'

Imogen!

'Sorry, darling. Did you just phone a minute ago? It's just that I keep getting these—'

'No. Look this is urgent. Mervin's had some more connections with Neil. He says that Neil just sent him a message saying that he's so fed up with technology and tech teachers and everything to do with computers that he's going to throw his phone and tablet into the sea. If that happens, Mum, you realise we'll lose all contact. We have to stop him.'

Trying not to laugh, Theresa bit her lip. She understood exactly what was happening. Now that they knew Mervin was behind the messaging, the two kids were playing up their ex-teacher. But how could she explain this to Imogen without letting on about Chloe's call? She took a deep breath, praying she was doing the right thing.

'A few minutes ago, Chloe phoned me, Imogen. I spoke to her.'

'What do you mean? Did you tell her to stop fooling about and worrying us all to death?'

'I'm trying to arrange a meeting.'

'What's her number? I'll phone her and make it quite clear ...'

Theresa knew that, if they were to have any success in getting the kids here, she must not give Imogen Neil's number.

'It was a Number Withheld, I'm afraid.'

'Damn.' Imogen sounded very disappointed. 'What were you saying about a meeting?'

'If things go as I hope they might, tomorrow, or perhaps the next day, Chloe will phone back and agree to meet me for lunch. I left the decision with her.'

'What do you mean, you "left the decision with her"? Mother, we are dealing with a teenage underage child who's on the run. You should have been firm. Someone has to stand up to Chloe and force her to come home.'

'Stop panicking, Imogen.' Theresa tried to sound calm and not let Imogen intimidate her. 'Remember "Softly, softly, catchee monkey".'

'Oh, for goodness' sake, Mother. We're not talking about a monkey. We're talking about a child – my daughter. My fifteen-year-old daughter!'

'My fifteen-year-old granddaughter.'

'You're impossible, Mother. I really can't waste time talking to you. But next time you hear from Chloe you *must* phone me instantly.'

'I would have done, but you phoned me before I—'

'I have to go now.'

And Imogen hung up.

Theresa felt sure she was doing the right thing. Wasn't she? At least this way they had some hope of seeing Chloe in person, and then, once she was here, reasoning with her.

Theresa was leaving when she noticed something lying on the doormat.

She picked it up.

Another photo of herself. This one was of her in her wedding gown.

As she flipped it over the front doorbell rang, and Theresa literally jumped a few centimetres into the air.

It was the postwoman, who handed her a parcel, got back on to her scooter and sped away up the hill.

The box announced that it was from a large online store. That was strange as Theresa had not ordered anything from them for months.

She crammed the packet under her arm, and started locking up. It was only while putting her keys in her handbag that she noticed the reverse of the wedding photo she had just received.

On the slightly foxed white paper, someone had drawn an ornate red heart pierced with a black arrow.

———

Sally thanked the lord that the first scene she shot was really simple. She had to walk out of a dark blue door, take a furtive look in either direction and then stride off confidently along a street peopled with extras. She clinched it in one take. The crew moved on and set up location at the boulangerie. Here she had to rehearse taking money from her pocket, passing it to an extra who handed her a baguette, which she stuck under her arm, and again walking off along the street.

On the second section Daniel suggested that Sally take a bite out of the loaf as she walked. She was in a dilemma, as she knew that this was something never done here in France, except by tourists. And as the movie was about two criminals who above all wanted to blend into their surroundings, she felt that her character, Louise, would not do this. Nor was it in the script.

She didn't want to seem difficult but knew that she was right in refusing to follow Daniel's orders for the sake of the film's credibility.

She tried to move nearer to him to explain, but the First Assistant insisted she stay on the spot as the crew was fixing up some supplementary lighting on her.

When the time came for the shot, Sally stepped out of the boulangerie and walked away, baguette tucked under her arm.

'Cut!'

Everything stopped.

'Sally, dear. You forgot to take a bite.'

'That's the thing, Daniel. I thought that the two crooks needed to be somewhat invisible and look like locals. If I take a bite I'd immediately look like a tourist.'

Daniel sighed.

'Very opinionated, aren't you, for an unknown?'

'I just thought—'

'It's not your job to think, luvvie, that's what I do. OK?' He made a signal to the First Assistant. 'Another shot, right away.'

Seething with rage and embarrassment, Sally moved back to the start mark and prepared, on the second take, to dig her teeth into the baguette.

After lunch they moved location again. The scene in the public convenience, where she changed into her disguise, went smoothly enough. There was a tricky moment when one of her false nails got caught in the netting of the wig, but she used it and they didn't need to do a retake.

As she sat in the back of the van which took her and the make-up girls to the final location of the day, Sally once more scanned her lines. She looked out of the window at the stunning views of Monaco harbour and mouthed the lines to her own reflection. She hoped that the bloke playing Gilbert was funny. It was easy to see that her laughs would depend on his delivery.

The van drew up outside a luxurious hotel on the seafront. The Third Assistant took them up to the suite where they would film the last scene.

'I'm afraid the other unit is running a little behind, Sally, so I'm going to walk through the scene with you now. Then, when your partner in crime turns up, we can go straight for a take.' He indicated the room. 'We've only got this suite for a few hours. So we need to wrap and have all of our kit out of here by eight p.m. at the very latest.'

When the tea break came round – a trolley with a platter of finger sandwiches, and polystyrene cups of coffee and tea – Sally took hers out on to the balcony and sat watching the sunset, making the most of the ravishing view, with all the twinkling decorations of the yachts going by, strung over with flags and coloured lights. Imagine being rich enough to take this room! How wonderful that would be. She looked down at the grim faces of people passing. The strange thing was that every trip she had made to Monte Carlo – and, earlier in her life, to another tax haven, Jersey – seemed to indicate that the richer you were the more miserable you appeared. What she saw now confirmed that.

She was chuckling to herself, thinking that there might be some balance in the world, and that not being on the top of the financial heap could have its benefits, when the Third Assistant called her inside to shoot the scene.

The others had arrived.

Daniel was standing in the corner talking earnestly to an actor who had his back to Sally. He was kitted out in a mind-boggling floral sun suit consisting of a short-sleeved jacket and matching shorts. She gave a quiet bravo to the costume designer. That costume was hilarious – a brilliant touch. Even from the back view, the man looked like an utter twit.

'First positions, please.'

Sally flopped on to the sofa and picked up the colourful mock cocktail which she had to fiddle with in the scene and eventually spill all over herself.

'Sorry, everyone. Especially Eddie, who's barely got his breath back from shooting the scenes up on the autoroute.' Daniel stepped forward. 'I know this is unusual, but don't blame me. Blame the stupid actors who ballsed up the schedule. Now, I'm going to turn on this rehearsal. So, though it's a rehearsal, can we treat it as a take, please? You never know.'

'Sound?' called the First Assistant.

'Speed,' replied the sound guy.

'Camera?'

'Rolling.'

The clapperboard operator knelt down in front of Sally, the clapper poised.

'Scene 102, take one.'

He snapped down the board.

'And ... action!' called Daniel.

'We did it, darling!' Sally took a sip of her drink and leaned back, kicking her shoes off and putting her feet up on the coffee table. 'Gilbert, darling?' She turned to face the windows. 'Shall we dine on the terrace? Champagne, caviar, the works? We deserve it after that haul!'

'What? Sorry, didn't hear you! The water was running.' The actor playing her husband came on to the lit area.

'But I say let's go for everything on the menu! Money no problem, now, eh? Kiss, kiss!'

As he dived down on to the sofa and grabbed Sally's face, she wasn't sure who was more shocked.

She could see the panic in his eyes.

They both struggled to continue the dialogue without going off script.

The actor playing her husband, with whom an on-camera full-mouthed snog was seconds away, was none other than Eggy Markham.

FIFTEEN

ONCE BACK IN THE RESTAURANT kitchen, Theresa took off her coat. Before she started the lunch proper, she decided she couldn't resist opening the parcel before anyone else came in. She ripped the cardboard strip along its length, and pulled out the further wrapping …

Lying in a shiny plastic box within was a very large knife. She flipped it over to see the brand. Sabatier. The top level of kitchen knives.

How odd. And how scary. She searched the packaging for any clue, hoping for some message or note indicating who'd sent it, but there was nothing. Just in case it had been dispatched to her by mistake, she put it back into the box, ready to return it.

But what kind of a mistake could that be? It had been sent to her home, not to the restaurant, so it wasn't a marketing thing.

She rolled up her sleeves and turned to the worktop.

What if it was some sign? Maybe Chloe had been kidnapped. Was she being held somewhere? When Theresa thought back on the phone call, her granddaughter had sounded subdued. Not at all the usual bright and flamboyant girl. When she rewound the conversation, Chloe had seemed very restrained; she'd actually been whispering.

What was going on?

Perhaps everything Chloe had said on the phone was a lie. Maybe she was being held by kidnappers, who were about to launch a ransom campaign. And the kidnappers had sent Theresa a knife, by way of a warning.

Marcel followed William into the kitchen from the dining room.

'You have to see, I was only giving a realistic price. If things are going as well as you say, then tell me why you're selling up? I thought I was doing you a favour, so that you could all be free of the place quickly and move on.' He turned and faced Theresa. 'You look upset. Has something happened?'

She was not in the mood to share her worries at this time. 'I'm fine.'

'If there's anything upsetting you, Theresa, remember I am your friend.' Marcel looked at her with that hang-dog face of his. 'You can always come to me with any problem.'

The nerve of him! How could he be offering help when he had just insulted them all with his meagre offer for La Mosaïque?

Theresa slid the opened package along the worktop.

'I'm fine, thank you, Marcel. It's just that I'm hot.' She held his waist as she squeezed past him to get to the storage fridge. 'No pork yet? Cyril promised.'

As though on cue, there was a knock on the back door and Cyril entered.

'*Voilà!*' He put his parcels down and went through with William to get a receipt.

'Don't you want a quick sale, Theresa?' asked Marcel once the others had left. 'Or don't you really want to sell?'

'Frankly, at the moment, Marcel, the sale of the restaurant is the last thing on my mind. My granddaughter has run away with some boy but she is somewhere in this area and I have to find her.'

'Chloe is fifteen, Theresa.' Marcel laid a consoling hand on her shoulder. 'She's practically an adult. I'm sure she can look after herself. Adolescents! You know!'

'Did you get my message?' Cyril was now hovering near the doorway to the dining room. He picked up the knife in its illustrated box. 'Phew! That's one good knife.'

Theresa faced him. 'Did you send me that, Cyril? A gift maybe?'

'Not a very romantic gift.' Cyril shrugged a no. 'I use knives every day, all the time. I gut chickens, and saw through bones with axes.'

'Do anonymous gifts have to be romantic?'

'*Bien sûr ...*'

'What message, Cyril? You asked about a message.'

Cyril pulled a face, meaning 'not here; not now'.

'You asked if I got your message. Spit it out. It can't be anything so private.'

'It's not important,' said Cyril, slamming the knife back on to the countertop. 'Really! Another time.'

Theresa was starting to get impatient with him. She had to get on with preparing the service. 'Do you need anything else, Cyril?'

'I just have to get past Marcel to reach the fridge.'

'Don't get into a sweat, Cyril,' snapped Marcel. 'I have important business here. You don't.'

Theresa stepped back to let Cyril by. Muttering to himself, he hastily started unloading the pork into the cool shelves of the meat refrigerator.

There was something disturbing about Cyril's presence this morning. Theresa turned back to continue her conversation with Marcel.

'You say "just fifteen" but fifteen years old is nothing, Marcel. You know how difficult an age that is. Remember you told me about your own son.'

Marcel's son had gone on to drugs at sixteen, and been found in a gutter one morning, overdosed. It had taken years of care to help him back to leading a good, healthy life. The boy, now twenty-two, was living in Paris, attending a college for pastry chefs.

'So, Theresa, what are you doing about your granddaughter?' Marcel shuffled from foot to foot. 'You don't want her to fall into the hands of bad people. Perhaps I can help. I can talk to you. Talk to her.'

'I have spoken to her today, and I'm hoping she'll contact me again somehow and that then we can arrange a meeting.'

'Hope? Why don't you simply phone her back?'

'She didn't use her own phone.'

'I don't envy you.' Marcel rubbed his chin with his hand. 'As you say, teenagers can be wily.' He seemed as though he himself might burst into tears. 'I'm so sorry about before.' He pulled his cap over his eyes and moved towards the back door. 'If there's anything I can do to help ...'

When he had gone, Cyril took his face out of the fridge and gathered up his empty boxes. 'It is love, you see,' he said. 'It is always love. Especially with adolescents.'

Throughout the lunch service Theresa's mind kept returning to Chloe. She wondered where she might be now; how she was eating; did she sleep with Neil; where *did* she sleep; what was Neil's father actually like? She couldn't imagine a man who was carefree about welcoming and then encouraging two underage children to play truant from school being really as lovely as Chloe had implied. She wished Chloe would come here, then at least Theresa could provide her with a decent hot meal and try to talk some sense into her. But then, with the kind of money Neil's father seemed to possess, she supposed Chloe would be fed well enough already.

She sent out the last of the desserts, a *poires belle Hélène* and a cheese platter, then hung up her apron. As she grabbed her bag she felt her phone vibrate.

This time a text message from a number she did not recognise.

'Meet me this afternoon, 15.30, Le Bar – Le Chat Bleu, Cours Saleya, Nice.'

This had to be Chloe or Neil making contact.

She glanced at her watch. She'd be lucky to get there on time. She ran straight to the station and caught a train into town; then, not wanting to waste precious minutes, took the tram down to the Vieille Ville.

Theresa trotted anxiously through the tiny back streets of the Old Town and arrived in the marketplace. Most of the stalls had packed up, and the restaurants, like her own, had just closed for the afternoon. She scanned the café terrace. No sighting of Chloe, but there were quite a few empty tables. She took a table in a corner near the back of the terrace to get a better view. From there she could see anyone approaching in any direction, and she would easily recognise Chloe from a good distance.

She ordered a *café express* and sat, while others all around her were chatting or reading the local paper. She looked at the time. Twenty to four. Surely Chloe would have given her more than a few minutes before giving up and going? The little white cup, only half-filled, but served with a slim biscuit, arrived and she tried to drink it slowly, savouring the rich aroma. It was difficult trying to dawdle over a coffee while not reading or fiddling with a diary, but she knew she had to keep her eyes forever scanning the crowds, in case Chloe was hovering, worried that this was a trap. A group of tourists briskly walked past, following someone holding up a flag on a stick. She saw that they were all wearing identical headpieces. There was a new position – a tour leader who didn't even have to talk to their followers, just press buttons and play them the commentary!

After half an hour, Theresa felt bad sitting there fiddling with an empty cup so ordered a glass of wine. Why not? She felt tense enough thinking about the whole situation: Chloe's running away, the mysterious gifts, the string of missed calls. And it wasn't as though she was going to be driving or operating heavy machinery. And she had more than an hour before starting tonight's service. She deserved, and needed, a drink.

She tried sending a text to the unknown number. But nothing.

After she had munched her way through a basket of crisps and drained the last drop of the wine, it was half past five. She knew in her heart that Chloe wasn't coming. But how much longer should she wait? Should she live in hope that Chloe would turn up, even after waiting two hours?

She ordered another wine.

At a quarter to six she knew she was cutting it fine. She'd be lucky getting back in time to start the dinner. Hastily she paid up, leaving a decent *pourboire* for the waiter who had very kindly not pestered her even when tables were starting to fill up with the aperitif crowd.

As Theresa cooked that night, sending out dishes to the dining room, borne by William and Benjamin, Carol assisted as best she could.

'We're overloaded out there,' she drawled. 'Better to help you out.'

'No deliveries to do tonight?' Theresa tackled a large steak, lifting it from the frying pan and laying it alongside the vegetables. It splashed juices over the edge, and she had to apply kitchen paper to the sides of the plate.

'If something local comes in I'll take it. But I'm not going off into the hinterland and getting stranded again. No siree.'

Theresa felt glad that she had Carol to talk to. The stress of the last few days was like a snowball; the more you worried the bigger the worry became. Time for a new subject.

'No word from Sally, I suppose.'

'Oh yes!' Carol prepared a mixed side salad in a small bowl. 'Milady Connor-Doyle has returned to the stage. Or should I say the movies.'

'She's gone back to acting? You're joking?'

'Absolutely not. She's on location, filming in Monte Carlo. And, from her tone, unrepentant. She left a message on William's machine. He went into a jig of anger which might or might not be interpreted as a war dance.'

'Well, at least someone's happy.' Theresa couldn't believe this. 'Talk about rats leaving a sinking ship.'

'Just leave the mugs to sort out the mess.' Carol drizzled vinaigrette over the salad.

'Is that Sally's game, d'you think? Swanning off to cavort around with film stars in Monaco while her friends have their noses to the grindstone trying to save their own and her arses?'

Theresa picked up an egg from the stand and it slipped from her fingers, smashing on the tiled floor.

'Damn!' She reached for a cloth to mop it up. The last thing they all needed was for someone, maybe herself, to fall and break a leg.

'You seem quite preoccupied this evening, darling?' Carol drained the new potatoes and laid a few on top of the gravy, which Theresa had ladled over the meat. 'I presume there's no word from the kid?'

'She texted me to meet in Nice, then she didn't show. I just don't know why she would text me then not come. I'm frightened something has happened to her.'

'She's a teenager, Theresa. They have social rules all to themselves. Maybe something better turned up. Perhaps she didn't feel that she could excuse herself from the boy's family.'

'Then why not text me to say she wasn't coming?'

'Don't you remember being young?' Carol laughed. 'In my humble opinion it's an intensely selfish period of life.' She picked up the plate and whisked it into the dining room, calling over her shoulder, 'You'll hear from the child in her own good time.'

But as Theresa left the restaurant at the end of service, she was disappointed that there were no vibrations from her phone – no voicemails or texts on her mobile. Absolutely nothing.

She strolled listlessly across the road and stood for a while gazing at the black sea, watching the lights of boats anchored in the bay. She was almost mesmerised by the slopping reflections of the moonlight, which spilled down on to the horizon, a rippling white stripe which ended in the slapping water at the sea wall near her feet.

If she was a teenage girl alone with a boy with whom she was besotted, would she have made an arrangement to meet her granny for a coffee? Absolutely not. Theresa knew she must have got it wrong.

As Theresa let herself inside the flat, she yawned. She was dog-tired. Not only from the hours she had been keeping and all the rushing about, going to London and back, but the stress of everything was starting to get to her. She had the worry about Chloe *and* La Mosaïque to cope with and she had not addressed either one mentally.

Before she'd had the time to remove her coat and check her answering machine for messages, the landline phone rang. With a sigh she picked up.

'Mummy? I'm coming over.'

It was Imogen.

'To Nice? When? Shall I make up the spare room?'

'No. It's too small and dark. I shall stay at that seedy hotel up the road – what's its name again?'

'Hotel Astra.'

'That's right.'

'But you could stay here—'

'No, I couldn't. I'm bringing the girls and I'm bringing Frances, so that, if I'm called upon, she can babysit.'

'But I could—'

'No, Mummy. You couldn't. You go out to work, remember? For us it's the Easter holidays, starting tonight. So we'll be arriving tomorrow morning. I just didn't want to surprise you by us bumping into one another in the street.'

'But I—'

'I have to go now, Mum. Packing. Passports. Tickets. Early start. Lot of organisation to be done.'

And she hung up.

Theresa went and looked at the spare room. It *was* small and dark. Imogen was right to stay away. For a guest room it was not very welcoming. Theresa decided, when she had the time and money, to get someone in to paint it a nice bright colour, put up some pictures, perhaps a mirror to give the illusion of space.

She flopped down on the empty spare bed and, feeling tired and unwanted, she wept.

After a moment or two she pulled herself together again. Though in her heart the fear was still whispering: Failure! Failure on every level – as mother, grandmother, wife, solicitor's secretary and now restaurateur.

It was all hopeless. What was the point of trying?

When you thought about it, everything came to dust.

She sat up, perching on the edge of the bed, and decided that the only possible solution was a cup of hot chocolate followed by sleep.

Depressed to her core, she moved back into the main room and switched on the kettle.

While waiting for it to boil she noticed something on the mat.

As the post had already come and gone long ago, it must no doubt be some junk mail – a local flyer for an astrologer, pizza delivery or a *vide-grenier*, the French equivalent of a car boot sale, perhaps.

She turned over the sheet of A5 paper. It was an odd collage of photos, artlessly done, one photo arranged higgledy-piggledy and photocopied to make one flabby mosaic-like design. Looking closely, she realised that all the little photos were of her. Some taken recently, but most were copies from her missing album.

The make-up girls were cleaning up the wagon, wiping down the tops and stowing things away, ready for it to move off.

As Sally came up the steps, Judy smiled and held out a jar of cold cream and a box of tissues. 'Quite a baptism of fire!'

Sally stooped to look at her face in the mirror. The lipstick was everywhere! When Eggy went in for a kiss it was like being sucked at by a wet Hoover. Sally hoped that she had looked as though she was enjoying it. The public always had the idea that these kissing scenes were likely to inspire you to run off and leave your husband or wife, it was all so exciting to look at. Little did they know about the reality.

'Is he an old friend of yours?'

Judy said this with an implied wink. She obviously imagined that they had once previously had an affair. Well, that was acting for you!

'I worked with him when I was starting out. We weren't really close,' Sally said, aware that that was a massive understatement.

During the shooting of the final scene of the day, after the kiss and the initial shock of seeing one another, Eggy had been rather subdued, she thought, and played the scene very efficiently, almost as if there was something weighing heavily on his mind. He seemed sheepish with her, although he did mumble encouraging noises. She remembered, when she was their ASM, that he had had a good side, and always had a wink and a sparkle in his eye. Over here he did seem a little bit like a fish out of water. Perhaps he was edgy because sometimes the crew spoke to one another in French. Sally was fine replying to them and obviously understood, particularly everything the script editor – or as Sally remembered in her day calling the continuity girl – said, but Eggy stood beside her looking lost, and *she* had ended up being the one encouraging *him*.

'Sally Doyle?' The Third Assistant was outside the trailer. 'Your car's ready.'

Sally dumped the soiled tissues in the waste bag and, waving goodbye to the girls, ran down the steps.

'Large silver vehicle.' The Third pointed across the car park. 'Hope you don't mind, but you're sharing a ride tonight with Mr Markham. The driver will drop you off first.'

Sally nodded and grinned, as her soul sank.

What would they talk about during the thirty-minute drive?

When Sally slid into the car Eggy was already waiting in the back seat. The car purred into action, swinging out past the car-park barrier and into the main road leading out of town.

While they drove through a street of high-rises, they remained together in a sticky silence. As the car moved on to the coastal road, Eggy spoke. 'Ravishing views round here.' He gazed out of the window at the black sea. 'It's a pity it's so dark. This morning I was intoxicated by the sight of that immense sparkling turquoise. Do you find it calming, too?'

Sally realised that she had lived down here so long now she took the beauty of the azure sea for granted. Perhaps she should gaze upon it anew, and let the sight soothe her nerves.

'It is calming. I'm very lucky. It's a lovely place to live.'

'Yes.' Eggy let out a little snort. 'You are blessed.' His phone rang out a jaunty melody. He glanced at the screen. 'Excuse me, Sally. I have to take this.'

What luck! For the moment, at least, Sally was off the hook in the realm of small talk.

'Today went very well indeed. No. No. Quite difficult … Yes. We're together in the car now driving us to our respective homes.'

Difficult to talk, Sally realised he was saying, mentally filling in the detail of the voice on the other end of the line. She could hear that it was a female. Probably Phoo.

She looked out of her window, watching the occasional garages, shops and bars along the way. People were seated out on terraces, heaters burning overhead, knocking back their evening glass of red. How Sally looked forward to quaffing her own. She remembered that someone had once accused Mary Tyler Moore of being an alcoholic simply because, on coming home from work, she drank one Martini every day. Well, if those were the regulations these days, Sally must be an alcoholic too. She was yearning for a drink.

The car passed into one of the tunnels leading through Èze. Instinctively Eggy started speaking louder.

'Of course I'm excited, my dear. But you're the one who got me stuck out here. I'd much prefer to be back in London, holding your pretty hand, helping you get by.'

Good lord! What could that mean? While they were going through the tunnel, Sally couldn't even pretend to be looking out of the window. But it was now clear that, whoever was speaking on the other end of the line, it wasn't Phoo.

Sally gulped.

She hated being in on other people's secrets. It was such a terrible responsibility.

With a whoosh the car returned to open air. But Eggy was still practically shouting. 'No, if it's a boy, you can't call it after me ... Because Edgar is such a silly, old-fashioned name ...'

Sally wondered whether her shocked gulp had been audible.

Totally embarrassed by what she had overheard, she started up a conversation in French with the driver which lasted until they were almost home. Eggy, ear glued to the phone, was still jabbering away with the casting director when the driver pulled up outside her house.

He glanced up, and mouthed, 'See you tomorrow,' bending his fingers in a mini-wave, as Sally climbed out of the car.

She waved back as the car continued down the hill.

She pulled out her key and opened up.

What a relief to be home and alone.

She went straight through to the kitchen and switched on the kettle. Old British habits die hard!

Next, she opened a bottle of Bandol, pulled out a glass, filled it and took a swig. Forgetting all about the kettle, Sally swung out into her living room and sat down on the sofa to replay her phone messages. She closed her eyes and listened to a blistering diatribe from William and slightly more reserved complaints from Carol and Theresa.

Yes. She *should* be helping them out with her physical presence. But if she could succeed in this film, she'd not only bring in enough money to save them all, but maybe the publicity would also be good for the restaurant.

She wiped the messages and lay back to study her call sheet for tomorrow. Some more tricky scenes, including one on a little motor boat – a cabin cruiser. Well, she would certainly look forward to that one as a fun way to end the day. She loved the sea, and she was an experienced helmswoman.

Smiling to herself, Sally took another sip of wine.

Eggy and the casting director! However much she tried not to put two and two together from the mobile snippets she had overheard, it was awfully difficult not to brood over the information. Had Eggy got the casting director up the duff? That's certainly what it sounded like. No wonder she'd landed him the role. Sally looked down the list of crew, searching for the woman's name. There it was. Right at the bottom. She had known many casting directors in her time but didn't recognise this one. But, then, that was hardly surprising as she had been out of the business so long.

She flipped open her laptop and quickly googled the casting director's credits, searching for a photograph. All the relevant pages showed a bright-looking woman in her mid to late thirties.

Gosh!

What on earth could she see in a stuffy old codger like Eggy? And what on earth would Phoo make of this?

The phone rang when Theresa was tucked up in bed, just drifting off to sleep.

Neither her tiredness nor the chocolate had done the trick. She had been kept awake not only fretting about the photos, especially this new, strange photo-collage of herself, but also by the sounds of a noisy quarrel taking place in the rented flat above. The man and the woman having a real humdinger this time. The woman was way more loquacious than the man, going at it hammer and tongs, while he only seemed to murmur rebuttals.

With this afternoon's café shenanigans, followed by the arrival of the photo-medley, Theresa was hesitant to answer the persistent clanging ring, but, just in case …

And it was lucky she did.

'Grandma? Could I meet you?'

Theresa sat upright in her bed and turned on the light.

'I think tomorrow we'll be going through Bellevue-sur-Mer. That's where you live, isn't it? So I wondered if I could meet you for breakfast.'

'Of course, darling. Do you want to come here? Either on your own or with Neil?' Theresa decided to wait till later to bring up the invitation to the Nice café.

'I'll be on my own. About nine?'

'Isn't that very early for you?'

Theresa noticed a slight hesitation in her reply. 'Neil has to go somewhere with his dad to pick some stuff up, so I'll be on my own.'

'Fine, fine. You have my address, don't you?'

'You won't have anyone else there with you, will you, Grandma?'

'Of course not!'

And Chloe hung up.

Wide awake now, Theresa couldn't stop thinking about the bizarre events happening around her. She gazed up at the ceiling.

She thought about her answering machine. When she got in from the café this afternoon, she had had a machine blinking at her, displaying the information that she had twelve messages, but no one had actually said anything. Just a row of silences and clicks. Could they all have been Chloe, trying to contact her to apologise about not turning up today or trying to set up tomorrow's meeting?

Theresa turned off the light, rolled over and stared out at the dark courtyard.

After a few minutes lying in the silence, she began to wonder if she was going mad.

Was it her imagination or could she hear someone saying her name, over and over?

She put her face to the window.

There was no one in the courtyard. How could there be, unless they had dropped down from the Hotel Astra or the upstairs flat?

Then she heard it again.

A whisper.

Theresa!

She pressed her face to the glass and scanned the entire space. No one was there.

Then she looked up towards the hotel.

She felt sure that a head bobbed back inside from one of the dark hotel windows.

Now she wished that she had curtains to draw but it had never occurred to her to get any as no one could see inside, unless they were standing in the courtyard and the only door to that was from her flat.

Slinging her dressing gown round her shoulders, Theresa got out of bed and tiptoed to the back door.

She peered up through the glass panels.

A few windows in the hotel were lit up, but what was strange about that? It was a hotel. Some rooms were occupied by people coming back from a night out, or sleepless with jetlag or excitement; others were empty or occupied by people sleeping.

She stood perfectly still, letting her eyes focus on the shadowy space, waiting for something to move, be it a cat or a rat ...

But nothing moved.

As she turned away she heard it again.

Theresa!

She wondered momentarily if she was hallucinating.

Or perhaps might ghosts be real?

This was getting ridiculous. It had been a long day. Actually it had been a very stressful *number* of days. No wonder her head was playing silly tricks.

Grabbing her blankets, she dragged them from the bed and through into the front room, where she curled up on the sofa.

Tomorrow she would get a roller blind or something put on both the bedroom window and the back door.

When finally she drifted off to sleep it was coming up to 5 a.m. But she was woken almost immediately by feet running down the stairs from the upstairs flat. Then the sound of a car door slamming, and pulling away with an expensive hum.

Theresa rolled over, cursing the buttons in the back of the sofa pillows.

PART FOUR

GNOCCHI NIÇOISE

You could of course save time and effort by simply buying a packet of ready-made gnocchi. That's what I do! Serves 6.

1kg floury potatoes, peeled
250g plain flour
1–2 egg yolks
1 large tablespoon olive oil
black and white pepper
salt
100g Gruyère cheese, grated
nutmeg, grated

To make the gnocchi, cook the potatoes in boiling water for 35 to 55 minutes, until very loose. Drain and mash. Stir in the flour, egg yolks, olive oil and a good grind of black pepper. Work the dough (as little as possible) until it is well mixed. Divide it up and place it bit by bit on to a floured worktop. Roll the pieces by hand until you get a cylinder 1cm in diameter and continue in the same way for the remainder of the dough until you have used all the mixture. Chop the rolls every 2cm. Roll each piece to form the gnocchi and press with a fork.

Preheat a dish in the oven and then drop the gnocchi into a large saucepan of salted boiling water. As it bobs up to the surface of the water, it is cooked. Usually this takes only a minute or two. Drain and place in the heated dish. Cover with the Gruyère and sprinkle with white pepper and nutmeg. Put under the grill until the cheese is golden and bubbling.

SIXTEEN

ESPITE THE UPSET OF having Eggy as her screen husband, and regardless of the snog with him and the shocking evidence of his affair with the casting director which had ended yesterday's working day, Sally was feeling high about being back in the acting saddle.

She wondered now why she had taken so much time out. She really enjoyed the frantic camaraderie of a location shoot. The laughs with the make-up and wardrobe department, joking with the crew while queueing to get the lunchtime catering tray, and sitting under canvas or on a bus with them all to eat it. Location catering had improved a lot since the old days, or perhaps this time it was because there was French money in the film, the caterers themselves were French, and thus naturally it was de rigueur to serve wine at lunchtime. Not that Sally touched a drop on set. She'd be far too worried about forgetting her lines. Also, after she'd reached fifty she found that drinking at lunchtime made her feel terribly tired for the rest of the day. But it certainly loosened up the camera crew.

Lunch on a British film set was a scant fifty minutes; here the *déjeuner* spread out to become the customary French two hours, giving her enough time to eat, relax and study the script for the afternoon's scenes.

She had risen that morning, dressed in the dark and made her way down to the waiting car. Eggy was already sitting inside grinning.

'I thought while we shared the car in we could go through lines,' he said.

Sally had been amazed that yesterday her words had come out in the right places and in the correct order, so was very happy to agree. They both had three speaking scenes today. One easy scene with few words, set inside an apartment in Monaco. Then lunch. After that a tricky scene, with lots of dialogue, to be filmed on a nearby beach, where they had to have a heated argument, much to the delight of onlookers, played by local extras. The final scene of the day was on the same beach as it started to grow dark, the two bungling petty crooks – she and Eggy – trying to climb into a boat and speed away.

But despite Sally's high hopes, so far this morning's scene had run to twelve takes.

The business was set in a dark room at night, where Eggy and Sally were trying to break into a safe. There were staccato lines interspersed with the movements of the action. Once they had got inside the safe, they had to pile the contents of boxes into a sack. But at that point they discovered they had forgotten to bring it, so ended up having to load wads of money and bundles of jewellery into Eggy's character's beret and down Sally's underwear. They then had to walk out of the apartment appearing deadpan.

Dark curtains blacked out the windows, and the lighting rig was arranged to make it seem as though the only light came from the occasional use of a torch and matches.

Everything technical which could go wrong had done so. The matches would not strike, the prop torch had flickered and cut out mid scene, then the safe numbers had all clicked correctly but the door was jammed and had to be levered open by the prop man. They'd tested it a few times, then gone for another take during which a helicopter had come over, flying low, and drowned out the sound.

This was followed by a near-perfect take, but one minute before the end of the scene the film cartridge had run out. So it was back to square one. Next take, a light bulb popped; after that when Sally pulled on the door handle, it came off in her hand.

Carpenters arrived and made good and the crew went for yet one more take. But by now Sally had gone word blind. Every time one of her lines came up she wasn't sure whether she had already said it, and then after a minuscule pause she got the line wrong. When Eggy came over and whispered, 'It's fine, love, just relax,' it had made her feel even worse.

Everyone was sent back to their start positions for the thirteenth time, and the clapper boy knelt before her and said: 'Scene ninety, take thirteen, let's hope this one is lucky for some.'

The rest of the crew guffawed. Daniel yelled, 'Cut!' and told everyone to pull themselves together. He reminded the crew that the shoot was already three days behind and Marina Martel would be arriving in France any day expecting results.

Sally glanced over to Daniel and could see that he was scared. She herself was terrified. By taking this job she had so much to lose. She could not foul it up. For sure she had to please Marina Martel. Sally was quite aware that, as Marina was the producer, the rushes would be sent to her each night for comment.

And at the same time, if the film was an embarrassment Sally would also have risked her friendship with the gang at La Mosaïque. And they were her everyday life. If she lost them, living in Bellevue-sur-Mer could become intolerable.

But that Daniel, the director, might also be worried, nervous that his work might be badly judged, had never occurred to her. She had been so wrapped up in her own fear she'd forgotten that she wasn't the only person on set who was feeling anxious.

Eggy gave her a nod and Sally smoothed down the front of her costume, ready to go for take fourteen.

'Don't mind me!' Sally heard a whispered voice in the dark ahead. 'I'm not really here! Sssssshhh! Ssssshhhh!'

She knew well the rounded tones of Eggy's wife, Phoo Taylor-Markham. Who had let her on to the set?

Sally tried to continue as though Phoo was not out there, watching her, hiding in the dark corner, lurking behind the script editor, the grip, the sound operator, the wardrobe assistants and make-up girls.

But she could not.

She found herself almost anticipating Phoo's rude remarks.

'Scene ninety, take fourteen.'

'And action!'

Sally began afresh but when her line approached the words all came out in the wrong order.

Daniel cut again, barking at the camera crew to keep turning.

'End slate!' Daniel ran both hands through his slightly greased hair and landed them with a slap on his thighs.

By the time they had a decent take, the crew were grumbling about their lunch break.

The location catering was set up in a car park, walking distance from the afternoon location. Daniel, checking his watch, asked the actors if they didn't mind losing some of their break so that they could go ahead to the beach and run through the scene a few times before the technical department arrived to set up. Eggy and Sally agreed.

They were both taken briefly to the location in a van then back to base.

Sally had not caught a glimpse of Phoo since they'd moved on from that unnerving seventeen-take scene and now wondered if she hadn't been imagining hearing her voice.

'I saw the rushes last night,' whispered Judy.

Sally felt a flash of expectant excitement.

'You looked good. We made the right choice with that shade of lipstick.'

Sally had forgotten that on a film set you were rarely paid a compliment; everyone was only really concerned with their own contribution. Therefore when make-up artists were watching the rushes all they looked at was the make-up!

The van drew to a stop and Sally got out.

A wardrobe girl rushed forward with an overall to cover her costume.

'Don't want you smeared with mayonnaise for this afternoon,' she said. 'There are no washing facilities down here.'

Sally made her way to the back of the queue, got her food and then walked to the tented area, where tables had been set up for everyone to eat.

And there was Phoo, seated at the tech crew's table, her arm around Eggy, holding up a large glass of rosé, throwing her head back and laughing, teeth bared.

'Oh, Sally was always such a klutz, wasn't she, Eggy? Absolutely hopeless at everything!'

Theresa was up by seven-thirty, making pancakes and all kinds of breakfast treats for Chloe. She wondered how best to handle the conversation. The most important thing was to establish a channel of communication, some way of being able to keep in touch, and to know where Chloe was at all times. But when Theresa contemplated this idea she also realised that it was rather threatening. Even as an adult she would find it horrible to think that someone might want to have tabs on her all day and night.

Obviously Imogen would have other ideas, but Theresa felt sure that the essential thing was, rather than capturing her and forcing her home, to get Chloe to go of her own free will.

She wished she had something more tempting to lure the child. Once a captive animal had escaped it was hard to get it back into its cage, unless of course the conditions outside were worse than the ones in. And from all accounts Chloe was currently living the high life. Theresa no longer even had the South of France as bait to lure her. Chloe already had that. And at the same time, the child was clearly being entertained by a very rich man and his son, whom she adored. How could she compete with that?

Once Chloe was here in person, Theresa hoped to entice her to meet up on a regular basis. Maybe invite Neil and his father to dinner at La Mosaïque? After that her mind ran dry. What other activities might she suggest to keep a grip on the girl? Everything she thought of, to use Chloe's own expression, sounded pretty lame.

At eight forty-five the doorbell rang, and Theresa went to open with a wide – she hoped – welcoming smile.

But it was only the postwoman who must have thought she was totally bonkers. With a brusque '*Bonjour*' she thrust a package into Theresa's hands and scooted off.

Theresa went back into the flat and opened the packet. A CD of Ravel's *Daphnis et Chloé*.

How strange. She had not ordered any such thing. What could that mean? And who had sent it? Might it have been Chloe herself? But that seemed rather a mature idea for a teenager.

Theresa opened the front door again, to let the sunshine in and take a peep along the front, just in case Chloe was in sight. Who knew, if Chloe was dropped off by car that would give a chance for Theresa to get the number plate. Though what on earth she could do with it after that she had no idea. It was just what people always did on TV series. It might be possible that Neil's dad would be in the car and Theresa could perhaps have a private word with him, maybe invite all three into her flat.

She crossed the road and sat on the sea wall, looking back at her own front door.

Carol pulled up in front of her. She was in the driver's seat of the restaurant's temporary van, windows down, sunglasses on, looking like a 1950s movie star.

'Taking the sun, my darling?'

'Waiting for my granddaughter.'

'You found her?'

'Not exactly, but she's coming to breakfast.'

'*Hola!* There's a start, anyhoo. See you later, darling. Off to get the seven loaves and two fishes.'

'We'll need more than that.'

'I know, sweetie – joke!'

Carol revved the engine and sped off up the hill.

Theresa looked up the road. No one was on the pavement; she could see no heads bobbing up and down behind the protective wall up the hill either. She turned the other way. A gush of people emptied out of the railway station. Theresa hadn't thought of that. Perhaps Chloe would arrive by train. There were stations all along the French coast into Italy. Wherever Mr Muffett was, Chloe could easily get here by rail.

She scanned the crowd as it thinned out and dispersed.

No Chloe.

'Theresa?' Marcel had crossed the road from his terrace. 'I was wondering if I could have a private word? Maybe I could come to your place later this morning.'

'I'm a bit preoccupied at the moment, Marcel. I'm waiting for my granddaughter.'

He laughed and pointed back at his terrace.

'Is that her over there?'

Theresa glanced at the tables of people taking *petit déjeuner* in the morning sun. Sitting alone near the door to the inside of the brasserie was Chloe, cradling a large coffee in both hands, blending in with the crowd. She seemed a little scrumpled, but that was teenagers for you.

Theresa leaped to her feet.

'God. I need my eyes testing. I was looking everywhere but ...'

'The meeting?'

Theresa couldn't think of that now. 'Whatever you like, Marcel. Just ring the bell. You're very sweet to offer.'

She ran over the road and stood before Chloe.

'Thank God you came, Grandma. It was only after I'd ordered the coffee that I realised I only have English money.'

'That's all right.' Theresa dug into her pocket and pulled out some coins. 'Shall I join you here, or do you want to come over to mine?'

'Can we go to yours, please.'

'Whatever you like.' Theresa felt strange being so subservient to a child, but realised it was necessary to keep her on side. 'Take your time.'

'That's all right. It's gone cold now, anyhow.'

Theresa was painfully aware that she must weigh every word she said. Whatever happened she must not scare Chloe off, and at the same time try to reason her around to going home.

'How long have you been sitting here?'

'Oh, ages.'

'You should have knocked at my door. I was up.'

Chloe stood up and stretched. 'I love the sun,' she said, stepping off the terrace. 'It makes everything feel so much more cheery.'

'Are you not feeling cheery?'

Chloe did not reply.

'I suppose Neil's dad has a huge mansion.'

Chloe stopped and looked Theresa in the eye.

'Why on earth should you think that?'

'I don't know. Something his mother said, I suppose.'

'You've met Neil's mother?'

Theresa thought back to the dishevelled drunkard in her run-down 'villa' in Streatham and wished she had not let that slip.

'Only briefly,' she said. 'In London. When we didn't know where you were.'

'They hate one another, his parents. It's so unfair,' said Chloe quietly. 'It makes life extremely difficult for Neil.'

Theresa nodded.

'Will Neil come here and pick you up today? To take you back to—'

'You won't get anything out of me like that,' Chloe snapped, then clammed up again.

This was going to be a tricky encounter, to be sure. Theresa walked at the child's side, rooting in her pockets for the front-door keys. She opened up and let them in.

'I made you some pancakes,' she said, pointing to the table. 'Dig in at will.'

'You haven't told Mum about me coming here, have you?'

'Of course not.' Theresa was pleased that she hadn't had to lie. 'This is strictly between you and me.'

Chloe licked her lips. It was clear that she was nervous and plucking up her courage to say something. Theresa prayed that it would not be anything awful, like announcing that she was pregnant.

She busied herself with the kettle, hoping it would leave Chloe more free to speak.

'Grandma?' Chloe said quietly.

'Yes?'

'May I have a shower first?'

Theresa was astonished that this was the thing which had made Chloe so nervous to ask.

'My bathroom is your bathroom,' she replied, heading for the cupboard and pulling out a clean bath towel. 'Take as much time as you like.'

As Chloe disappeared into the bathroom, Theresa regretted adding the last sentence. After all, Imogen had announced that she would be arriving in Bellevue-sur-Mer today. Who knew what time her flight would get in? Once landed she had to make her way from Nice, check in at the hotel and come down here – that was true. But it would certainly be better all round if, when Imogen turned up, Chloe was not here.

While the child was bathing, Theresa pondered on why, if she was staying in a millionaire's mansion, she wanted to take a shower?

Chloe's response to the suggestion that Roger Muffett lived in a large house somewhere down here certainly indicated that maybe he didn't. In fact if he did, surely the water would be connected and there would be bathrooms galore? Unless maybe it was one of those collapsed old farmhouses in the middle of being renovated? Perhaps Theresa's other imagined possibility was correct – that

Roger Muffett was living in a hotel and commuting around the area, property-hunting. But, seriously, these days didn't all hotels have bathrooms?

Surely they wouldn't be camping? Or even glamping, as people nowadays did. Glamping – glamorous camping! There was an oxymoron if ever she heard one. And, anyway, even if the Muffetts were on the downmarket side of camping, in France campsites were all very well equipped with showers and even jacuzzis and saunas.

It was a mystery.

Theresa wondered whether, when Chloe finally left here to go back to Neil and his dad, she shouldn't put on a mac and a pair of sunglasses and follow her, try to find out *exactly* where she was staying.

She had a last-minute idea to lay out the unsolicited knife and the CD she had received on the tabletop to watch if Chloe reacted to them. She ran round to get one from her bag and the other from the shelves.

The water stopped. Theresa once more went to the sink to fiddle with the kettle. She smirked at how tired this bit of business was, but it was the only thing she could think of doing which would enable her to turn away and seem insouciant.

Chloe, dressed and smiling, came in and perched on one of the bar stools.

'What a lovely spread!' She greedily pounced on the pancakes, drenching them with honey and scattering strawberries on top.

Theresa watched, fascinated. The girl seemed pretty hungry.

'When you go, would you like to take a sandwich or a slice of cake or anything?'

Still chewing, Chloe nodded, and Theresa set to work cutting and wrapping pieces of food.

Then she wondered if giving Chloe food wasn't a mistake. Wasn't she enabling her to stay away? But Theresa couldn't help herself. Food was her business. 'Shall I put it in your bag?' she asked.

Chloe snatched up her bag and held it open. There was another clue. She obviously didn't want Grandma digging around in there. Theresa was amazed at how easy it was to pick up signs from such little things.

She just wished she could make sense of them.

'How will you get back, Chloe? Will Neil's dad pick you up?'

Chloe laughed. 'Absolutely not!'

'Will you take the train? They're very cheap down here.'

'I know, Grandma. And the buses are even cheaper.'

'You can go as far as Menton or Cannes for €1.50, you know. Do you have to go far?'

'I'm not sure.'

Theresa's mind was racing now. Was Chloe fudging things, or did she really not know? 'How did you pay for your ticket here?'

'Oh God, Grandma, get off my case.'

Theresa retreated. She wished she hadn't said anything about the money now. 'Neil will call you, I suppose?'

'That's right.' Chloe fastened her bag, food safely stowed, and rested it down on the floor. 'Let's not talk about me, hey? What time do you have to go to work? Can I stay here, or should I come with you to the restaurant?'

'Whichever you like.'

'I'd like to come to the restaurant. I like your friends.'

Theresa was overwhelmed at how well this encounter was going.

'That's some knife, Grandma.' Chloe had picked up the knife and laid it down again. She ignored the Ravel CD, even though her name was part of the title. It didn't look as though she had had anything to do with the mystery gifts.

'It's lovely here, Gran.'

Theresa knew this easy chat was a good sign. Now she must make it relaxed enough for Chloe to want to come back. 'I'll get you my spare key, darling. Just in case. You never know.' As she opened the drawer next to the back door, she glanced out into the courtyard, and remembered the ghostly voice calling out *Theresa*. How different it all seemed in daylight.

She wondered …

'Last night … You and Neil weren't staying in the Hotel Astra, were you?'

'No.' Chloe used that upwards inflection which indicated that it was a stupid question not deserving a sensible answer. 'I haven't been in any hotels since I got here.'

As Theresa handed Chloe the key, she noticed somebody walk past the front window, for a second blocking out the sun.

Even before the doorbell rang she knew exactly who it was.

Imogen.

And she also saw that Chloe had seen her.

How to avoid this situation? There was no way. There would be an inevitable clash and she realised at this second she had totally lost Chloe's trust.

'You're a liar, Gran. A big fat liar. You bitch! How could you do this to me?'

'I thought she would arrive much later, Chloe.' Theresa tried to reason as best she could in the few seconds she had. 'I wanted to meet you alone. We're all desperately worried about you, darling. Especially your mother.'

'Is there another way out of here?' Chloe darted to the back door; then, seeing it was a dead end, ran back.

Theresa opened the front door to Imogen.

Chloe rushed past her. But Imogen was too quick. On the doorstep mother and daughter wrestled, Imogen pulling and tugging at Chloe's clothing and wrists. Chloe wriggled and bit her mother's arm, trying to free herself. Then, tearing herself away, Chloe ran off up the hill.

Theresa feared that that could be the last either she or Imogen would see or hear of Chloe for some time.

Imogen chased up the hill after her, but Chloe was young and fit and she soon disappeared into the dark, narrow alleyways of the Old Town.

SEVENTEEN

SALLY'S AFTERNOON WENT SLOWLY. On every take she was aware of Phoo, lurking behind the camera.

The scene was very wordy. And as the two characters were quarrelling, it was rather physical too, with slaps and hair grabbing.

After the master shot was completed, Sally was taken to one side to have her hair put back into the state it had been at the top of the scene, ready to start again, this time with the camera, over Eggy's shoulder, on a single close-up shot on her.

'Who is that peculiar woman lurking among the camera crew?' asked Judy, as she touched up Sally's mascara.

'She's Eggy's husband ...' Sally laughed. 'I meant his wife.'

'Ah, I see!' replied Judy, with a knowing nod. 'That explains it.'

'Explains what?'

'Oh, nothing,' said Judy. 'I need to do your lips again, can you ... ?'

Sally presented her lips. Silenced by the make-up brush, she went through it all.

She must not let Phoo's presence unnerve her. But it was hard.

She took her place and Daniel called, 'Action'. Every time she started a bit of dialogue she would catch eyes with Phoo. The woman had an uncanny way of moving around and getting into her eyeline.

Did Eggy also seem rather put out, or was she imagining it? He had none of the fire he'd had in earlier scenes. It was almost as though he was holding back.

They finished the quarrel on the beach to Daniel's satisfaction, although, if everyone hadn't been so pressed, Sally might have asked for another take just to make it that little bit better.

The next set-up was lower down on the beach, at the water's edge. A small motorboat was anchored there. She and Eggy, still fighting, balancing the spoils of their robbery, still visible in the beret, had to wade out into the sea, climb aboard and drive the boat away, doing some fancy curls on the water, as though they had no idea how to steer. But this was one of those things like singing. In order to make something look bad you needed to be really good at it.

Eggy was scratching his head. 'I don't know … I've never driven a boat before, I …'

'I'm qualified,' said Sally, stepping forward. 'I could take the helm.'

From the crowd, Sally heard Phoo's sarcastic laugh, clear as a clarion call.

'Thing is,' said Eggy, 'I get sick at the sight of water. I don't think I can even climb aboard without puking.'

'I don't really … I mean … Who planned this? We're fighting the light here.' Daniel was angry. 'We need to get on with it,' he roared. As he waded into the waves, he slammed his foot down in fury. 'Bugger this! Why didn't somebody book a stunt driver? Since when did bloody actors know how to do anything? Sod it, sod, sod, sod!'

The continuity girl ran forward and whispered something into Daniel's ear.

'All right. Apparently there is a boating chap on the way. Didn't realise that.' He glanced at his watch. 'Typical, though – he's stuck in traffic. Pity. It would be good to wrap this scene while we still have daylight. Once it's dark we'll be wasting our time and I'll have to reschedule it for late tomorrow, when we're miles away and we have tons of other stuff to plough through.'

'I'm not joking, Daniel.' Sally pressed on. She knew that capturing the light was essential today. 'I *really can* drive a boat. I have all the certificates you need for France. I'm a qualified helmswoman, or whatever the word is.'

Phoo stepped forward and took Daniel's arm, as he shook the water out of his shoes. She was swaying. Clearly much rosé had been consumed.

'Says the woman who couldn't even balance a tea tray! I won't have my husband risking life and limb …'

'There would be no risk to Eggy or anybody, Phoo. I reiterate: I have all the necessary qualifications. If I'd been warned I would have brought them here today to show you …'

'No. Sorry, Sally. You wouldn't be good enough for this stunt. It's all a major cock-up.' Daniel shook his head and turned to the First Assistant. 'What now?'

The First murmured to Daniel, and Daniel shrugged. 'OK,' he said quietly. 'Apparently, the stunt driver is parking his car. We might still catch the scene …' He squinted at the horizon through a rolled-up hand, then stamped again. 'But I doubt it. Bloody Frogs!'

'Daniel. I can do it.' Sally didn't know how to make him understand. Why was no one listening to her? 'I drive a much bigger boat than this all the time.'

'A boat!' laughed Phoo. 'Did you know, Daniel, that in her "spare" time Sally works as a waitress in a tired little restaurant in Bellevue-sur-Mer? And now she tells us she owns her own boat!' She cackled, and glared at Sally, lips pursed, eyes flashing. 'As if!'

Daniel appraised Sally for a moment, then said, 'No.'Fraid I can't allow it. Too big a risk. Bloody Norah!' He threw his arms up. 'OK, folks, that's a wrap.'

The crew started to pack up their equipment and shuffle off.

'Sally can easily do it,' said a firm voice. Everyone turned to see who had spoken. Sally only heard a man with a heavy French accent. He was coming towards her, masked by the lighting boards. 'I can vouch for her. She is an excellent helmswoman. I trained her myself in sea skills, and I signed her many certificates.'

'And who are you, exactly?' asked Daniel, to challenge the new arrival.

'I'm the stunt driver.' Holding out his pass, Sally's friend Jean-Philippe emerged from the throng. She had rarely felt so delighted to see anyone in her life. Jean-Philippe had not only taught her seamanship but had often hired her to reposition boats for him when he was unavailable.

'You may need to replace the Englishman. I could wear his costume … But, whatever, I think that Sally should drive.'

———

Theresa's day was hell. Imogen, of course, under the circumstances and understandably, had raged and ranted at her for at least two hours before she could escape by the necessity of heading off to work. Theresa, on the defensive, accidentally repeated the phrase which had infuriated Imogen before: 'Slowly, slowly, catchee monkey'.

'No, Mother. I'll tell you exactly what will "catchee monkey", and that's a bit of discipline and co-operation between us. We are supposed to be the adults, and Chloe the child. You are sixty, Mother. Not sixteen.'

Theresa wondered how soon before she was put into detention.

Just as she was walking out of the door to head for the restaurant to start the lunch service, she heard Imogen's phone bleep. Imogen glanced at the screen. 'Attagirl!' She looked across at Theresa. 'My secretary has been rummaging away and finally we now have the current mobile-phone number of Mr Roger Muffett. Excuse me one moment.' Imogen stabbed at the phone, then walked towards the front window and gazed out, her back to Theresa. 'Good afternoon. Am I speaking to Roger Muffett?'

Theresa could not hear the other side of the conversation, but as Imogen continued the call she understood that the reply was in the affirmative.

'I am Neil's former headmistress. That's right, Mrs Firbank. Well, obviously what you do with your own child is your own business, although I should point out to you that it is illegal both in England and in France to keep a fifteen-year-old out of school.'

Roger spoke.

'Ah. Neil is receiving home schooling, is he? From you? I see. And you are qualified in which subjects exactly?'

Roger spoke again.

Theresa knew she must go to work, but could not bear to miss the results of this call.

'Hmm. Be that as it may, Mr Muffett, I feel sure that Neil could better profit from being taught the normal curriculum rather than that of the "School of Life" as you put it. But that aside, I am quite keen to prosecute you for another matter.'

Theresa understood from Imogen's face that Roger let forth some nasty language.

'Excuse me. You are holding another minor, thus preventing her from returning to her parents and her school. Therefore, while we're at it, I will be informing the local police force, as well as the Met, Scotland Yard and Interpol, and anyone else who might be interested, that you currently are detaining a fifteen-year-old girl in your presence. A fifteen-year-old girl who should be at home with her mother in London. We might even call it kidnapping, Mr Muffett, which entails a hefty prison sentence ...'

A brief diatribe from Roger.

'I beg your pardon?'

Roger spoke again. His voice was clearly extremely agitated. It had risen in pitch, speed and volume, so that now even Theresa could hear the odd word.

'I'm talking about Chloe Firbank. Yes, Mr Muffett. That is my daughter, Chloe. And she is fifteen years of age.'

Another rant down the line.

'What do you mean, you have never even set eyes on Chloe? She is staying with you and Neil in your mansion or whatever it is you possess down here ...'

To Theresa's ear, Roger sounded so distraught and angry that it seemed as though he might be about to pop a blood vessel.

She actually heard the next sentences quite clearly:

'It's not a fucking mansion. It's a bloody boat. The bitch got the fucking house, the fucking car, the lot. I'm living on a bloody boat!'

Despite the barrage of swear words Imogen was seemingly unruffled. 'I don't care if you're living on board the wreck of the *Hesperus*, Mr Muffett, you will locate my daughter and you will return her to me in Bellevue-sur-Mer by seven o'clock this evening. You can bring her to the Hotel Astra, where I am staying. If she doesn't arrive here by that time, I will have no other option but to call the police and have you arrested.' She stabbed the call to an end and dropped the phone in her handbag. 'And that, Mother, is how you deal with a runaway child.'

'A boat.' Theresa looked out at the harbour. She was full of misgivings. From what she gleaned from the call, Roger Muffett didn't even know Chloe was actually staying with Neil. 'And the father didn't realise she was on board?'

'So he claims. But he would be quite capable of lying about that, I'd think.'

For Theresa things started to fall into place. It would certainly explain both Chloe's hunger and her desire for a shower this morning.

'I really do think he might not have known, Imogen. When Chloe arrived here earlier, she was hungry, she had no money and she wanted a shower. If she had come from that boat ...'

'I don't imagine his boat is big enough for it to be impossible for him to find Chloe. She's not a Lilliputian, and his boat can hardly be the *Queen Mary 2.*'

'She's not on board now, though, is she?'

'But Neil must know she's there. He made his siren call and Chloe came running.'

'And I suppose poor Neil is now with his father, getting an ear-bashing.'

'Believe me, Mum, Chloe's a headstrong and wily individual and, if you're right, I'm sure being a stowaway would be a wonderful adventure for her. But now that their little game is exploded, I presume Neil will have to give way to his papa and come clean. She'll be back here tonight.'

Theresa hoped that Imogen was right. 'You'd better take my key and get one cut.' She unhooked the flat key from her key ring and handed it to Imogen. 'Make yourself at home.'

Imogen took the key and said, 'I doubt I'll use it, actually. I will advise the people at the hotel to be on the lookout for a dishevelled and smelly teenage girl.' She looked at her watch. 'I'd say Chloe will be with us before darkness falls. Roger Muffett certainly meant business.'

When Theresa arrived at the restaurant she found Benjamin hopping enthusiastically from foot to foot.

'Total excitement, dear.' He picked up the bookings ledger and displayed it. 'We have celebs for dinner tomorrow. It seems unbelievable after the last time, but Odile de la Warr is making a return visit.'

Theresa had no idea what he was talking about.

'Odile! *The* Odile! Oh lord, Theresa! Catch up! You were here last time, weren't you? Oh no. You were in London. Well, anyhow Odile is *huge* and she's coming back here to dine. Don't you read *OK!* magazine? *Paris Match*? She's the Queen of St-Tropez. With customers like Odile as regulars we could easily survive. Plus ... she's bringing a famous English actress from London.'

'An English actress? Would I have heard of her?'

'You're certainly old enough to remember her.' Benjamin put the book down and sashayed off in the direction of the kitchen. 'William tells me she was in all those sitcoms in the 70s and 80s.'

Theresa remembered the name Phoebe Taylor, and would surely recall the face. Although she had never been a fan of sitcoms she did remember *Paddy and Pat*, a particularly poignant comedy series, in which Phoebe Taylor starred opposite Dermott Presley, a suave Irish comedian who had recently died. In the show Phoebe had played a bossy, posh Englishwoman who was on her uppers, but always at war with her neighbour, a working-class

Irishman who had recently won the pools. The role was played vigorously by Dermott Presley, a beloved star.

'William says that, in her day, Phoebe Taylor was a legend. She was here the other night with Odile, actually. They obviously like the place, despite Sally being rude to them.'

'Sally being rude?'

'You'd better believe it. She was a monster that night. IMHO, it's one of the reasons she hopped off.'

Theresa didn't understand about Sally, though. Upsetting diners wasn't her usual way. When serving at table she was always so bright and charming. Theresa wondered whether the stress of the Picasso episode hadn't slightly unhinged her. Doing a disappearing act was hardly in the spirit of things. Less the Blitz spirit than out and out surrender. Perhaps the situation and worry had all got too much for her. Otherwise why be a rat and desert the sinking ship?

Hopefully tonight's booking was good news for the remaining team, at last. Benjamin must know what he was talking about and it was certainly a grain of good fortune in a bucket of trouble.

But today it wouldn't be an easy ride. She still had other things to worry about, like the potential return of Chloe with Roger Muffett. It would be interesting to see the husband of the ex-wife who she had already encountered.

First she must get the luncheon service over. Then she could go up and join her daughter at the Hotel Astra and concentrate on the return of her granddaughter.

Theresa rolled up her sleeves.

'Oh ...' Benjamin spun round and pulled an envelope from his pocket. 'Someone left this for you. Another of your many fans, I presume. These days simply the whole world is sending you gifts.'

The envelope was covered in red hearts surrounding Theresa's name.

She ripped it open.

Inside was another photo taken from her photo album. In it she was standing, smiling, next to her ex-husband, who had his arm casually around her shoulder.

But someone had scribbled over Peter Simmonds's body with a black felt-tip pen and had scored away his face with a sharp knife. And on Theresa's chest they had drawn another bright red heart, this time with a sword through it.

———

Sally accomplished the tricky boat-stunt scene very fast. With Jean-Philippe at her side things were a lot easier. They communicated in French, making things clearer between them and at the same time foxing the sound crew, who were picking up everything they said from the mic fastened to the dashboard.

There were no lines to remember, but the mic was there to capture an excited squeal which Sally had to make as the boat roared off. She then had to continue making noises while the boat appeared to go out of control.

The scene later involved Sally falling out of the boat, and being hauled back in by Eggy's character, now being played by Jean-Philippe, before they thundered away and disappeared into the sunset.

As the boat pulled out for the final part of the scene, Sally, dripping from head to toe, took her place at Jean-Philippe's side. They both laughed.

'I think I should drive you home to Bellevue-sur-Mer,' he murmured. 'Leave them all behind.'

They heard Daniel's final: 'Cut. Check that. If it's OK, that's a wrap, folks. Thank you, ladies and gentlemen. See you tomorrow.'

'Seriously ... want a lift? I do have to drive past Bellevue-sur-Mer. We could have a drink?'

As she was due to share the car back with Eggy, which obviously now meant Phoo as well, Sally was delighted to accept Jean-Philippe's offer of a lift home, though she declined the drink. She had a lot to learn for tomorrow.

Jean-Philippe swung the boat round and sped back to the shore, where the wardrobe team held out warm towels for Sally.

Later, outside her house, by now in the dark, she climbed out of his sports car and paused on the pavement waving him off. She stood for a moment, watching his tail lights disappear up the hill.

Having declined the drink, she had arranged to have dinner with him the next possible evening when she had no early filming the following day.

What fabulous luck to have had Jean-Philippe on set! But then she supposed there weren't that many qualified boat teachers around the area who'd have been available for a shoot.

As she turned the key in the lock, someone ran down the hill towards her.

'Where on earth have you been? I've been waiting here for hours. I went to the restaurant but they claimed they had no idea where you were, so I ended up having an early supper there, rather than sitting on your doorstep all evening. They're furious with you, by the way!'

'Marianne? Was I ... ? I don't remember your saying you'd be coming here?'

'Just open the door, Mum. Why are you all caked with make-up? And who was that bearded bloke in the

Renault? And, eurgh, your hair's all wet and sandy? You haven't been naked night-swimming together, have you? Please don't let me keep that image in my head.'

Sally burbled some answers, but she realised that Marianne wasn't listening.

'You should have warned me, darling. I'd have arranged a key for you.'

'It never occurred to me, Mum, that you would have turned into a lady of the night. I just thought you'd be there at the restaurant as usual, or in your little van, or here.'

'You still haven't explained why you've arrived at such short notice – well, let's be frank: absolutely no notice whatsoever.'

'I've been told to get out of the office and advised to lie low for a week. And I couldn't think of anywhere else to go.'

Sally imagined that on her daughter's City pay there might be quite a few places she could have gone. But Marianne was still carrying on, while Sally hung up her coat.

'Then I thought, you know, if I hopped it to the Maldives or somewhere, it would look so awful. But coming home to see your mother. Well ... I knew that one would look fine.'

Sally gulped. This did not sound good. 'Marianne? What have you done exactly?'

'I just lost so much money in a deal, you wouldn't believe it. It's practically a Lehman Brothers situation. So I'm in hiding. And to warn you – if the press arrive on the doorstep, I'm not here.'

Press! Oh lord. Sally really couldn't cope with this.

She needed to be alone and quiet. She had so many lines to learn for tomorrow and, on top of that, a five o'clock start. She mumbled her excuses: 'I have to go to bed, darling.'

'No, Mum. Seriously, I've got to tell you all about it.' Marianne glanced at her watch. 'Anyway, since when did you go to bed at nine-thirty?'

Sally sat down.

She yawned.

Even if he had not bellowed his name at the girl behind the reception desk of the Hotel Astra, Theresa would have known Roger Muffett the moment he entered the cramped lobby. Tanned, with a crumpled white linen suit and panama hat, he had the look of a man who might be wearing a medallion.

Theresa had waited, with her daughter, in this entrance hall since around three-thirty. They sat in two faux-leather armchairs either side of a table laid out with brochures advertising local attractions. Theresa had suggested waiting in Imogen's room and relying on the hotel staff to alert her of their arrival, but now Imogen would have nothing of it. She wanted to be there on the spot when Chloe arrived. And it was earlier than they expected.

Imogen leaped to her feet and strode up to Roger. 'Where is my daughter?'

For such a confident and burly man, Theresa was surprised to see him flinch at her daughter's challenge.

'Now look, Mrs Firbank ...' He held his hands up in front of his torso in a gesture of self-defence. 'Honest Injun, I knew nothing about this ... I ...'

'You had no idea that your own son was living with my daughter in your little boat ...'

'It's not such a little boat, actually, but no. I didn't have a bloody clue. They've both been very duplicitous. Is that the right word? What I really mean is they're lying scum ...'

'Enough excuses.' Imogen shot him a dangerous look. 'Where is she?'

'I rented a car and drove them here.' Roger warily lifted an arm and pointed towards the front door.

Imogen strode past him out into the street, Theresa trotted along at her heels.

Chloe was sitting in the back seat, next to a young boy who Theresa presumed had to be Neil.

'I did put on the child locks,' Roger Muffett added timidly, holding up a hairy hand to shield his eyes from the sun's glare.

'Open up!' Imogen commanded.

Roger obeyed.

Cringing, Chloe edged herself out of the car. Imogen grabbed her arm and marched her inside, leaving Theresa in the street.

'It's been a difficult time,' Theresa said to Roger. 'We had no idea …'

'Nor me. Once I knew, I even contemplated handcuffs. But Jack the Lad in there won't be free to wander for many weeks, and to be honest I have sent for his mother. She was always better at handling him. So she's coming over to take him in hand.'

Theresa thought back to the morning when she met the inebriated Cynthia Muffett. If Roger Muffett had no control over their son, she wondered how on earth Cynthia would fare any better.

She stooped to look in at Neil.

Poor boy! He was just a kid. Theresa couldn't fathom why she was so shocked to see how puny and young he looked. She had always known that he was only fifteen, but in the flesh he appeared so much younger than Chloe, and with half the confidence.

'Hello, Neil,' she said, shaking her head. 'Very silly idea, I'm afraid. You do realise it couldn't have gone on for much longer.'

He looked up, right into her eyes.

'Are *you* Theresa?'

Theresa nodded.

'I've only ever heard very good things about you.' He fidgeted with his jacket buttons. 'You're a cook, aren't you? Please don't be cross with me. I did try to contact you … I ordered food from La Mosaïque …'

Theresa felt rather cruel now to be taking Chloe away from the boy. He looked devastated, and who wouldn't? His fate now was to spend his time between a brassy, loud father, who obviously wanted to be half his own age with no responsibilities, and a mother, who had turned to the bottle to assuage her loneliness. What a future!

She turned back to Roger, who was fumbling in his pockets for his sunglasses.

'You'll be sailing off to sea again tonight, I suppose?'

He slipped the glasses on, and they immediately slid down to the end of his nose.

'Maybe. Maybe not. The world's my lobster.' He pushed the sunglasses back up the bridge of his nose. '*Entre nous*, I prefer a good old cod and chips.'

A typical Englishman abroad.

Theresa tried not to smile.

'This is a very pretty place,' he said, glancing at blue sky, the stone walls spread with pink bougainvillea. 'Perhaps I'll settle down somewhere round here. Property prices aren't too bad. Better than London, anyway.'

'Make sure it's what you really want, though,' said Theresa. 'My friends in London all think that to live somewhere like this means you lead a life totally without care. The thing is, if you're running away from yourself, no matter where you go, you always bring it with you.' She laughed at her own chocolate-box analysis. 'What I mean is that you need to have an aim. Something to do.'

'You're absolutely right.' Roger gripped the handle of the hire car. 'Doing nothing is a pain in the arse.' He held the driver's door open, but before attempting to get in he said, 'Perhaps I'll go and sail the boat round here. I have to stick around a bit, while we're waiting for my ex-wife to turn up. Would you recommend this hotel?'

'Well ...' Theresa glanced into the car and she saw Neil's eyes light up. 'Actually there is no other hotel in the town, unless you go up to the top of the hill on the main road into Nice. There are many along that route. But it's not very nice up there.'

'It's not expensive?'

Theresa shook her head.

Roger bent to talk to Neil. 'If we stay here, on land, you promise to behave? No more lies. And no disappearing tricks?'

Neil nodded.

'OK.' Roger settled behind the wheel. 'Maybe see you later, Theresa.' He wound down the window. 'Neil tells me you have a restaurant.'

'That's right.'

'Great.'

With a loud rev, Roger pulled out.

As the car disappeared up the hill, Theresa waved then went inside and up to Imogen's room.

Chloe sat, forlorn, on the end of the bed.

Imogen made a face of exasperation at Theresa.

'Where are the other two girls?' Theresa asked, hoping that it might soften the anguish if Chloe was with her sisters. She knew from her own experience that having the spotlight thrown on you while you were alone only exaggerated the blow of the loss.

'Frances has taken them off on the train to Menton to see the Cocteau Museum and a weird place called the

Salle des Mariages, though I rather suspect things like that will be of more interest to her than to them. They'll probably be bored out of their skulls.'

Theresa walked across to the window and looked out. She was amazed that from here you could see the sea. She had imagined that her own building and the flat above it would obscure the view. She glanced down. She could see her own little courtyard, basking in the single hour of late-afternoon sunlight it got during the winter months. The buildings either side of her own were in shadow so that the panes of the windows seemed more like mirrors, reflecting only the walls of the hotel.

But she could see quite clearly through the windows of the flat above hers. A woman sat there, perched at the end of the double bed. She was talking on the phone. She looked very demure and not at all the *Fifty Shades* type. Theresa started to think that she might have a rather overdeveloped imagination, making dramas out of nothing.

Naturally Theresa couldn't hear the woman's conversation. But it got her to wondering whether the male voice she thought she had heard might simply have been her mind going wild. Why would a resident of the hotel open the window on a cold night and call out her name? Or might it just have been a coincidence? Someone calling for his wife or girlfriend. Theresa was hardly the most unusual of names.

' … wouldn't you, Mum?'

Theresa realised that her daughter had been talking and that she had not been listening. 'I'm sorry, darling. I was just admiring the view.'

'If we all stay for the rest of half-term, you'd take the kids off for a treat, wouldn't you?'

Theresa nodded eagerly, though at the moment she had no idea of a treat big enough to divert a love-struck teenager's mind from her thwarted romantic plans.

'They could come down to my flat, and I'll have a cooking afternoon with them all.' She glanced at her watch. 'I'm late. Would you all like to come down to the restaurant for dinner tonight?'

'No treats for runaways, I'm afraid.' Imogen grimaced at Theresa. 'We'll both stay in the room and when Frances and the other two come back, they can go out and get us some sandwiches.'

'But, Mum ...'

'No buts, miss. You're grounded.'

'Ah well.' Theresa shrugged. 'You know where to find me.'

'I'M VERY SORRY ABOUT yesterday. I really don't know what to say, I ...' Eggy had come into the make-up wagon expressly to apologise to Sally. 'But, well ... It's much more complicated than you can possibly imagine ...'

Actually, Sally *could* very well imagine.

The shoot today was taking place in a fancy house up in the hills behind Nice. After a very cold early start, by eight o'clock the weather was warm and sunny. The doors and windows of the make-up wagon had all been flung open. They sat side by side, talking to each other's reflections in the long, illuminated mirror.

As all of her scenes today were with Eggy, Sally had to accept his apology on behalf of his wife. Sally certainly could easily imagine that Phoo couldn't cope with seeing Sally back in the saddle.

When they first met, Phoo had been a major force in the business. Then Sally's star rose. Sally had given it all up to be a wife and mother and totally disappeared off the scene. Now, in Phoo's mind, to have Sally lording it over her and playing opposite her husband must have come as a horrible shock.

But Sally also understood that the fires of Phoo's anger had been seriously stoked up by having too much to drink during the lunch break.

'Really, Eggy, it's not important,' Sally said, trying to appease him as well as change the subject. 'We just need to concentrate on today. We have some hard stuff to do.' She was seriously worried about her lines and wanted to use this time to get as much learned as she could, as last night she had barely had a moment to glance at the script.

Make-up finished, Eggy sheepishly shuffled off to his tiny hutch of a dressing room in a three-way trailer, to put his costume on.

As soon as he was out of earshot, Judy bent low and whispered in Sally's ear.

'She wanted your part, you know, that wife of his. She's been nagging the casting director for days. But she was given strict words from above that it was to be you, you and no one else but you.'

This came as a shock to Sally. But of course if Phoo had wanted and *begged for* her part, well ... That confirmed so many more suspicions.

'Not only that, Sally, but I gather from the Second Assistant that Edgar Markham himself spoke *against* having his wife in the part.'

'He what?' Sally turned round in the chair so that she could see Judy's actual face, not just her reflection. Was this some deal that Eggy had made with the casting director?

'He didn't want her in the film. He phoned Daniel. Made it a hundred per cent clear.' Judy gave a knowing nod, twisted Sally round to face the mirror again and went back to soft-brushing blusher on her cheeks. 'The Second Assistant said that the wife has been phoning both himself and Daniel, non-stop. She obviously got hold of Eggy's call sheet and made full use of all the contact numbers and went on nagging. She was even calling him while you were standing there on the set!'

Sally was dumbfounded. When Judy leaned over to choose an eyeliner, she spun the make-up chair to scrutinise Judy's face, which told everything. The whole episode was clearly the hot gossip of the set.

'I think Edgar Markham wanted a little peace and quiet,' said Judy. 'That Phoebe is quite a handful. I've heard it from other girls in London.'

'But I thought everyone loved her.'

'The *public* loves her. National Treasure and all that.' Judy gave a nonchalant shrug. 'But in the business, it's quite another story. She's always rather been known for being cruel and catty to the wardrobe and make-up departments. Always complaining, throwing tantrums. She threw a hairbrush across the room on the last one. Smashed a mirror.'

'Good grief!'

Sally thought back to her own time as an assistant stage manager, the theatre's equivalent to make-up and wardrobe. Of course she herself had had similar treatment at the hands of Phoo.

Sally was rather sorry for poor old Eggy, who must by now be feeling pretty embarrassed at his wife's antics. To know that he himself had not wanted Phoo to have a role in this film spoke volumes. And it can't have helped his home life, either, especially if Phoo had the tiniest inkling of the truth. And then again … if Sally hadn't misinterpreted what she'd overheard in the car yesterday and Eggy was off getting young casting directors pregnant, perhaps Phoo had good reason for behaving badly.

'Mind you,' said Judy, clearly not wanting to seem to be bad-mouthing someone who was going to be around the set, 'I did love her in that sitcom she did with Dermott Presley.'

'*Paddy and Pat?*'

'Dermott was *such* a lovely man. A real charmer. And had such a lovely family too. We all adored him.'

Sally remembered seeing photo shoots of Dermott Presley riding horses with his wife and five children, or taking picnics with them on remote Irish beaches. He was the very picture of wholesomeness and family values. Always seemed to be smiling, and wearing those cream-coloured Aran sweaters and corduroy trousers. Sally wondered how on earth he had coped, working all those years with Phoo. *Paddy and Pat* had run for about eight series, with a couple of Christmas specials thrown in.

Judy gave Sally's face the final brush-down with powder and sent her back to her hutch, where she had to change into her all-black burglary costume, complete with hood.

Sally sat in her tiny trailer cubicle for a short time, studying her lines. She was shattered. The big scene wasn't till after lunch, which, after last night's surprise visitor, was just as well.

Marianne had talked solidly for hours and prevented Sally going to bed, with accusations that she, as a mother, ought to be interested in her daughter's life. Well, of course she was interested, but at that moment she had other things on her mind as well, like learning her lines for today. But she knew her daughter certainly wouldn't have understood that necessary task.

Marianne was a funny girl. They were so unalike that sometimes Sally couldn't believe she was her own flesh and blood. Marianne appeared to be utterly fascinated with money – percentages, deals, stocks and shares, financial indexes and all kinds of things about which Sally couldn't give a toss. In fact, the entire subject of money was something Sally would much rather *avoid* discussing. So while her daughter recounted, in minuscule detail, figures, share prices and statistics about the scandal she had seemingly caused back in London, Sally's mind glazed over. Marianne had apparently not noticed her mother's lack of interest and gone on talking till well after one in the morning.

Marianne did not understand either that, regardless of how late you might stay up while filming, your car still arrives at 5.30 a.m., and the driver expects you to be up and dressed, ready to go. Also that lines don't magically jump into your head.

Thus, having had less than four hours' sleep, now, slouched in the quiet warmth of her tiny roomette dressed in a black Lycra jumpsuit, it was not at all surprising that Sally fell into a deep slumber. Even though bits of script lay open on her lap, some pages had spilt on to the rough bit of matting.

She only woke to the sound of the Third Assistant knocking and opening up the caravan door, asking her to go straight to the set for a walk-through for camera. Bleary-eyed and groggy, Sally grabbed the pages of script to take with her. She still didn't know it.

But, as time was up, she followed the Third into the house, walking along carpeted hallways lined with canvas, on to the set: a very fancy room with gold-panelled walls and a beautifully painted ceiling. The ornate salon was crammed with antique furniture, which was roped off so that no one would sit on it. As this scene was set at night, all the windows were blacked out. The only light came from the warm spotlights.

'Morning!' Daniel grinned inanely. 'Let's keep it moving today, Sally. Okey-dokey, folks! Quick rehearsal, blocking it all. Then we'll get the cameras set up. Let's get the crew in to watch.'

This was terrifying. Sally only had the sketchiest idea of her lines in this scene.

Eggy was waiting, wearing his burglary attire. His was also a black Lycra suit, but it really was skintight and on him it was rather comical.

'OK, Sally, luv!' Daniel stepped into the acting area, while camera and lighting crew gathered behind him. 'Let's run through. Perhaps you could start crouched down behind that armchair.'

Sally got into position. Hiding the pages, she hastily got the first line into her head. She wished she'd had time to scribble some hints on to her wrists and palms.

'And action!' called Daniel.

Sally spat out her first line, and, as the scene demanded, bobbed up.

'Come on!' replied Eggy, in character. 'They've gone.'

Sally needed to glance down at the page she was gripping, hidden in her other hand behind the chair-back.

Eggy moved nearer, ready to grab her arm and make a dash for it. He murmured Sally's line under his breath.

Sally repeated it.

Eggy then spoke his line, and half-turned in order to whisper Sally's, which she duplicated.

'What's going on?' Daniel stepped into the scene. 'Miss Doyle? Don't you know your lines?'

'I got the scene number wrong. Sorry, Daniel, I'll be on it by the time we're actually shooting.'

'Buggeration!' Daniel threw his copy of the script down. 'This is all we need. Some bloody amateur who's lost her memory. You do know that you took the part from under the nose of a very well-known professional?'

All Sally could do was say again that she was sorry.

'I suppose you were out on the town last night, drinking rosé till the early hours with that hairy sailor friend of yours.'

Sally started to explain about her daughter's surprise arrival, but her voice faded out.

There was simply no excuse.

'Just for now, do it with the script.' Daniel let out a long theatrical sigh. 'But there's a lot of action in this scene, and I must point out, *once more*, that we are running behind and that we need *everyone* to be up to speed. *Comprendez?*'

Once they had blocked the scene, the crew moved into the acting space to set up the cameras and lights.

Eggy and Sally walked back to the trailers.

'I'll help you,' said Eggy. 'It's the very least I can do after yesterday. I really owe you one.'

Eggy came into Sally's cubicle.

'It's very sweet of you.'

'Don't worry.' Eggy squeezed down on the tiny seat next to Sally. 'You'll probably have to do the same for me, day after tomorrow. I'm going out on a rather exciting rendez-vous with a very exotic creature who's bound to lead me heaven knows where.'

Sally laughed.

'Right.' Eggy leaned back and closed his eyes. 'I'll give you a minute or two to look through,' he said, 'while I get a wee bit of shut-eye.'

'Lucky you. You can catnap?'

'In this business it's always worth having a few strange talents up your sleeve.'

While Eggy dozed, Sally started murmuring her lines to herself, covering up the script with a blank page.

———

While Theresa washed and chopped vegetables, Carol had spent the last fifteen minutes sitting on a stool near the dining-room door, burbling on about some bloke with whom she had fixed a luncheon date, and Theresa was bored. Not only bored but anxious and uneasy.

First, she felt whacked out from the back and forth over the last few days, with Chloe's disappearance and the ensuing trail of finding her. It was almost as though the relief of knowing that Chloe was back with her mother, and safe, had allowed Theresa to let go. Now she felt drained through to the bone. She wished nothing more than to go home, curl up and sleep.

On top of all this, she was feeling increasingly troubled about the string of bizarre events, gifts and photos. The whole thing was constantly niggling away at the back of her mind. She didn't want to talk about it because nothing about it was really that horrible, just disturbing.

There had been roses left for her, her answering machine was acting up, she'd lost her photo album and someone was returning the photos one by one, she'd been invited for a coffee and no one showed up, she had heard whispering – perhaps it had been her name – during the night. If she told anyone about these things, they would probably dismiss them as an unusual series of coincidences. But somewhere deep in her soul, Theresa was frightened that this chain of unimportant events was more sinister than the sum of its parts.

She opened the cupboard, principally to have a door to hide behind while Carol raved on about this man of hers who had a sexy voice.

On the eye-level shelf was a blue Tupperware box. It wasn't usually there, but with so many people working in the kitchen this week, it might simply be Benjamin putting something back in a different place.

'Well, Theresa, I can see I'm boring you, so I'll be off.' Carol jumped down and draped her coat around her shoulders. 'I can always sit in the van while waiting for the delivery orders to dribble in ... or not.'

Theresa pulled out the box and looked. On the top a handwritten name was stuck down with a Sellotaped label: 'Theresa'.

'Ta-ta!' Carol turned on her heels.

'Carol?' Now she thanked heaven that Carol was still there with her.

'Yes, darling?'

'What do you think this is?' Theresa gingerly took the box, holding it before herself on outstretched arms as if it was a sacred totem. 'I'm too scared to open it.'

'Why would you be frightened to open a box from one of your own kitchen cabinets? It's cheese or butter or cookies or something, isn't it? Didn't you put it there?'

'That's the thing, Carol. I have no idea what it is. And why has it got my name on it?'

'It'll be William.' Carol grabbed the box. 'He's so finicky about everything. Just the type of fusspot to start putting ownership labels on kitchen ingredients.' She ripped the top off, and looked inside. 'Yes. I was right. File under "cakes or cookies".' She pulled out a square of brown cake and inspected it. 'Chocolate brownies. Yum!' She put it back, popped the lid on and handed the box to Theresa. 'Mustn't tempt me, though. I have to watch my figure, you know. Especially as I'm going on a—'

'Hot date. Yes. I know.' Theresa felt silly now. Of course she didn't recognise the cakes. William and Benjamin must have made them and left them for her as a peace offering.

Carol gathered the collar of her coat and leaned back against the countertop. 'There's one thing puzzles me, though, Theresa. Why would a perfectly sane woman like you be hopping around like a cat on a hot tin roof about a Tupperware box? You're so jumpy. It can't be only the runaway child. And anyway, she's back, isn't she? So what's the beef?'

Theresa weighed up the situation and felt glad that Carol herself was asking her to talk about it.

She started with roses and the CD.

'*Daphnis et Chloé*, eh?' Carol gave a knowing grimace.

'I suppose that's because of my missing granddaughter.'

'Whad'ya mean?' Carol stood open-mouthed. 'That piece of music, my darling woman, is quite the most romantic bit of schmaltz *ever* written in the history of the world. Well, I suppose *The Firebird* might pip it to the post, but that's Stravinsky, so you have to wade through so much clink, clank, clonk before you get to the fabulous swooshingly dramatic bit. What else?'

'I got a knife through the post.'

'What kind of knife?'

Theresa grabbed her bag and took out the huge Sabatier.

'Whoo! Don't point that thing at me, as the girl said to the soldier.' Carol laughed and waved a hand. 'But then you *are* a cook. For *you* to get a knife isn't so much. It's a bit like a painter getting paintbrushes or a rally driver getting, well, whatever rally drivers use every day. Though if you weren't a cook, I'd be very worried. Let's leave that as a potential wrong 'un.'

Theresa explained about the rose petals, the answering machine and the voice whispering her name in the deep of night. She then mentioned the missing photo album and, before Carol could interrupt and offer to search the place one more time on her behalf, went on to say that, one by one, someone was sending photos from the album back to her. She dug into her pocket and presented the photo she had received last night.

'Oh my!' Carol gazed down at the picture of Theresa on her wedding day, beaming happily, arm in arm with a man who had been sharply scored out. 'No. No.' She passed the photo back and instinctively wiped her hand down her side as though it was contaminated. 'No. No. That's not good at all.'

THANKS TO THE PRICELESS antique furniture, which the location homeowner was reluctant to let the film crew touch, let alone move, and due to the fraying old carpet, which he said was historic, worth millions, and which he didn't want anyone stepping on, the set-up of lighting, camera and track for Sally's worrisome scene took hours. No one had anticipated this delay, which ran across the lunch hour and into the afternoon.

For Sally this was excellent news as it gave her more time to bang the lines into her head.

Eggy turned out to be a most solicitous screen partner. He ran the lines over and over with her, until they both felt confident and easy with the scene.

As a result, when the whole team finally got on to the set in the late afternoon, they were able to sail through, and even to add some sparkling moments. A little game of catch with a prop 'valuable' vase got a round of applause from the crew. It also caused a minor episode when the owner of the house mistook it for the real thing and, thinking it was another of his precious antiques about to be smashed, threw a tantrum and was only calmed down when the underside of the prop vase was displayed to him with its 'Made in Taiwan' stamp.

Once the scene was complete, both Sally and Eggy returned to the make-up department for the camouflage paint to be thoroughly removed by a series of very comforting hot towels dispensed from Judy's work micro-wave oven. They then quickly had to be made up again into their everyday look. After that, they were straight on to the set for a party scene, replete with extras. In this scene they were supposedly casing the joint.

Sally felt so grateful to Eggy for today. It really compensated for yesterday.

At 9 p.m., when the crew wrapped at the end of the day's work, Eggy popped his head into Sally's cubicle.

'Look, darling, I know the day's over, but we've got a late call tomorrow morning ...'

'How late?'

'Would you believe – eleven a.m., pick-up nine!'

'Wow! A real lie-in.'

'So, anyway, darling, how about exploring this village? It's bound to have a rustic square with a bustling bar full of colourful locals. I'll stand you a drink or two ... We deserve it.'

Sally felt rather relieved not to have to go straight back to Marianne and be forced to listen to further tales of financial skulduggery.

'But how will we get home later? Places like this don't have that many buses, you know.'

'Oh, don't be silly. I'll treat us to a taxi. You live in Bellevue-sur-Mer, don't you? That's where I'm staying.'

'Taxi prices are really prohibitive here on the Côte d'Azur, you know.'

'Who cares? Go on, Salz. I know we'd both enjoy a debrief on the film. Phoo's out to dinner with that monstrous Odile.'

'I thought you liked her.'

'You can have too much of a good thing. Anyway, I certainly don't want to go back to an empty rental flat. So depressing. You're avoiding your daughter and her tales of the financial times. We can spend a bit of time going through the scenes for tomorrow, if you'd like.'

Sally paused to think. It did sound like a pleasant-enough invitation.

'Go on, Sally. You know you want to. Why not? Just the two of us? A *bonne* peaceful *boisson à la Française*?'

———

'And we're off!' William appeared at the door, dangling an order between two fingers. 'Table for one. Boring little man in an ill-fitting wig.'

'One minute, William, before you head back into the fray ...' Carol stepped to the cupboard and took out the box of brownies. 'What have you to say about these?'

'Whoops! You got me bang to rights, gov'nor.' William winced and put his hand to his mouth. 'Let's just say Benj and I accidentally ate half the box the night before last. We labelled the box to make sure we didn't do it again. So there you are, girls. Enjoy!'

As William hopped back into the dining room, Carol took out a brownie and handed it to Theresa.

'I've barely had time to eat today.' Theresa took a bite. 'So it's just as well they left these. Mmmm. Delicious.'

She glanced at the order William had stuck to the board, polished off the rest of the brownie and washed her hands, ready to get back to work.

Benjamin rushed into the kitchen and spun straight out again, leaving himself only time to say, 'They're here! They're here! They're here!'

'Is she really such a big deal?' asked Theresa.

Carol shrugged. 'She's one of these people who everyone seems to know of, but no one knows what they actually do.

Like the Kardashians. Constantly photographed. Owns some pretty important places in St-Trop, beach restaurants, disco clubs where the only regulars seem to be European royalty and pop stars. You know the kind of thing.'

What with the hunger, the relief of Chloe being back and too little sleep, Theresa felt overwhelmed with emotion. She reached out a hand and patted Carol's arm. 'Thanks for being so understanding.'

'Shucks, Theresa!' said Carol. 'Don't get all schmaltzy on me.'

'Evening all!' The back door burst open and Zoe stood there in full evening dress. 'Sorry to be dressed inappropriately, but I was due to be going to some ghastly classical concert up at the Villa Rothschild and the young man who was to accompany me tells me he has caught the flu. A likely story! Probably just loathes Smetana and Rips-Yer-Corsets-Off. But then, who doesn't? Alas, the result equals the old adage: "All dressed up and nowhere to go."'

She stepped into the kitchen, swishing her train around as she closed the door behind her. 'So, my darlings, I thought to myself, where is there a nowhere I could go to without being laughed out of court? And natch, the answer is: here. I don't think I need to ask whether you have any free tables. As the song has it – I don't believe in miracles.'

While Zoe was talking, Theresa finished decorating the solitary table's starter plate.

William darted in with the new orders, which he stuck to the board. He handed one to Carol, a delivery this time, to be distributed to a local home.

Then he took in the sight of Zoe.

'Oh, God. I should have known that Cruella de Vil would turn up tonight.' He picked up the starter. 'Come to ogle the rich and famous, dear?'

'Rich and famous? Dining in La Mosaïque? Have you forgotten to take your anti-psychotics again, sweetie?'

'Says the Phantom of the Opera.'

'I'm only asking to whom you refer, William dear, when you say "rich and famous"?'

'Odile de la Warr.'

'No! That old rooster! Here in La Mosaïque? You *are* kidding me. Oh, this is too funny.' Zoe pushed past Theresa and Carol and peeped into the dining room. 'Oof! Someone should have told her to hold back on the filler and the fake tan.'

Theresa glanced at Zoe – bursting pout, eyebrows pulled up so high she could not affect anything but a look of constant surprise – and just managed to stop herself saying, 'Pot/kettle.'

William went back to work, but not before Zoe had linked her arm in his.

'I'll have the table beside theirs, please, darling. And I'll try to blend in.'

'Blend in?' squawked William. 'What do you think this is? Madame Tussauds?'

As she watched Zoe sailing into the dining room in her sparkling evening gown and glittering tiara, Theresa found herself laughing, holding her sides, rocking back and forth.

Zoe's arrival had somehow punctured the bubble of tension she'd been experiencing for the last few days, and suddenly she was feeling great again.

She turned to share the joke with Carol, but Carol had left.

Perhaps she too had gone into the dining room, pretending to be an ordinary customer.

Theresa roared with laughter.

When it wasn't tragic, life was really so funny.

She worked on the starter plates for Odile's table, chortling to herself.

Carol didn't come back. Maybe she really was next door, sitting down to dinner with Zoe. Then Theresa remembered that Carol had been given a delivery order and she must be out around the town, driving. Theresa recalled that, while she had been away, Carol had been stranded, the van broken down, but she had got it going herself. Theresa giggled at the thought of her lying under the chassis, blood-red varnished nails and impeccable make-up, sorting out the engine.

Suddenly, William burst into the kitchen, interrupting her fantasy.

'I can't witness another creepy fawning moment from my apparent beloved. Much as I am a fan of the opulent Odile, I'm feeling quite sick from the syrupy benevolence pouring out of Benjamin's every orifice … well, not every … that would be vile. But you know what I mean, Theresa. And no, before you say it, I can't afford a divorce.'

He spun around, seized an apron from behind the door and put it on.

'So, dearest? Where do you want me?'

Theresa was coping perfectly so didn't really want William in here at all.

'Isn't Carol off on a delivery?' she suggested. 'Will Benjamin be able to manage without you?'

'He'll bloody well have to, the sycophantic little crawler.' William grabbed a spoon and started pointlessly stirring a pan of stewed apples. 'The smarmy, toadying creep can certainly manage three tables on his own.'

'How's Zoe doing?'

William gave an exasperated groan. 'She only went up to Odile and said, "Good evening, you old slapper!" I could have died on the spot.'

'How did Odile take it?'

'She gave Zoe the up and down and replied, "From an old broad like yourself I take that as a sublime compliment."'

'Well, that's all right then.' Theresa laughed. 'Isn't it?'

'No, it isn't. Not only that, but the dusty little man in the corner is being quite demanding, when all we need to do is keep Odile happy.' He rubbed his chin and screwed up his eyes. 'I have an idea. How far on are you with everything in here?'

'Only dessert to go, and they're practically ready.'

He took Theresa by the shoulders and twisted her round till she was facing the dining room.

'Don't do that, William.' Theresa balanced herself by clutching the edge of the counter. 'You're making me feel quite dizzy.'

He untied the knot of her apron, then fluffed up her hair.

'Now, elegant Mrs Simmonds, you are going out to join Zoe at the table. Your duty tonight will be to keep Zoe under control. And, while you're at it, you can edge my "other half" away from Odile. There's nothing like overkill for ruining a good thing.'

'But, I ...'

'Go on.' He pushed Theresa towards the door. 'Go out there and make your country proud!'

As she stepped into the dining room, Theresa staggered a little. She felt pleasantly exhausted. She was looking forward to sitting down, maybe taking a little bite.

Zoe was seated at a table for two. Theresa took the seat opposite her.

'Oh, hello, darling. I was just telling these two how you and Sally are partners. Odile was sharing with us all the details of her new disco-bar in St-Trop. The Cockatoo.'

'*Non, non.* Les Cacatoès.'

'No need to show off, Odile, dear. We all understand French.' Zoe leaned forward and, inclining her head in the direction of Odile and Phoebe Taylor, whispered to Theresa, 'This conversation is classic. Wish I had a pen.'

'As I always say,' Phoebe blotted her lips with her linen napkin, 'there is no gathering which cannot be uplifted by a cock or two.'

Theresa blinked in disbelief as, deadpan, Phoebe Taylor ladled another forkful of food into her mouth. 'Tell you what I miss over here. You never see it in restaurants any more. But when I was in France at finishing school, it was everywhere. And that is coq au vin. No other way to travel.' She pushed her plate away and spluttered with laughter.

Theresa giggled.

Benjamin oozed forward, bearing dessert menus. '*Terminez, mesdames?*'

Odile nodded and waved at the plates as though she desired them to vanish instantly.

Benjamin laid down the menus, swiped up the plates, took the orders and briskly minced away.

'So, yes, Theresa,' Odile leaned across the aisle between their tables, bracelets clinking, 'as you all know, in the hospitality trade, things have been a little tricky for the last couple of years. Takings down everywhere after the … event. But it will get better. At least the Italians are back.'

'Much good that is for *us*,' said Zoe. 'Italians only eat at Italian restaurants, preferably those owned by Italians. This place is Anglo-Provençal.'

'True. But as I was saying, I'm opening Les Cacatoès next week. Then I'm putting my feelers out for somewhere new along the coast. A little nearer to Nice and the airport.' She looked around at La Mosaïque's dining room. 'Somewhere smaller. Cosier. More *intime*.'

Under the table, Zoe kicked Theresa's ankle.

'Ouch!' Theresa tried to cover her exclamation with a serene smile.

The wiry man in the corner put a hand in the air. When he failed to catch Benjamin's eye, he said aloud, '*L'addition, s'il vous plaît!*'

Benjamin turned briefly to acknowledge him before vanishing into the kitchen.

'I'm also fond of sausage.' Phoebe blinked and looked up as though resuming a continuing conversation. 'Aren't you? Not bothered whether it's German, English or Italian. I like it fat, long and spicy.'

Theresa started to laugh aloud, and could not stop herself.

Benjamin rushed from the kitchen bearing dessert plates. He plonked them down and made a goggle-eyed face at Theresa.

She couldn't make out what on earth he was signalling her to do. He looked as though he was on that ancient TV programme *Give Us a Clue*. She was tempted to sign back: 'Book and Film?'

Tonight everything seemed so funny.

She really had the giggles, in the same uncontrollable way she had had at school, sometimes in church or roll call.

Zoe was also now pulling a face at her, nudging her shoes.

To Theresa both Zoe and Benjamin looked like cartoon characters. She couldn't believe that everyone else wasn't laughing at them, and at Phoebe Taylor with all her double entendres.

Benjamin moved rapidly to the man in the corner and took his payment.

The man walked slowly from the restaurant.

As he passed her table, Odile smiled and wished him a very good night.

Phoebe leaned forward and squinted down at her plate of fruit. She thrust in a spoon and held it out in Theresa's direction. 'Kumquat?'

Theresa exploded with laughter.

'Cockatoo! I love birds.'

'Oh, so you *are* gay? I *was* wondering.' Phoo peered at Theresa as though inspecting a sweater and looking for moth holes. 'Sally talked about her "partner" Theresa, but I didn't realise ... I always picture her falling for some great big muscly chap. But I suppose "needs must when the devil drives". She was always a bit of a goer, that Sally. We all knew her as the Birmingham Rep bike.'

Benjamin was at Theresa's shoulder, trying to edge her to her feet.

'What are you doing, Benjamin? Can't you see I'm enjoying myself?'

'Theresa!' He was whispering, tugging at her dress.

'Sally's playing my part, you know, in some film opposite my husband Edgar. They offered it to me first. But I turned it down, of course. Not meaty enough for me. Less the *filet-mignon* role than a lump of old corned beef. But, bless! Someone has to take these tired little cough-and-spit parts. And as an actress Sally Doyle always was bloody hopeless.'

'I heard she was rather good,' said Zoe.

'Nonsense.' Phoebe slammed her hand down on the table. 'Sally had unwarranted and undeserved success.'

Theresa now didn't know what everyone was going on about.

She sat back, smiling at the room.

She felt serenely happy.

'Theresa? Are you feeling quite all right?' Zoe was scrutinising her face. 'You're looking very pale.'

'I'm just tired. And relieved after all the recent upheaval.' She sighed with contentment. It was odd – even after having eaten, she still felt starving. When she got home she thought she might rustle up a croque-monsieur.

'Croque-monsieur ...' she said aloud, with a raucous guffaw.

The little hilltop village certainly was picturesque. Winding cobbled streets, lined with small old houses painted in various shades of terracotta and ochre, led up to the square. Shaded by plane trees, the centre of the square was set up for pétanque. There were only a few shops – a clothing boutique, an artisanal jeweller, a gallery, a garage and a bike-repair station.

The sun had gone down, and the temperature dropped. Sally's clothes weren't nearly warm enough to handle it. As she walked along, peering into windows, deciding which of the two bars to patronise, she shivered.

'Can't have my wife catching cold the night before our big scene.' Eggy took off his jacket and draped it around Sally's shoulders.

They decided on the bar which did not have a loud sports television, blaring out a rugby match.

This one was quiet, with a few workmen gathered round a table playing cards.

They chose a red faux-leather corner banquette and on Sally's advice ordered a basket of *panisse* chips to go with their bottle of Bandol.

'We've not had time for you to fill me in on all the years between,' said Eggy. 'You must have had many adventures.'

'Not really.' Sally didn't want to go into a tedious spiel explaining how she'd landed up here. She just wanted to relax and be quiet after a long day's work.

'*Santé!*' She raised her glass.

'Cheers!' He raised his and they chinked.

Looking at him this evening, Sally felt sorry she had put him in the same bag as his wife. On his own, he was actually rather kind.

'You know, I really like a glass of wine,' said Eggy, knocking it back in one slurp. 'But what I'd really kill for is a cup of builder's.'

'When we next get some time off, you could pop over to my place in Bellevue-sur-Mer and I'll brew you a whole pot. How about the day after tomorrow?'

'Can't do that, I'm afraid.' Eggy nudged Sally in the ribs. 'I told you. Got a hot date in Nice.'

Sally recalled Eggy mentioning this before but had actually thought he was joking.

'Someone on the film crew?' she asked, intrigued at how, with his wife breathing over his shoulder, he could manage to fix up a date.

'No. Local. Lovely-looking woman, very striking. A random encounter.'

'When you were in St-Tropez?'

'No. Near you. We've rented a place in BSM, as it happens. A little first-floor flat, down on the seafront. Easier for the filming, you know. They offered me a hotel room, but I couldn't leave old Phoo on her own. And St-Tropez is all very well but it's quite a schlep.'

Sally worked out that the only possible place he and Phoo could be staying must be in the rental flat above Theresa.

Eggy gazed down into his empty glass, then mournfully picked up the bottle and refilled it.

'I feel rather badly about everything so far, you know, Sally. And I think it would be a decent gesture to ask you, please give us a second chance. And perhaps I could offer you and a friend – maybe that sailor chappie, or the nice lady you own the restaurant with – a little treat: dinner or drinks, somewhere really nice, to make all good. What do you say?'

To be truthful, another evening with Phoo wasn't exactly on Sally's bucket list, but she realised that there was no way she could refuse this invitation without seeming churlish.

'Drinks sounds like the better idea. After work one evening.'

'Why not tomorrow? It's good to wind down after filming.' Eggy took another swig of wine. 'Where's the poshest place for a drink around these parts?' he asked.

'Le Negresco,' Sally replied. 'It's in Nice.'

'Drinks at Le Negresco it is.'

Eggy once more lifted his glass to clink with Sally.

It was decided. Tomorrow she would go for drinks with Eggy and Phoo. Sally hoped she could contact Jean-Philippe and that he would be free.

After a slightly uncomfortable silence they got to chatting about mutual friends: actors and directors from Sally's past, some still working, others dead or retired.

Eventually the subject came back to the film of the moment.

'So, after so many years out, how did you get into this movie, Salz? Local contact?'

'It's complicated.'

'Complicated?'

Sally wished she hadn't used that word. How she was in the film couldn't be nearly as complicated as the way Eggy got the part. She decided that honesty was the best policy: 'I was asked by the producer.'

'Marina Martel?'

Sally nodded, hoping she didn't sound too grand.

'Wow!' Eggy gave a whistle of approval. 'For me, I'm just close to the casting director and she knew I was staying down here, and so, well, when the other bloke dropped out …'

'Close to the casting director? Really?' asked Sally, scrutinising his face for telltale tics.

'Yes, yes.' He waved his hand. 'You know how it goes. We've known one another for ages. Over the years I've had a lot of work through her.'

'I suppose she suggested Phoo for my part?'

'Erm … no.' Eggy blushed a deep red. 'No. Not at all.' He topped up his glass and took a gulp. 'Quite the reverse in fact.'

He really did seem profoundly uncomfortable. Sally knew that Phoo had pressed for her role and that Eggy had opposed it. But from the shade of aubergine flooding Eggy's countenance, Sally suspected there was a lot more going on than that. Something perhaps to do with a certain casting director's pregnancy?

Eggy raised his hand to attract the waiter. He pointed to the bottle, which Sally realised was almost empty, though she had only had two glasses.

She ordered a cheese platter and a plate of charcuterie to absorb some of the alcohol. Eggy was really knocking it back. At this rate he'd still be drunk by the time they were filming their scenes tomorrow. He was already moving into the maudlin stage of inebriation.

'Just make it two glasses, please.' Sally spoke to the waiter in French. Eggy wouldn't notice if another bottle didn't materialise.

While picking at the salami, his eyes filled with tears. 'It's hard work, you know, being married.'

Thinking about Phoo, Sally could certainly see Eggy's point, but also knew she was in no position to say anything. Those two had been married since Sally was in her teens, were still married, and tomorrow Eggy would be sober.

The two glasses of wine arrived. Eggy knocked his straight back.

'Everything in life is hard,' Sally said. A reply anodyne enough to mean absolutely nothing.

'Believe me. Marriage is the hardest.' Eggy's lower lip quivered. He stilled it by picking up his empty glass, pretending to sip at nothing.

'Are you not in love any more?' Sally threw all caution to the wind. Why not ask straight out? 'Is that it?'

Eggy didn't say anything. He just hung his head. The silence spoke volumes.

'If you really think like that, Eggy, perhaps you should consider separating.'

He turned to her, horror spread across his face. 'We can't do that!'

'Why not?'

'Because … because … because we're us.' Eggy looked at Sally with a childlike bewilderment. 'We're famous for being married. The Magical Markhams! That's us. Divorce? Can you imagine? No. No. Can't be done. Not now, anyway. Much too difficult all round.'

Sally felt very uncomfortable at having wheedled out this confession. What could she say? Better to appear disinterested, impartial. Though it all seemed tragic.

'Anyway,' Eggy hiccuped as he continued, 'poor Phoo has had a few setbacks recently. She *is* still my best friend. We rub along, you know. We both know about the business and how it works. Imagine trying to explain the days when you can't go to your wife's birthday party because you're filming in Monaco! She knows about all that stuff because it's the same for her. Plus – most important of all – we make each other laugh.'

Each to his own, Sally thought.

She imagined there might be better reasons for living with a person. But there you are.

Chacun à son goût.

She glanced at the clock. It was getting late. Almost eleven. She got the bill and asked the waiter if he could call them a taxi.

The waiter explained that there was only one cab service in the village, but he was an old man and he never worked after nine at night or before nine in the morning.

Sally asked for the time of the first bus.

'There are only four buses a day which pass through here. The first at nine-thirty,' he replied. 'And it takes about an hour to get to Nice *centre ville*.'

Well, that was a blow!

She turned back to Eggy. 'There are no cabs, Eggy.'

But it was as though he had not understood what she'd said.

'Very impressive, Salz, the way you just spin off into French without so much as a by-your-leave.'

As the waiter moved back behind the bar and started washing their glasses, Eggy rested his head on Sally's shoulder.

'It's a devil's life, sometimes, living with Phoo, you know. But, remember, we said "for better for worse", so there we are. We just have to grin and bear it, dontcha know. But I also think she's very misunderstood.'

Sally wasn't in the mood for marital confessions. Or for explanations of Phoo's foul behaviour.

The only thing on her mind was how the hell were they going to get back to Bellevue-sur-Mer.

They both had a company car picking them up at nine in the morning. They were due to go to Make-up and be ready to go on set at the location by eleven.

If the worst came to the very worst, Sally supposed they could take rooms somewhere in this village and phone the production company to see if they could get picked up from here.

She called the waiter over again and asked if there was a hotel nearby. He told her there was one, and it had one room available. He said it was owned by the bar – a kind of inn.

'Sally?' Eggy pulled his head up. He was starting to slur. He turned laboriously to face her. 'You know, I've always thought you were a very attractive woman …'

'Do you want to take the room?' the waiter asked them, in French.

Eggy returned his head to Sally's shoulder. Simultaneously his hand landed on her thigh and his plump fingers started squeezing at her flesh.

'No thanks,' she replied, briskly removing his hand. 'We have to get back to Bellevue-sur-Mer.'

How she could achieve this she had no idea.

'You know, I've not told anyone this, but Phoo and I, well, we've not lived together as, well, as husband and wife, for about forty years now.'

Sally realised he must be so drunk he was getting things muddled. They'd only been married for fifty years.

'Come on, Eggy,' she said, standing up and thereby shaking him off. 'Time to go home.'

As they made their way to the door, Eggy raised his hand and pointed at the WC sign.

While he was in the gents, Sally had a brainwave.

She phoned Carol and in as few words as possible explained the situation. Carol laughed and said she'd be right there.

Sally used the time waiting for the van to appear trying to get Eggy a bit sobered up. She took him out of the bar and walked him round the square, but he kept slipping down to the ground. He was very heavy to lift back to his feet. He must be all of six foot tall, and these days had quite a paunch on him.

In the darkness she pushed his arm over her shoulder and led Eggy down through winding alleyways to the main road which led up into the village. As they staggered along, Eggy continued trying to grope her.

'You don't want to do that, Eggy.' Each time she firmly shoved him away. 'We're working together tomorrow. You'll be embarrassed.'

A car turned around the sharp bend coming up the hill. The headlights lit them, blinding them both. Eggy's face slumped once more into Sally's shoulder.

As the van pulled up, Sally bent low to the driver's window to explain a bit more to Carol.

'He's totally plastered. We'll have to squeeze him into the front seat.'

Sally dragged Eggy round the bonnet and shoved him into the van.

Carol glanced at him, then did a double take.

Sally edged in, shunting Eggy along, and slammed the door.

Carol turned the engine over.

'Let's get you both home, eh? So, Sally, how do you know this old soak? New romance? Been keeping him a big secret from us?'

'No, no. Nothing like that.' Sally reached for the centre seat belt and strapped Eggy in, before clicking her own in place. 'I've known him for years and years. When I was starting out in the business I was a junior in a theatre company with him and his wife. You recognised him?'

'Oh yes.' Carol's voice carried a dark determination. 'So, you sneaked off for a secret date together?'

'No. No, Carol. We're working on the same project. Filming. It was a very long and tricky day and we decided afterwards to go for a drink. Who knew that this place was so utterly cut off? It was a mistake. He went on and on about his wife, who's staying in town with him. To be frank, it was grim. I should have gone straight home.'

'He's not divorced then?'

'Oh God, no. Very much still together with the wife.'

'At the very least I would have expected him to be a widower.'

'He's half of Theatreland's golden couple.' Sally's mind flitted to the conversation she had overheard with the casting director and she stammered out: 'They both came to supper at La Mosaïque a few nights ago. Don't you remember them? Eggy and Phoebe Markham.'

'Phoebe Taylor. Good lord. I rather believe that while you were canoodling up here with this old boy, down in La Mosaïque his wife was getting plastered with that blown-up doll, Odile de la Warr. Now I see why.'

'Well, there we are.' Carol's line was starting to annoy Sally. She'd done nothing, after all, except lend an ear. 'But, I must assure you, my relationship with Eggy is strictly professional.' Sally laughed away the notion which Carol had obviously picked up that she was up here in the middle of nowhere having a romantic tryst with Eggy Markham. 'Really, Carol. I wouldn't touch him with a pair of ten-foot tongs.'

'Hmmmmmm.' Carol was tight-lipped. 'Whatever.'

Eggy snorted and shifted in his seat.

'He's flat out.' Sally sighed. 'I wonder how his wife will take to him coming back unconscious?'

But Carol did not respond.

This was not how Sally expected going with Eggy for a little drink to end up. Carol, already disgruntled that she had flown off to do this acting job, was now also judging her as a cheat and a man-eater.

Sally knew that the more she tried to explain things, the worse it would get.

For the rest of the journey she and Carol barely spoke a word.

TWENTY

EARLY NEXT MORNING Imogen phoned Theresa to tell her that she was taking Chloe and the other two children directly to the airport and heading back to London. She had seen Neil hanging about the hotel, she said, and didn't want to allow any complications to develop.

Theresa suggested she might come up to say goodbye, but Imogen told her that they were all already sitting in the taxi, simply waiting for Frances to pick up her bill, so it would be pointless.

Theresa was quite upset. She had a slight headache. A ravenous hunger had also come upon her, but there was little in the cupboard, except the box of brownies, and she didn't much fancy them for breakfast. So, as a treat, to cheer herself up, she went along the road to Marcel's brasserie.

The morning was chilly, with no sun. An easterly wind was picking up dust and stray leaves and dancing them along the pavement. The brasserie terrace was deserted, but indoors the place was bustling.

At a table for two near the window she saw Roger Muffett, eating breakfast with Neil. He looked up, waved at Theresa and called to her across the room: 'Come and join us.'

'So you're still here,' she said, leaning against the back of a chair. 'I gather Imogen has taken Chloe back to London.'

Neil's face was the picture of misery.

'Little fellow's not very happy about that.'

'Good morning, Theresa.' Marcel came up and pulled out her chair. 'It's a rare day that you pay us a visit this early.'

'I'm lucky, Marcel. I am among friends.'

'And what can I get you?'

'*Un café crème, et une brioche, s'il vous plaît, Marcel.*'

Marcel lingered a little before moving off. Theresa wondered whether he was thinking of saying something else. Perhaps he wanted to try and sway her to make the others accept his pitiful offer for the restaurant. But after a moment he turned away, went into the kitchen and came back with her breakfast.

'What's that?' Neil pointed at her sugar-speckled bread.

'A brioche. Would you like to taste?' She pulled off a lump and put it on to Neil's plate.

'I suppose you must be thinking of getting back on the boat again now, Roger, and heading off into the great unknown? What an adventure it must be!'

'Really?' Roger sighed and topped up his coffee from the pot on the table. 'Must I?'

'It's dull today, I know. But don't let a spot of rain get you down. Usually the weather here is lovely. In the winter it's hot at midday and freezing at night. But at least most days we do get the sun. I think it would be gorgeous to go drifting out on to the Med. Even on a cloudy day.'

'Hmm. Good for you,' growled Roger. 'You're welcome to it.'

'My friend Sally drives a boat.' Theresa spread her brioche with apricot jam, then took a sip of the lovely strong coffee. 'I'm afraid I only go as far as driving a car.'

'I couldn't be more bored with the boat. Once upon a time it all seemed like such a good idea. But a life like this isn't at all as it looks in the adverts.'

'Nothing ever is.'

'Excuse me.' Roger laid down his napkin and rose, looking for the lavatories. 'Neil, please could you entertain Mrs Simmonds while I visit the little boys' room.'

Roger weaved through the tables to a door near the back of the café. Neil leaned in to Theresa. 'Poor Dad. He had all these horrible girlfriends, but they didn't like it on the boat either. They all went home. I got the idea that they thought because Dad lived on a yacht that he was a millionaire. They didn't understand that we live on a boat just because he doesn't have anywhere else to go.'

'How do you feel about it all?'

'I'd like to live in a house again.'

'In France or England?'

'You know, I really miss my mum. And, honestly, I miss my old home too. I even miss school.'

Theresa handed Neil another piece of brioche. Poor boy. In fact, Roger had looked so beaten she felt sorry for the pair of them. What a mess.

Marcel was back. 'I hear you took your coffee in the market in Nice a couple of days ago,' he said. 'Were you trying to avoid me? You usually come here.'

'Are you spying on me, Marcel?' Theresa looked him in the eye.

'No. Cyril told me he saw you there. He was taking photographs or something. I just thought that after our recent discussion about the price of your restaurant you might be …' He started fiddling with the table. 'The other gentleman is gone away?'

'Only for a minute.'

'I wanted to talk to you about La Mosaïque …'

At this moment, to Theresa's great relief, Roger emerged from the gents. She had no desire to be cornered by Marcel to talk money without anyone from the restaurant team to back her up. She was frightened she might say something in her poor French which Marcel would take as her agreeing to another minuscule offer. This was the problem when you spoke a language in the most basic of fashions. You might say something which actually meant something very different – like all those badly translated menus where *Crudités Variées* became Various Crudenesses, and *Gratin d'Avocat* – or avocado with grilled cheese – appeared as Cheesy Lawyer.

'Oh look. Here comes Roger.'

Marcel moved off. Roger sat.

'You know what, Theresa, I've had it with all the fancy French food, the wine, the coffee, the so-called "good life". I just want to slump down on the sofa with a football match and a packet of chocolate Hobnobs.'

'Followed by beans on toast,' added Neil. 'And a burger.'

'And chips, with tons of ketchup, and a fried egg.'

'Sausages.'

'Bacon.'

The way these two males were waxing on about English food reminded Theresa of the opening song from the musical *Oliver!* She half-expected them to put their hands to their chests, gripping imaginary braces, and start hopping from foot to foot in imitation of a Victorian street dance, all the while warbling manfully on the subject of shepherd's pie and mustard, fried-egg roll, toad-in-the-hole and jam roly-poly with custard.

'Have you got a busy day laid on, boys?'

'If only,' said Roger with a sigh, gazing out to the grey sea.

'I don't know whether this is an idea which would appeal to either of you, but Monaco is only just up the road. There's meant to be a wonderful museum …'

'Oh, not art. Please not. Or history. I left school thirty years ago, Mrs Simmonds.'

'No. It's motor cars. Race cars mainly.'

She noticed that Neil had looked up, his eyes gazing sheepishly at his father.

'You fancy that, nipper?'

Neil nodded.

'Right ho. Monaco it is.' He stood up. 'Breakfast is on me, Mrs Simmonds. See you around.'

Rather than stay there like a sitting duck to have Marcel explaining why she should take his offer, Theresa crammed the remains of her brioche into her mouth and left with the others. On the doorstep, Roger kissed her on the cheek and once again thanked her for her understanding.

She left the brasserie terrace, nipped round the back alleyway and went straight into La Mosaïque kitchen.

'Morning, old girl!' Carol was already inside, hanging up her coat. 'Letter came for you.'

'What's all this mess?' Theresa looked around at the countertops, which were cluttered with jars and utensils.

'Ugh. The boys never tidy up properly. Remember, you only did the beginning of the service last night. William was on his own at the end.'

Theresa realised that she had absolutely no memory of anything which had happened here the night before.

Carol sat on the countertop while Theresa put a jar of sugar back into the larder. 'So, anyway, darling, about last night. The hills were alive, not with the sound of music but with Sally, out drinking with some drunken Lothario.'

'How on earth do you know these things, Carol? Do you have CCTV on us all?'

'Caught them at it!' Carol smirked. 'In the deep of night my driving skills were requested, cos they got themselves stranded, stuck in some run-down bar in a no-taxi, desolate, long-forgotten, non-touristic, hilltop village.'

'What on earth were they doing there?'

'My guess is trying not to be seen by anyone. But, hard Cheddar, old beans. Sherlock Rogers came to the rescue.'

Worktops cleared, Theresa hung her jacket on top of Carol's coat and ripped open the letter.

'Why would Sally care about being seen by us? She's a free woman and over twenty-one.'

Theresa unfolded a piece of A4 paper and looked at it.

At first, she couldn't really work out what it was: a grainy picture of a sunny café terrace, people sipping coffee and wine, reading newspapers, chattering among themselves.

Why had someone sent her this?

Then she realised that the photo had been taken in front of the terrace of Le Chat Bleu in Nice.

And seated in the corner, there she was: herself, Theresa Simmonds, all alone, nursing an espresso cup, looking straight at the camera.

Why would anyone want to lure her to a café simply to take a photo of her, then print it out and put it in the post to her at the restaurant? You'd have to be deranged to go to all that trouble. And for what? At the end of it all what on earth had you achieved?

'You've gone all quiet and pale again, Theresa.' Carol jumped down from the counter. 'Are you feeling all right?'

Theresa held out the paper.

Carol squinted down. All she saw was a photo of Theresa sitting on the terrace of a café.

'Well? You'd better explain.'

Theresa told her how she'd been lured into the café in Nice the day before yesterday, how she'd thought the text came from Chloe, how she sat there all afternoon waiting for no one.

'What's it all about?'

'I have no idea.' Theresa snatched the paper back from Carol and crumpled it up in the palms of her hands. 'But I'm beginning to get really scared. And I have an idea I know who's behind it all.'

'You mean by "it all" – the photos, the gifts, the roses and all that stuff?' Carol stared at her, goggle-eyed. 'Who?'

'I think it's Cyril.'

'Cyril? The butcher?'

'I'd temporarily forgotten his occupation. Thanks for reminding me, Carol. Now I'm really scared.'

'But what makes you think it's him?'

'Marcel just told me Cyril had said he'd been in the market the day before yesterday, taking photos. And haven't you noticed how recently he seems to make his presence felt much more in here when he comes with deliveries?'

'Mmmm.' Carol held her chin in a pensive mode. 'Now that you mention it …'

'But why would Cyril do this to me? What does he want?'

'You tell me? It's obviously an obsession. Have you never got a sudden crush on someone? He's clearly infatuated with you. I think he may be angry with you too.'

'But why? What did I ever do to him?'

'Who knows? Sometimes people perceive a slight when none is intended. Or get jealous that you seem to spend more time on someone else.'

'But he's married to that lovely woman with the wonderful laugh.'

'Men are a law unto themselves. Being married doesn't seem to stop them these days. Look at Sally's friend.'

'But why me? Why now?'

'Love is a mystery and all that guff. Such things happen. You read about these stalkery obsessives all the time in newspapers. Usually when it's too late.'

'Oh my God, Carol, don't say that.' Theresa reached out and tapped a wooden spoon. 'You don't think it's to do with the restaurant and us reducing his order?'

'I think that when people get a fix on someone, logic flies out the window.'

Theresa's phone, lying on the counter, rang and she sprang away from it.

'Jumpy!' Carol held out her hand to pick it up. 'Shall I answer it? Just in case?'

Theresa nodded.

Carol put the phone to her ear. 'No … I'm afraid she's stepped away from her phone at this instant … I see … Really? Thank you. I will pass on that message.'

She handed the phone to Theresa.

'Well?'

'It was your daughter Imogen. I gathered that she thinks the airline people are a totally inconsiderate bunch of grasping charlatans who desired her to take out a mort- gage in order to change her tickets and, consequently, for the rest of the week, they are all returning to Bellevue- sur-Mer and staying at the Hotel Astra, because even four nights in that fleapit are cheaper than changing five seats on that two-bit airline.'

William came through from the restaurant.

'I'm not sure whether I'm talking to you today.' He stood for a second and glared at Theresa. 'However, I need to tell you the new plan. Zoe's idea, actually, and it's a good one. Like in Scotland, or so she tells me. We're putting out to tender. We have a set rock-bottom reserve price, one which won't leave us out of pocket but won't make us a profit. And we call for offers – sealed bids to be delivered in envelopes by a fixed date. The word is out.'

'Well, that's good, I suppose. Good on Zoe.'

'Anyway,' William continued. 'We have two tables booked tonight. Hardly a sell-out.'

'There'll be door trade.'

'We hope.'

'You don't sound as thrilled with the clientele as you were last night,' said Theresa, amused by how William was like a weathercock of moods.

'No stars of *Paris Match* or British TV, I gather?' asked Carol.

'I don't know why we bother.' William pursed his lips and hunched his shoulders. 'Instead of carrying on this masquerade, perhaps we should give ourselves a night off and just ask them round to our place for dinner.'

'I gather they're friends of ours,' drawled Carol, throwing a wink at Theresa. 'Not worth bothering about?'

'Sadly, yes, or is that no?' William pulled a pile of linen cloths from the cupboard by the door, ready to take them next door to dress the tables. 'Zoe – table for one. And a table for two for Cyril.'

Sally had had a better afternoon than Eggy. She was on top of her lines and, when he dried, fumbled about or came in on the wrong cue, she tried as best she could to cover for him.

She had hoped that, after the drunken state he had been in the night before, he might have forgotten his offer of drinks at the Negresco for tonight, but no.

'Phoo is very excited about our soirée,' he said, while they were being touched up between takes. 'I phoned and reserved us a table in the famous bar where the Beatles and Elizabeth Taylor drank.'

Sally felt pretty sure that the Beatles and Elizabeth Taylor might have stayed in the hotel but couldn't imagine any of them nipping down to the public bar for a quickie, while fans screamed outside on the Promenade des Anglais.

Just thinking about crowds on the Promenade at night caused her spit to dry up. She realised that, if she went to the Negresco with the others, it would be her first time walking along the Promenade in the dark since that terrible evening when the terrorist attacked in his speeding lorry.

She had to make sure she was not alone.

When she got back to her trailer to change costume for the next scene, she quickly phoned Jean-Philippe to invite him along. It wasn't simply that she couldn't face another night with Eggy's wife, but she doubted she could face the horror of revisiting her own trauma alone. After a number of rings, Jean-Philippe's voicemail kicked in. With a sinking heart, she left a message, now wishing she had asked him earlier. She knew his routines and, if he wasn't answering, the likelihood was that he was out at sea, either repositioning someone's yacht or giving lessons. He might be miles away, far along the coast, and, when he got home, no doubt his only desire would be to open a beer and lie on a sofa in front of the TV.

She flicked through her phone wondering who else she might invite. There was always Marianne, but the very thought of having her daughter there alongside Phoo chilled her. If Phoo went off on one of her rants, she couldn't face Marianne being a witness. Especially as she would quite likely spoil for a fight.

Everyone at the restaurant would be working tonight, though possibly Carol could manage to skive off, while ostensibly doing a delivery.

Or there was Zoe …

Sally's immediate reaction to that was NO.

A sharp rap on her door shook her out of the planning for this evening.

'Miss Doyle. We're ready for you on set now!'

While they both shuffled about, shifting positions between takes, Eggy kept whispering to her.

'Got your date arranged yet, Salz? We're quite open-minded, you know.'

Sally had no idea what he was talking about. Perhaps it was because Jean-Philippe was a lot younger than her. But he was only her good friend and companion. She opened her mouth then realised she couldn't be bothered to start explaining.

Another time Eggy leaned forward and said, 'Phoo is thrilled about tonight. She's never been to the Negresco before. It has quite a reputation. And, of course, she wants to stroll along the famous Promenade des Anglais …'

Again, at the very mention of that road, Sally felt her heart skip a beat.

It might have been a few years back now, but the memory of the fright always lurked beneath the surface.

As action was called, Sally realised that her mouth was dry. Her words came out fuzzy. She wondered whether she might not be able to pull out of this evening without being rude. But as Eggy was standing right here beside her it was obvious she couldn't throw a sickie.

Once the pair of them were wrapped for the day, Eggy walked her back to the trailers.

'Lucky we did that so efficiently. We've got a good long time to go home and get into our glad rags. It's all jackets and ties, isn't it? I'm sure you'll scrub up nicely. You always did.'

Inside the trailer Sally dialled Jean-Philippe again. No reply. This was horrible. She flicked through her address book. The only people she could come up with were Cyril or Marcel, but as they had little English, that wouldn't work at all.

If only the drinks were scheduled for tomorrow – the weekly day off at La Mosaïque – then she could have asked Theresa. Theresa was always reliable and oozed good manners. And she had been with her on that tragic night, so at least she would have someone with her who knew exactly …

During the drive back to Bellevue-sur-Mer, Eggy and Sally made arrangements about how they would get there, and eventually agreed they would go in Sally's car. At least that left her in control. And at the end of the evening she would be the one who would decide when they left.

It also meant she would have an excuse to have only one drink, which suited her fine.

Back home she alternated taking pieces of clothing from her wardrobe and phoning Jean-Philippe with no luck.

She squeezed herself into her black cocktail dress.

The front door opened. Marianne was home.

Again Sally toyed briefly with the idea of asking her, then imagined the conversation. She really could not have her daughter hearing all the spiteful things Phoo might come up with.

'Mum?' Marianne called up.

Clutching her mobile phone, Sally came down.

'Look!' Marianne displayed the screen of her phone. 'I've made the papers. Five lines on page thirteen but it does mean I was right to run here and lie low.'

Sally squinted at the article. 'You made a record loss. Isn't that the whole game of money? Like they say so quickly at the end of adverts, "Your investment may go down as well as up."'

'This time it just went down rather faster than usual.' She pointed at Sally's dress. 'Where are you going, all dolled up?'

'It's an actor thing. You know. Just the kind of thing you hate.'

'Somewhere posh, by the look of that dress.'

'Negresco.'

'No! I don't believe it. That's where I'm going.'

'Why?'

'I've met this rather dishy English bloke at the café. He's looking for financial advice.'

'In the light of what has just happened, Marianne, are you sure that you're the right person to be giving it?'

'Oh, Mum. To quote yourself, "Investment may go down as well as up." I'm only helping him consolidate his assets after a very nasty divorce. And, anyway, look, I only cocked up once.'

Sally realised that this news made her situation even worse. If her daughter was going to be there in the bar, sitting in another corner, coaxing a potential client, she really did have to find somebody to take with her to dilute the evening, even if only a little.

PART FIVE

OEUFS FARCIS DE NICE

Otherwise known as Stuffed Eggs Niçoise. Serves 6.

6 eggs
handful of black olives, finely chopped
fresh parsley, finely chopped
tube of cream of anchovy
3 dessertspoons mayonnaise
1 teaspoon mustard
salt and pepper
small tin anchovy fillets, drained
piment d'Espelette or cayenne pepper
green salad, to serve

Boil the eggs until hard (about 12 minutes). Remove the shells and cut the eggs in half. Take out the yolks and mix with the olives, parsley, a squirt of cream of anchovy, mayonnaise, mustard, salt and pepper to taste. Fill the half egg-whites with the mixture to get a rounded bump. On each half lay a fillet of anchovy, and sprinkle with *piment d'Espelette* or cayenne pepper. Serve on a bed of green salad.

TWENTY-ONE

A FTER HEARING THAT Cyril would be in the restaurant this evening, Carol would not accept any of Theresa's protests. She accompanied her over the road to her flat, after telling William and Benjamin that Theresa had a serious migraine and couldn't possibly cook.

'It's all too much, darling. You cannot allow Cyril to intimidate you in this way. So you're going home to safety.'

'But I ...' Theresa was torn. But knew deep inside that Carol was right.

'I'm on front of house tonight, and, while serving him, I'm going to delve, and see what I can pump out of him on the subject of you and all his stalkerish behaviour.'

The flat was dark. Carol strode ahead, checking every nook and cranny, even throwing open the back door and inspecting the small yard before allowing Theresa inside.

Then she demonstrated the flat to Theresa. 'All clear, guaranteed by Carol Rogers. OK?'

They both looked up at the Hotel Astra, its windows all lit against the darkness.

'Can you work out where the voice came from?'

'Don't think I haven't tried to work it out. But look! So many windows.'

'I know. Looks like a magical Advent calendar, doesn't it?' Carol sighed, and turned back into the flat. 'Can't you phone your daughter and maybe go up there and sit with them?'

Theresa mulled this over. But how to explain to Imogen, especially as she had her own problems? And even if she went up for the evening, once it came for time to go to bed she would still have to come back here alone, but then she wouldn't have Carol with her to check the place out.

Theresa decided it was best to stay put; after all, tonight they both knew exactly where Cyril would be, and Carol could keep an eye on him and warn her if he left the restaurant.

Theresa let Carol out and put on the kettle to make some tea.

While she was warming the pot, the phone rang.

Instinctively she moved to answer it, then realised that she shouldn't. She was either meant to be at work or too ill to be at work, so left the answering machine to pick up. The red display told her she already had one message.

During the playback of her announcement, the phone made odd clicking noises which she had never noticed before.

'So please leave your message after the tone ...'

Beep, beep, beep.

'Hello. Cyril here ...'

She took a step back.

'I hope you enjoyed your little present ...'

She rushed over to the phone, ready to pick up and challenge the man, but before she got to it, there was another beep, followed by a whirring sound.

She picked up.

Dialling tone.

She pressed Play on the answering machine, noticing that the display now said 'o' messages.

But nothing happened.

She pressed again.

Nothing.

She had just heard him leave a message and yet now there were no messages.

She was standing right by the window. It was dark outside but her lights were on. Anyone out there could see her. She took a step back, then pulled the curtain across.

Instantly the phone rang again.

She jumped, startled, then picked up.

'All right. Come clean. What do you want from me?'

'Well, actually, Theresa, I wanted to know if you'd like to come out for a drink.'

'Sally?'

It was.

'Don't worry, darling. I won't snitch. I phoned Carol first, you see. And she suggested you might be in need of some company.'

The very thought of getting out of this flat, where she felt like a sitting duck, seemed like a wonderful idea.

'All right, Sally. You're on.'

'Posh clothes, darling. We're going smart. I'll pick you up in ten minutes. Oh, and we're going with your upstairs neighbours. I hope you're on good terms.'

'I am,' replied Theresa, overflowing with relief. 'Phoebe Taylor was in the restaurant last night, and we had a laugh.'

'Me, not quite so much, but that's another tale,' said Sally. 'See you in ten.'

Theresa hastily put on some make-up and changed into a smart dress, and when Sally's car drew up was hovering by the front door. She heard Sally ring the upstairs doorbell. Immediately she opened her own front door and locked up behind her.

'You've saved my bacon,' she said, ducking briskly into the front seat of the car. 'Quick – before anyone sees me.'

Once in the passenger seat Theresa bent down into the footwell, pretending to do something to her shoe, until the two back doors had slammed and Sally revved the engine and the car sped up the hill.

———

Eggy ordered champagne, a bottle with four glasses.

Sally did the mental arithmetic – one and a half glasses each.

Conversation was pretty sticky. To Sally it seemed as though they were all tiptoeing around so many subjects, from Sally and Eggy's film job to the reason why they were sitting here together having a drink at all.

'I loved your sitcoms,' said Theresa during one of the leaden pauses. 'Very funny. Especially *Paddy and Pat*.'

'Thank you, Theresa.'

Sally watched as Phoo bestowed upon Theresa a condescending smile of the type usually reserved for fans.

'Compliments like that make my day. It was indeed a well-beloved show.'

And once again awkwardness reigned.

Eggy put up his hand and signalled for another bottle.

Just as the waiter was popping its cork and pouring, one hand smartly behind his back, Sally noticed Marianne enter with a well-built middle-aged man with dark hair, greying at the temples. She saw Theresa make a surreptitious wave. The man waved back at her. Trailing behind them was a teenaged boy.

At the same moment Sally's phone rang. She glanced at the screen. It was Jean-Philippe.

'I'm so sorry. I need to get this.' Sally took the phone out into the brightly lit hotel lobby. 'Oh God, Jean-Philippe. I've been trying to get hold of you all day. I wanted you to chum me to a drinks thing at the Negresco.'

Jean-Philippe told her he'd love to, and Sally had to explain that he was now superfluous to requirements. He laughed and told her that once he'd bathed and preened himself he might well 'happen' to pop in later. Don't worry, he'd make it seem a sheer coincidence.

As Sally made her way back into the bar, she was thinking how the whole quality of this evening was like a dream, or was it a nightmare?

She paused to greet her daughter. The man accompanying her rose to shake her hand.

'Roger Muffett, I'm the father of Neil, here, the little squirt who ran off with your pal's granddaughter.' He leaned his head to one side and squinted at Sally. 'I've met you before, haven't I? You look very familiar.'

Sally noticed that Neil was blushing tomato-red, his eyes popping at her as though he was trying to transmit a secret message. She also perceived the boy's slight shake of head, so said, 'I don't think so,' even though she really did think he looked familiar.

Marianne was also signalling at her. In actual words it would have been something like 'shove off and stop queering my pitch,' Sally realised, so she smiled and returned to her seat with the Markhams and Theresa. They were chatting merrily about British television of yesteryear.

'Phoo and Eggy were telling me about when they first knew you.'

Oh God.

Sally could imagine.

Without thinking, she took a large swig of champagne and ferociously bit off the end of a breadstick dipped in tapenade.

'I never realised you were held in such high esteem by everyone in the theatrical profession,' Theresa continued. 'Phoo has been telling me all about your wonderful interpretation of Natasha in *The Three Sisters*. I so wish I'd seen it.'

Sally took a deep breath and gaped at Theresa, then back at Phoo, who was gazing serenely into her champagne glass.

What on earth was going on?

'Well, isn't this nice?' said Eggy, leaning back in the sofa and taking in the room with its boiserie and gold-framed paintings of kings of France. 'What a lovely way to end a day's work.'

'Especially when we've got such a late call tom—' Before Sally could finish her sentence Eggy's foot lashed out under the table and kicked her ankle so hard she made an audible squeak.

'Late-ish,' he said sharply. 'These days I count a nine a.m. as a lie-in, don't you? So ten-thirty seems like heaven.'

Sally knew that tomorrow was scheduled as a night shoot.

And that their pick-up wasn't due till 3 p.m.

Theresa was also making small movements, which caught her eye. When she turned to look she appeared to be making secret motions in the direction of Marianne.

Sally pulled up her sleeve and gave her own arm a sharp pinch.

No.

She was awake.

'So have you been partners for years and years?' Phoo leaned forward and picked up a handful of herb-roasted nuts.

'No,' Sally replied. 'Must be around two or three years.'

Phoo nodded sagely.

'That's quite old to make such a sweeping change. Eggy and I have been together so long now we're practically welded.'

'Welded bliss,' added Eggy, stretching out his arm and putting it round Phoo.

Theresa was lifting her eyebrows and pulling a face at Sally. She appeared to be saying, 'Have it your way. I don't mind playing along.'

Why was everything tonight like a long course in the art of mime?

Sally was at a loss. Had Theresa given Phoo the impression that they were lovers? What on earth was going on?

'My friend Jean-Philippe may come along later.' Sally was determined to get things straight. 'I've been trying to get hold of him all day, but he was out at sea delivering a yacht for a client in Genoa. Then he had to take the train home. All tunnels.'

'Jean-Philippe?' Phoo was doing that wise-old nodding act again, all sympathy. 'Is he your beard?'

'He has a beard, yes.'

'No. I meant is he your "beard". I believe that's the expression, among the LGBTV community – you know, when you need to keep something about your private life covered up ...' Phoo started inclining her head now, bobbing her scalp in Marianne's direction. 'When the family is around the place. You know.' She was bouncing her head so regularly she was giving a fair impression of a toy dog in a car rear window. 'When ... family ... is nearby ...'

Nod, nod, nod.

'Why would I need to cover it up from Marianne? She knows all about the restaurant ...'

'No. I'm not talking about the restaurant.' Phoo laughed, still shaking her head. 'I mean ... you know ... The L word.'

Phoo now wiggled her eyes back and forth between Sally and Theresa.

When Sally looked to Theresa for some support, all she got back was the same wide-eyed stare. This time it said: 'You got yourself into this; you can get yourself out of it.'

Sally wondered if this was anything to do with Carol. Had Carol spoken to Theresa about her being stuck up in the hilltop village with Eggy? Did Theresa believe that she and Eggy were at it, and so now she was spinning some lie which she had told Phoo to cover for her? Or did Theresa, for some reason of her own, need to make Phoo believe that they were lovers? She wished that someone had let her into the rules of whichever charade everyone was playing. She would then willingly join in.

Suddenly Marianne's date had crossed the room and was looming over her.

'I know who you are now,' bellowed Roger. 'You're that bloody delivery-woman with the stuck-up health food which lost me my girlfriends.'

Sally glanced past the man and could see his son shaking his head, making 'Sorry' gestures.

'If I needed a lecture on healthy eating I'd buy a book by Jamie Oliver.'

She saw the thick twists of dark hair curling over the top of his shirt collar and remembered where she knew him from.

It was 'Snooky' from the yacht with the long and ghastly name which she couldn't quite remember. '*The Wife Got The House*?'

'Oh, so the bitch has been speaking to you, has she?'

Sally's question seemed to have popped his bubble somewhat.

'I heard she was coming over here.'

'No, I ...'

Marianne arrived on the scene.

'Come on, Roger, let's not make a fuss, now, eh?'

Marianne took his arm and led him back to their table, where Neil sat hunched up, his face in his hands.

'Our first and only Shore-to-Ship delivery. It was a disaster.' Sally said it more for something to say than to explain herself. 'We gave him a delicate fish, and a cheese platter, when he really wanted baked beans on toast and chips.'

'That's what *we all* really want,' said Eggy. 'With ketchup and a nice cup of tea.'

Sally remembered something else about the encounter. 'The boy called me Theresa.'

'Neil?' Theresa peered across at the boy.

'So often happens with couples.' As she nudged Theresa's elbow, Phoo's speech was slightly slurred. '*Did* you get the house, darling? Well done you! Eggy and I have a Beamer.'

It was all too much for Sally. Everything had become so surreal. It was exactly like one of those actors' nightmares where you are on stage in the middle of an obscure play by someone like Eugène Ionesco, but you have never even read the play and have no idea of your role, let alone the lines. And you look down to see that you are naked.

Sally grabbed her champagne glass and downed it in one.

When she looked up she saw that everyone was squinting towards the doorway, where some people were hovering, waiting to be seated. It was Odile de la Warr, accompanied by a gaggle of Italian men.

Phoo raised a hand and waved. Odile murmured something to the Italians and they all turned away, and left the bar, heading for somewhere else to drink.

'I don't think she saw us,' said Phoo.

But Sally knew that she had.

What she wasn't sure of, though, was which one of them Odile de la Warr was avoiding.

As they all came out of the hotel, stepping warily down the white marble steps, Theresa realised that she had got rather more drunk than she had intended. But even this did not soften the pounding of her heart when a passing motorcycle backfired. Instinctively, as she had on that terrible night a few years ago, when they had stood yards away from this spot as the lorry barrelled towards them, she reached out and grabbed Sally's hand. From the strength of her friend's grasp, she knew that Sally had experienced the same shock.

They rounded the corner and broke into a run as they had that night, stumbling together along the pavement of Rue Cronstadt.

They ran onwards until they turned the corner leading into Rue du Commandant Berretta. Even though they could hear Phoo behind them, calling loudly, 'Hey there, you two, wait for us!' they ran on.

As they came to a halt, both panting, they leaned against the wall, and Sally burst into tears. Theresa put her arms around her friend.

Last time, it had been the other way round. It was she who had broken down in tears once they reached safety, while Sally had remained stoical.

'I thought we would be over it by now,' Sally sobbed. 'It's such a beautiful place. To have that loveliness tainted by something so horrible …'

'I know,' said Theresa, holding her tight. 'We were so lucky. I'm sure the fear will fade one day.'

Sally wiped away her tears with the back of her hand.

'Come on, darling.' Theresa reached out and stroked her hair. 'Let's go home.'

'We can't.' Sally burst into tears again. 'I drank far too much. I'm way over the limit.'

'Me too,' said Theresa. 'Those ruddy waiters keep topping up the glasses. You can't count. You really have no idea you've drunk too much till you can't walk straight. Should we phone Carol?'

'She wouldn't thank us,' said Sally. 'Last time she was quite snippy with me.'

'Isn't that because you were canoodling with the married actor, fella-me-lad?' Theresa signalled with her head.

Sally jerked herself away. 'Me and Eggy? Good God, no. Is that what she told you?'

'There you are!' Phoo was bearing down upon them. 'Break it up, you lovebirds. You can get your nookie once you're home.'

Both Theresa and Sally shook their heads and opened their mouths and closed them again, realising there was no point even trying to explain.

Eggy ambled round the corner. 'Can't remember which car is yours, Salz, old girl. Is it the blue one?'

'I remember,' said Phoo, strolling towards Sally's car and slapping it on the boot. 'It's this one. Isn't it?'

While Theresa rooted in her handbag for a tissue to give to Sally, Phoo put her knee up on the bonnet of the car. At first no one had any idea what she was intending to do.

Next thing she was clambering up over the windscreen, dragging herself on to the sunroof. Once on top of the car, she stood up.

Theresa lurched forward and offered Phoo a hand, trying to lure her back down.

'I *am* somebody.' Phoebe Taylor started beating her chest. 'You can all get lost.'

Theresa looked to Sally, who was gaping up, open-mouthed, still wiping away her tears.

Then Phoebe started bouncing up and down, as though the roof of Sally's car was a trampoline, and, while she bounced, she chanted, '*Paddy and Pat, Paddy and Pat …*'

Theresa looked to Eggy, but he remained still, standing there. But he wasn't looking at his wife. He stared down at the pavement, as though searching for lost keys.

When Theresa glanced up again, Phoebe was tearing at her pink cashmere sweater, pulling it over her head, revealing her plump, naked top, covered only by a greying brassiere.

'We have to get her down,' said Theresa, tugging at Eggy's elbow. 'She'll hurt herself. She's ruining Sally's car, and ... well ... if anyone gets a photo of this, it'll be the end ...'

'The end of what?' Eggy looked Theresa in the eye. 'You see ... That's exactly the problem.'

'*Paddy and Pat*, Paddy, Paddy, Paddy ...' Phoo was still bouncing, all the while grabbing at her own back, trying to unfasten her bra. 'Paddy's dead. Paddy's dead.'

'My sunroof,' muttered Sally, leaning back against the wall.

'There's nothing I can do about this.' Eggy spoke with a mournful solemnity. 'And the main reason for that is that I am not Paddy.'

'Paddy! Paddy! Paddy!' Phoo continued calling out the name of the character played by the recently deceased beloved Irish actor.

'For the last forty years she's loved him.' Eggy shrugged. 'And now he's not here any more.'

'Eggy! You've got to help! That's my car.' Sally stood beside Theresa, turning to stretch an arm out towards Phoo. 'Apart from anything, it's very dangerous for her.'

'She won't come for me. Only Paddy could have got her down.'

'Oh God, no!' The imperious tones of Odile de la Warr rang out. 'The woman's not *still* banging on about that tiresome man. She is a complete idiot.' She pushed through them all and stepped forward to the car. 'Phoebe! Stop it! Give me your hand, darling. This is neither the place nor the style in which to air your grief.'

Phoo stopped calling out the name Paddy and looked down at Odile. It was as though she was waking from a dream and was not sure where she was.

'Odile?'

Theresa had a terrible realisation. Phoebe Taylor, one half of the 'Magical Markhams', the most constant wedded couple in showbiz, had for years and years been having an affair with Dermott Presley. Dermott Presley! A man utterly celebrated for his 'family values' and devotion to his homely wife. A man rarely photographed without his children and dogs at his side, Aran sweater brightening his face from below, always a smile of quiet contentment, adding a twinkle to his tranquil expression. As she stepped forward to help Odile, Theresa decided she would never believe another thing she read in the newspapers.

Sally's phone rang. She spoke urgently into the handset. 'Jean-Philippe! Thank God. There's been a bit of an incident. We're round the back of the hotel.'

At the same time a bright flash illuminated the dark side street.

Hearing the noise, a gaggle of tourists had gathered to see what was going on. More than one of them had already captured the moment on their phone.

Theresa knew that, even if none of these people recognised Phoo, by dawn those photos would be on Twitter. It wouldn't take very long for someone to work out exactly who was bouncing up and down topless on a car roof behind the famous Negresco Hotel calling out the name of her dead lover.

TWENTY-TWO

THERESA WOKE WITH a start and looked around her. For a short time she had no idea where she was. She recalled the stalker situation and her heart skipped a beat. Had she been kidnapped?

Then she remembered.

After the uncomfortable scene behind the Negresco, Sally's friend Jean-Philippe had kindly driven her and Sally back from Nice to Bellevue-sur-Mer, while the Markhams went with Odile de la Warr. Sally's car had been towed away by a mechanic. The roof was dented, the windscreen smashed and the ceiling inside now too low to get safely into the driver's seat.

Theresa had explained to Sally, en route, her fears that Cyril had developed a strange crush on her and that she was frightened to be alone, so Jean-Philippe had offered to walk through Theresa's flat, checking it out for her. Sally had decided that that wasn't good enough. She insisted Theresa stay up the hill in her house. And Theresa had willingly accepted.

As she lay staring at the ceiling of Sally's spare room, she remembered that La Mosaïque was closed all day today, on its weekly *congé*, and that Sally was due to go off working on the film set. Where could she spend the day?

Theresa did not want to be alone. Whoever was stalking her might be watching, following her, taking photos again.

But she couldn't stay at Sally's place. Sally must have things to do and lines to learn.

Theresa got dressed quietly, wrote Sally a thank-you note and left the house, then strolled down to the seafront to take breakfast at the brasserie.

It was a lovely spring morning. The sun had burned through the mist, leaving a gorgeous sparkling day. Theresa wished she had her sunglasses with her.

She took a corner table on the terrace. It was heaven to be able to gaze out at the deep-blue water while feeling the sun warm her through. Taking a deep breath, she leaned her head back letting the sunlight spill over her face.

'Good morning, Theresa.' Marcel was poised to take her order. 'What can I get you?'

'I'll have the full breakfast, please, Marcel. Orange juice, *café crème*, croissant.'

'Can I bring you the local newspaper?'

'Thanks. Yes.'

Theresa looked back at the front door of her flat, then cast her eyes up to the windows of the apartment above. She wondered, after the shenanigans of last night, how things were going inside. Sally had implied that Phoebe was a difficult woman but, lord, last night had been a real eye-opener. And to have all her own illusions shattered. So these famous people's lives were as imperfect as her own.

Theresa couldn't imagine how the woman had got that drunk. She knew that after three glasses of champagne she herself had been on the tipsy side but ... well ...

Would Phoebe Taylor be paying for the repairs to Sally's car? she wondered.

Would her affair with Dermott Presley be all over the tabloids?

'Hello!' Theresa's thoughts were interrupted by a woman who she couldn't exactly place. 'Mind if I join you?'

As the woman sat, Theresa recalled who she was. Frances, the drama teacher whom she had met briefly while in London on the trail of Chloe.

'What a gorgeous spot,' said Frances, pulling her chair out better to catch the sun. 'You're very lucky.'

A short silence was broken only by the sound of fishing boats, clanking together along the quay.

'I gather Roger was rather rude to your friend last night in some bar in Nice.' She took a puff of her electronic cigarette and exhaled a billow of strawberry-scented mist. 'I met them coming in last night. He'd been having a financial meeting with your friend's daughter, he said. So he couldn't have embarrassed himself more if he had tried.' Another cloud of fruity smoke wafted past Theresa's face. 'Poor Roger! I think he's realising what a dreadful mistake the whole business is.'

Theresa could see that Roger being so brutish towards Sally wouldn't have done him any favours with Marianne.

'The Muffett divorce should never have happened,' Frances continued. 'Problem is that they're both too proud to back down. Really, they were made for one another. Both wanted the same things – the glamorous life, a few months every year in the sun, to be surrounded by the latest gadgets ... You get the drift.'

Theresa did get the drift – of strawberry-scented vapour – and realised she preferred the smell of tobacco!

'Then they also both got the idea that they wanted younger lovers. And that didn't work out well for either of them. Once you reach forty it's better just to admit it. Teenagers or even twenty-year-olds ain't going to be sticking around for long.'

'You do strange things when you start to panic about growing old.' Theresa thought back to her own little crisis a few years ago which led to her moving here. 'But some-times it works out all right. Look at me.'

She remembered her meeting with Neil's mother, Roger's ex-wife. 'Mrs Muffett seems very troubled.'

'You had a husband leave you, didn't you, Theresa? Did you not find yourself pouring one too many large gin and tonics. And then another ...'

Theresa remembered the dark days after Peter had run off with the Italian au pair. She had turned to the bottle. There had been days when she never got out of her night-dress, days when she fed herself standing at the fridge taking bites out of blocks of cheese. She let herself go. For months she had been inconsolable. 'You're right.' Theresa winced at the memory. 'It wasn't gin and tonic – it was whisky and soda. But yes, there were some very difficult weeks.'

'Some days you get by fine, others it's really not at all OK. That painful fear of an unknown future, when you thought you had it all worked out.' Frances laid down her electronic cigarette, tore off a morsel of Theresa's crois-sant and popped it into her mouth. 'I think it's the double whammy. You realise you are old and past it, and at the same moment you see that you are no longer desirable to the man who'd always loved you. And, for us women, that starts rolling on into visions of a future sitting alone in a dark empty house, knitting, darning or some other boring pastime resting on your lap, a couple of cats curled around your feet, and that's it ... for ever.'

Theresa knew Frances spoke utter sense. She couldn't imagine anything so soul-destroying.

'I think also that when you're one of those socially ambitious women, like Cynthia,' Frances continued, 'it all gets muddled up with so many kinds of anxiety which I never had to deal with – like "How will they think of me at the golf club?'" She gave a bitter laugh and picked up the electronic cigarette.

'Could they get back together, do you think?'

'They ought to.' Frances shrugged. 'But I have a feeling they're also too stupid, not to mention conceited and self-righteous, for it to ever happen.'

'Poor Neil.' Theresa thought back to his absolute embarrassment last night, as he sat cringing at his father's behaviour. 'He does seem to be a very nice boy.'

'He's impulsive. Like them! Doesn't really think ahead. Gets an idea and runs away with it without considering anything even nearly related to reality. It's all great, that kind of thing, in the drama classes but, oh, so utterly totally hopeless in real life.'

A shadow fell over Theresa.

'*Bonjour, Theresa!*' It was Cyril. '*Vous avez reçu mes cadeaux?*'

Theresa shrank back in her seat.

Cyril tapped the bridge of his nose. '*Je comprends! Pas de problème.*'

As though seeing her discomfort, Marcel was suddenly beside Cyril, calling him by his name, inviting him into the brasserie.

'*Bonne journée, mesdames,*' Cyril called over his shoulder as he was dragged inside. '*Et, Theresa, à tout à l'heure.* See you soon!'

When Theresa turned back, Imogen was coming on to the terrace, with Chloe beside her.

'So this is where you are! I've been ringing your flat and your mobile for hours.'

Theresa saw that Imogen was grasping Chloe's wrist.

'I wasn't at home ... my mobile had ...'

'I'm not interested, Mum. This child has been sitting in the hotel breakfast room in the company of that boy, Neil.

Frances? Did you know he and his father were actually still staying there in our hotel?'

Frances said no, but Theresa couldn't miss the blush blooming on her neck.

'I thought they were living on a stupid boat down in the marina here! But it seems he sensed out my daughter, persuaded his father to come ashore and now they're together again.'

Theresa wasn't quite sure what they were supposed to do about that. You couldn't forbid a man from coming to stay in the same hotel as you.

'Right.' Imogen swung Chloe around. 'From now, until we finally get on that plane home, you will keep Chloe in your flat and under your care.'

'Where are the other two?' Frances laid down the menu and stood up. 'Not on their own?'

'As you had disappeared, Frances, I've had to leave them in the breakfast room. I needed to get this young lady immediately out of the radar of Neil Muffett.'

'I don't think Neil will be here long. His mother is due any moment to pick him up and take him home.'

'If she can stand up.' Imogen flopped down in the seat next to her mother's. 'Well, as we're here, and we've now missed breakfast up at the hotel, I suggest that Chloe and I join Theresa, while you, Frances, go back there and see to the others. After we've eaten, Chloe will be going to the restaurant to help her grandmother.'

'It's our weekly closed day.'

'Of course it is.' Imogen sighed. 'Then you must take her home to your flat. Until Neil Muffett is extracted therefrom, Chloe is suspended from the Hotel Astra.'

Theresa gave her daughter a sideways glance. Why was she now talking like a comedy headmistress from St Trinian's? 'Suspended from the Hotel Astra' indeed!

Theresa worried that at any moment Imogen might set her a hundred lines: *I shall not lose my granddaughter; I shall not lose my granddaughter* ...

Sally mooched about in her dressing gown. She was slightly disappointed that Theresa had crept off so stealthily, as she had been looking forward to a debriefing session about the embarrassing and startling events of the previous evening.

She wondered how Eggy was doing now. And had Odile continued the lecture she had started with the Markhams while she shoved them into the back of her chauffeur-driven car?

And that awful Roger man. *The Bitch Got The House*? Really? Ugh. She was looking forward to Marianne waking up and trying to explain what she was up to knocking about with a man like him. And he also appeared to be at the centre of the plot with Theresa's disappearing grand-daughter. So much trouble everywhere.

She gazed out over the rooftops at the sea.

Fancy Phoo having been at it with that smarmy Dermott Presley all those years. She tried to do the maths and calculate if the affair could have been going on when she had worked with Phoo and realised they must certainly have been an item before the Markhams' appearance on *Sssssaturday Ssssslamerama!* as Sally remembered making jokes about their characters, asking whether, after Phoo was glooped, Paddy would be coming to give her a brisk rubdown. Oops! Poor old Eggy. The meaning of his odd remark about not living with Phoo as man and wife for forty years suddenly became crystal-clear. No wonder he was looking out for hot dates in Nice.

Today the sea looked so gorgeous and inviting. So blue, its colour enhanced by the spots of white, curling across the vast horizon. But white horses meant wind. A storm must be coming up, which was not good news for tonight's filming. She went back to double-check on the call sheet for today's night shoot. Yes. It was a scene where she and Eggy once more drove some boat away, only this time it was a small one, and to be shot at night from the rocky shore at Èze. Oof! The sea could be tricky at the best of times around there. Lots of undersea rocks and lethal currents.

Ah well, Sally would be surrounded by a film crew, cameras whirring, so she would not be alone.

'Morning, Mama.' Marianne appeared, fully dressed and made up. 'So which mystery man did you bring home last night? I heard someone furtively sneaking out a couple of hours ago.'

'It was Theresa.'

'God, Mum, you haven't gone gay?'

'For heaven's sake, Marianne, don't *you* start. I've already had too much of that from the barking Markhams.'

'Oh, you mean that awful actress you were with last night? I remember her from when I was a kid. Wasn't she the woman on that dire show *Paddy and Pat*?'

'Marianne, please stop.' Sally blocked her ears with the palms of her hands. 'I never want to hear that phrase again as long as I live.'

'What? That awful actress you were with ...'

'No. *Paddy and Pat*, stupid.'

'Isn't her husband in that film with you?'

'Yes. So what?' Sally threw up her arms in exasperation. 'And anyway, what on earth were you doing drinking with that hairy ape who ruined our first, and only, boat delivery from La Mosaïque?'

'He might be an irritating twit. But he has money problems. I thought I'd help out. Who knows? Might be a fee in it for me. I have to earn money somehow, now that I've been fired.'

'Given your recent history, I think Roger would be safer getting financial advice from me.'

Ignoring her remark, Marianne continued. 'He's quite good-looking, though, Mum, you must admit. I could do worse.'

'Marianne! Can't you see that the man is trouble? For a start he's married.'

'Divorced. That's the source of all his financial woes.'

'And his son ran off with Theresa's grandchild. Please don't complicate my life any more than it is already. And by the way, his wife is due in town at any moment.'

'*Ex*-wife. And anyhow, what's sauce for the goose ...'

Sally was trying to form the words to respond to this when there was a sharp rap on the front door.

'That'll probably be him.' Marianne strode towards the door and opened up. But it was Eggy, standing there on the doorstep, looking penitent, stooped and beat.

'Do you mind if I have a few words with your mum?' He hovered, without stepping inside, wringing his hands, the very picture of misery. Marianne turned to her mother, pulled a face and strode past him and out. 'See you later, Mum.' Then she made a condescending face in Eggy's direction. 'And please may I say, Mr Markham, that I do *so* admire your work – both your own and that of your charming wife.'

And she was gone.

As Eggy stood there, looking pitiful, instinctively Sally rewound both Marianne's very convincing compliment and her own life, realising that when members of the public volunteered such lavish praise they were probably lying, and had only flattered you for something to say when confronted with the presence of a famous face. A kind of nervous embarrassment. How very disappointing!

'Please come in, Eggy.'

'Thank you, Sally.' Cautiously he stepped inside and closed the door. 'Look. I'm so sorry, Sally. I don't know where to start …'

'Let's both sit down, shall we? Would you like some tea, toast?'

Eggy shook his head. Sally realised he really must be feeling bad. Tea and toast were normally top of his wish list.

She sat down in the armchair opposite the sofa, where he perched, picking at the fabric of his trousers.

'First, I will of course pick up the tab for the repairs to your car, and if you want can provide you with a hire car while you're waiting.'

Sally's reflex was to tell him it was fine and that he didn't have to, but she realised that really he should pay.

She stayed silent.

'Phoo is going through a very difficult patch …'

Again Sally held back a sarcastic retort.

'Nobody knew that for most of our life together she was in a very passionate relationship with Dermott Presley, family man, beloved of the nation, blah-blah-blah …' Eggy sat back into the sofa. 'I had to read all the newspaper obituaries, too. And the glowing eulogies in the red-tops. And watched all those saccharine TV memorials.' He shook his head slowly, thoughtfully. 'He was a friend of mine actually, Salz. Before. We'd worked together at Liverpool Rep, back in the day. And when the TV show was looking for a partner for Phoo, in the sitcom, 'twas I who put forward his name. Anyhow, one thing led to another. You know what it's like when you're off on location in the middle of nowhere. I thought it would pass. But no. They managed to carry it on in a most furtive manner right up to his death. I myself knew nothing, till a few years ago, when Phoo became very anxious, and confessed all. She was like Niobe, all tears, as she sat and told me her worries – that Dermott was seeing someone else.'

'Not his wife, by any chance?'

'He was married throughout, and seemingly the most assiduous husband … It appears that his wife never had an inkling. Still doesn't. In fact, when Dermott was told by the doctors that he didn't have long, he called my agent and asked me to come into the hospital for a private meeting.'

'He wanted to say sorry to you?'

'No.' Eggy gave a sad smile. 'He wanted me to do him a few last favours. One was to find a suitcase full of letters tied up in pink ribbons – his correspondence with Phoo, over the years. He didn't want his family finding and reading them, after he was gone.'

Sally was speechless. What an absolute horror for poor Eggy.

'The other task was to remove and dispose of a box full of pornographic magazines hidden under the bed in his study. And let me tell you, we're not talking *Playboy*. It was … well … appalling stuff.'

'Did you?'

Eggy nodded.

'Did you read the letters?'

Eggy shook his head. 'Burned them on the barbecue.'

'How did Dermott keep up such a pretence for so long? You'd think the papers would have been on to him.'

'He wasn't the first.' Eggy shrugged. 'I imagine he won't be the last. But he always handled it majestically. Neither the public nor his family will ever know. Not unless a handful of people, including me, spill the beans. But you see, we all have so much to lose. Why would I do that to myself? To make muggins here look like a prime fool? I'd only come over as a vindictive cuckold having his last revenge on his "love-rival"? I don't think so.'

He shuffled around a little on the sofa. 'Actually, Salz, darling, if you don't mind I will have that cuppa.'

Sally rose and moved into the kitchen. While fiddling with the kettle and rooting out some bread for the toaster, she reeled back the years in her mind. Really, it was so obvious. But, as everything was done in plain sight, Phoo and Dermott managed to get away with it. Paddy and Pat were the loving couple, always squabbling, but clearly besotted with one another. That's how the public saw them. It's how everyone saw them. And now Paddy was dead. And Pat, sad old Phoo, was left all alone. All alone with the man who let it happen.

Sally laid a tray and carried it through. She was bursting with a thousand questions which she knew she could never ask.

'So anyway, Sally. I beg you to be a little understanding of Phoo's situation. She's really been through the mill these last few months. That's why I brought her down here. For a break. Of course her initial mourning was helped because the public always associated them as a screen couple. When she broke down at the funeral, it seemed quite natural. The family simply took it as the typical over-the-top behaviour of some mad actress with whom their own beloved real-life husband/father had worked. An embarrassingly dramatic thesp overplaying her moment. But, you see, really her grief was gargantuan.' He took a bite from the toast and chewed it slowly and deliberately. When he had swallowed he continued. 'Covering his tracks, naturally Dermott left Phoo nothing in his will. Not even the tiniest keepsake. So she is doubly bereft. She took it as a kick in the teeth from beyond the grave. And I know she shouldn't take it out on you, but … believe me, she's taking it out on me too. I pity poor Theresa. Every time Phoo sends a plate flying towards me and it ends up smashing on the wall of our flat she must hear it downstairs.'

'She is angry with *you*, Eggy? But to me you seem to have been too understanding?'

'Ah!' Eggy took a sip of tea. 'She's furious. Poor old Phoo can't stand the fact that it was Dermott who died, not me. She'll never forgive me for being alive while he's lying rotting in some North London cemetery.'

He cradled his cup in his hands and hung his head.

Sally saw a tear fall.

How to deal with this?

Up to now, Sally had thought that Phoo behaved like she did due to Eggy playing around, but it seemed they both were as bad as one another.

Now was the moment …

'But you weren't always the faithful old dog, darling, were you? Admit it!'

Eggy looked up, puzzled.

'The casting director of this film?'

Eggy swallowed and gave a slight shake of his head.

'You're a smart one, Sally, and no mistake. I suppose this is from a few snatched words you might have overheard while we were together in the car, no?'

Sally shrugged.

'Clever old Sal. You worked out a bit of the story. But certainly not the whole picture.'

'So you're not responsible for her, erm, current situation?'

Eggy gave a little snort. 'God, no. I'm far too old for all that baby malarkey.' He sighed a sigh which came right up from his feet and through him. 'I do my best in life. Or try to. Looking after that poor little girl was my third errand, dispatched from the hospital bed.'

'Not Dermott? Dermott was the father?'

Eggy nodded.

Sally could barely breathe as Eggy continued.

'Phoo was right to be nervous. Dermott really was seeing someone else. It had been going on a few years. Not only that, but the someone was young enough to be his granddaughter. Hers too. I suppose the old dog thought it would give him an edge in the TV world, get him that longed-for film role which would let him be someone other than Paddy in the eyes of the public.'

'But the baby? God, Eggy. These are consequences that will last a lifetime ...'

'As I said, Dermott was very careful when writing his will and testament. He had to preserve his precious reputation: Paddy the family man, the Irish darling with the heart of gold, the scally who upheld old-fashioned values. So, naturally, he made absolutely no provision at all for the forthcoming arrival. Poor girl. I gave her a bit of money. Not nearly enough. And I've offered to help wherever I could. She in turn tried to help me out by getting me this film. Even if I was only the last-minute standby!'

'She didn't cast Phoo, though?'

'Oh, she knows all about Phoo and Dermott. When Dermott was with her Phoo regularly made abusive calls to him, calling her – the unknown mystery woman who had stolen him away – every vile name under the sun.'

Eggy wrung his hands then polished off his cup of tea. What more was there to say?

Reeling from the convolutions of the whole saga, Sally decided to change the subject. Tonight's filming would be their last scene together. The final shoot for both of them.

'Ah well, Eggy,' she said. 'Thanks for letting me know all this. I shall think of Phoo in quite a different way now.'

'Thanks for that, darling.'

'And now …' Sally stood up. 'I suppose we'd better start preparing for tonight. I hear Marina Martel is already down here on the Côte d'Azur, ensconced in her hotel in Monte Carlo. Perhaps she'll turn up on set today.'

'I hope not. Not today.' Eggy winced. 'Will you be taking an afternoon nap, Salz, before the rigours of tonight?'

Sally nodded.

'Me too. But first remember I've got that hot lunch date. I just met this woman – I told you. And she made me laugh. These days I need all the laughter I can get. So hopefully a laughing lunch.'

Eggy chomped through the last slice of toast.

'One thing I have learned from Dermott, Sally, and it's a lesson for all of us, is that we *have* to make the most of *now*. We're none of us going to live for ever. But we're nearer the precipice than most.' He got up and moved to the door. 'Thanks for the tea. See you on the green, old girl.'

COOPED UP IN THE FLAT with Chloe, Theresa had spent an excruciating afternoon. While they ate lunch, seated at the glass table, Chloe had told her all about Neil. How wonderful Neil was, how kind Neil was, how good-looking Neil was, how Neil was the only person in the whole wide world who understood her, how Neil should be an actor, how Neil had been so brilliant playing Friar Laurence.

Theresa held her tongue. After her own experience last night with a tableful of actors, she didn't think she would be recommending that occupation to any sane person.

As the afternoon dragged on, Chloe gave up flicking through the French TV channels, took out her mobile phone and started typing frantically on to the screen. Theresa knew that this had to be a conversation with Neil and wasn't quite sure whether she was meant to prevent it. Imogen had left no regulations regarding her daughter's utilisation of electronic equipment, only that Theresa should not let the girl out of her sight.

While Chloe was hunched over the phone Theresa took out a book and tried to read, but she couldn't concentrate. Her mind kept going back to two things: the awful embarrassing evening with Sally's actor friends and the threats, or veiled threats, which someone was sending her. And it certainly looked as though that person was Cyril.

He had obviously picked up her album from the counter-top at La Mosaïque, and was sending the photos to her; he had lured her to Nice where he had taken a picture of her, and sent her gifts, roses – a knife, for God's sake. All butchers had knives galore.

Suddenly she had an idea and decided to listen to the CD, *Daphnis et Chloé*.

As the ravishing music started, filling the room with its swirling mystery, Theresa stayed behind the kitchen counter, tidying up.

'What's this?' The music had been playing only a few seconds when Chloe looked up. 'It's lovely.'

'It's named after you, sweetheart. *Daphnis et Chloé*. It's a ballet by a French composer, Maurice Ravel.'

'A ballet!' Chloe exclaimed, leaping up and spring-ing around the room like a gazelle. 'I love it. OMG. It's wonderful. It's exactly how I feel about Neil.'

Chloe dashed into the kitchen space, then she bent low and backed out on tiptoes, arms outstretched. Up in the air she sprang at great speed. Theresa just caught a vase Chloe had skimmed before it toppled. She was now wish-ing she had not put the darned music on. But while Chloe was so enchanted, it would be churlish to rip the CD from the machine half-played.

So, instead, she pottered around the flat, avoid-ing collisions with Chloe who performed an animated dance-drama involving the sofa, the four chairs around the dining table and the entire length of the kitchen counter. At one point Chloe even grabbed the feather duster from the corner and flung it about like a magic wand, running it along the countertop, pointing it fero-ciously towards Theresa, who wasn't really sure whether she was supposed to make some dramatic gesture in return.

'Can I put it up louder?' Chloe cried, leaping over Theresa's pouf, grabbing the knob of the hi-fi and turning it up to full. 'It's sooooo wonderful!'

Although, with the volume this high, Theresa would normally be worried about disturbing the occupants of the flat upstairs, at this moment she didn't give a flying fig; in fact, after last night, she'd be rather glad if she could upset them.

Feeling exceedingly childish, Theresa flung open the back door and let the music swell around the courtyard.

As the music reached its dramatic finale, Chloe, panting, flung herself along the length of the sofa, both arms outstretched, one leg pointing upwards towards the ceiling. Then she mimed total collapse and let her whole body go as floppy as a rag doll.

In the subsequent silence Theresa moved to the window to look out at the sea. Suddenly, with a jerk, Chloe jumped up, rushed past Theresa and out into the courtyard, shouting,

'O Romeo, Romeo! Wherefore art thou Romeo?
Deny thy father and refuse thy name.
Or, if thou wilt not, be but sworn my love,
And I'll no longer be a Capulet.'

Theresa realised before the long verse that the music had gone entirely to the child's head.

While Theresa wiped down the countertops, Chloe was standing outside the door speaking Shakespeare to the sky.

Theresa supposed there was no harm in it. Most parents, especially schoolteachers she'd have thought,

313

would be only too delighted to have children who could spout Shakespearean speeches at the drop of a hat. Chloe even seemed to be putting on a slightly lower voice to play Romeo's lines.

'I take thee at thy word:
Call me but love, and I'll be new baptised ...'

Moving through the flat, Theresa hovered near the back door.

'Henceforth I never will be Romeo.'

'No,' shouted Chloe towards the windows of the Hotel Astra. 'Because you'll always be my darling beloved Friar Laurence!'

Theresa looked up to see, leaning out of a tiny window, Chloe's Romeo, Neil Muffett.

———

Sally had been in Make-up a good half hour, before she went back to the trailer to put on her costume. Eggy had not come into the dressing room this evening with his usual bright hello.

After their conversation earlier, Sally felt really bad. She worried for him. Perhaps he was avoiding her, embarrassed at how much she now knew of his wretched life with Phoo.

When the car had arrived to pick her up this afternoon, Eggy had not been inside. The driver told Sally that Mr Markham's wife had come down to tell him that today Mr Markham was making his own arrangements.

Sally wondered whether she should go looking for him, but knew that that was the job of people on the crew, who would be well aware of where he was.

She perched on the seat in the trailer, all decked out in her costume. An evening dress, high heels and copious jewellery. This scene followed the pair of second-rate crooks doing a spectacular but accidental robbery at a party. They were only there to case the joint. But their presence coincided with the real robbery by professional robbers (Marina Martel and Steve Baxter). The principals had amassed the jewellery and stashed it behind a plant pot, ready to take it home at the end of the evening. But Eggy and Sally had to get there first. They fortuitously came upon the pile of diamond necklaces, rings and bracelets which the pros had removed from the safe. They then had to walk calmly out of the party with all the stolen jewellery plainly on show, around Sally's neck, fingers and wrists, with the odd bracelet sticking out of the pockets of Eggy's dinner jacket.

Sally stood in front of the mirror and tried working her wrists. With all this junk around the joints of her arms and hands, it was going to be rather hard to operate the throttle in the boat, but it had to be done. She wondered whether the boat would have similar controls to the last one.

A sudden gust of wind shook her trailer.

That did not bode well.

She didn't fancy being out in the dark on a small craft in a high sea.

She slung the chain of the evening handbag she had also been given around her wrist and picked up her mobile phone.

After a few more practice flicks she decided to go and visit Eggy in his wee trailer, just to say hello or something. She had to break the ice, to normalise things, otherwise tonight could be hell.

A rap on the trailer door.

'Ready for you on set, Sally!' It was the runner. 'Your car is the grey one, to the left of the chuck wagon.'

Sally delicately climbed down the caravan steps in her high heels, scooping up the skirt in her be-ringed fingers.

'You look great, by the way.' The runner put out a hand to help her. 'This scene will be very funny.'

'Where's Eggy?'

The runner hesitated before replying. 'We're getting hold of him. But we need you to run through the rehearsal for the lights and camera. After all, you'll be the one driving the boat.'

Sally sensed that the man was keeping something from her. Had something happened to Eggy? What did 'getting hold of him' mean? Eggy was clearly not at the location yet, otherwise the runner would have said, 'He's in Make-up' or 'He's grabbing a quick bite at the chuck wagon.' 'Getting hold of him' meant he was not here.

She fiddled around with her handbag and realised that she had inadvertently dropped her mobile inside. Phones were banned on set, so she'd have to hand it to someone later, but for now it could prove useful.

As the car pulled out of the car park, the film-set base today, on to the main road, she dialled Eggy's mobile number. No reply. Just voicemail. She tried again. No luck.

What if he had done something stupid? Sometimes confessions led to deep depressions.

She remembered her own horrible marriage situation all those years ago, but it came nowhere near poor Eggy's.

Sally sat back in the car seat and wondered what she could do next.

She didn't have a number for Phoo or she would have called her.

Then she remembered that Phoo and Eggy were staying in the flat above Theresa, so she hastily dialled her number. She'd ask Theresa to run upstairs and find out from Phoo when she had last heard from Eggy.

That was the answer.

————

'Grandma!'

Theresa went to the back door, where Chloe was still standing, gazing upwards.

'There's a man up there, making strange faces at me.'

'Not Neil?'

'No.'

Theresa looked up. It was starting to get dark, and the setting sun caught the hotel windows, turning them into red mirrors.

'I don't see? Where?'

Theresa feared that it could be Cyril looking down. Certainly someone had been up there that night a few days ago, whispering her name into the well. Could it be him again, alerted by the two kids larking about with their Romeo and Juliet routine?

'Has he been there a long time?' Theresa squinted up and still could not make out any faces framed in the red glow of the setting sun's reflection.

'There was some other creep earlier, but he disappeared when I came out and started up the Shakespeare rap.'

'Some other creep?'

'That creepy man who came up to you at breakfast, Gran. You remember?'

So it *was* Cyril up there.

'Which window?'

'Not the same one as the weird man. He was in one of the low windows. Bottom floor at the near end.'

Chloe's finger was pointing up, then she shifted it. 'But this weird bloke's still there, making faces. Look. One, two, three, fourth-floor centre ... Looks like he's got no clothes on ...'

Theresa's mobile phone rang. She ran back in to fetch it.

'Theresa? It's Sally. Sorry to disturb you. But I'm on my way to the set and Eggy seems not to have shown up today. Could you do me a favour and run upstairs to ask his wife if she's heard from him?'

Theresa glanced at Chloe in the courtyard, gazing up at the Hotel Astra, where her beloved Neil was. While Neil was in sight, Chloe would hardly notice if she popped out, just for a second. At least not while they were still talking to one another and making dramatic mimes.

Phone pressed to her ear, Theresa left the flat and walked up the steep stone steps leading upstairs. She rapped on the door. After what felt an eternity Phoebe Markham opened up.

She was clearly drunk.

'I've got Sally Connor on the line.'

'Who?'

Theresa remembered that the Markhams would only know Sally by her maiden name – her stage name.

'Sally Doyle.'

'What does she want?'

Theresa passed the phone over.

From Mrs Markham's responses Theresa gathered that she had not seen her husband since early this morning when he had gone up to Sally to run through some lines and had told her that he was getting a cab into work today.

Phoebe then thrust the phone back at Theresa and slammed the door in her face.

Standing on the tiny landing Theresa continued the call: 'All done?'

'I'm very worried,' said Sally.

'They're both mad as hatters,' Theresa replied.

'You don't understand, Theresa. There are reasons. For both of them, actually. But, please, I beg you, if you see Eggy, call me at once. I am worried for him.'

Theresa gripped the handrail and slowly clomped down the vertiginous steps. She turned and re-entered her flat.

All was quiet.

She put the phone back on to the charger and went out to the courtyard.

But Chloe was not there.

Panicked, Theresa ran back inside, shoving open the doors to the spare room and then her own bedroom, then banging first and opening the bathroom door.

The flat was empty.

Chloe had fled.

Heart now hammering, Theresa ran out into the street and looked both ways. There were only a few people on the quayside. She rushed along the front, hoping that the child had gone in the direction of the brasserie.

As she came to a stop a sudden gust of wind almost pushed her over.

Marcel was out front, gathering up tablecloths and condiment bottles which would otherwise fly off. 'Something wrong, Theresa?'

'Have you seen my granddaughter?'

'Not since she was here with you this morning.'

'She ran out of my flat a few minutes ago. You didn't see her?'

Marcel shook his head.

'Are you sure – you can see my door quite clearly from here?'

'Too busy with all this.' He caught hold of a salt cellar which had jittered to the edge of a table.

'If you get a glimpse of her, please call me at once.'

She ran back home.

Once inside she grabbed her mobile and, with shaking hands, tried dialling the number Chloe had last used. But the phone went immediately to answer. She realised that this meant that Chloe had either turned the phone off or was on the line to somebody else. No doubt Neil.

Still gripping her phone, Theresa ran out again into the courtyard.

If Chloe had gone anywhere it would be to the company of Neil up there.

But the boy was no longer hanging out of his tiny hotel window.

She counted up and along, noting the window from which he had earlier been poking. Second floor. Third along from her right.

It was then that she saw the weird man. His face was squashed against the window, like a pig in one of those Spanish restaurants. He was mouthing panicked words into the glass. His torso, so far as Theresa could see it, was, as Chloe had said, naked.

But it was not Cyril.

It was that actor friend of Sally's, Edgar Markham.

And he was obviously in serious trouble.

Without taking her coat, Theresa left the flat and ran up the hill to the Hotel Astra.

TWENTY-FOUR

SALLY WAS SHOCKED TO SEE that the boat for tonight's stunt was not a mini gin palace like before, or even a little fisher, but an open, orange rigid inflatable boat. It had the usual steering wheel on a centrally placed control console. Behind that there was a black leatherette motorbike-style seat for two.

This was going to be a dangerous stunt in so many ways.

Sally looked out at the sea.

There was a definite swell building.

She needed to make things go as smoothly as possible, so she talked briefly to the First Assistant, pointing out that it would be extremely unwise to enter a rigid inflatable boat wearing stiletto heels. Daniel wanted her to keep them on but, after some discussion, the First, clearly worried, relayed Sally's concern and persuaded him. Foreseeing the boat deflating, stabbed by a stiletto, before they could complete the scene, the First took Sally aside and worked out a routine in which she could appear to try getting into the RIB in heels, lose her balance on the pebbles and, in a moment of anger, take the shoes off and fling them furiously into the carcass of the boat before she herself jumped in after them and took control of the throttle.

The scene could be very funny, especially as she was in an evening gown, sparkling at all points.

Wanting to get it right, while the camera crew were focusing the lights, Sally walked down to the water's edge and went through the sequence a few times by herself.

It was difficult to do it properly without Eggy. She tried to put the stilettos back on. But she realised that when jumping on the stones without shoes she had laddered her tights. That would be fine later, but would look all wrong at the top of the scene when she was supposed to appear like any other guest leaving a posh party.

She jammed the shoes on and ran, or rather hobbled, at speed up the beach to the wardrobe mistress. A runner was sent up the slope to the cars to drive back to base and fetch a few pairs of fresh tights from the wardrobe wagon.

While Sally was hanging around behind the camera crew, Sophie from the wardrobe department brought a warm coat and slung it around her. Sally asked if anyone knew where Eggy had got to.

Everybodys' shoulders hunched.

'Nobody has a clue,' said Sophie. 'No reply from his phone. No call in to anyone on the crew. Wife hasn't seen him since this morning.'

'What if he doesn't turn up?' Sally shivered and hugged the coat closer. 'Will they put off shooting this scene till tomorrow?'

'They can't do that,' said the Third Assistant, pulling away from the gaggle of make-up and wardrobe girls, cradling a cup of coffee. 'Tomorrow we have to start on the principals. Marina Martel and Steve Baxter. No possibility of rescheduling anything. It's now or never. If he doesn't show in the next ten minutes, we'll have to put someone else into the scene wearing his costume.'

'What about the lines?'

'We'll keep his back to camera, then post-synch. Get him in for an ADR in London or something.'

Sally knew that this would be a very sad way of finishing this job – having to do her last scene with one of the crew.

Plus she knew from experience that it was far easier to get your laughs – and this scene could be hilarious – if you were fed the cues by an actor, an expert, which Eggy assuredly was.

She walked slowly back down to the water's edge. The RIB was being seen to by various tech guys.

'We're putting in some lighting, hidden by the outboard.'

'And how will we communicate?'

'We thought we'd tape a mobile phone to the console but it's too noticeable.'

'No point anyway.' Sally looked around at the rocks either side of the bay, the craggy hill looming up behind the beach. 'You lose signal quite early out there.'

'Like your co-star,' Daniel pulled his face away from the camera and laughed sarcastically. 'Well, I'm sure it'll work fine without any communication. You just drive out to the horizon and then you turn back.'

Sally resisted the urge to ask whether the director belonged to the Flat Earth Society. Didn't everyone know that as you move forward so does the horizon?

Well. She'd work all that out later. Now she just wanted to get on with it. But where was Eggy?

———

Gasping for breath after her run up the hill, Theresa entered the Hotel Astra. She climbed up the stairs to the second floor and banged on the door of the room which she hoped would correspond with the window Neil was using to talk Shakespeare to Chloe.

Roger opened up.

He looked tired and depressed.

'Is Chloe in here?'

Roger pulled a face of incomprehension. 'Should she be?'

'Where's Neil?'

'I don't know.' Roger shrugged. 'A few minutes ago, he was locked in the bathroom, babbling to himself, then suddenly he shut up and raced out of the room like a lightning bolt.'

'So did Chloe.' Theresa hoped Roger knew how serious this situation was. 'Chloe was staying down in my flat for safekeeping. They've obviously run off again.'

'Oh bloody hell.' Roger turned and grabbed a jacket. 'We've got to find them. I don't want that bloody bossy bitch of a schoolteacher on my back again.' He paused and winced. 'Oops. Sorry. She's your daughter, isn't she? Ah well. No time for manners now. Let's go!'

Theresa followed Roger down the corridor to the stairs. Her phone buzzed. She answered, praying it would be Chloe.

'Theresa, it's Sally. Please could you try Phoebe Markham again. I have to get Eggy here. I'm so worried.'

Theresa was now torn. She had to get out and search for Chloe. But it would be too petty not to tell Sally that she had seen him.

'I know where he is,' she replied. 'Hotel Astra.'

'Jesus!' cried Sally. 'What the hell is he doing there?'

'Look. We've lost Chloe again. I'll do my best.'

Theresa hung up, but as she passed the hotel reception desk she paused to tell the clerk that there was a man trapped in a room on about the third or fourth floor.

'Oh that's all right,' said the clerk. 'We know all about that. It's an actor rehearsing a part. The lady with him told us he was not to be disturbed.'

'Grandma!' Theresa spun round to find Lola grabbing at her skirts. Roger, she noticed, had also been stopped and was now in a tense conversation with a woman who looked very like his ex-wife Cynthia.

'I think you should definitely check on him,' Theresa explained to the desk clerk. 'He may be acting but he doesn't look at all well.'

'But I ...'

'Just do it!' snapped Theresa.

The clerk slithered out from behind the desk and ran up the stairs, skeleton key in hand.

'Have you come to visit your special room, Grandma?' asked Lola. 'Cressy and I found it the other day when we were exploring.'

Over the child's shoulder, Theresa could see that it was actually Cynthia, who now looked extremely elegant and self-contained. Nothing at all like the drunken woman they had visited days before.

She was standing close to Roger, but the couple were quarrelling – and the subject was their son Neil.

Theresa moved across to them.

'We should go, Roger,' she said. 'They can't have got far. I just have to take my other granddaughter back to her mother.' Theresa took Lola by the hand. 'Where's Mummy, darling?'

'Mummy's gone out to see the ballet at Monte Carlo. We're sitting in the bar with Frances, the magic dragon. She can make smoke come out of her nose. Come along.' Lola tugged at Theresa's hand, pulling her along the passageway.

'Roger, Cynthia,' she called back over her shoulder. 'Please wait for me. I can't be responsible for the loss of two grandchildren in one day. I won't be a minute.'

Both Roger and Cynthia stood together still, stabbing at their phones, presumably trying to contact Neil.

Lola turned off the corridor and pushed Theresa through a door marked 'Storeroom. No Entry'.

'This isn't the bar,' said Theresa, pulling back.

'No. It's your room, Grandma.'

As Lola marched into the tiny room, Theresa remained on the threshold, not believing her eyes.

The walls were covered with photos of herself. Photos blown up to gigantic size. The photo of her on the terrace. Photos from the album. Photos of her walking along the quay, sitting on benches, having breakfast on the terrace of the brasserie this morning. A photo of her in her nightgown, staring up in the darkness.

'Did you do this?' Theresa didn't know why she had asked such a stupid question. This was clearly not the work of a child. She glanced along the countertops and shelves. Boxes marked *Serviettes*, *Plateaux* and *Nappes*, piled high. There was a glass-fronted refrigerator.

Inside were more boxes, marked *OEufs*, *Bacon* and *Saucissons*.

It was obviously the storeroom for things the hotel used for breakfasts and room service. And by the look of the refrigerator, Cyril had recently been here.

A touch on Theresa's shoulder and she leaped into the air. But it was only Frances.

'Lola! You little rascal. Theresa! Thank goodness for that. I thought Lola had done a runner too.'

'How did you know?'

'My God! A shrine!' Frances stopped short and peered over Theresa's shoulder. 'What's this all about? Is it an art installation of some kind?'

'I have a stalker.' Theresa lowered her voice to reply into Frances's ear. 'It seems that Lola has just discovered his hideout.'

'Come along, Lola.' Frances raised her voice and stretched out a hand behind her. 'Let's get back to that jigsaw, eh?'

As Frances shoved Lola along the corridor, she turned back to Theresa.

'What did you mean when you said, "How did you know?" You haven't lost Chloe again, have you?'

'Between you and me, Frances, yes, I have.' Theresa shut the door of the room which was a strange place of devotion, dedicated to herself. 'But it was literally minutes ago that she ran out of my front door. And we all know she's gone to Neil. His parents, Roger and Cynthia, are at reception. We've got to find them. Now!'

Theresa took a step away. Once more Frances touched her shoulder.

'And who was responsible for that little reliquary inside there?' Frances tipped her head in the direction of the storeroom. 'Do you know?'

'I think it's a man called Cyril. He's been weird to me for a few weeks now.'

'And who is Cyril? An ex?'

'Absolutely not.' Theresa was appalled at the very thought. 'He's the local butcher.'

'Butcher!' Frances pulled a face of horror. 'Good luck with that, Theresa!'

Theresa ran out to join Neil's parents.

When she reached reception she found Edgar Markham standing there, naked but for a towel. He was yelling loudly in English to the desk clerk, telling him that he must call him a cab, pronto.

Such was the state of Edgar's agitation the clerk could not understand a word he was saying.

Theresa hastily translated.

'That bloody woman of yours.' Edgar spun round to face Theresa. 'She tied me up. Took away my clothes. Your friend. And Sally's.'

Theresa hadn't a notion what he was talking about.

'Tall. Blonde. Very strong ... as I discovered when I tried to fight her off.' He ran his hand over his bald patch. 'God. I'm so late on to set. This is a disaster. A disaster! And it's my last filming day.'

'How do you know she's a friend of mine and Sally's?' asked Theresa, edging towards the front door, where Roger and Cynthia were still standing, squabbling.

'Because she bloody drove up to that godforsaken village to pick Sally up that sodding night when we both got stranded. Or so she told me today. I was too bloody drunk to remember her. But I met her for lunch because I was labouring under the mistaken impression that she was going to be fun.'

A wardrobe girl ran down the beach and thrust hand warmers into Sally's icy hands. 'You'll die of cold, darling.'

'What a mess.' Sally held her coat tight but in the gusting wind it made little difference. 'Where is he?'

One of the runners was getting into Eggy's costume and the scene would soon be ready to shoot.

Sally turned towards the sea, pulled her phone from her handbag and hastily tried Eggy's number once more. Voicemail. After leaving another desperate message she went to turn the phone off again but it rang in her hand. She picked up.

'Hi, Mum. I thought you'd be at work.'

'Marianne?' Sally stooped over the phone. 'I *am* at work. What do you want?'

'Oh, charming. Well, I was phoning to tell you there's been a change of plan. I'm sitting in the bar of the Hotel Astra, and, well, the bloke who I've been after, you know, Roger ... well, his wife's turned up.'

'So leave him alone, then.'

'But they're divorced …'

'What has it to do with me? Do what you want.'

'I wondered if you had any tips. How I can keep hold of him.'

'Oh, for God's sake, Marianne. I'm at work. Go and get a copy of *Barbara Cartland's Guide to Dating* or something. But don't disturb me again.'

She hung up and slipped the phone into her prop handbag.

One of the runners, dressed in Eggy's evening suit, sidled up to her. 'Hi. I'm Mike. I know I'll be dubbed, but do you want to go through the lines with me? I really have never acted before and …'

Jeez! This was all Sally needed. But obviously it would be better for her if she was given her cues in the correct order. So, for a minute or two, they bantered the lines back and forth.

Sally's phone rang again. 'Mum. Your friend Theresa was here! And some hubbub with that actor bloke you were with at the Negresco. They were naked in a room or something …'

'What?'

'Now Theresa's gone off with Roger and his wife.'

'I've got no time for this. Sorry.' She swiped to end the call and dropped the phone back into her bag.

While the runner muttered Eggy's lines, Sally tried to make sense of what Marianne had said. Theresa had been naked in a room with Eggy at the Hotel Astra. Marianne was obviously bonkers; either that or desperately trying *anything* to get her attention. Well, fine, she would phone her back later, when work was over and she was in the make-up wagon getting her slap off.

They tried to go through the lines again, but the First Assistant came running down to the water's edge and interrupted them. 'Sally! Urgent.' He was holding out a phone. 'It's Marianne. Hotel Astra?'

Sally couldn't believe her ears.

'What?'

'She needs to talk to you right now. It's very important.'

'For crying out loud! Honestly, I've had enough of today. Seriously?' Sally took the phone. 'Look, Marianne, why don't you just piss off and leave me alone. You're getting on my nerves. So just bugger off and sort out your own boring love life. I'm too busy for this puerile crap.'

When she handed the phone back she saw that the First Assistant's expression was one of shock. His mouth had fallen open. He was almost a comedy picture of astonishment: eyebrows raised, eyes wide open and a gaping O for a mouth.

'What?' she asked. 'What? Why the face?'

'You do know who you were just talking to?'

'My daughter Marianne, from the Hotel Astra.'

'No, Sally. That was the producer and star, Marina. Marina Martel calling from the Hotel Astor.'

Sally's intake of breath was so severe she almost lost her balance. She reached out for the mobile phone. 'I misheard you.' She stuck out her hand, pleading. 'Give me that thing. Call her back. Call her again for me. I thought it was my daughter, Marianne. Stupid hotels with names so alike.'

The First Assistant was still gaping at Sally. 'We can't phone her. They won't put us through. When she needs us *she* phones in.'

'Oh, no.' Sally put her face into her hands. What had she done? 'Can this evening get any worse?'

As Roger, Cynthia and Theresa ran down the hill, Theresa shouted out, 'Where exactly are we heading?'

'How would I know?' cried Cynthia Muffett. 'I've only just arrived.'

'I thought you knew, Theresa.' Roger stopped in his tracks. 'We can't just run around aimlessly, like headless bloody chickens. We need a plan.'

'Perhaps we should check my flat again, in case they've gone back there.'

'Whatever ...' said Cynthia. 'Honestly, Roger. I knew that stupid judge should never have let Neil choose where he wanted to live. You're incapable.'

'I know I am.' Roger let out a sob. 'I know. Really. I'm so sorry. I made such a mistake.'

'Doing what?'

'Everything!'

The three turned on to the quayside, scanning the street for a sight of the two teenagers.

Cynthia jammed her phone to her ear, trying Neil's number again.

Theresa opened up and ran through the flat, searching all the rooms.

'Have they taken any food?' asked Cynthia, standing on the threshold. 'Could you check?'

Theresa hastily threw open the fridge and looked. 'No, nothing. Oh wait. They took some chocolate brownies.'

'Typical kids,' said Cynthia. 'Always fantasy over reality.'

'Oh buggeration!' Roger was agitatedly patting his jacket pockets, checking them all in a frantic manner. 'My keys. They've taken my ruddy keys.'

'The keys to what?' Cynthia turned to him with an ominous stare. 'The keys to what, Roger?'

Roger threw his hands up and shouted, 'To the bloody boat, that's what.'

'I can see that it would be a good place to hide and be alone,' said Theresa. 'Where is your boat moored?'

'Here. In Bellevue-sur-Mer.'

'Good. Let's go.' Leading them, Theresa ran along the quay towards the Gare Maritime and the tiny *port de plaisance* behind it.

Darkness was falling fast. The street lights flickered on.

Desperately out of breath, the three turned into the small harbour, and stood together, panting at the water's edge.

'Which pontoon?' asked Theresa, looking out at about fifty boats moored in lines of white.

'This one.'

'What's the boat's name?'

Roger and Cynthia spoke at once –

Cynthia: '*Sea Nymph 2*.'

Roger: '*The Bitch Got The House*.'

There was a short pause while Cynthia took this in.

'You changed the name of the boat? Don't you know that it's unlucky, Roger? You should *never* change a boat's name.'

'Superstitious rot.'

'Fine. Could you repeat the name, please, Roger?' Cynthia took a small step back. 'And slightly louder this time?'

He hung his head and said quietly, '*The Bitch Got The House*.'

Cynthia turned and slapped his face.

'Ow! That hurt.'

'So did the new name of our boat.'

'Mr and Mrs Muffett! Please! We need to get on to your boat. Now.'

Theresa followed Roger along the wooden pontoon.

He looked around. 'What?'

His face wore a sudden look of horror.

'Where?' Panicked, he turned in each direction.

'Where's it gone?'

'What do you mean, "Where's it gone?"' Cynthia was pulling at Roger's jacket. 'Roger? Roger! Please tell me you're joking.'

'No, Cyn.' Roger ran both hands through his hair. 'No, I'm not.' He put his palms up, covering his nose and mouth. 'Our boat's not here.'

'Now, Roger!' Theresa stepped in, trying for some sense. 'You're *certain* that this is where you left it?'

'Yes!' Roger flung his hands out in a wide circle. 'Of course I'm bloody certain this is where I left it.'

'There's no need to be rude, Rog. The poor woman is trying to help us.'

'And find my granddaughter.'

'Oh yes. Yes.' Cynthia peered into the dark. 'Do they know how to turn the lights on? You can't go floating out on a boat at night with no lights ...'

'They don't know anything.' Roger started to weep. 'I never let him drive. He hasn't got a clue.'

'Neither of them can drive a boat.' Theresa was very frightened indeed. And worst of all, she knew that it was her fault for letting Chloe out of her sight. 'Come on, you two. This situation has just got very serious.'

'Does this boat with a pathetic name still have a tracking device?' asked Cynthia.

'I haven't an inkling.' Roger shook his head. 'I never really worked anything much out except stop and go.'

'Come on, Rog. Concentrate now.' Cynthia stroked his elbow. 'For God's sake, man. It must have a tracking device. These days even a mobile phone can be tracked, let alone a million-pound boat.'

'I have an idea.' Theresa pulled out her phone.

There was one person of her acquaintance who would certainly know how to track a missing pleasure boat.

Sally was standing at the water's edge with Eggy's stand-in. She was so cold she could barely feel her feet. Judy was fussing around with her hair, Sophie was photographing how the jewellery was positioned, getting her ready for a take, when the Second Assistant came bounding down the beach with the news that Eggy had not only been found, but he was a few minutes away, in a cab heading straight for the location.

Mike, the stand-in, was hurried up the beach and divested of Eggy's costume.

One more time Sally turned away from the crew and took out her phone. She had tried every ruse she could think of to call Marina Martel and apologise, try to explain the nature of the misunderstanding. But at the Grand Hotel Astor, Monte Carlo, as at all hotels when hosting a mega-star, Marina Martel was booked in under a code name and, unless you knew that, no one on the switchboard would even admit that she was a resident, let alone put you through.

Sally moved over to the First Assistant for a further conversation on the subject, but he was adamant. Marina Martel called the set. The set did not call Marina Martel.

'Sally?'

One of the tech guys called her down to the boat.

'We'd like you to get in place and get the engine going. Just so we can time things.'

Sally removed her high heels, giving her feet a quick rub in the hope they might regain some feeling, and hopped into the boat. She looked at the motorcycle-style double saddle.

'I'm in evening dress,' she said. 'How on earth can I get astride that?'

'Daniel would like you to try taking her out while standing up … if you could.'

'But there's nowhere to stand,' she replied, pointing to the console. 'I'll need Wardrobe to put a slit in the dress. Wouldn't that be noticed? Where's the camera boat?'

'There won't be one,' said the cameraman. 'We're close in on your getting up and setting off, then we're doing a long shot. You saw the sparks team installing some lamps to a battery hidden down at the back …'

'Stern,' said Sally automatically.

' … the stern,' the cameraman corrected himself. 'Well, the plan is that they'll keep you well lit all the way out to sea, so that we can follow you precisely. Hopefully we'll keep turning till you're a mere spot on the horizon.' He glanced at his watch. 'Daniel? While we're waiting for Mr Markham, perhaps we could switch the shots?'

Daniel looked across at his assistant.

'I think we ought to do the long shot first, whatever. This wind is picking up and I'd like to get that one in the can before it's too late. With a rising sea like this we can work in the waves at the water's edge, but I imagine it'll be hard to keep the boat in focus if it's bouncing all over the place out there.'

Sally looked out to sea. From the look of those waves the RIB would certainly be bouncing all over the place, even if she left this minute. She'd have a job keeping it upright.

'You? Stephane, is it?' The cameraman signalled to one of the grips. 'You're wearing black. As long as we make a thing later of Mr Markham removing his top hat in the first shot, when he climbs aboard, we can use you on the long shot ...' He pointed towards the boat. 'In you get.'

As the chief electrician came out of the RIB, which was now brilliantly lit, tentatively Stephane climbed in.

Sally helped him get astride the pillion, while she had no option but to ride side-saddle.

'OK, folks.' The First Assistant signalled to the crew to prepare. 'We're going for a take on this.'

The clapperboard went into position.

'Sound?'

'Speed.'

'Camera?'

'Running.'

'Scene 198. Take one.'

'Stop!' Eggy panted as he trotted down the sand, fastening his shirt buttons as he came towards the boat. 'I'm here. WAIT! I'm here!'

'And cut.' Daniel sank back on to his shooting stick. 'Quick as you can now. And look, while we're here, let's shoot Eggy getting in, with the lines, please.' He turned to the First Assistant, then looked up at the sky, then at his watch. 'Let's run it all into one scene. Do the scene with Sally already in the boat. OK? Just for now. We can fiddle it in the edit. But at least we'll have something.'

The First Assistant nodded and held up his hand for silence. 'Start positions, everyone!'

Stephane moved away and Eggy stood a few feet back from the boat.

'Turn on the engine, please, Sally.'

Sally fired up. She so wanted to quiz Eggy about where he had been, and what the hell Theresa had to do with it.

'Take her out a little from the shore.'

The crew pushed the back of the boat forward, and it started bucking on the wave crests.

'Sound?'

'Speed.'

'Camera?'

'Running.'

'Scene 198. Take two.'

'And ... action!'

Eggy stood poised and Sally waited for the call to start the lines, but all they could hear was the roar of the engine.

'And cut!'

The First Assistant waded out to the boat.

'Did you not hear us call "Action"?'

'No!' shouted Sally and Eggy in unison.

'All I can hear is the motor,' Sally explained.

'Me too,' said Eggy.

'Mr Markham, maybe you could turn slightly towards me now and on Action I will give you a visual,' shouted the First. 'Watch for my signal.'

He made his way back to the beach.

'Miss Doyle, you will know when to drive away because Mr Markham will be climbing on to the seat behind you.'

'Sound?'

'Speed.'

'Camera?'

'Running.'

Eggy turned to look out for the signal.

'Scene 198. Take three.'

'And ... action.' The First's hand slashed downwards.

Eggy waded into the waves, shouting, 'Don't go without me, old girl!' then clambered over the orange rubber side of the boat, and took his position behind Sally.

'Hold tight!' she cried. Part of the script. 'Next stop Bank of England!'

Sally pushed the throttle and the boat took off into the bay.

'I'm so sorry, Sally. You cannot imagine ...' Eggy shouted into her ear but the wind swallowed most of his words.

'Not now, Eggy.' Sally would have loved nothing more than to punch his lights out. But not while the cameras were turning.

As the little RIB smashed into an oncoming wave, it jolted and then crashed down into the trough behind.

'Jesus!' Eggy cried as he slid off the seat, then rapidly clambered back up. 'Bloody hell! This is more than I was expecting.'

Sally gritted her teeth. 'I did say "Hold tight."'

Eggy flung his arms around Sally's waist. Sally still had her prop handbag dangling from one arm. As they shot out into the deeper bay, it started really annoying her, blowing all over the place, thumping against the control console, slamming into her chest.

'Take my bag, Eggy!'

'What?'

'TAKE MY HANDBAG! HANDBAG!'

'Righto, Lady Bracknell.' Eggy held on with one hand and slid the bag from Sally's arm with the other. 'It's vibrating!'

'Jesus!' Sally knew what this would be. She turned back towards the shore. She hoped they were far enough out now. 'It's my phone. It'll be Marina Martel. Answer it.'

'WHAT?'

'My phone. ANSWER IT.'

Eggy opened the bag and put the phone to his ear.

'What? Who? Right. Hello. Well, we're ... Yes, I'll tell her.' He slipped the phone back into the bag.

'Well?'

'It was your friend Theresa. Her granddaughter and the boy Neil have taken his father's boat out on their own from Bellevue Marina and are lost at sea. How do you track it?'

'What?'

'As Theresa hung up she said something very odd: "The Bitch Got The House".'

'How do we know when they've said "Cut"?' Sally looked over her shoulder to Eggy. 'Do we just keep on driving till we reach Corsica?'

Eggy turned round, still acting his role, then faced Sally. 'They look as though they're still turning. No one's waving us to stop or circle back or anything like that.'

Obviously Sally couldn't phone Theresa to tell her, but she realised that somebody had to call the coastguard as soon as possible.

'OK.' She stared towards the horizon. Either side of the bay, dark, rocky crags loomed, jutting out of the water. She knew from experience that the most dangerous rocks were invisible, lurking feet, sometimes inches, beneath the surface.

Keeping right in the centre of the bay, Sally opened the throttle. 'Let's go!'

Their boat was now leaping wildly out of the water, slamming down hard on the ever-increasing waves.

Sally estimated from the direction of the wind and tide that tonight, in these conditions, whichever way a pleasure boat leaving Bellevue-sur-Mer was headed, it would be swept towards this bay. The wind was howling in from the west, and the swell was also surging eastwards.

Sally herself was finding it hard to keep this little RIB on a straight course, so God knows how amateurs, let alone kids with no experience at all, would fare on a sea as high as this one.

She looked down at the console. Thank goodness, it was a normal one. No one had tampered with the layout. There was a speedo, a couple of other gauges, on her right the throttle, and on her left a ship-to-shore emergency radio. The receiver with its curling wire was in its cradle. If she caught a glimpse of the lost boat she could call in. Sally remembered that the boat was very big and very white. But there was no use doing anything now, as the radio would only locate this boat, the RIB that she and Eggy were in.

She continued her drive towards the horizon.

Stupid bloody kids.

'I don't feel very well.' Eggy, still gripping Sally's waist, was now resting his head on her shoulder.

'Head up, Eggy! Keep looking at the horizon.' Sally pushed the throttle further forward. 'And whatever you do, Eggy, do not be sick down my back!'

———————————

Theresa, Roger and Cynthia stood on the quayside stabbing at their phones, trying to find out how you called the French coastguard. Cynthia said she remembered reading stories where some English tourists, lost in the Mediterranean, had phoned the coastguard back in Falmouth, who then sent out emergency calls to the local forces in Italy or Greece or somewhere.

'That's all very well,' said Theresa, 'but we don't have a number for Falmouth either.' She shoved her phone back in her pocket. 'Look. There's no point standing here and getting cold. We'd be better off going back to my place and making calls on the landline. I've got a laptop there too.'

But Cynthia and Roger said they preferred to stay out near to the water's edge.

Theresa decided that, as she walked home, she would call the general emergency number, 112, in the hope that someone there knew what to do. But just as she started to dial, her phone rang. She answered.

'Is that Theresa?' It was a very laid-back English male voice. 'This is Mervin. The tech guy from Mrs Firbank's school. Calling from London.'

'I really can't talk now, Mervin. There's an ongoing emergency situation.'

Theresa had no idea why she was suddenly talking like Mervin.

'I know all about it, Mrs S. That's why I'm calling you. I just received a message from young Neil. He appears to be in distress. They motored out into the bay on his father's boat and they turned off the engines thinking they'd stay where they were but, what with wind, tide and all that, they're running adrift. They seem to have floated out to sea. I called Falmouth coastguard, but when I told them the boat's name – *The Bitch Got The House* – they told me to stop messing them about and hung up. So I made a few more calls and found out that you need to call somebody down in the South of France called John Darmarey who's with the Mary Team.'

'Who?'

This time Mervin spoke the words together as one phrase.

'John Darmarey, Mary Team.'

Theresa understood. 'Thank you, Mervin. I shall phone them.' She could see how, to an English tech-head, the words Gendarmerie Maritime might sound just like that.

She recalled the name was on a list of emergency numbers hanging in her kitchen on the fridge door.

'Presumably Mr Muffett can take control of the boat ...' Mervin continued. 'And all will be well.'

Theresa looked over the road at Roger Muffett, who in her opinion looked far from being in control of anything, let alone his own boat. 'No, Mervin. He's not on board. The kids took the boat without his permission. Thanks for the info. I'll just tell his parents, who are frantic. Hold on.'

She ran across to the Muffetts.

'Neil!' Cynthia had her phone to her ear. 'Neil! Pick up the bloody phone.'

'I've got the school's tech guy on the line.' Theresa spoke to Roger, who was pacing around, forever wringing his hands, like a domestic Lady Macbeth in some soap opera. 'He's been in touch with the boat. I'm going over there to my flat.' She pointed. 'It's behind that parked van. The blue door. I'm going to call the French emergency services.'

As she ran back across the road, heading home, she resumed her call to Mervin.

'OK. Call this number again if you hear anything more. I'm going home right now to call the Gendarmerie Maritime. Bye.'

Theresa had her finger resting on the red button to cut off his call when she heard his anguished cry.

'Wait! Wait! Don't go, Mrs S. I'm just getting another message from Neil. He says the boat has stopped now.'

'That's good news. Isn't it?' Theresa hoped that if the boat was not moving further away, they might have the chance to catch up with it.

'Erm, it *should* be good news.' Mervin's voice had taken on a new, sinister tone. 'Except that Neil says it stopped because they just hit some rocks ... And there seems to be water coming in.'

Theresa squeezed past the bumper of the little parked van, noticing that her front door was ajar and her lights were still on.

She obviously had left so quickly she couldn't have shut up properly.

She shoved the door open, simultaneously slipping the phone into her pocket so that she would feel it vibrate if Mervin should call back. She walked briskly inside, heading straight towards the kitchen counter and the landline telephone.

Quickly consulting the magnetic list of emergency services on the fridge, she picked up the receiver.

'Theresa?'

Theresa spun round, to see a man emerging from her bedroom.

It was Cyril, and in his right hand was a large, sharp knife.

TWENTY-FIVE

WHEN SALLY TURNED AROUND to look for Eggy, who was no longer holding on to her, she could see him on his knees, grabbing hold of the ropes along the side. He was heaving.

She immediately slowed the boat down so that she could be heard.

'Eggy!' She waved her free arm at him. 'Do NOT lean over the side. You could be thrown into the water.'

'What can I do?' he wailed. 'Help me, Sally.'

She cut the engine off. The boat was now floating on the rolling sea, bucking up and down worse than when they had the thrust of engine power propelling them over the crests of the waves.

Sally looked around for a receptacle. It was usual always to keep a bucket on board small craft.

'Here.' Sally grabbed Eggy's top hat, which he had jammed under the seat. 'Use this!'

From where she sat, the shore was now nothing but a speckle of tiny lights.

'They can't want us to go further than this,' she shouted. 'They have got to have captured their shot. I'm turning back.'

She wasn't sure whether or not Eggy had heard her. The noise from the wind seemed to swallow her speech.

The RIB was now tossing from side to side, water sploshing over the transom.

She had to get the engine back on and start moving. Then the boat would be once more under her own control rather than drifting at the whim of the sea. She tried to get a purchase on the saddle, but, with her long, tight skirt, now that the leatherette was covered in spray, it was impossible to hold on.

'Sod this!' Sally bent down, gripped the bottom of her dress and tore it up the seam to her waist. 'They'll have to make a repair for the other shot when we get back to shore.'

'If we ever make it back to shore,' Eggy whimpered.

Sally managed to climb astride the wet saddle, and face the console.

She turned the key to start the engine.

It spluttered.

'Not now, not now,' she murmured to the controls. 'Come on. Come on.'

She turned again.

The engine engaged for a brief moment then cut out.

'Come on, old thing! COME ON! For God's sake.'

Once more she turned the key.

This time a mere gurgle, followed by nothing.

Sally took hold of the radio receiver. Now she knew she had to call at least a pan-pan signal, indicating to the local coastguard that their boat had a mechanical failure.

She prayed that the radio was real and not a dummy stuck on by the props department.

Sally looked to the east. The rocks were getting nearer. Simply on the power of the tide the boat was racing towards them at great speed.

She switched on the radio and pressed the Urgency Alert button. She waited for the decreed fifteen seconds, pressed the transmission button and shouted into the microphone. 'Pan-pan, PAN-PAN, PAN-PAN.' She left a pause. She had no name for the vessel, nor an exact position. 'Bay of Èze. Engine failure. Require a tow. Two persons on board. Pan-pan, pan-pan, pan-pan. Over.'

As she slid the radio mic back into its holster, she realised that the nearest coastguard station was in Nice and, unless a ship happened to be already on a nearby call, they would be waiting out here a good half hour before anyone could reach them.

She looked at her watch. She had forgotten that Wardrobe had taken her own watch and replaced it with an idiotic, female-sized minuscule evening thing, with a clock face which was impossible to read without a microscope.

She guessed it must be about nine o'clock.

She had another go at starting up the engine. When nothing happened she shouted a hail of curses up to the sky.

And it was at that moment that, straight ahead, she saw the end of the white gin palace which bore the asinine name *The Bitch Got The House*.

The words were clearly visible on the prow.

The boat itself was on the rocks, slamming hard against them. The pointed white bow reared up out of the water, the aft end of the craft was submerged. The transom was obviously shattered.

Sally could just about make out two human shapes, perched at the top of the only part of the boat untouched by water. The kids were clinging to the shining silver rails of the foredeck, screaming for help.

Once more Sally grabbed the radio mic and made a call: 'MAYDAY, MAYDAY, MAYDAY.'

———

Theresa dropped the receiver.

Cyril took a step towards her.

'Let me explain ...' He spoke slowly and in French. 'I am here to save you ...'

Theresa put up her hands, though what defence could they provide against a knife?

She could try to talk him down. But as her French was poor and his English even worse, she knew it would be too difficult.

Then she had a better idea. She pulled open a drawer, reached inside and pulled out the very knife which he had sent her.

She held it out before herself, gripping the handle with both hands. They stood still, facing one another like pistol carriers at a duel, looking one another in the eye, each holding steady.

Nobody moved.

'What do you want, Cyril?' Theresa's heart was pounding so hard she feared it would burst. 'Why are you here, holding a knife towards me?'

'A bad man is hunting.' Cyril glanced down at the knife in his hand. 'I came to tell you.'

'Cyril! Please put the knife down.' Theresa slipped slowly around the edge of the counter and took a few steps back towards the front door. 'Why are you pursuing me? What do you want?'

'I am married.' Cyril swung the knife down, dangling it at his side. He started speaking in a stumbling English. 'My wife. I give you cake. My wife is drugged. But at Hotel Astra I have room of you ... Lovely photos! *Attention!* I am love you.'

Theresa was near the front door, which she had left ajar for Roger and Cynthia to follow her in.

She took one more step back and was able to kick it wide open.

'*Theresa! Non! Non! Attendez! Attention!*'

Edging backwards through the door, Theresa yelled out for Roger, then turned and fled into the street.

She physically bumped into William, strolling along with Carol.

She pointed back towards her flat.

'Cyril,' she gasped. 'With a knife.'

'Oh God!' Carol grasped Theresa by the elbow and dragged her along at speed in the direction of the brasserie. 'Let's get you somewhere where there are lots of people around you.' She turned to William and told him that Cyril had gone mad and taken to stalking Theresa.

'That's not all, Carol, William. Please help me. I've lost Chloe again. This time she and Neil took his father's boat and they're out there, somewhere floating around in this rough sea. They've nothing to eat but those chocolate brownies—'

'They've what?' William stopped and dramatically put his face in his hands. 'The brownies? You are joking?'

'No. The ones you left me. They took them.'

William's mouth wiggled into about seven contrasting positions before he finally said: 'The brownies are hash.'

'What?'

'They're dope brownies. Marijuana. Cyril's wife left them for you. You got really high, remember, when you ate them? That night when Odile de la Warr deigned to grace us with her imperious presence.'

'I was drugged?'

'Well … sort of …' William shook his head in exasperation. 'Yes. But in a good way.'

'God in heaven! Call the emergency services, NOW. I have to save those bloody children. They're adrift, lost at sea, and, thanks to me, stoned out of their minds.' Theresa staggered up the step on to the brasserie terrace.

'Oh God. If only we had a boat, we could go after them ourselves.'

'Theresa? Is something wrong?' Marcel stepped forward to welcome them. 'You should have come to me. I do have a boat, you know.'

'Really?' Theresa looked at him. 'There's too much going on to explain. Cyril has gone mad. And when she gets back from the ballet, my daughter will kill me. And ... poor Chloe. Oh God.' She teetered, feeling as though she might faint from sheer anxiety.

'Come along,' said Marcel forcefully. 'You should take a brandy.'

'No,' Theresa replied firmly. She really wanted her wits about her until she had Chloe and Neil back on dry land.

'Come this way, Theresa.' Breaking into a run, Marcel led her across to the quay. He turned back and shouted to Carol and William. 'We'll find them. Have no fear.'

Marcel's vessel was a little fisher boat, not much more than a canopy over the helm and an open rear deck. He leaped into the well of the boat and held his hand up to help Theresa down.

Once she was settled on the back seat, a simple white board across the transom, he threw her a life jacket and sprang up on to the jetty to untie the guy-ropes. Keeping hold of the last rope wrapped around the iron capstan, he stepped inside and moved under the canopy to get the engine going. Then he pulled in the rope and stowed it beside him at the helm.

Just as the little boat started edging away from the stone quayside, there was a loud shout from the shore, and Roger Muffett leaped aboard.

With the sudden weight balance the boat rocked violently.

'Wait for me.' Cynthia ran towards the edge of the quay, but, without turning around, Marcel opened the throttle and they sped away.

'We should go back for her,' shouted Theresa. 'Her son is on the missing yacht.'

But Marcel clearly did not hear her plea, for the boat's speed increased. They pulled out of the sheltered harbour, heading towards the dark horizon.

Roger stood up. He took mini steps towards the wheel-house, until he was standing just behind Marcel.

Theresa was still seated right beside the outboard motor, so couldn't hear their conversation. But Roger was gesticulating wildly towards the shore, while Marcel shook his head.

Roger shrugged and walked towards Theresa. He was pulling a grimace. They were not turning back for Cynthia.

Then Marcel stopped the engine.

Roger smiled and made a thumbs-up at Theresa.

Marcel ran towards Roger and grappled him from behind.

Theresa was so startled she had no idea what was happening.

The two men struggled, causing the boat to rock peril-ously. Roger lost his footing and put out his hand to steady himself. At that moment Marcel gave him a sharp shove, toppling him over the side.

Roger splashed into the black water.

Theresa looked to Roger, then back up to Marcel, who made a gesture of wiping his hands and moved calmly back to the helm.

Theresa was horrified. She looked around for something to throw after Roger – a lifebuoy or something, anything that he could grab on to, until they could fish him out. There was nothing.

'Help! Help!'

Roger was bobbing up and down, gasping for breath.

'I can't swim.'

Theresa pulled off her own life jacket and tossed it into the sea. As it hit the water, it immediately inflated.

'Roger! Grab that,' she cried, hanging on to the side of the boat and leaning out.

'Marcel,' she called forward, 'do you have a boathook or something to help pull Roger aboard?'

But Marcel kept his back to her.

He started up the engine again.

'Watch out! Marcel!' Theresa was anxious lest Roger get caught up in the current and pulled under, or, worse, cut up by the rotor blades. 'Marcel! Turn off! Marcel! *Coupez! Arrêtez!*'

But Marcel simply thrust forward the lever and the boat raced into the darkness.

Theresa looked back, tracing the pale wake, trying to see where Roger was.

If only he could swim.

The nearest point of the quayside was a mere twenty metres away.

She got to her feet and, hunched over to grip the sides, edged forward towards the wheelhouse.

'Marcel?' She stood as soon as she reached the canopy. 'Why did you do that? Marcel?'

Marcel continued to look straight ahead.

Then he turned and glanced at Theresa.

He twisted around to look back towards the shore, which was now simply a necklace of tiny lights.

'Marcel! You can't just throw people overboard.'

Marcel cut the engine for the second time.

Good, thought Theresa. Now he's going to turn back and rescue poor Roger.

'Why can't I?' He looked Theresa in the eye. 'Roger was not invited.'

Marcel stooped. It looked to Theresa as though he was about to tie a shoelace. But he flipped a handle in the blank wall.

A hatchway opened.

It led down into a tiny cabin.

Marcel gently slid his arm around Theresa's waist and edged her to the open hatch.

'Don't they say three is a crowd?'

From the threshold Theresa could see that the space was completely filled by a bed.

The bed was strewn with heart-shaped cushions.

'Now, at last, Theresa,' whispered Marcel, 'we are alone together.'

Shock froze Theresa to the spot.

Every inch of the curving, white fibreglass walls of the boat's hull was decorated with photographs of herself.

'So many things have transpired to keep us apart, my darling. But, out here, no one can disturb us till dawn, my beautiful, beloved Theresa.'

Sally let the little RIB drift close to the wreckage of the large gin palace.

The wind was whipping her hair around her face, and when she tried to shout the gusts seemed to thrust the words back down her throat.

'Come down with us, into this boat.'

Chloe was sobbing.

Neil leaned forward to shout down.

'It's too scary. What if we slip?'

Sally looked at the remains of *The Bitch Got The House* and realised it would only take a few more large waves to break the bow completely away from what was left.

Any wave coming in would also knock the two kids back and on to the rocks.

Still astride the seat, Sally stretched out a hand. The rubber edges of her RIB were rubbing along the white walls of the larger boat, squeaking.

'Come on.' She tried to sound calm. 'Come now. One at a time.'

Neil shot Chloe a look, then, holding on to the back of her T-shirt, he edged her forward until she flopped down from the white boat and landed on the inflated side of Sally's RIB.

'Now you, Neil.'

Scrambling, face up, on all fours, like a crab, Neil moved downwards, then jumped. In his anxiety to avoid colliding with the people inside the RIB, he missed his footing on the wet rubber, and slipped into the raging water.

Together, Sally and Chloe reached out but he was too far away and being pulled by the swell.

Sally was terrified another wave might slam him back on to the rocks or sweep him out to sea.

She wrenched up one of the emergency oars which were fixed to the sides of the RIB, and thrust it out towards the rocks, resting the paddle end on the top of a crag.

Neil stretched up, clasped it from below with both hands, then inched along, walking his hands forward as though dangling from a rope.

When he reached the rubber side, he let go of the oar and, with Chloe's help, hauled himself aboard.

Throughout all this drama, Eggy was bent over at the rear of the boat, retching into his top hat.

'OK, you two. Now we have to get this boat away from those rocks and on to the tide.' Sally wrenched the other oar free from its clips and handed it to the two kids. 'Do not let that oar wash away. It's all we've got.' Still holding on to the first oar, she angled it against the rock. 'Get yours and do the same as me. OK?'

She looked across. Their oar was touching the rocks.

'And on a count of three – heave away. Push with all your might!'

The others gripped their oar which now lay parallel to Sally's.

'One, two, three – and heave!'

They pushed hard enough to edge the RIB away from the wreckage.

It moved off with the sea, bucking on the waves like a horse at a rodeo.

'Put the oar inside the boat now. Sit low on the floor and grab hold of those ropes on the side. Huddle up, but – do NOT let go.'

Sally returned to the console.

She prayed that the engine had simply been flooded and that by now it might engage.

A great wave hit them and swept them further out. Another wave followed in its wake and broke on top of them, drenching them all.

The RIB took on a lot of water.

Sally turned the key – a splutter.

She shouted down at Neil. 'Get the hat off Eggy. Empty it over that side ...' she pointed to the leeward side ' ... then use it to collect as much water as you can from the floor of the boat.'

'Look!'

As Neil turned back to face Eggy, Chloe gasped.

'The boat we were on ...'

The wave which had inundated them had scooped up the prow of *The Bitch Got The House*.

The whole boat was now nothing but a mess of broken white pieces, floating on the waves. Before their eyes the largest remaining portion sank down into the depths. All that was left was the name, bobbing on the water, slamming itself against the rugged crags.

Sally counted to three and once more turned the key.

Theresa pulled away from Marcel.

He had managed to tumble her down on to the duvet. She struggled to sit up. There was no floor to stand on; the entire tiny cabin area was filled with bed. On all fours, Theresa crawled across the heart-shaped cushions, her head scraping the ceiling, trying to reach the little hatch-way out.

Marcel grabbed her by the ankle. She was amazed how strong his grip was. She thrashed around like a floundering fish, pulling herself forward inch by inch. His hand moved up under her skirt.

'I know you love me, Theresa. You let me know all the time, my darling. And when I heard you might go back to London I panicked.'

Theresa couldn't remember saying she was going back to London, except to look for Chloe.

'There was that message on your answering machine. An office in Hampstead …' He was up beside her now, face to face. 'When the others say cruel things you are always the one to soften their words with your sweet loving heart.'

Theresa cursed the day she had ever tried to be the peacemaker.

'Soon we can be together all the time. We can anywhere, together. You said once you were free of the restaurant you could spend lots of time with me. And so you can. For I will be free too and have money. You will have anything you desire.'

Theresa twisted her head around to make sure she was looking him in the eye as she said, 'Marcel – I did not mean any of that personally. You have misunderstood me. I have no feelings for you. None. As for the restaurant ... it was all just ... the things people say and don't really mean ...'

'You do mean them. And you love me. You know you do! You told me so many times. *Je t'aime. Je t'adore.* You've said it.'

'Never! Never have I said those things.' But even as the denial came out of her mouth, she wondered whether, when reaching for a compliment in her basic French, she might have accidentally said, '*Je t'aime, je t'adore*' when she really meant *Je l'aime, je l'adore*. I love IT, I adore IT.

'You give me signs, Theresa. All the time you give me signs. You left the book for me. All those lovely photos of yourself. You felt sexy with me.' With some horror Theresa realised she must have made the elementary error of saying '*Je suis chaud*' – 'I feel sexy' – when she meant '*J'ai chaud*' – 'I am hot'. Marcel was still speaking: 'You are a lonely woman; I am a lonely man.'

As Theresa stretched forward, trying to push open the hatch, Marcel once again launched himself towards her, his hands fumbling clumsily at her breasts.

His face was close to hers now. He rolled on top of her.

She tried to escape his kiss but, as she rolled and tumbled through the mess of bedding, still aiming for the doorway, Marcel's wet, cold lips slithered over her ear.

Simultaneously he caught hold of the edge of her blouse and yanked at it. She heard the fabric rip. Buttons flew off.

She attempted to cover up her flabby body and too-tight bra. But Marcel's hands seemed to be everywhere, palpating at her flesh.

She kicked against the hull and tried to use the solid surface to lever herself forward, but with his dead weight on top of her it was impossible to get anywhere.

To make matters even worse, the little boat had started rocking violently from side to side.

Every time Theresa thought she was making progress, she would lose her balance and roll away from the hatch.

Marcel was now tugging at her skirt, trying to pull it up, stroking the naked flesh of her legs.

The boat started jerking up and down while still rolling.

Was it sinking? What was going on? Had they been sucked into a whirlpool? Would she now drown, going down with the ship, like Rebecca in that book?

Marcel was no longer trying to grope her. She looked down and could see why. He was fumbling at his fly buttons.

Twisting her body, Theresa curled into a foetal position, then suddenly stretched out and kicked the hatch open. She turned around once more and squeezed herself through the hole leading to the open air. On hands and knees, she scrambled up the step on to the deck. She lay panting for a second; then, pulling down her clothing, she clambered to her feet. Using the wheel to get herself upright, Theresa came face to face with two men.

'*Madame? Avez-vous besoin de notre aide?*'

Two burly, helmeted coastguards stood on the rocking deck of Marcel's craft.

Theresa saw the slanting French flag on the grey side of the lifeboat. She looked up. The rest of the brigade who'd come to save her were standing ready with a ladder.

'*Oui.*' Theresa collapsed into their arms. '*Oui!* Please, please help me. *S'il vous plaît.*'

SALLY'S BOAT, COMPLETE WITH three passengers, limped towards the shore. A welcoming party was waiting on the beach. The whole team was running towards them, bearing gold emergency blankets, hand warmers and hot drinks.

Sally saw the whirring blue lights of an ambulance waiting on the road above the shore.

'The poor old boy has been so ill,' she told one of the paramedics who came down to meet them.

Face white as paper, Eggy climbed out of the boat and the paramedic steered him up towards the ambulance.

Other paramedics rushed down to check out the two shivering children.

While they were rowing against the raging sea, with intermittent help from a spluttering outboard motor, the kids had told Sally that neither of them had a desire ever to run away again. All they wanted now was the warmth of a house, a home. They even told Sally, who kept them talking all the way as a protection against hypothermia, that if they had the liberty to see each other from time to time, they'd be good and go back to school in London.

Job well done, thought Sally.

More than this, Neil told her that he was going to write to the judge who saw to his parents' divorce and tell him that he had made a mistake because he really wanted to live in London, not on a boat. Never again on a boat.

Although exhausted, as Sally trudged up the shingle, while wardrobe staff surrounded her, pulling off the costume jewellery and throwing warm blankets over her wet evening dress, something about tonight's escapade made her want to dance and sing.

'Hope there wasn't a hair in the gate,' she called out as she passed the camera operator. 'Call me unprofessional, but I'm not willing to do a second take on that one. And if you don't like it you can sue me!'

'I take my hat off to you, Sally,' he replied as he started packing up his equipment. 'We caught most of what happened on a zoom lens. We'd stopped rolling, but I assure you that we never let you out of our sight.'

'You are quite the heroine,' added the First Assistant. 'Talk about sangfroid.'

'I could have done with having some way of communicating with you, actually,' she replied. 'It wasn't a good idea to let us go out there willy-nilly.'

'My bad!' Daniel, apologetic and hunched, scampered to Sally's side. 'They all wanted to give you a walkie-talkie or something, Sandy—'

'Sally!'

'I thought it might show, or you'd start using it too early and it might ruin the scene or ... it would take away from the authenticity ...'

Sally threw him a glance in disbelief.

There were no words.

'It's lucky for you, Daniel, that I know how to use a ship's radio. At least I could call in for emergency help, even if I did manage to save us before they reached us. Oh. Yes. Someone better phone them and say we've made it to land.'

Sally noticed that other members of the crew had started looking out to sea once more.

'Looks like they've got here.' The First pointed out into the bay, where a large grey lifeboat, searchlights scanning the water, was thundering in their direction.

Someone from the boat was talking through a loud-speaker.

The First Assistant grabbed his megaphone and replied in French. 'The two children are safe. They are here with the SAMU. Their boat is destroyed. Over.'

'Their grandmother is here with us, on board,' called the lifeboat. 'She wants to come ashore. Can you assist? Over.'

The First Assistant grouped as many of the crew together as he could, and they waded out to pull in the small tender, which a few minutes later carried Theresa to the shore.

Hearing the interchange, Sally turned and rushed down to the water's edge to join them, torn evening dress twinkling in the reflection of the searchlights.

'Come along, darling!' Sally looked at Theresa's clothing, which was also ripped and ruined. 'What happened to *you?*'

'Long story,' Theresa panted. 'Where are they?'

Hand in hand, the two women scrambled up the beach to the ambulance, where, wrapped in gold foil blankets, Chloe and Neil sat sipping warm drinks.

'Thank God,' cried Theresa.

Chloe jumped up and ran into her arms. 'Oh Gran! I'm so sorry.'

The two stood hugging one another for a long time.

'I'm sorry too, Mrs Simmonds.' Neil crept forward. 'My dad is going to kill me,' he said in a low voice. 'We sunk his boat.'

Theresa put out her other arm and wrapped it around Neil, at the same time hoping Roger was all right.

Sally backed slowly away. But not before overhearing the strangest snippet of conversation: 'The chocolate brownies which you took from my kitchen?'

'We didn't have time to save them. They went down with the ship before we even tasted them.'

'Thank God for that!'

Mystified, Sally moved over to the nearby seat where Eggy sprawled, exhausted, but at least displaying some colour back in his cheeks. He sat up and shot her an embarrassed smile. 'I'm so sorry, darling.' He stood and spoke to the paramedic who had been helping him. 'May I?'

The paramedic indicated that it was fine for him to go.

'I have to say, Salz, that that was one of the worst days of my whole life.' Tottering slightly, he limped along at Sally's side. 'But in the end it was worth it. Because I witnessed you being so brave and so calm. Thank you.'

'I've got to go to Wardrobe and get out of this dress.' Sally pushed her damp hair out of her face. 'And while we walk, you can tell me now why you were late on set today.'

'Oh dear,' Eggy grunted. 'You may recall I told you I had a hot lunch date.'

Sally lowered her voice to say: 'Don't tell me it was with Theresa?'

'Theresa? No! Whatever gave you that idea? It was a woman I had met on the seafront in Bellevue-sur-Mer. I invited her to lunch. I thought we would have some fun.'

'By the sound of it much too much fun.'

'She told me she had a hotel room waiting, and … well, I'm just a man, Sally …'

Sally sighed. The same old story.

'But it seems that the woman had some axe to grind with me. She's the one who came up to rescue us from that village. Actually I don't remember a thing about it.'

'Carol?'

'Yes. Carol. She had got it into her head that I was casting my favours around a little too liberally and decided to teach me a lesson by tempting me to a hotel room, where she told me she'd give me a massage ...'

'Oh Eggy!' Sally didn't know which of them she was most cross with ... or disappointed by.

The two actors climbed the steps of the wardrobe van.

'So, anyway, I undressed and lay, face down, on the bed. She knelt behind me, and I really thought she was going to give my shoulders a nice rub. But she tied my wrists. I tried to struggle but, believe me, that is one strong woman.'

Sally knew this, but now was not the moment to explain why.

'Then, once I was tied, she calmly left the room, taking all my clothing with her, and told the hotel desk that if they heard shouting coming from the room, it was just me practising my lines.'

Bloody Carol! Since when did she become the avenging angel?

Sophie emerged from the rows of costumes at the back of the wardrobe wagon door. 'Who's first? Sally?'

'Let Eggy go first.' Sally stood outside, making the most of the warm air blowing from the wardrobe caravan's fan heater.

'Don't make a fuss, will you?' called Eggy through the billowing fabric which covered the door. 'I asked for it, really.'

Sally heard Eggy sigh. 'I'm just a silly old fool.'

Sophie asked him: 'Where is the top hat?'

Before he could reply Sally called out. 'Ruined, I'm afraid, Sophie. We had to use it to bail out the boat when we were inundated.'

'I made such a fool of myself, over and over, today, didn't I?'

Sally remained silent.

'I am such a stereotypical Englishman,' he said. 'It's too embarrassing.'

'What's that got to do with anything?'

'As you know, I love Marmite, I can't live without my marmalade, or a nice cup of tea. But I am English, Sally, and you know it is every Englishman's duty to be seasick.'

The Third Assistant came up to Sally. 'While you're waiting, why not get your make-up off? It's very warm in the wagon.'

Sally trudged up the hill.

Daniel, phone stuck to his ear as normal, was lurking near the make-up van door.

'Sally!' He put the phone away so quickly that Sally wondered if there had been anyone on the line at all. 'I just have to reiterate how sorry we are and … if there's anything …'

Same old claptrap.

She wondered if she asked for a Steinway grand piano, would he come up with it? Actually she felt like slapping his face, but instead she turned and said, 'Thank you, Daniel, I'd like a whisky, please. Laphroaig, one ice cube.'

'Right. Whisky. Laphroaig. Fine. I'm on it.' Two steps of darting forward, then Daniel stopped in his tracks.

Sally knew there would be a catch, even to this simple request.

Suddenly Daniel went into something like a Uriah Heep-type grovelling bow, and his voice took on an irritating unctuous quality. 'We are so flattered …'

Sally looked up to see what or whom had so vividly caught his attention.

Wearing a cashmere coat, with silk scarf, slacks and trainers, walking down the slope which led to the film unit, came Marina Martel. She looked every inch the world-famous movie star that she was.

'Sally! My sweet! Look at you!' Marina raised her hands as she beheld the sight of Sally: ripped evening gown, littered with grit and seaweed; make-up smeared down her face; hair as unkempt as Struwwelpeter's. 'Oh, Sally, it's as though you were back on *Sssaturday Ssssslamerama!*'

'Except tonight we've reversed roles,' laughed Sally. 'Oh, Marina, please forgive me. I'm so sorry I shouted at you earlier. I thought you were—'

'Your daughter, Marianne.' With a wave of a hand, Marina brushed away any idea that Sally had insulted her. 'They explained that to me. I was only calling you because I didn't want you running away the minute you were wrapped, without us having a chance to catch up. I wanted to invite you to dinner right after the shoot. But after what happened tonight, it doesn't look like such a brilliant idea, so I suppose that's it.'

Despite the anguish and danger she had gone through, Sally felt exhilarated.

The principal thought in her mind was jubilation that she had survived.

They all had survived.

It was something to be celebrated.

'Do you know, Marina,' she replied. 'If you're still up for it, it won't take me ten minutes to smarten up. But I have to warn you – I could eat a horse.'

'They do that in France?' asked Marina.

Sally nodded. 'But, frankly, I'd prefer a pizza!'

PART SIX

MACARONI NIÇOISE

Serves 4.

small packet of macaroni (or ziti, bucatini or spaghetti)
1 onion, peeled and chopped
olive oil
1 aubergine, chopped
1 red pepper, deseeded and chopped
1 courgette, chopped
4 cloves of garlic, crushed
handful of black olives
large tin of tomatoes
squeeze of tomato puree
½ teaspoon *herbes de Provence*
salt and pepper
Parmesan or Sbrinz cheese, grated
fresh basil

Boil the pasta in a large pan of salted water until al dente, then drain and set aside. Meanwhile, in a large frying pan, fry the onion in a good glug of olive oil until tender. Add the aubergine and red pepper and, once they are softening, drop in the courgettes. When all is nicely cooked, add the garlic, then the olives and tomatoes. Finally add the tomato puree and *herbes de Provence*, with salt and pepper to taste. Put the pasta into the sauce and stir over heat. Serve topped with Parmesan or Sbrinz and a leaf of basil.

TWENTY-SEVEN

In the cold light of morning, the world seemed a different place.

Nowhere was that more true that day than in the little town of Bellevue-sur-Mer.

Theresa opened the front door and took a deep breath of the warm sunny air.

She wondered if she needed a coat at all, took a jacket from the hook and rested it over her arm.

She locked up carefully. She must remember to get someone in to change the locks again.

She crossed the road and walked along the quayside.

Now that the water was still, shiny as a pale-blue plastic sheet, it was hard to believe the terrifying antics of last night had actually happened.

Rather than walk alongside the front of Marcel's brasserie, Theresa stayed at the water's edge.

She had no idea where he was, but after telling the coastguards what had happened, she had no doubt he would at least have been taken in by the police for questioning.

The brasserie was all closed up, the shutters pulled across, tables and chairs all inside.

She entered La Mosaïque through the front door.

William and Benjamin were seated with Zoe at one of the tables.

'Poor Theresa!' William rose to greet her with a warm embrace. 'Once you had gone off in that boat, I got talking to Cyril and we realised there had been completely crossed wires between you two. You and your bad French. And his bad English.'

'When Cyril entered your house he was in a terrible panic,' said Benjamin.

'And his English wasn't up to the crisis,' added William.

'Why did he tell me he'd drugged his wife?' Theresa was winding back the conversation, attempting to make sense of it.

William laughed. 'He was trying to explain that he and his wife were your friends and that they had given you a gift of their special home-made brownies.'

'He really wanted to warn you about Marcel,' said Benjamin, pulling out a chair. 'He saw your front door open, the lights on, and so grabbed a knife from his van, just in case he needed it, to protect you.'

'He was so shocked, you see,' William said. 'By what he'd just seen in that storeroom of Marcel's at the Astra.'

'He took us all up to see it,' drawled Zoe. 'Looks like some weird artwork that Tracey Emin might have cooked up.'

'Anyway,' continued William, 'Marcel, I suspect getting the idea from us, has been doing a delivery-style breakfast for the Astra while their kitchen is being renovated this last week. It was meant to be just the normal Continental. But with so many English and Germans staying there, they needed meat: sausages, bacon. So then Marcel phoned Cyril who brought the meats around to the brasserie. But later Marcel remembered he'd forgotten sliced ham, a favourite with the Scandinavians, and asked Cyril to bring it over yesterday afternoon. He thought Cyril would bring it to him at the brasserie. But Cyril thought it would be quicker to go straight to the

Hotel Astra. The desk clerk pointed out where Marcel's storeroom was and …'

'Marcel had that room to himself,' explained Benjamin, 'and obviously didn't think that anyone else would go in there. Why would they?'

'But Cyril did.' Theresa felt so sorry for her mistaken belief that it had been Cyril who was up to no good when he was only coming down to warn her. 'And so did my granddaughters – always poking about where they shouldn't be.'

'But anyway,' Zoe chipped in. 'Poor you. Having that squelchy oyster mouth of Marcel's land on you must have been quite a revolting experience.'

Theresa had another worry niggling at her.

'Roger?'

'Over and out,' replied Zoe.

'He's not … ?'

'Dead? Oh no. Sorry! Joke!' said Zoe. 'That wife of his dived in, fully clothed in her twinset and pearls, like a Home Counties Esther Williams, crawled out there, like Weissmuller, and pulled him to the shore. Gave him the kiss of life and everything. It couldn't have been more like a movie.'

Carol swept in from the kitchen, bearing a tray with teas, coffees and a basket of Viennoiserie.

'So anyway! Today's the day …'

'The day?' Theresa wondered if she hadn't forgotten something. 'The day for what?'

'When we open the offers.' William spoke to Theresa as though to a child.

'I hope we're not accepting any offers from Marcel.' Theresa recoiled at the very thought of the man.

'God, no! Over my dead body,' said Zoe, crossing herself, and whispering a prayer towards the ceiling.

'Where's Sally? Shouldn't Sally be here?'

'I am here.' Sally slammed in through the front door, pulling off her coat and grabbing a seat at the table with the others. She looked at her watch. 'I'm not late, am I?'

'Just totally absent for a bloody week,' murmured Zoe into her polo neck.

'Oh, and, Carol, I've a bone to pick with you.' Sally gave Carol the evil eye. 'But later!'

'Come along, everyone. The candidates should be here shortly.' William took an official tone to start the meeting. 'But we have two sealed offers before us. As you know, there was a reserve price set, so no more joke offers like Marcel's.'

'Good,' replied Theresa. 'No more anything from Marcel, thank you.'

'So let's open them.' Benjamin folded his arms, ready for battle.

'Who wants the honour?' William held up two colour-ed envelopes.

'It should be Sally and Theresa.'

'The two women who deserted their posts,' muttered Zoe.

'I agree.' Carol's low voice drowned out Zoe's remark. 'They've both been through the mill, so ...'

'And opening an envelope is going to make it all better?'

Carol shot Zoe such a look that she was silenced.

William handed the pink envelope to Theresa and the blue one to Sally.

They both tore them open, pulled out the pieces of paper and held them up, displaying numbers, in euros.

Both numbers were well within the price range which would bail them out, and one even gave them all a little profit.

William glanced from pink to blue and back.

'The pink wins.'

They turned to one another and embraced, smiling and laughing.

William twisted to face Zoe who seemed not to be as delighted as the others. 'Smile, won't you?'

'What do you mean?' Her face did not move. 'I *am* smiling.'

'Oh darling,' said Theresa, flopping back in her chair with relief. 'If that's a genuine offer, it's saved our old bacon. What would we say here in France? Saved our lardon. No, that sounds too like—'

'What's that?' William shut her up. 'Someone's knocking at the back door?'

Carol jumped to her feet and ran through the kitchen to open it.

Simultaneously there was a demanding rap on the front door.

'The warring parties, the pink and the blue, make their entrances from different sides of the stage,' whispered Sally. 'How fitting.'

'It's open,' called Benjamin.

The tinkling sound heralded the arrival of Odile de la Warr who stepped forward and stood proudly on the threshold. 'So ... when do I get the keys?' She jangled her bracelets, and swayed, hands on hips.

Carol came back from the kitchen, leading Roger and Cynthia Muffett.

William stood up and brusquely handed the blue note back to Madame de la Warr.

'No deal, Odile.'

'You mean we got it?' Cynthia swirled around and kissed her husband on the cheek.

'That's fine with me,' said Odile, already on her way out. 'Yesterday afternoon I bought next door from that pervert who's now up at the police station. It's going to be the biggest Italian trattoria this side of Genoa.'

And she was gone.

Cynthia stepped forward.

'Not only that, but you should be the first to know: we've decided to remarry. We're getting married tomorrow at the Salle des Mariages in Menton and you're all invited.'

'Will there be a reception?' asked Zoe.

'We didn't know where?'

'Why not in here?'

The restaurant front door swung open again.

'Oh God, I hope it's not Cruella de Vil, back to put a spell on us all,' whispered William.

'That would be Maleficent, actually,' corrected Benjamin. 'Cruella would want us to serve dog stew.'

But it was Imogen, with her three children and Neil Muffett, who ran across the room to join his parents.

'I gather, from the departing party, that you got your price,' said Imogen. 'Congratulations!'

'I think we all need to get up to a notary and sign some papers,' said William, rising. 'I think we can put the Closed sign up today.'

'We're going to be bridesmaids,' said Lola. 'In the room with fantastic walls.'

'There's a flying horse, and angels juggling.' Cressida was very excited. 'A man whose eye is a fish because he's a fisherman.'

Zoe leaned in and added, 'And some man on that same wall is going to hit the husband over the head with a club because he didn't marry his ugly sister.'

Theresa pulled a face in Zoe's direction.

'Why are you rolling your eyes like that, Theresa?' asked Zoe, all innocence. 'You're not a slot machine.'

'Will Neil be pageboy?' asked Theresa, anxious to change the subject.

Neil squirmed. 'That would be just too weird,' he said.

Lola edged up to Sally. 'There was a picture of your daughter on the walls there too.'

Theresa was aghast. Not the whole Marcel saga over again, but this time with Sally's daughter.

'Frances told me it was a picture of Marianne,' Lola confided. 'But it didn't look a bit like her. And she is the cymbal of France. But I play cymbal in percussion band and frankly the painter made a mistake because there was no cymbal.'

'Come along!' William was already at the door, ushering everyone out.

The gaggle continued to talk among themselves as they climbed the hill to the notary's office.

Sally, lagging behind with Theresa, noticed Eggy and Phoo coming down the stairs of their flat, carrying their suitcases.

Marianne, who had been keeping her eyes on the English newspapers, had shown Sally the photos of Phoo in this morning's edition. She wondered if the Markhams had seen them? Maybe by the time they got home to London the storm would have blown over, and, to use the old term, become today's fish and chip wrapper.

'That's us off home to Blighty,' called Eggy.

Phoo stepped forward to speak to Sally. 'Edgar tells me you saved his life last night. I thank you from the bottom of my heart. I really don't know how I could go on without him. He's my best friend, you know.' Phoo dropped her suitcase into the boot of the BMW and took Sally by the hand. 'And I realise I've been cruel and insensitive towards you. You were a sweet kid, really. Still are.'

She climbed into the passenger seat, then wound down the window and called back to Sally: 'Enjoy the rest of your holiday!'

As Eggy pulled open the driver's door, he turned and gave Sally a wink. 'We're going to take the drive very slowly. Stay in some little French hotels en route. In a week or so I'll be in front of the telly with a nice cup of tea.'

Eggy had been so desperate to get home that Sally knew that he must have seen the news about his wife and was not going to let her get back to London until the storm in a teacup had calmed down.

With a feeling of melancholy Sally watched the car speed off up the hill, tooting as it passed the straggling gang from La Mosaïque, both past and future.

'We mustn't fall out again, darling,' said Sally to Theresa. 'We've been through so much recently, both together and apart. And there are some things which only we two understand.'

A tear filled Theresa's eye as she replied, 'How about we do all this signing stuff, and then head off somewhere lovely for lunch?'

Sally thrust out a hand to shake.

'Deal!'

Postscript

Marcel was found guilty of assault and attempted rape (of Theresa) and of actual bodily harm (to Roger Muffett). At his trial it came out that not only had he taken Theresa's photo album, he had also 'borrowed' her keys from their peg in the cellar cupboard. Once inside her flat, he had fiddled with the answering machine, setting up a remote code by which he could listen to and even erase her incoming messages. His cell phone was found to be filled with images of Theresa, including a few of her standing in the dark at her own back door, wearing a nightie. When he knew Theresa was expecting to hear from her missing granddaughter, Marcel had lured her to Nice to sit alone in a café so that he could watch her for a whole afternoon. He is serving a seven-year prison sentence.

After her mini-scandal died down, Sally's daughter, **Marianne**, went back to London. She will never forgive Cynthia Muffett for showing her husband the article in the British tabloid in which her huge financial gaffe was exposed. But the City has a short memory, and Marianne has just landed another prestigious job in Canary Wharf. On the office wall she has a photo of her mother standing beside Marina Martel taken outside the Grand Hotel Astor, Monte Carlo.

Odile de la Warr opened her Italian trattoria on the seafront at Bellevue-sur-Mer. It bore the name, in letters of green, white and red, Il Gatto e la Volpe. The locals have not decided whether Odile is the Cat or the Fox. Quite possibly she is both. All summer the terraces echo with Italian-speaking tourists. The customer numbers have been swelled hugely by the locals and visitors, plus the occasional outpouring from a passing cruise ship. The menu has recently been altered to reflect the reality of the clientele and now includes Hamburger Italienne with fries.

Cyril and his wife continue to live happily in Bellevue-sur-Mer. They both still enjoy making gifts of slightly illegal chocolate brownies to friends who appear *un peu stressé*.

Roger and Cynthia Muffett remarried in a delightfully opulent yet romantic ceremony at the Salle des Mariages in Menton. They live together in the big house in Streatham (previously owned by 'The Bitch'). Roger is having a pool installed in the garden, where Cynthia will teach her husband how to swim. While their new brasserie, renamed Folie à Deux, is being decorated and expanded, they commute to Nice for business meetings. They hope to open to the public very soon, in time for the summer rush. They are seeking out a flat to buy near to the restaurant. While Neil is still at school, they plan to spend all their holidays on the Côte d'Azur. They have offered William and Benjamin the job of the hands-on management of the restaurant on a permanent basis; the two are considering the offer.

For the next school play, **Frances**, the drama teacher, has chosen *The Way of the World*. **Mervin**, the tech guy, is providing state-of-the-art lighting and a musical score.

After their Côte d'Azur adventures, **Chloe and Neil** are both happy to be back together at school in London. They will be starring as Millament and Mirabell in *The Way of the World*. Recently the kind father of a mutual school-friend invited them to join the family for a week-end on his white motor cruiser moored on the River Thames near Maidenhead. They politely declined.

Lola and Cressida were proud and excited bridesmaids at the Muffetts' wedding. Three weeks later they were both given detentions and suspended after having been found responsible for painting huge psychedelic eyes on the inside walls of all the school lavatories. The sisters later explained to their mother/headmistress that it was only what the famous French painter called John Cockatoo would have done. He hated a blank wall.

Despite their ever-increasing ages, **Phoebe Taylor** and **Edgar Markham** continue to delight British audiences. They are currently rehearsing a new TV sitcom, written especially for them. They play a married couple divided on how they treat their ditzy housekeeper. The role of house-keeper was offered to Sally.

She turned it down.

They have no idea why she didn't want the part.

Carol has promised Sally that she will no longer be judge and jury on married men who have the audacity to flirt with her.

William and **Benjamin** have opened a small antique shop in the town. They hope that if they take up the job at Folie à Deux, they can manage to do both things at once.

Zoe is in two minds about her favourite Swiss plastic-surgery clinic, now that it has just opened a branch in nearby Nice. The week's 'holiday' in Switzerland provided her a far better excuse to cover for her escapades with Botox and fillers.

Sally has a new London acting agent. She continues to live on the hill in Bellevue-sur-Mer, occasionally popping over to London for meetings and to film the odd TV role or commercial. She has been invited to the Hollywood premiere of her and Marina Martel's new movie, *Côte d'Azur Capers*, early next year. She has already packed her case.

Among the messages left on **Theresa**'s phone, but wiped out by Marcel, was a job offer. Her old office asked if she would like to return to London and take up the position she had been retired from a few years back. Her replacement, a much younger woman, is going on a year's pregnancy leave. They desperately need someone to fill in. Theresa turned them down.

But she is not pining. She has teamed up with Carol to do a home-delivery service. It gives them both a bit of income and is something which they can do from their own flats.

In order to improve her French, and to avoid further misunderstandings, Theresa has taken up a course at Alliance Française in Nice. She now knows well to avoid saying *'je t'aime'* when you mean *'je l'aime'*, and NEVER EVER to say *'Je suis chaud'*.

Despite everything, each morning as she opens up the curtains of her flat, and looks out at the ever-changing sea, she still thanks the heavens she made the move and settled here in Bellevue-sur-Mer.

ACKNOWLEDGEMENTS

Multiple thanks, as ever, to all my friends in Nice: Lina, Raymond, Charles, Cyril, Gilbert, John, Sebastien, JF, Richard, Daniel, Monsieur B, Fabrizio, Karine, Gianni, Flory, Tony – *Issa Nissa!*

To the wonderful staff at Alliance Française in Nice, who are helping me *améliorer mon français*. In particular to Jean Phillipe, Marlène, Martine, Nadia, Emilie M, Emilie P, Patricia and Marilyn. Also their counterparts at the Alliance Française in Los Angeles, especially Paz.

To my *QM2* friends: Robbie, Paul, Jo, Declan and Viktoria.

To the team at Bloomsbury: Alexandra, David, Ros.

To my agents and managers: Robert K, Dallas, Sophie, Sarah, Alex, Shelley, Jared and Hannah.

To my publicists: Alexa and Erin.

To Pamela Adlon.

To all my friends at the Regal Cinema Club.

To my pal Fidelis, who keeps me laughing.

To my son Angus.

A NOTE ON THE TYPE

The text of this book is set in Adobe Caslon, named after the English punch-cutter and type-founder William Caslon I (1692–1766). Caslon's rather old-fashioned types were modelled on seventeenth-century Dutch designs, but found wide acceptance throughout the English-speaking world for much of the eighteenth century until replaced by newer types towards the end of the century. Used in 1776 to print the Declaration of Independence, they were revived in the nineteenth century and have been popular ever since, particularly amongst fine printers. There are several digital versions, of which Carol Twombly's Adobe Caslon is one.